The Hallowed Blood Bonds
of the Eternal

Michelle Morningstar

Volume Two of
The Blood Bond Canticles

IBSN: 979-8-218-31493-4

Second Edition: October 2023

Cover design and logo by Michelle C. Stewart

www.michellemorningstar.com

For Azrael, the only adult in the room.

Special thanks to Shanley Gunderson for devoting her time and efforts to editing this story.

Special thanks to Brian R. Luedtke. Your exceptional talent and dedication to this story helped to create the most amazing battles and scenarios.

Thanks to Jason Armstrong, Judy Aguiar, and all my friends and chosen family. Thank you so much for your support and encouragement.

Unsichtigkeit wolluß vnd pracht
Die edelkeit vnd Kleider pracht.
Großs namen reichtum vnd macht
Ist nur allein ein draum der nacht.
Der dodt ist allen gantz gewiß
Keiner ist frey von seinem biss,
Den dodt entgeen Keiner Kan
Ehr sei ein weib Oder ein man.

Luxus, deliciæ, pompaque sæculi,
Fastus, nobilitas, Stemmata, purpura,
Nomen diuitiæ, fluxaq gloria.
Ecquid sunt aliud, quã breue somniã?
Certo veniunt ordine Parcæ,
Nulli iusso cessare licet,
Nulli scriptum proferre diem,
Recipit populos vrna citatos.

Ioye, delices, du monde caresses
Des Princes couronnes renommees, noblesse
Fame estendue richesses et puissance
Ques ailtes, qui sommeil et vain ioyssance?
La MORT par my le monde voyageant
L'heure et le iour destine va finissant
Nulle personne la peult certes eschapper
Apreus a mourir pendant la petit esperne.

G. Allenbach exc.

PROLOGUE

*"The heroes, the villains, the daring decisions. My wings will
pull me up into the sky."*—Switchblade Symphony

Austin, Texas. Two years earlier…

Adelia inhaled and exhaled as she bent down, placing her
hands on top of her knees. She attempted to open her lungs
as much as possible. Straightening her back, she paced
around as she slid the back of her hand across her forehead
to wipe the waterfall of sweat from her brow. The increasing
Texas temperatures made running especially challenging.
She felt the vibration of her cell phone, tucked tightly against
her neoprene leggings. She pulled it out and pressed the
answer button.

"Mare, what's up?" She continued to pant and pace
around her car in the driveway.

"Where are you?" Marilyn asked.

"I just finished a run around the arboretum. Back home
now," Adelia's breathing slowly returned to normal.

"Did you check your mailbox?"

"Not yet. Why?" She looked up at her mailbox on the
street and headed towards it. She flipped down the aluminum
door and fished out a small stack of envelopes.

"Check it. Now!"

"I am! Relax! Let me put you on speaker." Adelia pressed the speaker button and set the phone on the top of the mailbox. "What am I looking for?"

"You should see an envelope from Osmus and Berg. It's from a law office. Open it."

Adelia nodded and flipped through the envelopes. The last envelope was from the law firm. "Okay, I have it. What is it?"

"Brace yourself."

Adelia eyed her phone suspiciously. She turned the envelope over and peeled off the auspicious wax seal. She slowly slid out a sharply creased white paper and unfolded it. A small slip of paper slid out and drifted slowly to the bright green grass below. Adelia looked down and leaned her head to the side to read it upright. Her eyes widened in disbelief.

"What the…?!" She slowly bent down to pick up the small rectangular paper. She held the slip of paper up to her eyes.

"Yeah! Right?! Marylin exclaimed.

"Mare! This is a check for two hundred and fifty thousand dollars!" Suddenly realizing her voice was incredibly loud, she quickly looked around nervously to see if anyone had heard her. "How? What? I mean…" Adelia struggled to find the right words.

"Gramma left us some cash in her will. Pretty awesome, huh?"

"Okay, why are we getting it now? Gramma died last year."

"I dunno. I called, and they said something about probate, blah blah blah, legal shit, legal shit. Whatever, who cares? Is a two hundred 'n fifty grand!"

Adelia picked up her phone and slowly walked to her front door, unable to pull her eyes off the six-digit number on the check.

"What are you going to do with it?" Marylin asked.

"I…I don't know." She unlocked her front door and stepped inside.

"Del, allow me to offer a proposal?"

"Okay, what are you thinking?"

"What if we could invest it and turn our five hundred thousand into a cool million?"

"How do you suppose we do that?"

"Ever heard of a town called Bonfire? It's about twenty miles north of Dallas, so roughly three hours from you."

Adelia's eyes shifted as she tried to figure out where her sister was going with this proposal. "Yeah, vaguely, but I think it's a bit of a ghost town."

"*Was* a ghost town. Our company has been inundated with an influx of building requests in the area over the past couple of years. The town is attempting to revitalize, gentrifying if you will, and those old houses are going for dirt cheap. I say we grab one while we can and flip it."

"I dunno, Mare…That sounds like a ton of work."

"But you don't have to do anything! I'll take care of it."

Adelia sat down on her couch and stared at the check again. She bit the inside of her cheek, deep in thought. "You really think we can flip a house and sell it for a million?

"Think? No. I know we can. Possibly even more."

"Let me think about it. I'll get back to you later this week.

"Great! I'll get to scouting. I'll come up to your place in a couple of days."

"Mare, I didn't say yes."

"I'll see you Friday!"

Marylin hung up the phone.

Adelia shook her head and rolled her eyes. She focused back on the check, her mind racing with possibilities.

✝✝✝

"GPS said it should be up on the right side there," Marylin said. She pointed her finger off the steering wheel straight ahead on the cottonwood tree-lined residential street.

Adelia looked out the passenger side window at the residential neighborhood on Historic Bonfire's north side. Some houses desperately needed repairs, and others looked far too gone and would probably need to be torn down. Still, some looked stable, and some were recently updated and occupied. She couldn't deny that this neighborhood would be beautiful if it could be returned to its former glory.

Marylin stopped the SUV in front of 313 Bradley Street. Adelia turned and looked at her sister suspiciously. She raised an eyebrow.

"Don't judge yet. Come on!" Marilyn popped open the door and climbed out of the SUV.

Adelia followed and walked onto the sidewalk facing the house. It was an absurdly humid Texas day. The locusts were screaming, and she could smell the distinct scent of petrichor from the heavy overnight rains. She noticed the new, eight-foot-high, chain-link fence surrounding the property with a *Do Not Enter* sign placed right above the padlock. She looked through the fence to the two-story, dilapidated Victorian home. Marylin walked over to her and stood at her side.

"It's really not as bad as it looks," Marylin started. "It's solid—surprisingly, no serious termite damage but a bit of rodent damage. The wiring and plumbing are shot to hell, but the foundation is great, and there's some mold and warped floorboards. Easily repairable."

"So, what are we looking at as far as an investment?" Adelia asked. She still wasn't sold on this idea.

"I think I can pick it up for about $175. The owner is asking $250, but there's negotiation room. I mean, clearly, this place is going to take a bit of work. Do you want to go inside?"

"Is it safe?" Adelia scrunched her nose.

"Oh yeah, totally. As I said, it's not that bad. The outside is the worst part."

Adelia shrugged. "Well, let's see it then."

Marilyn unlocked the padlock and held the gate open for her sister to pass through. Adelia looked down at the broken porch stairs to the front door. The door was decomposing, but the oval-shaped stained-glass window was, surprisingly, still intact. She turned and looked back at her sister. Marylin tossed her a heavy key ring with three skeleton keys which Adelia caught and eyed curiously.

"Are you kidding me right now?" Adelia asked.

"Open it up."

"I've never used a skeleton key lock before."

"It's really not much different than any other lock."

Adelia inserted the well-worn iron key into the lock and turned it with a loud clink. She stepped inside the hallway foyer. The hardwood floor seemed to be stable but warped in places. The railing on the stairs leading up to the second floor was missing most of its balusters, and the handrail was cracked in multiple places. Cobwebs were strewn about, and the house smelled musky, like moldy, wet paper, rotted fibers, and damp wood.

She slowly and cautiously walked through the parlor as the floor creaked with every step. The room was bright, with large windows that faced the street. The tops of the windows had an ornate stained-glass design at one time, but most of it was broken or missing. The fireplace was black, with clusters of plaster millwork grapes and vines protruding on either side of the opening. A large, empty frame hung over the fireplace—it possibly held a mirror or maybe a painting at one time. A few gas sconces lined the walls. To the right of the parlor was a large opening that led to a dining room. The walls were reddish in color and consisted of a hand-painted floral pattern.

Marylin stood behind her sister and leaned against the wall inside the dining room.

"This wall treatment is gorgeous. I mean, look at it! I bet this place was amazing when it was new," Adelia said.

"Yeah, it looks like it. What do you think so far?" Marylin asked.

"You really think we can do this?"

"Yep!"

"So why doesn't the owner fix it up and sell it?" Adelia asked. She couldn't understand why someone would offload such an amazing treasure if it truly had this much potential.

"So, this is what I was told," Marylin started. "The current owner is the granddaughter of the original owner. She inherited it about five years ago. She lives in New York City and has no desire to keep it. Her father died and left it to her. I have no idea why he didn't do anything with it either."

"This place is just getting passed around?"

"It would seem so." Marylin shrugged.

Marylin's phone vibrated in her pocket. She pulled it out to check the notification.

"Woah!" Marylin exclaimed.

"What's wrong?" Adelia asked, concerned.

"I just got a text from Dad. I guess your friend Drucilla's brother died."

"What? Drake? Are you serious?"

"That's what Dad said."

"Wow. I don't talk to Drucilla nearly as much as I should, just a couple times a year. I know she and Drake had a falling out a while ago, and she dislikes talking about him. Hopefully, they patched things up before he died," Adelia said.

"I think I met him a couple of times. Wasn't he that super-hot Mediterranean-looking dude? The one with the really cool hair?" Marylin asked.

"You mean the ex-governor of California? And they're half Egyptian."

"He was a governor?"

"Mare, Christ's sake, what planet do you live on?"

"I don't follow politics! I didn't know him that well. You guys were two years behind me in high school, but dang, he was hot!"

"Mare, you're gay."

"I can recognize attractive men, Del."

"Okay, fair. But none of us really knew him. He was a hard guy to know," Adelia admitted.

Adelia moved into the kitchen area. In the middle, covered in a thick layer of dust and cobwebs, was an antiquated, oak kitchen table with one chair. An old ceramic double sink and a tall icebox were situated on the other end. To the left was a black iron stove with a pipe attached to the side of the wall going outside. She continued to move out of the kitchen into a large room. The room appeared to be an office space with a dust-covered, mahogany desk. The wallpaper was clearly original, and it was cracked and peeling in most places. Much of it had fallen and was scatted around the floor like dry paper leaves. A large window faced the backyard looking out on the overgrown, dead lawn, dried weeds, and pecan trees in the back. Adelia looked down and noticed the floor in front of the window was moderately burned in a small two-foot area. She bent down to get a closer look.

"Be careful. I don't know if that's stable," Marylin warned.

"I wonder what happened here," Adelia said. She ran her hand over the floor, pushing away the debris.

"Who knows, probably knocked over a candle or something. It's easily fixed. I think I can salvage most of the wood flooring. I can match the parts that need to be replaced."

Adelia stood back up and wiped her hands on her jeans.

"Well? What do you think? You wanna go for it?" Marylin asked.

"You know this place has got to be haunted as hell, right?"

Marylin rolled her eyes and crossed her arms at the stupid comment. "I don't think that's true."

"What do we know about the original owner? Did he die here?"

"No, Del. He died in Colorado during one of his performances."

"Performances?" Adelia quired.

"Yeah, I guess the original owner was a well-known magician, illusionist, or something back in the early 1900s. I can't remember the name. Violet or something. I forgot. Whatever, it doesn't matter. Regardless, I think we should pull the trigger on this place before someone else does."

Adelia walked back through the house the way she came, ignoring the upstairs, and stepped out onto the porch. She looked onto the street at the other homes that lined the road. "Are you positive this is a good investment?"

"Absolutely."

"If it fails, I'm taking two hundred and fifty K out of your ass. You know that, right?"

"My ass is ready." The moment Marylin let those words escape her mouth, she knew that was the wrong thing to say. Adelia glanced at her, pressed her lips together, and blinked rapidly.

"Shut up, Del."

"You said it!"

"Shut up, Del!" Marylin scolded again.

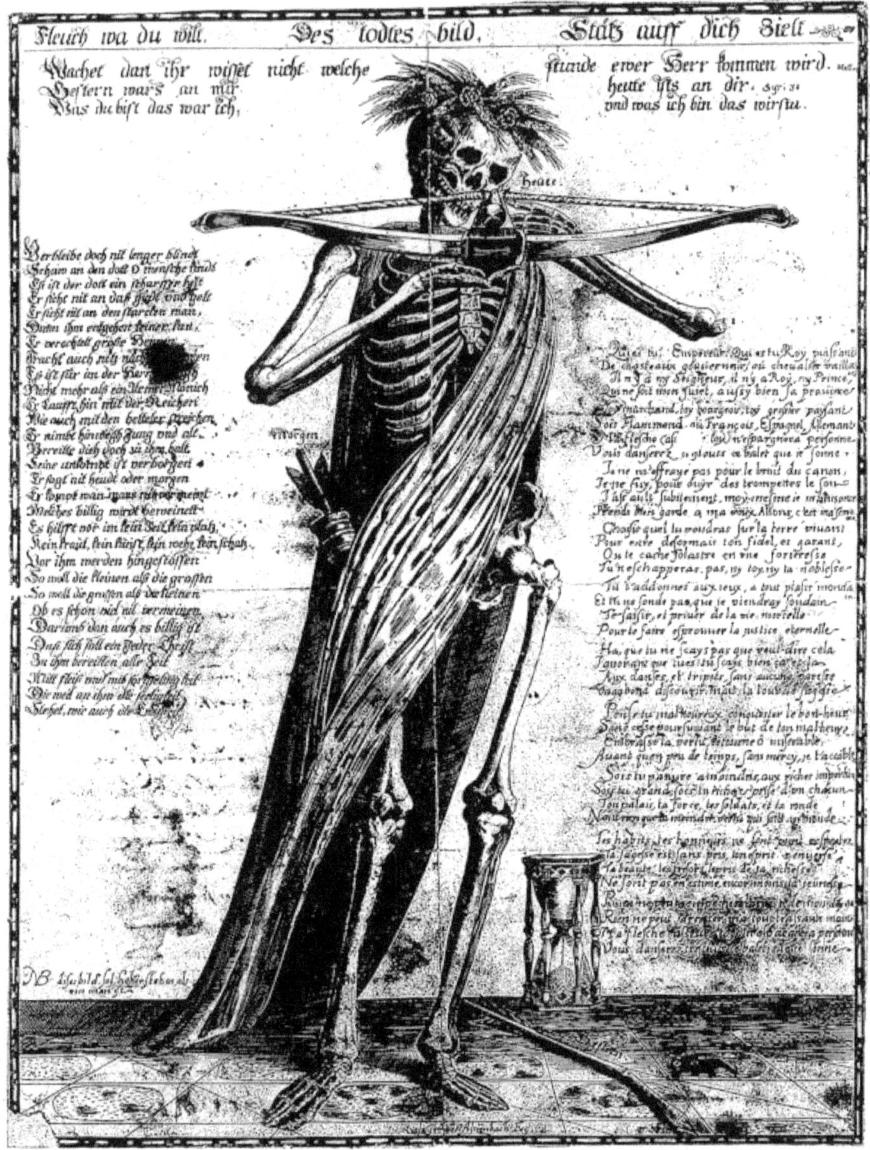

Fleuch wa du wilt.   Des todtes bild.   Stäts auff dich zielt
heute
morgen

CANTICLE ONE

"No one will find us as we walk through the dark tonight. The cold invades you to sleep." —Twin Tribes

"Adrian!" Drucilla called out.

"What?" Adrian responded. He descended the stairs into the living room.

"Adrian?"

"Dru, what?"

Drucilla frantically moved from room to room, searching.

"What are you looking for?" Adrian asked.

Drucilla stopped in her tracks. She inhaled. Tears began to well in her eyes. She placed her hand over her mouth and squeezed her eyes closed. A single tear streamed down her cheek.

"Dru, what's wrong? What's happening?" Adrian reached out to touch Drucilla's shoulder, but his hand passed through. He looked at his hand. He wasn't corporeal.

"Dru, can you hear me?"

Drucilla wiped her cheek with the back of her hand. She slowly walked into her living room, sat on the arm of the couch, and placed her face in her hands. She wept softly. Adrian followed and stood directly in front of her. He looked at her chest and noticed the amulet of Thoth no longer adorned her neck.

"You can't see or hear me anymore, can you?" Adrian asked quietly.

Drucilla stood up and headed for the staircase.

"Fuck," he whispered. Adrian watched her walk away.

Adrian felt a sudden and powerful tug at his chest. He lunged forward momentarily as if an invisible force was trying to extricate him from this plane of existence.

"Not this again," he said loudly to anyone who could hear him. "I'm not going!"

Azrael stood stoic and statuesque, arms crossed, in the center of the living room behind Adrian. His massive stature looming and foreboding. Adrian turned around and almost ran into him.

"Azrael." Adrian looked upward, surprised by Azrael's unexpected appearance. "Make Drucilla see me!"

Azrael cocked his head at Adrian as if the request was out of place or unusual.

"What? Why won't you help?"

Azrael looked toward Drucilla but otherwise remained motionless.

"Well, then tell me what's going on."

"Drucilla believes the ability to interact and make you corporeal is a result of Calliope's relic," Azrael started, "she does not understand that it is she who is keeping you tethered to her."

"So, she doesn't need the amulet?"

"She never did."

"Why haven't you told her that?" Adrian demanded.

Azrael ignored his question. Instead, he turned fully to face Adrian again and crossed his arms.

"Adrian, it is incumbent upon you as a human to return to the Agglomeration, now. Your life is ended, and I've entertained Drucilla's wish long enough. Come. Let's go."

Azrael lifted a single finger of his long, white, nearly skeletal hand from its rest upon his arm, and suddenly Adrian felt the pull in his chest again.

"No! I refuse!" Adrian yelled, planting his feet, and clenching his fists even as he slowly slid backward across the floor.

"You cannot."

"Why not?! I've heard ghost stories, and I've seen other ghosts. Why do *I* have to return?"

"Your soul needs to rejoin the others in the Agglomeration to strengthen the pool of Cosmic Essence. Future souls will benefit from the knowledge you have gained from your time on Earth. Those that refuse to rejoin are doomed to fade away, and that'd be a shame for you."

"Drucilla doesn't want me to go. She needs me. I won't abandon her like her brother did."

Azrael lowered his finger. The pull on Adrian ceased.

"Very well. You can rot here, in this house. Your soul will eventually decay until you are nothing but a distant memory in someone's book of photographs…"

Adrian clenched his jaw.

"Or," Azrael cocked his head again, "you can choose to do something meaningful with your death."

"What do you mean by meaningful? I am Drucilla's family. I give her life meaning just as much as she gives mine. I'm not going to leave her."

Azrael peered down at Adrian. "So be it. You can continue to exhaust your spiritual energy here, and eventually burn yourself out. You will never interact with Drucilla or Dominic ever again. You may see The Beast from time to time, but I doubt he will be sympathetic to your plight. Lucifer is consumed by his own schemes and strategies."

Adrian creased his forehead at the Cataclysm.

"Maybe," Azrael spoke flatly, "in time, you can learn how to push coffee mugs off tables." He turned to leave. "I will leave you to it."

"Wait! What was the other option again? Something about giving my death meaning?"

Azrael relaxed his arms and turned back. "Adrian, you are unique. Your soul is ancient. Not just here, but in any realm. Nearly eight hundred times you've lived, reborn from the Agglomeration whole and intact each time. An infinitesimally rare occurrence." He reached out and brushed his hand through Adrian's spirit, dissipating it like he was made of incense smoke, before watching it congeal back together. "If this were three thousand years ago, you would have become a Seraph. But your existence is better served as something much more valuable than a foot solider in the Celestial Empyrion."

"What could possibly be more important than becoming

an Angel?" Adrian scoffed.

"Have you ever heard of a Noden?"

"No. The Hell is a Noden?"

Azrael raised his hand. A small orb of light the size of an apple appeared within his palm. He rolled the orb within his fingers. "The Nodenti are a particular sect of soul healers. Their primary function is to heal fractured souls and scarring within the Agglomeration. There is usually only one, rarely two, Nodenti in existence at the same time. Currently, there are no Nodenti."

"What happened to them? Do they retire after a while or something?"

"In a sense, yes."

The answer left Adrian feeling uneasy. He shook it off and changed the subject. "What are these fractured souls?"

Azrael turned his attention to the orb in his hand. "When a soul is forcefully removed from the Agglomeration, outside of the natural process of rebirth, it is fractured." The orb in Azrael's hand instantly formed thousands of small cracks that snaked over the orb completely. As the orb cracked, the light waned, and many small fragments of the orb dislodged and fell to his palm. "You do not get a full soul back when you pull it out of the Agglomeration in this way. You get a fraction of it. How much of a fraction depends on how long the soul has been in the Agglomeration before removal. The longer a soul has been part of the cosmic pool, the less is there to retrieve as it disseminates into the cosmic mass. All souls taken in this way fill in the missing gaps with the souls surrounding it. This leads to a fracturing of that area of the Agglomeration the soul was taken from. When Drucilla performs Necromancy, for instance, she is causing this very same damage."

"And a Noden puts the parts back together?"

"That is a function. The Nodenti are the ones that heal the scarring. The Agglomeration can self-heal over time, but that takes eons. And the machine still churns despite the damage. Even during normal rebirth, souls sourced from fractured regions of the Agglomeration produce fractured souls in new human bodies." Azrael closed his palm, and the orb disappeared. "It is an ever-growing problem without Nodenti to smooth the cracks."

"How can I be a Noden? I'm not saying I will do it, but if I did."

"It will not be easy. Only the Throne of Life can forge Nodenti. You will need to convince Gaia you are worthy. Seek from her a Globe of Dawn, a seed of life she creates from her heart. Obtain this, and you will have her blessing and guidance to become a Noden."

"A Throne? How the Hell am I supposed to find a Throne? And what if she doesn't find me worthy?" Adrian queried.

"I will relay your willingness to her. She will come to you. Or I suppose she will not if she does not find you worthy."

"You're not giving me much to work with here, Az."

Azrael winced at the sound of his shortened name.

"Adrian, I need you to understand that this path will not be easy. You will face many challenges. Situations that will challenge your ethics, your pride, and your patience. From what I know of you, I believe you will weather these obstacles with confidence and decorum. When you are ready, you should leave this house."

"I can't. I'm bound to the ashes in the urn on the mantle." Adrian pointed to the sleek black box above the fireplace.

Azrael appeared to glance at the mantle with his blackened eye sockets, then turned his attention to Adrian. "You are not. Binding you to the urn was another one of Drucilla's subconscious decisions. While she thinks she cannot summon you, you are free to leave whenever you wish."

Adrian glanced at the mantle and then back to Azrael. Adrian slowly stepped toward the front door. He plunged his hand through the heavy oak door, and it passed through without resistance. He pulled his hand back out and examined it. "So, just wander the Earth like Caine, huh?" he grinned at Azrael.

Azrael frowned in confusion.

"That's a Kung Fu joke— You know what, never mind. Wish me luck." Adrian said. He held Azrael's stare for a moment. Azrael gave no response.

Adrian exhaled. "Okay, then." He passed through the door, his Cosmic Essence trailing behind in a blur.

MVNDANÆ FŒLCITATIS GLIA

CANTICLE TWO

"Where are the dreams that I've been after?"
—Metallica

Drake sat patiently at the head of a long, black rectangular table in the center of the oratory, but his patience was growing short. He held his hand in front of his face and watched the streams of orange light course through the palm of his hand. He turned his hand over and watched the energy move over the top of his hand. Drake's body was burning with an orange glow beneath the skin of his exposed hands and head. Swirls of light seeped through his finely tailored black suit. His eyes, like hot, white fire, illuminated with intense light.

Drake recalled the battle at the Hellgate, one of the breach points on Earth in a forest of the Olympic Peninsula. He did not intend to join in the confrontation but could not pass the opportunity to take Thoth for himself, even if it meant releasing Drucilla from her mortal body. He saw such an opportunity when Drucilla was fighting Calliope. Drucilla's body was on fire with what could only be seen as pure blue rage. Her expansive blue-grey wings, with sharp serrated feathers, were tough and impenetrable as plate armor. With Drucilla struggling to decapitate Calliope, Drake noticed Calliope's sword unattended and lying at her feet. He could not pass up the chance to use it against her.

When Calliope fell, the Throne's energy departed its physical form in search of a suitable host. Drake, being the closest infernal, absorbed Calliope's essence into himself. Wild with power, he saw the opportunity for the real prize, Thoth, the Thone of Knowledge and Wisdom. Interference by Lucifer prevented him from taking Drucilla's life. Calliope's essence would have to be enough for now.

Breaking his daze of self-amazement, Drake impatiently turned to Leviathan. Leviathan, the King of Lechery, retained his appearance of a Virtue. His long, silver hair tied back neatly at the nape of his neck and his beautiful and perfect angelic features made him stand out in Hell among the other Kings. His flawless silver wings were meticulous, choosing to keep his original angelic appearance rather than take on the form of a demon. He took pride in himself, almost more than Lucifer.

"How much longer is this going to take?" Drake ran his hands through his hair and straightened his suit. "I feel as if I've been sitting here for centuries." Drake stood up and paced.

"This is just a formality. I am certain Raziel will clear you of all allegations."

"After all, Calliope faced no implications for her role in slaying Thoth," Persephone chimed in. She sat to the left of Drake. Her hands dripped with precious emeralds and diamonds. Her long, wavy, black hair piled loosely on the crown of her head. A few loose tendrils of curls framed her vampish face and bright, cadmium-yellow irises.

"Calliope acted in defense, and Thoth isn't exactly gone. You are aware of that, Persephone," Leviathan retorted.

Drake creased his forehead at Leviathan's comment.

The sudden clanking of the heavy oratory door slid open. Oriens, the ruler of the cardinal direction to the East and Prince of Hell, emerged and held the door open for three Seraphs to enter. Leviathan stood up and faced the Seraphs.

"Raziel, welcome. I appreciate you agreeing to meet with us," Leviathan said.

Raziel was considerably smaller than the other two Seraphs that accompanied him. He resembled a humanoid man with golden, shoulder-length hair and a plain fitted stone-grey suit.

"I appreciate your cordiality, but I would prefer to settle this issue as quickly as possible," Raziel responded as he tousled his blonde locks and adjusted the vest of his suit.

"Understood," Leviathan nodded.

They both took a seat as Drake walked back to the head of the table and sat down.

"You're Seraphs. Since when were angels allowed to enter Hell?" Drake peered at the Seraphs in contempt.

"Drake, this is Raziel. Raziel is the arbiter of Celestial Law," Leviathan advised. "Raziel has liberties in certain circumstances. One of them is jurisdiction in all realms."

"I see. And what of these winged enormities?" Drake asked. He motioned to the tall black-winged Seraphs.

One of the larger Seraphs stepped closer and stood behind Raziel. "We are what is known as Cataclysms. I am

Samael. I am here merely to recount the events that happened on Earth during the battle." Samael stood a towering eight feet high with long, somewhat curly, auburn hair and black wings that rested in a collapsed position upon his back. He turned his attention to his companion of equal size.

Azrael stood back near the door. With his short black hair and almost skeletal features, he gave the impression of being unapproachable and apathetic. Evidently, he was obligated to attend this meeting, most likely under duress. Visibly annoyed and unwilling to move closer, he crossed his arms. Samael started, "This is Azrael, the—"

"Ah yes, Azrael!" Drake exclaimed. "The Angel of Death, the Grim Reaper. Legendary. My sister was a big fan. I have heard so much about you. All good things, don't worry."

Azrael said nothing. His hollow eye sockets, a black void of nothingness, gave no indication of emotion.

Drake narrowed his gaze at Azrael. Drake wasn't accustomed to Celestials making a show of superiority over him without consequence.

"We would have preferred to meet in a more neutral territory, but it appears that Hell has been cut off from Earth," Persephone said.

"Yes, of course. That was clearly a violation of Celestial Law. We are working to have that annulled," Raziel explained.

"It is unnecessary to concern the Celestial Empyrion.

The barrier enchantment will be nullified shortly," Leviathan said confidently.

"Fine, let us proceed, shall we?" Raziel prompted.

"Of course," Leviathan responded.

"Raziel, because you are the arbiter of Celestial Law, I suppose you intend to judge my action and have these Cataclysms execute me? Is that what is happening here?" Drake's skin began to glow brighter. He gazed at them intimidatingly, daring them to make a move on him.

Without so much as a flinch, Raziel glanced at Drake. "We are here to understand if a law has been broken. If it has, we will take the proper and necessary steps to rectify the situation. Understand that there has been an accusation that you intentionally slew Calliope. We are here to decide if that was the case or—"

Drake sat up stiffly and shouted over Raziel. "I was protecting my sister!"

"That is exactly what we are here to understand," Raziel said calmly.

Drake forcedly leaned back in his chair and folded his hands in his lap. His eyes slowly began to glow brighter with his increasing annoyance.

Raziel stood up and paced for a moment before speaking. "Our prime mission is to protect Earth. It is our planet. All life on Earth is a divine creation of the Thrones…"

"Yeah, I know how this works. Lucifer explained that years ago."

"Then you understand that humans are under our

protection. Any threat to humans by the Infernal Sphere will be met with swift, and potentially, lethal force."

"What does this have to do with me ending Calliope?"

"You are no longer human. You are Unholy. You are afforded no protection from the Seraphs. Calliope is of the highest divine order, and although she resided in the Infernal Sphere, she is still a Throne. The slaying of a Throne by an infernal is punishable by the banishment from all realms. If it is found that you intentionally slew Calliope, you will be executed, and your Cosmic Essence destroyed."

"I told you—"

"Yes, you were defending your sister. I understand. I also understand that the conflict had nothing to do with you, and it was between Drucilla and Calliope. Drucilla is the Throne, Thoth's host, acting on his behalf."

"Then you understand why Drucilla needed to be defended." Drake interrupted.

"However, the conflict between Thrones is not a concern for the Seraphs nor the Infernals. The concern is the truth. To make that case, we need evidence."

"Hundreds, if not a thousand, infernals could tell you that I was acting in defense of my sister."

"We must see for ourselves, and what we have is the recollection of Samael." Raziel motioned to Samael. "Through Samael's eyes, we can view the battle's events."

"How do you do that?" Drake asked.

"Can we move that?" Raziel asked. He pointed at the large, egregious bronze sculpture of four demons tearing apart a Seraph that sat prominently in the center of the long rectangular table before them.

Leviathan looked at the statue, which must have weighed upward of seven hundred pounds, sliding it effortlessly across the table with his eyes. It fell to the floor with a heavy clunk. He shifted his gaze back to Raziel. "Please, continue."

Samael stepped closer to the table. With only his eyes, he projected a three-dimensional recollection of the event on Earth when Hell broke through. Drucilla was in front of Calliope, fighting to decapitate her. Drake could be seen picking up the sword that Calliope dropped and rushing to her. Drake drew the sword back and plunged it into the center of Calliope's back. The sword narrowly missed Drucilla as Drake pulled the sword upwards. The sword slid through Calliope, cutting her in half."

"There! Do you see? I was protecting Drucilla."

Raziel glanced at Drake, then turned his attention back to the image. The swirling energy mass plunged into Drake as Calliope's essence bonded with him. A moment later, it appeared that Drake attempted to strike with the sword again, but the angle made it unclear who he was trying to hit. The sword's swing was interrupted when Lucifer shoved Drake into the portal to Hell he had created with Erato Falx, Dominic's relic.

"Curious," Raziel started. "We can see that you attempted another strike. It is unclear if you were attempting to hit Drucilla, but had you landed the blow, you would have slain another Throne. That is interesting." Raziel turned his attention to Drake.

Drake glanced up at Raziel. "That's preposterous," Drake laughed incredulously, waiving it off. "Why would I attempt to slay my sister? Ridiculous."

"Azrael was there. Perhaps he had a better view?" Persephone chimed in.

Drake's eyes quickly shifted to Persephone, and he furrowed his brow.

"Azrael informed me that he was not there at the time of this particular incident," Raziel explained.

"Possibly…" Persephone said. "However, he was there at the beginning of the fight. I suppose he neglected to say that he eviscerated an entire legion of lesser demons for Drucilla to raise and attack Asmodeus and Belphegor."

Drake smirked at Persephone and directed his attention to Azrael.

Raziel glanced at Azrael and then at Drake. "Cataclysms function on their autonomy. What Azrael does to protect Earth is entirely under his control. If he, in fact, massacred a legion of lesser demons, he made the decision based on his mission as a Seraph to protect humans. They could hunt, kill, or possess humans if they escaped the area. From what I understand, there was a human in attendance. Is that correct, Azrael?"

"Yes, Dominic Novikov was the human present," Azrael responded, his voice gravelly thick with a low resonation. "He has bonded with Erato Falx and wields its power. He is Drucilla's ally and aided her in the battle."

Persephone chuckled ruefully to herself. "You were not preventing anything. You slaughtered them to help Drucilla get the upper hand and slay Asmodeus and Belphegor! You didn't do this to protect the human! He's lying to you, Raziel!"

Expressionless, Azrael slowly turned his head to face Persephone.

"Unfortunately, we do not have the advantage of viewing through Azrael's eyes," Raziel responded.

"Why not? I demand to see what he sees!" Persephone shouted.

"Because I do not have eyes, you duplicitous strumpet." Azrael shot back. He stared at her with the blackness of his hollow eye sockets.

Persephone, visibly offended, dropped her jaw and gasped. "You callow conspirator!"

Drake groaned and shook his head. "Enough!" he shouted. "Look! Am I guilty of slaying Calliope intentionally or not? If I am not guilty, I would ask that we end this conference. I have more important matters that require my attention. If I am…." Drake stood up and pulled at his cuffs. "Then this is going to get very interesting." Drake stared down Raziel.

Raziel held Drake's stare for a moment. Neither appeared willing to back down. Raziel finally broke the tension, "It would appear that you acted in protection of your sister. As you have familial bonds with Drucilla, I would consider this an act of defense. Calliope's essence still exists within you, does she not?"

Drake crossed his arms. "I intend to be her host."

"I will address that in a moment. However, I am interested in who you intended to strike with the second attempt."

"What difference does it make?" Drake asked, annoyed. "Can we adjourn this hearing?"

"Unfortunately, no. Drake, now we move on to the second part of why I am here. We now must establish if you are fit to possess a Throne."

"What does that mean?"

"Calliope is the Throne of Death. You are a king. Your current duties are only of benefit to the infernals. Thrones are beholden to the universe in its entirety. Calliope is not dead. Not in the way you perceive death. She has moved into a new formation," Raziel explained.

"I am still me. I don't feel different. Granted, I feel unfathomably powerful, but I retain my own mind."

"As you will for the time being. As the Throne takes residence within your body, your Cosmic Essence is eventually forced out. You can think of this as a virus. You are infected with an entity that will grow and consume. I am afraid that if you want to continue to host the Throne, you will eventually be consumed by Calliope."

"So, you're saying this is going to kill me?"

"In a sense, yes. Your essence will be replaced with the one currently developing within you. You will still be *you* in physical form only. Eventually, even that will dissipate over time.”

“That doesn’t make sense. Drucilla is a Throne. How can Drucilla still be Drucilla and not be taken over by the Throne?” Drake demanded.

“Because Drucilla is not a Throne, she is an Ophanim,” Azrael interjected. “A Throne is a power and a title and has nothing to do with what has happened. Thoth’s blood mixed with Drucilla’s blood. She died as a result. When she returned, she returned in a symbiotic relationship with Thoth. In the simplest terms, you were infected with a Throne—Drucilla was reborn as an Ophanim.”

“She had to die first.” Drake pondered that revelation as he began to pace.

Drake stopped, glanced at Azrael, and then back to Raziel. “To clarify, when you say, ‘fit to possess a Throne,’ you mean physically, not mentally.”

“Precisely.”

Leviathan and Persephone glanced at each other. Drake looked down at the floor for a moment in contemplation, then back to Raziel. “If I am unable to physically contain the Throne, then what?”

“The Throne would be exorcised from your body and placed in another vessel.” Raziel peered at Drake with a piercing gaze. “You must understand that Calliope cannot die. If she were to perish, the transition to death would no longer occur. There would be no process of death. At all. Every human under the ground would awaken. Every disease-stricken or fatally maimed human would persist in agony for eternity."

Drake winced slightly at the information. "How much time do I have?"

"How much longer will you remain, Drake? Quantifying Earth time in this realm is difficult, but I would say possibly two hundred years, perhaps less."

"Two hundred?" Drake asked. "That hardly seems imperative."

"Two hundred in *this* realm. A hundred years may pass in this realm for each year on Earth. From an Earthly perspective, you will have less than two years."

Drake sat down and put his face in his hands.

Azrael felt a sudden familiar presence nearby but was unable to understand it. He glanced at Drake. Then, he shifted his eyes around the room. Samael caught onto Azrael's change in demeanor.

"What is it, brother?" Samael asked quietly.

"I do not know. But I feel a familiar presence. Something is here that does not belong."

"Another Seraph, perhaps?"

"Possibly… It is familiar, but I cannot gain a firm grasp on it."

"There are no other Seraphs here. I assure you," Leviathan insisted.

Drake looked up at Azrael and narrowed his eyes. He knew what Azrael was feeling. Drake stood up and walked over toward him. He stopped and stood a few feet in front of him. Azrael looked down at Drake.

"Celestial Deal," Drake said.

"What are you implying?" Azrael said.

Drake turned away from Azrael and looked at Raziel. "I have a pact with Lucifer."

"Indeed," Raziel responded.

"My agreement with Lucifer is that I will rule indefinitely in his stead until he deems it appropriate and returns to take his seat among the seven kings. I must exist until the deal is complete, right?"

Raziel leaned back in his chair and interlaced his fingers. He put his index fingers to his chin and contemplated.

"Then there has to be a way to suppress the Throne until the deal is complete," Drake surmised.

"Hm. You are correct, Drake. According to law, you must exist until the deal is fulfilled." Raziel raised his hand to his forehead and summoned a divine tome made of light that manifested in front of him. The book opened, and pages flipped frantically until it finally stopped. Raziel glanced down at the open tome. He read briefly, then waved the tome away, it dissipating before him. "Regrettably, we do not have an immediate solution. I must consult the Virtues." Raziel stood up and straightened his suit. "I will contact you after we have found a solution. Leviathan, thank you for your cordiality."

"It's not going to be a year, is it?" Drake asked, irritated at the lack of conclusion.

Raziel had already disappeared along with Samael. Azrael stood silently facing Drake with his hollowed-out eye sockets. Drake looked back at Azrael in confusion. They held each other's stare briefly. Drake shrugged at him, "What? Was there something more? I believe your time here has run out." Drake snarked and grinned deviously.

Azrael smiled, the feature fitting unnaturally on his face. He gestured toward Drake, passing his finger through the air. Drake felt something stir inside him, the tickle of a cough in his lungs that wouldn't fully manifest. And in response, he could feel Calliope shift. "Your soul shines brightly, Drake. Shines like a lighthouse to ships at sea—for now. I'll return when it's time to collect it." Azrael disappeared.

Drake's smug expression faded slowly into uneasy foreboding and a disquieting panic.

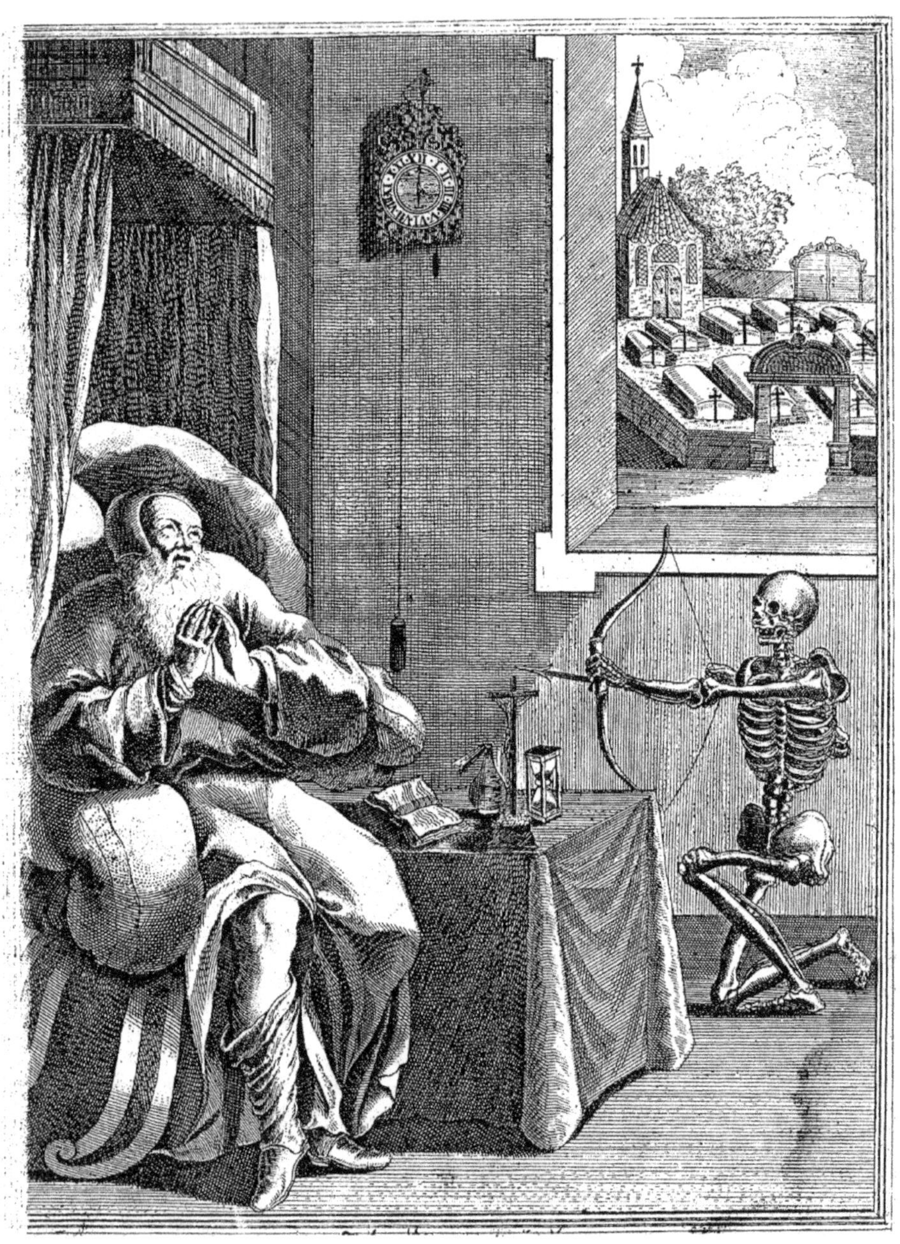

CANTICLE THREE

"The sky is turning grey; bodies walk around me. It's just another day, waiting for the dream." —Killing Joke

Adrian stepped out into the crisp early morning air. The sun was barely peaking over the horizon. A slight cast of orange light slid back the sheet of navy-blue sky. He could feel a shallow breeze blow through his Cosmic Essence, expanding and contrasting with the wind's direction. He looked at the forest across the street from the front porch. The trees abruptly formed a break, as if of their own volition, in the dense, dark forest that boarded Drucilla's neighborhood. Adrian raised an eyebrow with suspicion. He took a few steps down the porch and looked over his shoulder. Azrael stood motionless on the porch behind him for a moment, finally nodding for Adrian to proceed.

"Do something meaningful with my death," Adrian reminded himself.

He proceeded across the street to the entrance of the forest. He took a final glance back to Azrael, but Azrael had vanished. The sun emerged from the horizon casting a bright white glow over the top of the forest. Stripes of light and shadows filtered through the trees and lined the forest floor. Adrian followed the path as it slowly revealed itself, step by step, while he moved deeper into the woods. Eventually, he reached a ridge of broken trees, upturned rocks, and recently disturbed foliage. He stood upon the ridge and looked down to the gouged Earth below. The massive boulders below seemed to act as a barricade to something hot contained within—streams of smoke filtered upwards through the spaces between the rocks.

"What happened here?" he whispered to himself.

Adrian walked down the ridge to the dredge below. He stopped before the boulders and looked around the wreckage of ravaged Earth. The area was still and eerily silent.

"Nothing will grow here," a small voice cracked the silence.

Startled, Adrian turned to his left. A small girl turned her gaze to him. Her curly, auburn locks spiraled down her shoulders. She wore a long gown made of leaves and twigs that blended into the ground below her feet. Her child-like eyes were deep purple and contained millions of points of light like a nebula full of stars. Her pouty bright pink lips smiled with slightly turned-up corners.

Adrian appeared perplexed at the odd child. "What do you mean nothing will grow here?"

"It's scarred," she responded in a child's voice. She moved behind Adrian to his other side.

"Scarred?" he questioned. He glanced to his right side; the child was now a woman. His eyes widened at the transformation. She stood equal to him in height with the same curly, auburn hair. It was clearly the same little girl, only older.

"It will take eons to heal or for any living thing to return."

She looked out over the landscape, then slowly turned her gaze back to Adrian. Her galactic eyes peered into him. Adrian felt uneasy at the strange humanoid and turned his attention back to the decimated landscape. She turned and moved away from him.

"Are you Gaia?" he asked. He turned to face her, but she was gone.

"I am the Throne of Life, Adrian," she was directly behind him now.

Adrian turned to face her. She now appeared as an older woman. Her once auburn locks were now strewn with strands of grey and silver threads. Her cosmic eyes blazed like a thousand suns.

Again, the jarring transformation caught Adrian off guard. "You know who I am?"

"I do know you. I have known you for over a hundred thousand years. I was there when you emerged from the primordial sea. I watched as you learned to use stone tools and as you learned to cultivate and harvest your food. You've been the sons and daughters of spiritual leaders, lords, kings, artists, scholars, and doctors. You think I am talking about all of mankind, but I mean you, Adrian. Your essence is unique. You have acquired such vast knowledge through nearly infinite lifetimes. Your soul was among the first created, durable and enduring. You and your rare brothers and sisters are the reason the Agglomeration exists today."

"Why don't I remember any of it?"

The Throne walked up to Adrian and stood in front of him. She placed her hand on his cheek. "You will if you choose for me to free you. You will have access to all the memories of your previous incarnations." She moved past him.

"Wow, really?" Adrian turned around to face her.

The Throne of Life turned into a small child again. "Yes. Or you may choose the path of the Nodenti," she said in a child-like voice. "Like this Earth, the Agglomeration is scarred." She motioned to the devastated grounds.

Adrian slowly scanned the surroundings. It was evident that a tragic and catastrophic event happened here.

"Your friend Drucilla helped save this planet from destruction by the Unholy."

"Is that what happened here?" Adrian asked.

Adrian turned to face the Throne. She appeared as a woman again. "Yes, she, along with Thoth. But that's not what is vital right now. You can heal the Agglomeration. You can save the souls within and those who are yet to return from devastation by fracturing. Instead of taking eons to heal, which could cause greater fracturing, you can heal it instantly. You alone can fix the ruin contained within. We have been without a Noden for centuries. The Agglomeration needs you."

Gaia's chest began to illuminate in a bright purple glow. She gently placed her hand on her chest. As she pulled her hand away, a flower bulb emerged from her chest into her palm. It resembled that of an orchid, the size of her heart and emitting a blue radiance. She extended her arm out to Adrian to hand him the bulb.

Adrian looked at the bulb that she presented to him for a moment before placing his hand on top of it and accepting it from her. He held the bulb in his hand, then looked back to her face. Gaia had taken the form of the older woman again.

"You have choices to consider. You can consume this seed, this Globe of Dawn, and it will unlock your memories. You can give this seed to The Fates, and you will be trained as a Nodenti, and learn the alchemical process of healing the Agglomeration. Lastly, this is the most important choice: you keep the seed and may resurrect one human from death. You may resurrect yourself."

Adrian gasped, "I can be alive again?"

"That is correct. If you choose, you may live again, Adrian. I will leave you to your choice," Gaia said.

Adrian looked down at the Globe of Dawn, emanating a blue glow in his hands. Azrael's words echoed in his head. *You will face many challenges. Situations that will challenge your ethics, your pride, and your patience.* When he looked up again, Gaia had circled the maw in the Earth and knelt at its edge. Carefully, lovingly, she plucked from the scarred Earth a dying plant and inspected it. Her form continued to change from girl to woman to elder each time Adrian blinked. As he stood and watched, he felt the Globe in his hands. It felt like it was getting heavier.

"How do I choose?" Adrian asked himself. He held up the Globe.

"Memories. I could get back all the lifetimes of memories my soul has. Hundreds of lives worth? A million experiences? A multitude." Adrian rolled the Globe in his hand and thought for a moment longer. "And then what? I'm still dead, right? Would any of that knowledge help me now? Do I chance it on a toss of the dice that I was a necromancer in a previous life? A dead man who knows everything."

Gaia was true to her word, leaving Adrian to contemplate on his own. When Adrian looked for her again, she was gone. He could still feel her presence, but she had taken from the soil what she had come for and moved out of sight.

"Or I can resurrect myself. Okay. Yeah. That one's obvious. I'm alive again. But I've been dead a while. I can't just go back home. I can't just re-enter my old life. And what does regaining my life do? I'll just die again someday and be right back here again. I'd just be prolonging the inevitable."

Adrian paced about the edge of the crater. He looked out over the craggy Earth and at the devastation that had been wrought.

"Or, I can become a healer of souls. Heal the engine that gives us life. Fix the breaks in it before they get worse and undo the damage. Sounds important. But if it was so important, then why…"

Adrian looked up. "Gaia? I have questions. Can I ask you questions about this?"

"Of course, you can," the womanly voice came from behind him, and as he turned, Adrian could see her adult self.

"If the Nodenti are so important, why are there none

now? Why not train more before now?"

Gaia smiled. "Azrael was right about you. And, yes, you deserve to know the caveats to your choices before you make one." Adrian blinked, and Gaia was once again her elder self. "To be a Nodenti, you have to be in possession of a rare soul. One capable of staying whole each time it is imbued with new life. That alone makes the candidates extremely rare."

Adrian nodded. "And years ago, those souls would become Seraphs, right?"

"Right, if they made that choice. They could become Nodenti, otherwise. So, as you can imagine, the relatively unknown role of healer had even fewer souls choosing the path."

"Right. And what happened to the Nodenti? Why are they no more?"

Adrian blinked, and Gaia was a child. She looked up at him. Her face darkened. "The good ones faded away. And the bad ones were destroyed."

"What?" Adrian's jaw dropped, and he looked away in shock.

"It requires your spiritual energy to heal the fractures in others, Adrian." Gaia's voice was, once again, more soothing in her womanly form. "The path of the Nodenti is one of learning how to best spend your energy to reweave soul fabric and to do it as efficiently as possible. Sufficiently mastering the power, you could still exist for a millennium before finally exhausting your essence."

Adrian felt cold. There it was, the negative of this choice.

His shoulders sunk. He watched as elder Gaia moved into his eyesight before him.

"Why not heal it yourself? Surely you or another Throne could just undo the damage or remake the Agglomeration."

"We could remake it, yes," Gaia's old face looked stern. "And lose everything the souls have put into it over the eons. Sacrifice them all for a fresh start." Her voice matched her face, conveying almost displeasure at the statement. Adrian shied away from her gaze.

"And, sadly," she continued as a child once more, "no Throne remains who is of the same as the Agglomeration. No god or power compatible to heal it. None else to delve it, save for you."

Adrian watched Gaia as she spoke, noting her words and how they fit. And how they didn't. He never got the impression she was lying or hiding the truth. In fact, he was sure she wasn't, but he could still sense she was holding something back. As he blinked and her adult form reflected back to him, he couldn't help but shake the feeling time was running out. He closed his eyes and shook his head.

"And the 'bad ones'? What happened?"

The lines on Gaia's old skin creased, enhancing her sobering look. "Destroyed for violating their station for their own ends."

"Violating how?"

Gaia regarded Adrian with a look suggesting she was about to chastise him for asking, but the stern look gave way, and she continued instead.

"Some of the Nodenti decided that giving up their essences in service to the Agglomeration was too high a price to pay. But rather than giving up their station, they formed a sect and experimented with their soul weaving. Eventually, they discovered they could unravel the Cosmic Essence of Celestials and used that instead of themselves. Dozens of Celestials would die at their hands before they were put down for it."

"My god... They killed angels and demons to heal the Agglomeration?"

"No, they killed them to heal the Agglomeration *and* to prolong their existence. An ounce of celestial energy was like a dozen Nodenti or more in terms of raw power. One could sustain a Noden for an age."

"And so, they were killed for murdering Celestials."

"No, they were killed because they were playing with power that, with one mistake, could have blown the entirety of the Agglomeration to an irrevocable end. They thought themselves above the natural order and were willing to destroy it to prove it."

Adrian fell silent as he thought, biting his thumb, and letting his eyes cast down.

"It is a lot, but now you know." The child's voice broke the silence. "There's none left without you. And something big is coming, something Azrael says could shatter the Agglomeration if we don't have help. He's trying to stop it, and he thinks you can do it."

Adrian shook his head and clenched his eyes shut,

making them sting. He felt a hand on his shoulder and looked to see Gaia's adult form reaching out to him, looking to reassure him.

"And so do I," she said as she smiled pensively at him.

Adrian looked at Gaia. He drew in a deep breath and clenched the Globe of Dawn. Meeting Gaia's nebulous eyes. "Alright. I've decided." He screwed a look of determination into his face. "Take me to the Fates. This is for them."

Gaia smiled again and took the hand in which Adrian held the Globe. Gently, she unwrapped his fingers, took the Globe from him, and pressed it against her chest. It blazed alight in a golden hue as it dissolved back into her body. When the light subsided, she met Adrian's gaze again. "It is done. The offering is accepted."

"Wait," Adrian gasped. "You're the Fates?"

"Was it not obvious?"

CANTICLE FOUR

"We all have a monster inside. The difference is in degree, not in kind."— Douglas Preston

"Excuse me, sir, but are you Nate D'Silva?" the young man asked, staring starry-eyed at the A-list celebrity standing before him.

A wide grin stretched across Lucifer's face. "Why yes, yes I am."

"Oh, my God! Can I get a pic?!" the young man asked enthusiastically.

Thursdays at Drucilla's Corvidae Gallery were generally slow and low-key. The shops and galleries on this street cater to tourists on the weekends. But today, the unusually large crowd could have partially been attributed to the abysmal, dreary late-autumn weather and chilly temperature of the Pacific Northwest that compelled the townsfolk and tourists to migrate indoors rather than their usual window shopping. Drucilla's gallery offered a contrast to the grey outdoors, a warm and beautiful arrangement of fine art in bright, bold colors and textiles. Drucilla loved being able to talk with random patrons about the artwork and the artists that she hosted on her walls. Engrossed in her conversations, Drucilla often failed to notice anyone outside of her immediate bubble. Today was no different.

Lucifer put his arm around the young man's neck and smiled as he held his phone up to face them. Other gallery patrons began to notice the celebrity's presence and hastily made their way toward him, clamoring for a photo. Like a rippling effect, one-by-one people quickly whipped out their phones to take videos of the spectacle.

The sudden commotion near the entrance of the gallery interrupted Drucilla's conversation with her client. Hordes of people poured into the lobby from the street. Many folks were pointing through the large windows from the outside and holding up their phones.

"Mr. D'Silva! Nate!!" random voices shouted.

Drucilla pushed her way through the gathering crowd. Her petite stature made it difficult to see over the tops of heads.

"Drucilla, how are you?" Lucifer beamed brightly. He continued to take photos with the crowd of fans surrounding him.

Drucilla crossed her arms and let out a heavy, annoyed sigh as she closed her eyes and rubbed the bridge of her nose. Everyone in and around the gallery saw an A-list celebrity, save for Drucilla, who was well adapted to seeing through Lucifer's facade.

"Nate, I thought you were going to call me before showing up for a private viewing?" Drucilla said angrily.

Hordes of hands reached out with pamphlets and magazines demanding a signature, and others fought to get behind him while holding up their phones for quick selfies and videos of themselves near the A-lister. Lucifer attempted to keep up with the pens and papers shoved in his face. He amused himself, smiling for the photos in between, quickly scribbling out his name on the papers.

"Thank you! Thank you!" Lucifer repeated over and over to the growing crowd.

Drucilla had enough. "Can we stop, please?" she shouted loud enough for everyone in the gallery to hear.

In an instant, everyone stopped moving. The room went silent. The elaborate, steampunk-styled grandfather clock near the front door ceased its constant ticking. Drucilla's wide eyes made a pass around the motionless patrons, eventually locking with Lucifers. Seeing he was equally shocked at the silence, she covered her hand with her mouth and slowly walked around the room.

"What…what did I do?"

"You slowed time, obviously." Lucifer shrugged at her ignorant question.

"I've never done this before."

Lucifer chuckled to himself.

Drucilla's eyes shifted around. "How do I make it go again?"

"It is going, but extremely slow. Time does not stop, Drucilla, but you can affect how it flows."

"Okay, how do I make it go back to normal speed?"

Lucifer crossed his arms. "You have had entirely too much guidance. It is time that you learn to figure things out for yourself."

Drucilla pressed her lips together in annoyance at Lucifer's response. She exhaled heavily through her nose. *I can do this. I'll just yell at it to start like I did to stop it.* "Continue!" Drucilla implored.

Nothing happened. The room remained still. Lucifer laughed quietly. "Continue!" Lucifer mocked and giggled. "You lack conviction. Drucilla, demand for time resume."

"I thought I did?"

"Clearly, you did not."

"This is stupid."

Lucifer continued to chuckle to himself. Drucilla remembered in movies, when someone wanted to start time, they would snap their fingers. Drucilla held up her hand and snapped her fingers. Time didn't resume. Lucifer laughed harder.

"Why can't I do this?" Drucilla yelled.

Lucifer snapped his fingers. The gathering crowd resumed and continued to demand Lucifer's time. Lucifer watched Drucilla while still chuckling to himself.

"What did I do wrong?!" Drucilla shouted.

"Nothing, it was me the whole time. I did it," Lucifer shouted back, laughing.

Drucilla stiffly dropped her arms and stormed off to her office.

"Please excuse me. I have an appointment," Lucifer told the crowd as he pushed past to follow Drucilla. He opened the door to Drucilla's office and closed it behind him.

"You're a real dick sometimes. You know that?" Drucilla growled.

"Oh, do not be so cantankerous. Genuinely, you grow less humorous as time continues. Honestly, you are becoming a bit akin to Azrael every day," Lucifer complained.

Drucilla narrowed her eyes. "And why the Hell do people think you look like Nate D'Silva?!"

Before he could answer, the abrupt ringing of Lucifer's phone reverberated through his chest pocket. He opened his blazer, fetched the small electronic device from his pocket, and hit the answer button. "This is Nate…"

Drucilla cocked her head to the side and squinted at Lucifer.

"One moment, please," Lucifer said and looked at Drucilla. "It is my agent. I will only be a moment."

"Agent? What?"

Lucifer put his finger up to Drucilla and went back to his call.

The abrupt knock on the office door startled Drucilla. She walked over to the door and cracked it open to see Dominic's face between the door and the frame.

"What is going on, Dru?" Dominic asked in a panic.

Drucilla reached for Dominic's wrist as the crowd leaped up to look over Dominic's massive shoulders to get another glimpse of the celebrity. She pulled him through and locked the door behind him. The banging on the door and yelling of Nate's name became louder and louder.

"What is the commotion about—" Dominic's jaw dropped at the sight of Nate.

Lucifer grinned at Dominic as he ended his call.

"Mr. D'Silva, I am a huge fan!" Dominic said excitedly as he reached for Lucifer's hand.

"Dom, it's Lucifer. It's a façade," Drucilla interrupted.

Dominic stopped and quickly blinked as if to clear his vision.

"Oh, all right." Lucifer reluctantly dropped his glamour into his natural state for Dominic.

Dominic crossed his massive arms. "Far be it from me to question why you'd choose a popular celebrity as your persona, but aren't people going to wonder how you can be in two places at once? How do you navigate that?"

"What do you mean? I am here. Nate is here in Port Townsend," Lucifer explained.

"I mean, these photos are definitely going to be posted on social media. You don't think folks are going to see the real Nate D'Silva somewhere else at the same time and wonder how you're in two different places?"

"Dominic, there is only one Nate D'Silva."

Drucilla and Dominic looked at each other inquisitively.

"Wait, you mean you really are him?" Drucilla asked.

Lucifer grinned his prideful and arrogant grin.

"I don't believe it." Drucilla flung open the laptop on her desk and typed in a search engine. "Naaaaaate D'Silvaaaaa," she said aloud as she typed his name into the image search. Shockingly, every photo that Drucilla scrolled through was a photo of Lucifer. Drucilla sat back, slack-jawed. She rolled her eyes up to Lucifer's face.

Dominic rubbed the top of his head and folded his arms as he glowered at Lucifer in irritation. "Drucilla, his name is an anagram."

Drucilla blinked rapidly. She quickly shuffled the letters in her head. "Devil Satan? Are you serious right now?"

Lucifer arched his eyebrow.

"Dru, you really must get back to the gallery. You don't need these people wrecking the place. Also, you should know the police have barricaded off the entire street for one block due to the enormous crowd," Dominic stated. He glanced out the office window to the street.

"Fuck's sake, Lucifer!" Drucilla yelled.

"You might want to get some help. I don't think you can run this place on your own anymore. I mean, not if this guy is going to be making random appearances."

Drucilla threw up her arms as she reached for the office door, exited, and shut it behind her.

Dominic vigorously shook his head. "This really drifts into the realm of not my business, but what brings you to this wasteland of a planet? You have the entire celestial empire to run amok. You can't possibly be bored already."

"Oh, Dominic! It is so tedious and trite. I do not know how the Seraphs tolerate such blandness. It is cloying. I feel myself becoming increasingly perturbed." Lucifer rubbed his hands together, seemingly to alleviate tension.

"Well, what do you do up there?"

"Up? No Dominic. Heaven is not *up*. It is another dimension. If anything, it is approximal, juxtaposed, the same as Hell. Portals to either realm exist all over the planet."

"Okay, so what do you do *over* there?"

"The Seraphs condition and run drills for entertainment." Lucifer crossed his arms. He leaned against a structural beam in the center of the office.

"Like a military?"

"Yes! Exactly."

"That sounds, uh, boring."

"Quite boring! However, being an action film star on Earth requires my frequent attendance to fulfill my obligations. It is either that or an attempt to get back into the good graces of the Infernal Sphere. With Drucilla's brother running the place, I do not think Drake will welcome me with open arms."

"Yeah, Dru's brother..." Dominic's face faded from curiosity to paranoia.

"Did I say something wrong?"

Dominic shook his head and looked away from Lucifer to the floor.

"What has you troubled?"

"You remember when you were teaching me how to use the portal with the stylus, and you put some random images in my head?"

"Of course."

"I saw something. I don't know exactly what I saw. I can't be certain, but—" Dominic abruptly stopped. "You know now that I'm saying it out loud, it's stupid. Never mind."

"Please, continue, Dominic."

Drucilla swung open the door and interrupted the conversation, "Finally!" she exhaled. "Everyone is out. I told them that Nate had exited through the back entrance. You wouldn't believe how fast the gallery cleared out." Drucilla noticed the concerned look on Dominic's face. She looked back at Lucifer. "What did I miss?"

"Nothing, really," Dominic answered. "Lucifer was just telling me how he was not enjoying his time in the other realm."

"Well, I guess you could always move back into Drake's old house now that he's…well, you know, King of Hell." Drucilla shrugged. "If you don't mind living amongst us plebians."

Lucifer gave Drucilla a surprised look. "You would not mind?"

"I'm never going to live in Drake's mansion. I guess I should think about selling at some point."

Lucifer looked at her conspicuously.

"You've been there. There's art in that house worth millions. Some of it is priceless. I don't think I could keep any of it. I mean morally and ethically, possibly legally." Drucilla sat down at her desk. "I don't know how Drake obtained all of it and—"

Lucifer snorted loudly and cut her off by chuckling to himself.

"What? What are you laughing about?" Drucilla demanded.

"What do you mean, 'what?' Drucilla, you are the female embodiment of Indiana Jones. You have more priceless artifacts in your bunker than any single human has any right to own."

"That's different, Lucifer. No one even knows that stuff exists. It's not, like, famous or anything. Drake probably has the goddamn Mona Lisa in that house."

"He does."

Drucilla threw her hands up, rolling her eyes as far back as they would go, and exhaled deeply. "Of course, he does. I don't know what I was thinking."

"Thank you, Drucilla. I appreciate your generosity."

"Whatever, have at it. Burn it down for all I care. Any reminder of Drake isn't something I want to hang on to at this point."

"Understood," Lucifer conceded, and he turned his attention to Dominic. "Dominic, we shall talk later about your concern."

Dominic stared at Lucifer for a moment before nodding his head. Lucifer blinked out.

"You okay?" Drucilla asked.

"It's nothing, really. I thought I saw something weird in Hell when Lucifer was teaching me to use the portal."

"I'm pretty sure there's lots of weird shit in Hell."

"Dru, I don't know what I saw, and honestly, I didn't think about it until Lucifer brought up Drake. It's really not a big deal."

"Well, if it's stressing you out, it is."

Dominic exhaled deeply. "I saw…I saw Drake sitting at a large round table, and to his left was—"

The ringing of Drucilla's cell interrupted the conversation. She glanced down at the phone screen as it lay on her desk. "It's my mom. I have to take this. We'll talk later, okay?"

"It's fine. I got to get back to the shop."

Drucilla nodded at Dominic as she pressed the answer button.

CANTICLE FIVE

"So, where's the grace? Where do we find it?"—Hocico

†

Drucilla took one last look around the gallery before she closed for the night. She checked and double-checked, the front desk to ensure she locked the cabinets.

"Ms. Blackwood?" The voice of a young man came from behind her.

Startled, Drucilla turned around, "I'm sorry, I'm about to close. Is there something I can help you with?"

"Hello, I am Ash," he said. He approached Drucilla and extended his hand. "Ash Palm. I observed on your website that you're looking for an assistant. Are you still looking?"

"Wow, that was fast. I just posted that an hour ago. Yes, I am still looking. You are the first to answer." She extended her hand to shake his. "Tell me about yourself, Ash."

Ash was a slender young man, average in height, and appeared to be in his early twenties. His dark, reddish hair was neatly coiffed, his face clean shaven, with intense light caramel-colored eyes. His style was business casual, a neat and crisply ironed shirt. He appeared to take a bit of pride in how he looked. Drucilla couldn't tell if he was from a wealthy family or if he simply put a lot of effort into his appearance.

"I recently moved from Tampa. I graduated from the University of Florida with a BA in Art History." He handed Drucilla his resume on heavy, white paper.

"Wow, fresh out of college. Why come to a small town in Washington state? Certainly, you have better career opportunities on the East Coast?" Drucilla took a cursory glance at his education and skillset.

"My father is not doing well on his own. He needs help. I will be spending the next year here."

"I'm sorry to hear that," Drucilla responded empathically. "Well, Ash, this job isn't very glamorous, and it's part-time…late afternoons mostly. The pay is average, and you must be available most weekends. I close the gallery to the public on Mondays and Tuesdays, although I will be here those days. I pretty much work constantly. Basically, I need someone who can perform clerical tasks and help out with packing and shipping. Do you know how to build wooden crates?"

"I can. I can also design and set up displays."

"Great. I may also need you to open and close the gallery at times. Shouldn't be too often." Drucilla wandered the gallery and pointed at random works on the wall. "You'll need to familiarize yourself with the artists and even deliver items locally at times. Is that a problem?"

"No issues at all. In fact, that particular painting you're standing in front of was made by Margret Clark. She grew those sunflowers in her garden."

Drucilla quickly blinked in shock. "How in the world did you know that?"

"She's my father's neighbor."

"That would make sense." She nodded. "Have you ever worked in a gallery before?"

"I have not been employed by a gallery, but I did spend a summer at the Kolby College Museum of Art assisting with displays and lighting for various exhibits." Ash flipped through the images in his portfolio. He handed Drucilla a photograph of a pop exhibit consisting of shelves with various colored canning jars. The names of the colors were crudely written with a pencil on top of white masking tape for labels. It looked like a supply cabinet of someone who created custom glazes for pottery. "It's the artist demonstrating a crucial role in creating his works. To give you a kind of glimpse of the laborious and sometimes unrewarding task that goes into creating just the right color combination to give the piece its own personality and emotion that the piece is trying to convey."

Drucilla peered curiously at the photo, then back to Ash, then back to the photo.

"Wednesday, 11 a.m.?"

Ash nodded slowly and smiled.

CANTICLE SIX

"I am weary of days and hours, desires, dreams and powers,
although it makes me weep." —Clan of Xymox

✝

Drucilla excitedly flung open the door of Dominic's shop. His brass doorbell dislodged from the doorframe and flew again into the wall behind Dominic's head.

"Dru! 'The hell?!'"

"Guess what? I have a new assistant!" Drucilla blurted, ignoring Dominic's protest.

"Uh, cool?" Dominic gave a single thumbs up. He bent down to pick up his newly dented bell, staring up at Drucilla, unamused.

Drucilla crossed her arms. "Dom, I essentially have two jobs right now. I really needed the help."

"Dru, I know. It's why I suggested it." He set the bell on the countertop.

The smile from Drucilla's face faded as she walked over to the hand-carved antique dining table that had become a permanent fixture in Dominic's shop. Dominic watched Drucilla as she ran her finger over a chair's intricately carved mahogany cresting rail.

"You, okay?" He noticed the change in her demeanor.

"Why wouldn't I be?"

"I'm not blind, Dru. Over the past year, you only had fleeting moments of happiness here and there since the battle of the Hellgate. I never know quite how to approach you. Your mood swings are quick, like a light switch. One minute excited, the next minute you're lost in your own head."

Drucilla's eyes shifted as if she were processing what he was saying.

"I don't know if it's because of seeing Drake or because you've lost the ability to communicate with the dead. I mean, that's kind of become a part of your identity. You've been able to do it for years. I know Adrian is part of that. And you never want to seem to talk about anything. We don't really communicate like we used to. Every interaction since has been superficial. You're like a swift-moving undercurrent. The surface seems calm, but underneath, you're raging. You wanna talk about it?"

"Nope."

"Okay. I'm here when you're ready."

"Okay."

"So..." Dominic started, searching for something to change the subject. "Azrael still MIA?" Dominic asked, changing the subject. He looked down and sorted through his receipts.

Drucilla shrugged. "I don't know what's going on with him. I haven't seen or heard from him in months. Maybe that's a good thing. Maybe if he does show up, it means things are about to go sideways."

"That's probably the right assumption. He is Death, so we should probably take his absence as a sign that things have calmed down. For now, at least."

Drucilla looked around the shop, deep in thought, then turned to Dominic. "I think about the barrier spell a lot. I lay in bed at night, wondering if the dam is going to break any minute. Like, when I'm most vulnerable. It's intrusive in my thoughts. Do you ever think about it?"

"Sometimes, but I also know that we have Lucifer and/or Azrael that would alert us if there was even a slight possibility that shit would go awry."

"Have you been back to the forest since it happened?" Drucilla inquired.

Dominic wrinkled his forehead. "No, I don't have any reason to go back."

Drucilla stared at him for a moment before nodding in agreement.

†††

Drucilla stood on the edge of the ridge. Her glowing, ethereal, blue eyes looked down into the barren pit of gouged Earth and the mound of enormous boulders that kept the entrance to Hell barricaded. Locals passed off the incident as a possible earthquake or a lava tube that tried to surface. With the amount of volcanic activity in the area, it wasn't that far-fetched.

The bright blue veins pulsating through her arms and shoulders stretched across her back and gave way to blue-grey wings as they unfurled. The multitude of eyes lining the ridges of her four Ophanim wings allowed her to see all directions, simultaneously. This usually caused chaos in her brain, but she learned to compartmentalize her visual signals over time. The transition from human to ophanim was far from smooth since becoming the host for Thoth. Somedays, she wished she had never laid eyes on the relic that transformed her. Other times, she felt empowered to change the universe.

She glided down to the bottom of the pit and glanced at the area where Calliope met her demise. Not even a crumb of charred debris remained. It had all washed away over the year, almost like it never happened. The area was eerily silent. Not a bird or a squirrel had returned. She walked towards a group of boulders and stood in front of them. She could hear sounds coming from under the boulders but could not understand what they were, possibly water or flowing lava. She was about to turn away when something caught her eye. A strange silver rock glinted in the daylight.

"What is that?" she whispered.

Her eyes lit up when she realized she was in *the* spot where Calliope had destroyed the amulet. Drucilla bent down and picked up the slab of silver. She held it in the palm of her hand. The object resembled nothing of its former self. She recalled the ancient vestige of Calliope, the hollow, crystal beads that once held divine blood, and the silver talisman of Thoth, the Throne of Knowledge. She had effectively removed a Divine relic from the world by taking the blood of the Ophanim into herself, becoming the host for Thoth. As a teenager, Drucilla remembered when she found it in the Catacombs of Palermo, spending hours admiring the depiction engraved into the surface. Now, there was nothing.

"Drucilla," a familiar voice drawled with the ubiquitous damp, Earthy scent.

Drucilla turned around to face Azrael. He looked down at her and turned his head to the side. He appeared to be studying the slab of silver in her hand.

"The former relic of Calliope?" he asked.

"Well, what's left of her rosary, anyway." Drucilla held the chunk of silver between her fingers. She looked back up at Azrael. "Where've you been?"

"Wars, famine, disease, pestilence, that sort of thing."

Drucilla grinned. "Whatever. It's good to see you. I haven't seen you in…forever."

"It is good to see you too, Drucilla. How is Dominic? The Beast enjoying his time in the Celestial Empyrion?"

"Dominic is doing well. Did you know that Lucifer is an A-list celebrity?"

"Which celebrity? He is a few…"

Drucilla glanced at Azrael. "You know what? I don't even want to know. Forget I brought it up."

"You seem out of sorts. Are you unwell?"

"I don't know," Drucilla shrugged, looking out onto the rocky landscape. "You know, this is the first time since I was seventeen years old that everything has been quiet? The rosary had put my life in constant chaos and turmoil. Now, I'm not even sure how to function as a normal human."

"You aren't human, Drucilla."

"You know what I mean."

"Do you feel you have become mundane? You are fortunate in that you are always free to experience human interests." Azrael gestured toward the ground. "There's always archeology."

"I dunno, I guess. And no, that part of my life has passed. The truth is, it was way more exciting and engaging to watch my mother be the archeologist. I guess that's probably what I really wanted. I wanted to be like her."

"Hm. Give me the silver," Azrael imposed. Drucilla looked at him curiously, then complied.

Azrael held the silver in his hand. His eyes emitted an eerie purple hue as his fingers closed around it. He looked down at his hand and opened his palm. He held the newly reconstructed amulet between his long, spindly fingers. He looked at Drucilla and handed her the amulet.

Drucilla's eyes widened as she took the amulet and held it. "Does this mean I will be able to see Adrian?"

"Yes."

"Can I also—?"

"Yes, but don't. Don't perform necromancy."

"So, I can?"

"No."

"Kind of?"

"No."

"A little bit?"

Azrael sighed.

"Honestly, Azrael, I don't see the big deal. So, I raise a

couple of dead bodies out of a bazillion dead bodies that have died over the centuries. Why does it matter so much?"

"There are many reasons why Necromancy is forbidden, Drucilla." Azrael stepped past her and gazed at the landscape as if seeing some far-off thing. "Divine, as well as Unholy, understand the ramifications of removing souls from the Agglomeration and abide by a tenant to never do so unless necessary."

Drucilla watched Azrael, peering at him intently. Azrael caught the impetus to continue explaining. He bent over and scooped up a clump of dirt, rolling it into a ball in his hands. Holding it in one hand, he gathered another smaller clump and turned toward Drucilla.

"When a human dies, their soul returns to the Agglomeration. There, it is slowly rejoined to the unaspected mass of soul matter, the individual dissolving away." He pressed the smaller clump into the larger one, leaving a discernible bump on its surface. "It is a process, and it takes time. The longer a soul is in the Agglomeration, the less of it remains intact." Azrael then smoothed over the bump until it looked the same as the rest of the ball of dirt.

Drucilla watched, unsure whether she should be insulted by the visual aid.

"As you know," Azrael continued, "souls go into the Agglomeration and disseminate their knowledge and experiences. The mass learns, and with a soul rejoined, future humanity is improved by that small, profoundly important amount. And then, when the call arises, the

Agglomeration offers optimal souls to be joined with their new human bodies."

Azrael held the ball in both hands as if it were a revered relic. "The only time you can ever return a soul fully intact is if you can catch it before it rejoins the Agglomeration—a feat in itself, since travel to the Agglomeration is nearly instant. But, if you are quick to block it from rejoining, it is possible to grab it and bring it back."

"Like when Dominic died, and Lucifer brought him back?"

"Precisely. But, for a soul that's rejoined the Agglomeration, if it's only been a little while, most of the soul comes back. If it has been longer, then much less. Until the soul reaches a point where none of the original soul is left to return, but a human vessel can't be animated with anything less than a full soul. So, when you take a soul from the Agglomeration to put it into a vessel, you have to take more, damaging the area where you took it from. We refer to this as fracturing."

"Fracturing? What's fracturing?" Drucilla asked.

Azrael dug a finger into the dirt ball and gouged out a small lump. He then turned the ball so Drucilla could see the hole.

"Fracturing is what happens when you are commanding the soul to return." He held up the gouged dirt and rolled it between his fingers. "It's incomplete. It must infuse with soul matter that is not theirs to fill in the broken gaps. How much of this bit of dirt was part of the original I had pressed into this mass?"

Drucilla thought on this while Azrael continued.

"This can have dire consequences, depending on what parts of the soul were filled from the Agglomeration. Whatever makes you unique, such as your identity, is usually the last to go, with every lesser banal thing you cared about being the first to dissolve. What's brought out is only a fraction of the original soul, and you are cursing it to live fractured with soul matter that is not theirs. If enough of the original soul is intact for it to be sentient, you've condemned it to a kind of Hell in a corpse's shell."

"Oh, I see…."

"That is not the only reason, Drucilla. You must understand that the Agglomeration does not heal quickly from this kind of scarring. When the soul matter is returned, it does not go back neatly into the gaping hole from whence it came." Azrael smashed the small lump back into the ball with no heed to the hole that was still present. "The hole remains. The result is a span of miasmic space that takes eons to repair naturally. The scarred area cannot naturally give up soul matter to create new life as needed properly. Souls given life that come from that area are, at creation, broken and scarred."

"Do these souls exist on Earth?"

"Some. Less so now than has been in the past, thanks to adherence to these rules." Azrael dropped the ball of dirt at his feet and wiped his hands. "We call them 'The Fractured,' and you would likely know them for their negative impact on themselves and humanity around them. Think of those who do evil for evil's sake. Or those who are compelled to perform horrific acts in full remorse for them but are unable to stop. It's unpredictable. The more fractured, the worse the outcome, and usually quite destructive here in life and more so to the Agglomeration once they rejoin."

"Is it always that bad?" asked Drucilla, looking at the disturbed dirt on Azrael's shoes.

"No. A necromancer possessing skill and precision, not unlike that of a world-class neurosurgeon, could conceivably excise the soul without causing scarring. A clean cut, taking only what was needed, can heal quickly enough. But we are talking about a caliber of skill not likely found beyond myself. More so, a similarly skilled healer could smooth the harsh edges of a living Fractured and give them a measure of peace."

Azrael paused.

"You are fortunate that Adrian has refused to pass over to the Agglomeration. You are also fortunate I didn't force him to." Azrael gestured to the amulet. "You may communicate with him now."

Drucilla beamed with excitement. She stuffed the amulet in the pocket of her jeans and smiled brightly at Azrael. "Thank you. You have no idea what you've done for me." She expanded her wings, but Azrael caught her as she was about to leave. She looked down at where his hand wrapped around her wrist, confused.

"Drucilla, while I am elated that I was able to help

you, you must understand that your abilities have consequences. Others may be negatively impacted by your decisions. You must try to find a balance between your desires and those of others, so none are bound to your will and your will alone. I am speaking beyond necromancy."

"Thaaat's cryptic."

"It is not."

"You know, I could have used your support over the past year."

"You never called upon me."

Drucilla put up her finger as if she was going to argue, but he was right. She had never called on Azrael since the battle. She put her hand down and furrowed her brow at Azrael.

"Point taken."

CANTICLE SEVEN

"In this cruel place, your voice above the maelstrom." —Sisters of Mercy

Drucilla bolted up the front porch steps and threw open her front door with such force that she didn't bother to unlock it. The front door bolt bent under pressure, tearing out part of the doorframe.

"Adrian!" Drucilla yelled.

"Adrian?"

Drucilla slowly walked through her house, peering into dark corners and under furniture, as if playing a game of hide and seek. She clenched the rosary pendant tightly in her fist.

Adrian's eyes snapped open. Forcefully, he was jerked from his meditative state. Something wasn't right. He stood up and faced the moving, spiraling helix of the innumerable souls swirling around him in a cosmic dance. He was responsible for monitoring the Agglomeration at the edge of the universe as the only living Noden. He felt a sudden and intense pull. The pull wasn't like the pull of the Agglomeration itself. This was significantly stronger. It was demanding. He couldn't fight it. It was as if his will was disregarded. This was a summoning. Adrian could feel his Cosmic Essence tearing away from his current reality. He could perceive the threads of time stretching and snapping off all around him. It was almost audible. In an instant, he was transported and appeared before Drucilla in the center of her living room.

"Adrian!" she exclaimed. She threw her arms around him.

Adrian was solid, corporeal like he used to be. He could feel her tight embrace as she wrapped her entire body around his ribcage. He peered at his hands over her shoulder and turned them over multiple times, inspecting their front and back before returning her hug. She finally released him and looked into his amber eyes. She was beaming with excitement at the reappearance of her best friend.

Adrian placed his hands on his arms and chest to feel his body. He had been in his spiritual essence for so long that he had forgotten what it was like to have a solid form again.

Drucilla stared at him momentarily. "I lost my amulet. I couldn't see you. Could you see me?"

Adrian wasn't sure how much he wanted to divulge about his new life. He pondered if Drucilla was ready to learn about his path as a Nodenti. He paced the living room for a minute to decide what to say.

"I was here when you came back from the battle," he responded.

"So, you know what happened? I came home to tell you all about it, but..." Her face fell. She remembered how excruciating it was to lose contact with Adrian. She inhaled to quell her anxiety. "We beat back the Unholy. They came up from the ground. Dominic and I fought them off until Azrael and Lucifer joined. The Seraphs showed up at the end. They blocked off the Hellgate with boulders so the Unholy couldn't reemerge. I am not sure how long it will hold."

"Wow, that's incredible. You did it!"

Drucilla nodded. "Dominic died, but Lucifer brought him back."

Adrian narrowed his gaze at Drucilla's words. "How long was he dead?"

Drucilla shrugged. "I don't know for sure. It could have been five minutes, could have been fifty. It doesn't matter. He's alive and well. Why do you ask?"

"This is probably a conversation for another time," Adrian responded.

Drucilla moved to her couch and sat down. She looked up at Adrian. "So? Where have you been up to for the past ten months?"

Adrian held Drucilla's stare for a moment before he finally spoke, "I was, uh, giving my death meaning."

Drucilla blinked rapidly. "What do you mean?"

Adrian clasped his hands and bit the inside of his cheek while he thought about how to respond.

"Well?" Drucilla asked impatiently.

"At the edge of the universe. The beginning and end of life. The Agglomeration." he answered reluctantly.

"What? Agglomeration? Why?"

"As I said, doing something meaningful with my death."

"Why do you keep saying that? You're being awfully cagey." Drucilla pressed her lips together tightly. She felt like he was purposely trying to keep information from her. "I thought we gave each other meaning. We're family!"

"Not like that, Dru. I'm special. I mean to the universe."

"I could have told you that!"

"Dru…"

"Fine, what were you doing in the Agglomeration? Don't tell me you're a Cataclysm now."

"Don't you have to be a Seraph to be a Cataclysm?" Adrian asked.

Drucilla rested her chin on her hand. "Why won't you tell me what's happening?"

"Dru, I can explain later, but right now isn't the time. Just trust me on this, okay? Please."

Drucilla rolled her eyes, realizing she wasn't getting anywhere.

"Dru, you don't do necromancy anymore, do you?"

"I've only done it like…" she glanced at the ceiling momentarily to count the times she had used the rosary beads since she was 17. "Ten times. Why?"

"Don't do it anymore."

"Oh, you're not going to get on my ass about it, too, are you? You and Azrael both, I swear!" Drucilla complained.

"Dru, you don't know what you're doing. You aren't trained," Adrian scolded.

"Um, I'm Thoth. I can do necromancy, thank you very much!"

"Please don't. I can't keep cleaning up your messes."

"My messes? What does that mean?"

Adrian looked at Drucilla and crossed his arms. "Just do me this one favor, please? Don't use necromancy anymore from now on, okay?"

"I won't. I already told Azrael I won't. You're both really uptight about the necromancy thing. What happened over there?"

"There is a lot to tell you, and I swear, I will. But for now, I need to return."

"Like Hell you are! I just got you back!" Drucilla yelled.

"Dru, I'm working on something very important. Right now, I need you to trust me. I'll be back before you know it." Adrian looked around the house. "When was the last time you dusted?"

"I do it all the time!" Drucilla growled.

"This mantle though," Adrian clicked his tongue.

"I'M SHORT, OKAY?!" Drucilla hollered.

CANTICLE EIGHT

"She will call it by name while embracing it."
—Cancerslug

Drucilla sat at her desk, pulling up random searches on the internet for A-list celebrities. She wanted to see how many of them were Lucifer. It had become a bit of a game.

Ash poked his head into Drucilla's office.

"Your gentleman friend is here." Ash motioned over his shoulder toward Dominic, who stood near the gallery's front door with a smirk.

"It's not like that, Ash." Drucilla stood and picked up her backpack.

Ash smiled and nodded. A gesture that made Drucilla feel like he didn't believe her. She shook her head as Dominic entered the gallery and walked towards them.

"Dominic! This is Ash. Ash, this is Dominic."

Ash stuck his hand out to shake Dominic's hand.

It was clear to Drucilla that Dominic immediately disliked Ash, almost dubious at Ash's presence. "Hey," Dominic said unenthusiastically. He stuffed his hands in his pocket. It was unlike Dominic not to shake someone's hand. Ash looked perplexed and studied Dominic's face for a moment before lowering his hand.

"Okay!" Drucilla said. "Uh, Ash, we're gonna head out. I will see you tomorrow."

Ash smiled and nodded again. Drucilla turned and headed for the door, but Dominic would not take his eyes off Ash. Finally, he turned away and started following Drucilla out. Before making it to the door, he looked back. Ash responded by giving the most maniacal smirk he could manage. Dominic's eyes widened, and he hurried to catch up to Drucilla, who was about to walk up the stairs to the pub.

✝✝✝

"I don't like him. He gives me the creeps."

"Stop, you're being dramatic," Drucilla scoffed and sipped her beer.

"He's a creepy dude."

"What is so creepy about him?"

"He's perfect. He's like a Stepford child or something. Young dudes don't look like that. Not unless they're psychotic or sociopathic trust fund babies. I'm telling you, Dru. You need to watch your cat."

"What?"

"I'm serious. Dudes like him will become obsessed with you, and then you'll come home to find your cat, Diablo, strung up in your bedroom with a heart shape cut out of his stomach and a rose between his teeth."

"What the f…?"

Dominic shrugged. Drucilla rolled her eyes, ready to change the subject.

"Well, you seem delightful today. Bad weekend with your family?"

Dominic snarled and sipped his beer, then set it down before him. "Okay, so Baba, my grandma, is old-fashioned, right? She went on this tirade about how much Aleksei, and I disappoint her by not being married and cranking out grandchildren."

"God, I'm glad my mom is progressive," Drucilla remarked. "So, what did you do?"

"So, to Dad's disapproval, I told Baba that maybe one day, when Aleksei can settle on one girl, I'm sure he would give her many grandchildren."

"I take it she wasn't satisfied with that answer?"

"Of course not. She started hollering at me about being a disappointment to the family. It was ridiculous."

"So, what are you going to do?"

"Nothing. There's nothing to do. Because, quite honestly, I don't need to be in a relationship with anybody. If being a theology-obsessed, multi-linguistic bodybuilder that fights demons with an Unholy javelin makes me feel like a complete and whole person, then I don't need or want anything else. And if that makes me a bad person, then I'm the worst."

"I don't think that makes you a bad person, Dom. I think it makes you the coolest person. You and I live in a different world from one else. Let's just figure out how to navigate that for now."

"Agreed." Dominic nodded.

"So, I have something to tell you…"

Dominic peered at Drucilla as she pulled the amulet from around her neck and slid it across the table in front of him. Dominic's eyes enlarged. "Where did you get that? I thought Calliope destroyed it."

"I went to the Hellscape a few days ago and found a chunk of melted silver. Ran into Azrael there. He did this. I wanted to wait and tell you in person."

"He made you another amulet?"

"Nah, he restored it."

"How do you know?"

"I know every cut, crease, chip, and dent in this relic, and they're all present and accounted for," Drucilla said enthusiastically.

"Wait, what? Can you, uh…"

"See Adrian? Yeah, he's back. However, he's up to something secretive. I don't know what it is and he won't talk to me about it. All he will tell me is that he's special, nothing more."

"Strange. It's unlike him to keep things from you. I'm sure he has his reasons, I wouldn't take it personally, Dru. I'm sure the past year has been an experience for him. So, what about the, uh…you know," Dominic asked, changing the subject.

"Yeah, I can. All of it."

"You mean to tell me he's fine with you defiling the dead?"

"Nope! He said absolutely no to the necromancy."

"But you have the ability?"

"Yep, and as far as I'm concerned, that's the same as consent," Drucilla said smugly.

"Dru, where did your mother fail you?" Dominic exhaled in defeat.

†††

Drucilla entered her house, slid off her jacket, hung it on the hat rack, and kicked her shoes onto the floor. The sound annoyed Adrian, so he peeked around the corner, pointed at Drucilla's shoes, and then at her.

Drucilla threw up her hands. She picked up her shoes and stacked them neatly in the cubby hole near the door. "Satisfied?"

Adrian glared at her and popped back into the dining room.

"Christ, it's like living with Joan Crawford," Drucilla mumbled to herself.

"Don't think I can't hear you!" he shouted from the other room.

"Damn, I left my laptop in the car," Drucilla whispered to herself.

Refusing to put her shoes back on, Drucilla hobbled barefoot down the porch steps and gingerly tiptoed across the walkway to her Jeep. She opened the passenger door and pulled out her laptop bag. As she turned back, she came face-to-face with Lucifer.

"Well, hello, Mr. A-List," Drucilla said with a bit of sarcasm. She pulled the laptop bag over her shoulder and crossed her arms.

"Good evening to you, Drucilla."

"What brings you by? Shouldn't you be leaping off twenty-story buildings and driving exotic cars going a million miles an hour?"

"No, of course not. That is for the stunt doubles."

"Just how many celebrities are you?"

"Including the Chilean president's wife? Sixteen."

Drucilla's jaw dropped as she blinked rapidly.

Lucifer glanced down at the amulet that hung mid-way on her torso. He peered at it suspiciously, picking it up and examining it between his long-clawed fingers.

"I see you and Tobit have been in communication." He continued to examine the amulet and then looked into Drucilla's eyes.

"What makes you think I got this from Azrael?"

"Drucilla, unless you have suddenly become proficient in spatiotemporal manipulation, which is quite literally far too advanced for you at this stage, I do not think this is your doing. And, because I did not do it, it leaves only one other possibility."

Drucilla snatched the amulet from his hand.

"If you wanted it back so badly, you could have asked for my assistance. I would have reconstructed it at your request."

"It doesn't matter. All that matters is that Adrian is back." Drucilla walked past Lucifer and headed up her porch steps.

"You do know you do not need it, Drucilla."

"Actually, I do." Drucilla sat down on the top step. "It's been really hard. I've been emotionally exhausted. Everything may be calm right now, but I feel something big is coming, and I don't know when. Having just one person in my life, one constant, more often than my mother, means everything to me."

"I am not attempting to be unempathetic to your dilemma, but you have many constants—" Lucifer stated.

"You don't even have empathy. What would you know of it?"

Lucifer felt slighted by her jab. He exhaled and sat next to Drucilla. "You have experienced a substantial adjustment. I will disregard your insult."

Drucilla glanced at Lucifer for a moment, then at her amulet.

"I want you to understand that when I say you do not need the amulet, it is because you do not need it to interact with Adrian. It's a placebo."

Drucilla looked at Lucifer in confusion. "What are you talking about? I couldn't interact with him for a better part of a year until I got the amulet back."

"You must understand that Adrian has an important job. He cannot be tethered to you for eternity."

"Adrian has free will, Lucifer. When he died, he hung around on his own. I was at his funeral. I wasn't even there for a few days after he died. He stayed around before I knew I could see him, even before I brought his ashes home. I wasn't even an Ophanim when he died. Adrian hangs around because he wants to, although lately, he hasn't been around much." Drucilla said that last part quietly. She stood and picked up her laptop. "Now, he kind of just pops in and out on a whim."

"Understandable," Lucifer remarked. "He still feels the need to watch over you."

"Look, I know he has some huge, important job. One that I still don't know about. Apparently, it's a big secret, since no one will tell me what it is. I doubt you will either." Drucilla glanced up at Lucifer, hoping for an answer.

"That is for Adrian to decide. I can tell you that he is not working alone. But what Adrian is doing is vital to the continuation of humankind. Adrian is special."

"He said that too. That he was special, I mean," Drucilla added.

"Adrian is what is referred to as an Original Soul. This is why he is special. Rather than making large groups of earthly inhabitants, as we did with the Nephilim, we started with a small, controlled group of humans."

"Less clean up, in case they go rogue, I suppose." Drucilla quipped.

"We created one hundred. These one hundred souls are unique. They can manipulate their Cosmic Essence."

"What do you mean, manipulate?"

"They are the blueprints. The template to which all human souls derive. These souls can change how their essence works. Some can use their essence to heal, some to influence, some to help like true prophets, while others can leave their bodies entirely. They merely have to will it."

"Am I an Original Soul? Is that why I'm special?"

Lucifer chuckled to himself. He looked at Drucilla and chuckled again. Drucilla narrowed her gaze at him.

"No, I'm afraid not." He chuckled once more as if her question was beyond absurd.

Chauin. fec.

CANTICLE NINE

"Questions are a burden. And answers are a prison for oneself."— Iron Maiden

Lucifer stood atop a wide, lush cliffside in the Celestial Empyrion's Blue Garden. He slowly ambled towards a tall woman with long, golden hair that rolled in curls softly over her silver pauldrons. His hands were deep in the pockets of his finely tailored black suit, and his appearance was his natural, translucent-skinned state. "You know, Valor, when we were first created," Lucifer started. "Your father was the most self-assured and authoritarian Seraph I had ever known."

Startled, Valor quickly turned to face Lucifer with her right hand gripping the hilt of the sword strapped at her side. Lucifer leaned casually against an enormously tall pillar in the courtyard, glancing over the cliff. The large, blue, flowering trees hovering above created a billowy, aqua canopy over Valor and Lucifer, like gentile, inverted ocean waves.

"I did not mean to startle you," Lucifer apologized.

Valor released her grip from her hilt and crossed her arms. She turned away from Lucifer and looked at the Seraphs training in the valley below. "What do you want?"

"To chat. I know you do not have a favorable opinion of me, but I thought we may try to build a rapport."

"No, thank you."

"I am going to be making many appearances here while I work with Sariel, at least for the foreseeable future. We cannot go about our existence ignoring each other…"

"My father welcomed you here, and I didn't have a say. If I had—"

"You know, Sariel and I were very good friends at one time. He was, and still is, for that matter, an over-achiever, lawful, boring," Lucifer chuckled. He plucked a bloom off the tree above his head and yanked the petals off individually.

Valor didn't respond.

"Until *she* came along…" Lucifer pulled himself away from the pillar, walked up to Valor, and stood a few feet behind her. "No one knows from where Persephone came. Are you aware of that fact?" Lucifer paused and looked around as if he were processing a possible explanation for her existence.

"What do you mean?" Valor spoke in a calm, monotone voice.

"As I said, she is not a creation of ours. At least not as far as the Celestials know. She appeared one day. Maybe, she came from a dream. No one is certain." Lucifer stood parallel to Valor and leaned his back against a tree trunk. He crossed his arms and looked up at Valor. "Sariel was absolutely captivated by her. Although, he would never admit it to anyone, much less himself. He would treat her as he would anyone else in the realm."

Valor turned to Lucifer. "Why are you telling me this?"

Lucifer stared at Valor for a moment before he spoke. "We are also not entirely sure from where you came. One day you appeared—a young sprite. You looked human. Everything about your appearance was that of a human child, but we knew you were not. You are both Persephone and Sariel in one entity. You were like nothing we have ever seen—half Seraph, half Lilim. How could this be? You are fascinating."

Valor exhaled in annoyance.

"Unfortunately for Sariel, Persephone chose me. I mean, can you blame her?" Lucifer laughed. Noticing Valor's disinterest, he quickly composed himself and turned to her. "I did not send you to live with the Priestesses of Hathor when you were a child. That was not my influence. Persephone decided that for herself."

Valor slowly side-eyed Lucifer. "No one said you had."

"Your mother was raw, powerful, clever. She refused to be anything less than equal to any demon or angel. That is why I was intrigued by her. There are very few beings who have outmaneuvered me. She is one of them. She did not want you in the Infernal Sphere. She felt you were special and would be better suited to live with the Egyptians. Humans are weak. She felt that they needed a protector; they needed you. Persephone has an affinity for humans. She cares for them as one would a pet, I suppose."

"I still do not know where you are going with this, Lucifer. I do wish you would get to the point."

"Tell me Valor, do you think your father loves you?"

Valor blinked rapidly at the absurdity of the question. She turned to meet Lucifer's gaze. "Why would you ask me something like that?"

"It is a simple question. Do you feel that Sariel loves you?"

"Yes." Valor's answer was sharp.

"Then why are you not on the council of Virtues?"

"It has nothing to do with love, it is about diplomacy. He does not feel I can be diplomatic enough to handle the position. But I am going to prove to him that I can."

"But why? Why is a Virtue that has more than earned their respect in Celestial Empyrion, who is more powerful and lethal than any other Seraph or Virtue in existence, required to earn their place on the council? You single-handedly defeated a battalion of four hundred Cambions that broke into Heaven. Do you think any other Seraph could have done what you did? I would even go as far as to say that you are more powerful than your father."

"Stop it!"

Lucifer chuckled.

"Why are you laughing?" Valor demanded.

"Because it is just so ridiculous! Valor, had you performed in the Infernal Sphere as you did here in Heaven, I would not have hesitated to make you a general, a president for that matter. Instantaneously, with full privileges."

Lucifer moved closer to Valor and stood directly in front of her. "Sariel's dismissive attitude towards you defies all reason. You deserve better than a meaningless, honorary title." Lucifer exhaled. "Unfortunately, I do not believe he will ever grant you a seat on the council."

"And why not?" Valor snapped.

"The task he has given you is futile."

Lucifer paused to allow his words to penetrate, then continued. "The chosen humans know they are not to surrender any relics, and they will not."

"How… how do you know?"

"Because I had warned them never to surrender the relics. Valor, I have their trust, and they have my guidance. The Virtues and Seraphs do not want a war with the Infernals; their only interest is protecting Earth. In turn, anything that happens in Hell is not their concern."

"But what if the war happens in Hell? What about the humans?"

"What about them? Sariel is to protect Earth, not the humans in the Infernal Sphere."

"But Drucilla's tribe. Why would we not protect them?"

"Ten humans are not an entire populace of Earth. Sariel has his directive, and it is not to protect Drucilla's tribe."

Valor pondered Lucifer's statement. "Then what could we do to protect them?"

Lucifer crossed his arms and shrugged. "I suppose you could gain the trust of the Infernal Sphere. You have an advantage in that you are half Lilim. Hell is open to you. No one would have the temerity to question your entitlement to enter."

"If I enter the Infernal Sphere, Sariel will certainly strip my title."

"A title you never had in the first place," Lucifer refuted.

Valor inhaled deeply.

Lucifer grabbed her hand and placed his hand on top of it. "Valor, although you are not my daughter, I do care for you. This may be your best course of action if you want to help Drucilla's tribe."

Valor pulled her hand away warily.

"You are worthy of being a Virtue. If Sariel will not grant you the position you are entitled to, perhaps you can get it elsewhere. Being half Lilim should never be a limitation. Instead, it should be an impressive augmentation. You are exceptional, Valor. You deserve to be feared and admired. Persephone created you for a purpose, and I assure you it is not to be a foot soldier in an army whose general disregards your formidable talents."

Valor turned away. She was feeling uncomfortable with the thoughts of revolting.

Lucifer stepped behind Valor and whispered in her ear. "You and you alone could destroy worlds. No Virtue in existence has the boundless power that you possess. Sariel knows this and wants to keep you under his thumb. You need not exist this way."

Valor quickly turned around to face Lucifer, but he had vanished. Her eyes darted around, processing his words. She gritted her teeth as her eyes flared with a bright yellow flash.

"I want to assist," Valor announced.

Sariel focused his gaze upon Valor. "In what capacity?"

"Let me prove myself to you," she turned to Sariel. "Let me show you that I can be diplomatic, and I want to earn your confidence."

Sariel rubbed his chin. His large, imposing size, on par with a Cataclysm, made him look powerful, influential, and difficult to defeat. It was easy to see why he was the General of the Virtues,

He turned his attention to a massive floating globe that resembled Earth in the center of a vast strategy room and crossed his arms. "I do have a small task...I had intended to give it to Ramiel. However, I would be willing to designate it for you. The Grigori have informed me that the Tempest is in the possession of an Eoethrian woman. I would like for you to find her. Find out what she knows and how she intends to use it. Gain her confidence and obtain the cauldron. If you succeed, return it to me, and I will speak to the council about possibly allowing you a place among the council."

Valor peered at Sariel curiously. "Possibly?" Valor was not happy with that word.

"I can still offer the assignment to Ramiel if you do not feel confident—"

"No! No, that will not be necessary. I accept. Thank you, Father." Valor turned and headed for the large doors of the chamber.

Valor stopped short of the door and turned to Sariel. "What if she refuses to offer it?"

"You want to prove your diplomacy. This is your opportunity."

Valor nodded.

"Valor, one last thing. Do not involve yourself with human conflicts or concerns. You may find yourself tempted to help—this is not our place. Our engagement with them is to be brief and only when necessary."

"I understand. One question, if I may. What do you intend to do with the Tempest?"

"We must ensure that we maintain possession of Eorthe just as the Thrones intended."

"You plan to use it against the Infernals."

"Do as I ask, Valor, and. I will discuss with the Virtues your participation in the council."

CANTICLE TEN

Drucilla rested her chin on one hand. The other hand fidgeted with a bar magnifier she found on Dominic's table. It was a lazy, calm Saturday afternoon. Drucilla's life consisted of her gallery or hanging out in Dominic's library. Although she appreciated the calm versus the rigorous pace of the prior year, she was becoming bored. Drucilla sat up, picked up the amulet around her neck, and studied it momentarily.

"Dominic, I think we've made a huge mistake."

Dominic peered at Drucilla in confusion. He set his book down and sat at the table across from Drucilla. "What's going on, Dru?"

"I'm hurting the Agglomeration with the necromancy spells we've been playing with. Remember when we rose all the Civil War soldiers in the cemetery last year? We are interfering with the Cosmic Order. We're breaking the system. I didn't understand at first what Azrael was telling me. I get it now."

Dominic looked remorseful. He sat silently for a moment.

"Not everything is bad. Some positives came out of the battle at the Hellgate. I mean, I qualify to become a Seraph.

Sariel did offer me a place when I kick-off this mortal coil. I don't know why." Dominic attempted to change the subject away from the Agglomeration.

"You wield Nova's pen. Maybe that's like an instant get-into-heaven-free card?"

"I also died in battle protecting the Earth from the Unholy. Maybe that's a qualifier too?"

"Yeah, there's that." Drucilla nodded.

"It's too bad. If there were cards, I could hand 'em out to Adrian, my mom, my grandfather…" Dominic mused.

"Your mom? You never talk about your mom. Where is she?" Drucilla said. She walked over to Dominic and watched him peruse his library.

"She died when I was twelve," Dominic responded. He faced away from Drucilla as he scanned his bookshelves. Drucilla waited for Dominic to offer more information, but he didn't say anything further.

"Oh, Dom. I'm sorry. What was she like?"

"What do you want to know?" He glanced over his shoulder at Drucilla, then turned his attention back to the shelf.

"I dunno. Tell me about her. Like, what did she do? What did she look like? How did your parents meet? Things like that." Drucilla repositioned herself on the swivel stool.

"Well, that's an interesting story." Dominic decided on a book and slid it out of the bookshelf. He opened it and glanced at the inside for a second before closing it back up and sliding it back into place. He continued his search.

"My dad was working one night at the hospital. He was making his rounds before heading home for the evening. For lack of a better term, he had a patient who was not long for this world. I guess she was a follower of the Capitoline Triad, some Hellenism. You know Jupiter, Juno, that kind of thing." Dominic grabbed another book, turned around, and placed it on the table.

"His patient was in her room praying with another woman. As Dad explained, the woman turned to face him, and apparently, she was the most beautiful woman he had ever seen in his life. Dad was recently divorced from my older brother's mom, and he wasted no time getting together with my mom. They were married four months later. I came into the world a year later. Her name was Mona, and she had recently immigrated from Santa Maria, a small island country off the coast of Spain. She was tall, about six-one, very strong, and muscular, but feminine. She had long, brown hair and bright, green eyes. She liked to run, climb, and swordfight."

"Swordfight?" Drucilla asked, amused.

"She was into different fighting styles with swords, staves, various stabbing weapons, etcetera."

"Maybe that's why it comes naturally to you?"

Dominic approached his desk and picked up a family picture in a small black frame. He handed it to Drucilla. "On the right side, my dad and Aleksei. On the left, my mother and, of course, me."

Drucilla inspected the image of Dominic's family. She was surprised to see the distinct size difference between Dominic and his mother in comparison to his dad and brother.

"You definitely take after your mother," Drucilla said. "How did she pass, if you don't mind my asking?"

Dominic sat across from Drucilla at the table, pulled a book titled *How to Communicate Through Dreaming* toward himself, and opened it to the table of contents. He paused for a moment.

"We don't really know. Her heart just gave out. Dad always said she was in perfect health. It took everyone by surprise. The peculiar thing is, I think she knew she was going to die. Oddly, there was a lot of preparation work done before she passed. It's hard to explain, but it's like when she died, everything was in place. You know? The house and finances were in order. She had funeral expenses paid up and left everything where we could find it easily. Even her clothes were clean and neatly put away. She died in the neatest way possible. I think she didn't want us to worry about anything."

"That's interesting. You think maybe she didn't want to spend the remainder of her life with the family being depressed and anxious?"

"That's exactly what I think, but Dad was her physician. He would have known if anything was wrong with her. The autopsy just came back as natural causes. It was always too perfect."

"Is she buried here?" Drucilla asked. Her morbid curiosity was piqued.

"Her dry remains are in solid limestone in an ossuary box in Milan. She's among the monks in the catacombs of an Italian church. I haven't been there. I don't really have the desire to go."

"If you ever change your mind. You know I can take you there."

Dominic nodded.

"So, is that book for me?" Drucilla leaned her head to the side to read the title.

"For me, actually. I keep having these intense dreams lately."

Drucilla peered at him with curiosity.

"It's been the same dream every night for two weeks. These large, ornate, silver double doors open outward, revealing an enormous celestial garden. The garden is contained by tiers of white marble walls and platforms with cracks of silver lighting, that appear to be alive, branching within the marble itself. I mean, they respond to my movement when I walk past. The cracks move in pulsating waves throughout the walls, like blood through veins and capillaries. The floor is sand, but not sand, as you would see at the beach. This sand is black with millions of points of light. It looks like you're standing on a field of endless stars and galaxies. Above, the sky is billowy, consisting of purple and teal hues with flashes of lightning streaking across, like a nebula cloud."

Drucilla stared at Dominic inquisitively as he relayed his dream.

"A large door on the opposite end of the garden, similar to the one I entered, is guarded by four large, winged beings. I can't tell if they are real or monuments, but they're a hundred feet high. A woman approaches me, but I can't determine who she is. She's very blurred. I can't see her face, but I can make out auburn hair and silver armor. I'm certain she's a Seraph, but she doesn't appear to have wings. As she approaches, I see she's incredibly tall, about twenty feet high. She reaches down and puts my face in her enormous hand. She speaks to me, but I can't understand her. The only thing I can make out is "Custos Dominicus." Her voice hisses in whispers as she gets brighter. I have to shield my eyes from the light because I can't take the growing brightness."

"Weird," Drucilla said.

"Then I wake up. But it happens over and over again. I'm fairly certain someone is trying to contact me. I need to figure out how to communicate."

"What's 'Custos Dominicus'?"

"Custos is Latin for Guardian, and Dominicus is the Latin version of my name."

"That's just bizarre…"

"I'm trying to see if I can actually control it. It's too complex for it to be just a dream. This has to be some precognition or retrocognition. I just don't know right now, but if I don't figure it out, it'll make me crazy." Dominic sat down with his book and started reading.

"So, Dom, it's your birthday next week," Drucilla said, changing the subject to lighten the mood.

"Yeah, I suppose." Dominic continued to flip through his book.

"I want to throw you a birthday party."

Dominic shook his head at her. "No"

"Screw your 'no.' I'm gonna."

Dominic glared at her disapprovingly.

"Look, Dom, you and I have been through Hell and back, figurately. I would like to do this to show my appreciation for you and our friendship. It would mean the world to me to give this to you."

Dominic paused to look at Drucilla for a moment. "Jesus Christ, Dru. You didn't need to go that hard with it."

"Good! Next Friday night. My place."

Chovin fecit
19

CANTICLE ELEVEN

Drake stood atop the parapet of his lofty, extravagant palace. The dwelling was ancient and fortified with intricately carved stone, inlaid with ostentatious and lavish fine gold filigree. His castle-like villa was one of seven that surrounded a central square. This was the King's quarter of Hell. Drake peered over the ledge to the countryside beyond the quarter. The area looked much like the surface of Earth, just inverted. Blue is orange, rivers are red, and death is eternal life.

Persephone approached Drake. She slowly drew her fingertips across Drake's shoulders to indicate her presence. "I know what you're thinking," she whispered in Drake's ear.

Drake shifted his eyes in her direction and then back to the countryside. "Oh? And how do you know that?" he responded, unimpressed by her perception.

"She won't give up the entity," Persephone lifted herself backward onto the railing and sat with her legs crossed as she faced Drake.

"She won't, or she can't? Certainly, there are other ways." His eyes flared with a burst of orange light.

"You plan to rip Thoth from her by force? I think you underestimate how powerful she's become." Persephone turned away from Drake. "I feel her strength growing with each passing moment. The entire Infernal Sphere does. I know you do, too."

Drake scoffed. "She doesn't intimidate me. I know who she is. She's still Drucilla. She still has affection for who I once was."

"You plan to ask her to join you?" Persephone slowly turned her gaze back to Drake, looking for confirmation.

"Obviously I don't need to ask her to join me."

"Underestimating her could be to your detriment—"

Drake abruptly turned his head to face Persephone, cutting her off. "Azrael. Tell him I want to meet with him immediately."

Persephone nodded.

Suddenly as if beckoned, Azrael manifested on the parapet behind them. "No need, Persephone," Azrael said. He slowly walked over to Drake and stood beside him. Drake turned away from his view and leaned against the railing. He peered into Azrael's deep black eye sockets.

"You're helping my sister. Why?"

Azrael held Drake's stare.

"Aiding humans is interference, correct? That's why you have..." Drake made a small gesture towards Azrael, "Certain restrictions?"

"Drucilla is not human," Azrael responded.

"I suppose that's true. But she is still my sister, and as her brother, I want to know your intentions."

"Intentions?" Azrael drew out a pause. "We align in a cause."

"What cause would that be?"

"The realms at peace." Azrael's black sockets seemed to deepen, "Isn't that what you should want?"

Drake narrowed his gaze. "How do you intend to achieve that?"

"Via all the power of my station."

"Including cutting off the Unholy's access to Earth?"

"Your accusation is off base. And it is of no matter. Your access appears to have been rectified," Azrael responded.

"What has she offered you in exchange for your allegiance? Whatever it is, I am certain I can offer a better deal."

"What she offers, Drake, is that she is not at all like you."

"Why do you antagonize me?" Drake seethed. He attempted to grab Azrael's scarf to gain control. Drake's hand went through it. Drake stopped and looked at his hand. He tried to snatch Azrael's scarf again.

Azrael scoffed. "The law of dominion. The Beast's bastion of control. I am not really here and haven't been in an age."

Drake pressed his lips together.

"I took you for a diplomat," stated Azrael as he turned his gaze forward, "I would have thought you'd study every facet of the rules and laws your master put in place."

Drake paced for a moment. He couldn't make sense of Azrael's deflections. "Tell me, why is she necessary to you?"

"Necessary?" Azrael said, returning his gaze to Drake. "As a child, she possessed the Sanguis Deus. It gave her the ability to manipulate and control the dead. Poorly. I could not abide by such reckless use of the souls I shepherd. I had to rectify her mistakes and thus began a relationship of mentor and defiant student. A role of even more import now that her power is inborn. That much should be obvious."

Drake cocked his head to one side. "Azrael, you are first and foremost a Seraph. From what I understand, Raziel informed me that your duties are to protect humankind above all else. My sister should not have to live her life as a host to a Throne. She is cursed, her life stripped away to serve as nothing but a prison to another entity. This is unreasonable. Is this why she was resurrected, to serve as a vessel?"

Azrael pondered for a moment. He put his hand up to his chin and tucked his other hand under his other arm. "We know nothing of her resurrection. When she died, I was summoned to collect her. However, when I found her, she was alive."

"How was she brought back?" Drake probed.

"We don't know. Something higher granted her life again."

"Was it Thoth?"

"No. Thoth was little more than blood and essence. Another would have had to intervene."

"Can she die again?"

Azrael studied Drake for a moment. "Are you asking me to reap your sister?" He turned fully toward Drake, "Or do you want the entity Thoth torn from her? Isn't that what you're really asking?"

"Drucilla will eventually join me here, and Thoth will undoubtedly join her. I do not want to take Thoth from my sister, but I do want my sister to be free of her obligation by the time she arrives. I would prefer to take on the burden of Thoth onto myself to alleviate her, to grant her an after-life free of the entity. I request that you allow me to attend when Drucilla departs Earth, when you reap her."

"That is untenable," Azrael stated flatly. When Drake's expression revealed his expectation of an explanation, Azrael continued. "Drucilla has somehow become a singular being. Not human, as none could ever hold a Throne and not burn, yet she does so easily. He does not consume her as Calliope will you. He, instead, changes her. She is Ophanim in part, becoming more so as Thoth resides within. She'll not die in any manner we can predict."

Azrael paused. He shifted his sockets around, as if unsettled. He glanced down at the courtyard below, then back up as if trying to make sense of something in his head. Something didn't feel right. Something was off. It was the same feeling as before, when he met with Drake and Raziel. He shifted his gaze back to Drake. "Why do I sense Drucilla is here?" Azrael asked pointedly.

Drake's grin faded to a cold, sober stare.

"Here? Why would she be here?" Drake sounded moderately defensive. "Maybe you are sensing my human side. We are twins, after all."

Azrael stared solidly into Drake's eyes.

Drake held his stare.

Azrael turned away as if he was trying to listen for something. He turned back to Drake. "If you'll excuse me, I have duties I must attend," Azrael declared.

"One more thing, if I may?" Drake asked but did not wait for a reply. "Something has been bothering me. When Raziel asked about what you had witnessed at the battle, you neither confirmed nor denied aiding Drucilla nor how she got the upper hand on Asmodeus and Belphegor. Granted, they were ineffective, and their demise was nothing short of relief, but I can't for the life of me figure out why you wouldn't explain your involvement."

"Should I ask of yours, kin slayer?"

"Interesting."

Azrael straightened his coat.

"Think about what I propose," Drake offered.

Drake confidently, and quickly, walked back into his villa. As Azrael watched him leave, he crossed his arms in contemplation before disappearing.

Memento Mori memorare novissima.
Cum Priv. Sac. Cæs. Maj.   D. 4.   Johann Christian Leopold excudit Aug. Vind.

124

CANTICLE TWELVE

"I got such a fright seeing them in my dark cupboard with my great big cake." —Altered Images

Adrian and Drucilla rushed around the old Victorian home with last-minute preparations for Dominic's birthday party. Drucilla groaned, frustrated with her petite frame and inability to reach the overhead beams to secure the string lighting around the edge of the wrap-around porch, even with her tallest stepstool.

"Adrian, is it cool to throw string lighting on the floor? You know, like ground lighting or something? Is that a thing that interior design people do?" Drucilla looked around the porch floor. She thought the autumn leaves that gathered around would create an interesting ambiance.

Adrian glowered at Drucilla peculiarly from the living room through the front window. He looked at her like she had an aneurysm and was speaking nonsense. He creased his forehead and turned his palm up at Drucilla as if to say, *what is wrong with you?*

"Just wrap it around the banister! Do I have to think of everything?" Adrian muffled through the glass.

"Give it here. I'll do it." Dominic quickly walked up the porch steps.

"You're early." Drucilla wrapped the string lights around her arm.

"I didn't have much going on, I figured I'd get here before Aleksei and Dad showed up. You know, to make things less awkward."

"Oh, you don't think I have the people skills to keep your family entertained?" Drucilla mused.

Dominic paused and stared at her for a moment. "Yeah. Yeah, pretty much. Uh-huh," he said, deadpan and nodding.

Drucilla leaned her head to the side, trying to parse what she had heard. She wrinkled her nose at him disapprovingly.

Dominic smirked, grabbed the string of lights from Drucilla, and moved the stepstool out of the way.

"There's hooks already embedded up there, so you should just be able to throw them on."

"Is Adrian staying?" Dominic asked. He glanced through the window at Adrian toiling around the living room.

"He knows to be cognizant of his corporealness and has agreed not to go through walls. That's about the best I can do."

Dominic nodded. "My dad, he's uh, he's extremely rational… I guess that is the best way to put it. I don't know what seeing a ghost would do to him. Most likely, he'd commit himself. On the other hand, Aleksei might pass it off as an acid flashback."

"Azrael will not make an appearance, but he did leave you a gift," Drucilla mused.

"Oh God, do I want to know?" Dominic looped lights around the embedded hooks in the porch rafters.

"I have no idea what it is. He said it's something you, of all people, will appreciate."

"That doesn't sound suspicious at all," Dominic said under his breath.

"Dominic, I feel horrible. I didn't have the time to get you anything."

"Dru, I don't need anything. The fact that you put effort into pulling this party together is more than I deserve." He smiled while he continued to hang lights.

"Yeah, but still…"

"Dru, you know what you could do for me?"

"Tell me." Drucilla tilted her head to the side. At this point, anything Dominic could ask would never be enough for what he'd done for her.

"Try and be a little more open with me. You've been shut off for almost a year. You're my friend. You can come to me with anything, and you know I will never judge you. This whole thing is new for me, too. I am also human. Even though you technically aren't, you still navigate life as one. This is just as new to you as it is to me; let's commiserate together. I could use your support as well."

Drucilla smiled and nodded in agreement.

✝✝✝

One by one, the guests began to fill the house. Aleksei and Edik, Dominic's father, arrived about an hour later. There was a decent turnout of guests. They mostly consisted of Dominic's lifelong neighbors, friends, and family, many of whom Drucilla was meeting for the first time. Lucifer also decided to grace them with this attendance. Drucilla always felt second-hand cringe when he introduced himself. Although his façade was an illusion, he had no problem giving up his real name. At least this time, he chose a random glamour, not a disruptive one.

Adrian strolled out with a gorgeous, lit vanilla bean pistachio cake that he had spent the last twenty-four hours perfecting. He claimed that it was his best work yet. Dominic was so excited that he attempted to stuff an entire slice in his mouth in one bite.

Lucifer held out his arm and presented Dominic with a bottle of Zakharov, a rare Russian vodka. Dominic took it from him and turned the bottle as he read the label. Edik grabbed the bottle from Dominic and analyzed it.

"How did you manage to get this?" Edik asked in a very thick Russian accent.

"It can only be purchased from a small distillery in Derevy outside of Petrozavodsk," Lucifer proudly stated.

"Yes. I know, but how did *you* get it?" Edik asked again.

"I got it…" Lucifer glanced at Drucilla. Drucilla's eyes widened. "When I was in Petrozavodsk on business."

Dominic and Drucilla both looked at Lucifer and then back to Edik. Edik raised an eyebrow suspiciously at the bottle and then back to Lucifer. He seemed curious about how an average American could happen on an obscure distillery that nobody had heard of outside of Petrozavodsk, let alone Russia.

"Business, eh? Okay. Well, open it up, syn!" He laughed and handed it back to Dominic. Dominic let out the breath he'd been holding, a sigh of relief. He opened the lid, took a drink from the bottle, and passed it to his father.

"I have glasses, you know," Drucilla said, offended at his barbaric display of alcohol consumption.

"I suppose next you'll tell me I should put it in the freezer for a few hours?" Dominic scoffed. He wiped his mouth with the back of his sleeve.

Drucilla exhaled unamused, picked up a worn leather messenger bag underneath the antique buffet table, and handed it to Dominic. He eyed her suspiciously. "It's a gift from your friend 'Dave Vanian,'" Drucilla smirked.

Dominic took the bookbag from Drucilla and put it on the dining room table in front of him.

"An old satchel," Dominic mumbled, unimpressed.

"Pretty sure there's more," Drucilla advised.

He unbuckled the straps and slid his hand inside. He partially pulled out an antiquated, heavy, flat wooden box. He paused with a peculiar look on his face. He slid it the rest of the way out and placed it on the book bag. He opened the box, glanced at the inside for a fraction of a second, and then dropped the lid quickly. He took a step back and analyzed the box. He appeared to be alarmed at the contents.

"What is it?" Drucilla asked quietly, leaning her head toward Adrian. Adrian glanced at her and shrugged, then turned his attention back to Dominic. Dominic acted as if he had opened a box containing a cobra or other lethal animal.

Dominic put his hand on his mouth and tucked the other under his elbow. He seemed apprehensive about opening it again. Drucilla looked at Dominic's face trying to figure out what was concerning him.

Dominic stepped forward to the table and flipped the lid on the box. He glanced at Drucilla as she looked inside the box. Inside she found yellowed, frail pieces of papyrus paper with Egyptian hieroglyphs painted on them. They both stared at each other in disbelief.

"What is that?" Aleksei asked. He stepped up to the table and looked in the box. He attempted to reach his hand inside, but Dominic snatched his hand before he could touch the fragile pieces. Aleksei looked at him with concern.

"Aleksei, don't touch them," Dominic warned.

"Why? What is it?" Aleksei asked.

"What you're looking at is the Egyptian Book of the Dead," Drucilla said softly. She tried not to disrupt the papyrus with her breath.

Dominic stood in disbelief, unable to form a comment. Lucifer walked up behind Dominic and looked over his shoulder.

"Ah, old paper. Neat." Lucifer tossed back the rest of his scotch and walked away.

Dominic and Drucilla looked at Lucifer, and then at each other. They shook their heads.

"I don't know what to say," Dominic whispered. Clearly, this gift had caught him by surprise. "Uh, thanks, Dave."

†††

Drucilla stepped out from the backdoor of her kitchen with a large garbage bag full of paper plates and plastic cups. Trying to keep her house in order with this many people proved challenging. Drucilla dragged the plastic bag down the steps to the patio and hiked it into the large garbage receptacle. She dropped the lid and turned to head back into the house, but she heard footsteps. Someone wearing heels was walking up the stone path from her backyard to the patio. Drucilla looked to see who it was, but it was too dark. She assumed it was a party guest and didn't think much of it. She reached for the handle to pull the door open.

"Drucilla," the woman's voice said.

Drucilla paused and turned in the direction of the voice. She stepped away from the door and back onto the patio. Slowly, a beautiful, raven-haired woman emerged into the glow of the string lights surrounding the back patio. She wore a deep red, tight-fitting, low-cut dress with a snug, taffeta duster trimmed in black fur and a wide-brimmed hat. Her fingers dripped in jet and ruby jewels. She emitted a familiar scent. Drucilla couldn't quite place it, sweet but with smoky incense. Her eyes cast a brief but subtle yellow glow as she lifted her head to Drucilla.

"I'm sorry, have we met? I don't remember you being at the party." Drucilla then concluded her thoughts internally…*and I'm not entirely sure you're human…*

"We have met—a year or so ago. We met under—unconventional circumstances."

Drucilla paused to study her. She was certain she had seen her face before but couldn't seem to place it. Her brain struggled to make the neural connections.

The back door swung open, and Dominic leaned out of it. "Dru! Come do shots!" Dominic yelled.

Drucilla turned to Dominic and back to the woman. Dominic followed her stare before exiting the house and down the steps to the patio beside Drucilla. The mysterious woman smiled at Dominic.

"Happy Birthday, Dominic," she said.

"Uh, thanks. Who are you?" Dominic asked.

"She's not with you?" Drucilla peered at Dominic. He looked at Drucilla and shook his head.

The back door swung open again. "Are we moving the party out here?" Lucifer asked. He stepped down onto the patio. He looked at Drucilla and Dominic and then over to the woman. The woman smiled at Lucifer.

"Lucifer." The woman nodded slightly.

"Oh, it is you," Lucifer said unenthusiastically.

"Who is she?" Drucilla looked at Lucifer.

"Drucilla, Dominic, this is Persephone. Persephone, this is Drucilla and Dominic."

"I know who they are. Thank you, Lucifer." She peered at Lucifer as if he were a simple child.

"I knew you looked familiar!" Drucilla exclaimed. "Wait. How did you get out of Hell?"

Dominic furrowed his brow at Persephone.

"Persephone is a bit of a sparrow," Lucifer proffered.

"A sparrow? What's a sparrow?" Drucilla asked.

"It means like a spy," Dominic whispered.

"Did you really think a spell could keep *me*, of all Celestials, in or out of anything?" Persephone laughed. "You know me better than that, or have you forgotten who created Hell?"

"Persephone has her own agenda. It is best to steer clear of her. Do not trust her." Lucifer advised.

"Do not trust *me*? This coming from a King of Hell?" Persephone narrowed her gaze and crossed her arms.

"She is also my…well, my former companion, for lack of a better nomenclature." Lucifer motioned to Persephone. "But do not worry. She means nothing. I have no feelings for her."

"…what?" Drucilla asked.

"Are you courting?" Persephone pointed at Lucifer and Drucilla.

"Yes," Lucifer confirmed.

"NO!" Drucilla shouted simultaneously over Lucifer.

"Not presently. You know, it is only a matter of time." Lucifer smiled brightly at Drucilla.

"Well shit, if it's gonna be that kind of a party." Dominic grabbed a bistro chair, flipped it around, sat on it backward, and threw back a vodka gulp. "Proceed," he said with a slight belch, covering his mouth.

"Lucifer, if you think for a second that I—" Drucilla pointed her finger at him and scolded.

"What are you doing here, Persephone?" Lucifer cut Drucilla off.

Persephone walked up to Lucifer and stood directly in front of him. "It would appear that Drake would like to extend a generous offer," Persephone paused and turned to Drucilla. "To Drucilla."

Drucilla shifted her eyes to Dominic. Dominic stood up.

"Whatever it is, she isn't interested," Dominic answered in her stead. He pulled out his stylus and held it at his side.

Persephone looked mildly confused as to why this man was answering for Drucilla. She glanced at Dominic and then back to Drucilla. "Drake specifically requested for you to come home. He would like his sister to be at his side."

"Am I correct to assume you are firmly attached to Drake's other side?" Lucifer asked, crossing his arms.

"I must think about self-preservation," Persephone slowly lifted her gaze to Lucifer's eyes.

"Of course, you do. Why would you think of anyone other than yourself? No, that is not what he is really asking. Is he Persephone?" Lucifer turned to Drucilla. "He wants Thoth. Not you."

Drucilla looked at Persephone curiously. "Why would Drake send you?"

"Drake did not send me. He does not know I'm here. He requested Azrael to deliver you to him, and I am merely here to warn you of his offer."

"Bullshit. Azrael is a dick, but he wouldn't do that to her. Not after everything we've been through," Dominic growled.

Drucilla felt her skin get hot underneath her clothes. She looked down at her hands as her veins began to crank up the wattage. The glow caught Dominic and Lucifer's attention.

"Dru, calm down!" Dominic commanded. "We got this!"

"I'm—I'm not doing it!" Drucilla exclaimed. Her eyes shifted back and forth, trying to make sense of what was happening. Drucilla looked up at Lucifer, her eyes glowing like dwarf stars, as bright blue capillaries branched across her face and neck.

"Drucilla! Control yourself!" Lucifer shouted.

"I can't! I can't stop it! It isn't me!" Drucilla stepped backward away from everyone.

Drucilla felt two rigid arms from behind. They pinned her arms against her sides and around her chest. She looked down and saw Azrael's familiar long, white, spindly fingers grasped together.

Lucifer suddenly realized that Thoth was attempting to gain control of Drucilla's body. "Get her out of here, Azrael!"

With a blink, Azrael and Drucilla disappeared.

Persephone looked back up at Lucifer. "Drake has requested that Azrael deliver Drucilla and the entity to him, and you just let him take her."

Lucifer looked uneasy.

"We know Azrael. He's not going to give her to Drake," Dominic said, picking up on Lucifer's concern.

Persephone looked at Dominic and back to Lucifer. "Can you be certain? I hope for your sake that you are correct."

"Bro," Aleksei said, standing in the doorway. "I'm so trashed right now. I thought I just saw the Reaper take Drucilla. I'm gonna, uh, head to the house and lay down. I'm done drinking." He looked at Lucifer and Persephone. "For, um, ever."

Aleksei stepped back into the house and slowly closed the door.

CANTICLE THIRTEEN

*"Why can't you be like this? Why can't you be like that? I don't
know where I am or where, or where I'm at."*
—Missing Persons

Drucilla stood on an icy, dilapidated, rusted oil rigger in
the middle of the frozen tundra. The sun was in a setting
position on the horizon and didn't move. It was as if time
didn't exist there. Drucilla's body started to dim, and her
skin returned to its typical, light-olive complexion. Azrael
leaned against a rusted railing with his ankles crossed and
his hands tucked in his overcoat.

"Where are we?" Drucilla looked around.

"Antarctica. An ideal place for you to explode, I think,"
Azrael explained. "Are you okay?"

"I think so?" Drucilla looked at the palms of her hands.
"What's happening to me?"

"Drucilla, you must promise never to reenter Hell."

"Ugh, it was one time!" Drucilla bemoaned. "Well, okay,
I almost did it a second time, but Dominic was all, 'No, we
can't do that…Lucifer said we can't use the pen for that, blah
blah blah.' So, we didn't." Drucilla said, animating her
hands in a sarcastic, wringing motion.

"The Infernal Sphere has plans for you. Never enter
again if you wish not to see them carried out. It is far too

dangerous, too hard for anyone to back you up there. Do you understand?"

Drucilla threw her arms up. "Fine, I wasn't going to anyway."

Azrael regarded Drucilla for a moment. He then turned his eye sockets toward her center of mass.

"Thoth attempted to take over your body. And I think it won't be his only attempt. It's time you communicated with him if you intend to continue to host him."

"Communicate? I don't know how to communicate with Thoth. I haven't figured it out."

"If you will allow me, I'd like to try." Azrael pulled himself away from the railing and walked towards Drucilla.

"Okay, how?"

"I will put you to sleep as I did before," Azrael said with a slight hint of distaste of his recollection. "After a few minutes, I'll bring you back and awaken you."

Drucilla nodded. "Okay, if you think it will help."

Azrael stood before Drucilla and gently placed his cold, boney hands on either side of her face. Drucilla looked into his soulless eye sockets. She felt herself drift and become lighter. Drucilla closed her eyes.

"Thoth," Azrael took his hands away from Drucilla.

Thoth's eyes popped open with bright, blue beams of light that slowly dimmed to a subtle glow.

"Old friend," Thoth said. "Lucifer, the Unholy has me trapped in this body."

"Not trapped. Incubated. Your host has allowed you to take up residence within her body so you can heal and regain your form. Without her and this body, you could not exist."

Thoth looked up at Azrael in anger and confusion.

"I'm sorry, old friend. Calliope struck you down and had your essence fashioned into a rosary, trapping you there for eons. Your host, Drucilla, found the rosary and freed you. You now live inside her."

Thoth looked down at Drucilla's hands and feet. He placed his hands on her stomach and breasts. He looked back at Azrael. "I am in a Seraph?"

"Human, not Seraph, though also something more. I assure you that you could not have asked for a better host. She is called Drucilla."

"She is Lucifer's companion!" Thoth angrily cut off Azrael.

"Indeed. And Lucifer is an ally welcomed back to the Celestial Empyrion. Much has changed."

"This is deception!"

"It is true. Lucifer earned his place among the Seraphs."

"Lucifer is no Seraph. He's Ophanim," Thoth paced around the deck of the oil rigger.

"Ophanim?" Azrael asked, confused by the correction.

Thoth turned to Azrael. "Lucifer cannot be trusted."

"Of this, we agree. But… Ophanim?"

"Lucifer is an abomination. He is a bastardization. The sum of all Thrones. He consists of a fragment of each Throne in one entity. He was to be the savior of Earth, the Throne of

Humankind. Humans, with their free will, worshiped their own gods. This deviation rendered Lucifer's design to be without purpose. He should have been destroyed. He is unpredictable, far too powerful, and efficacious. He is anathema in any dominion. Lucifer will be the undoing of everything in every universe!"

Azrael turned his head and looked towards the floor. He seemed to be putting things together in his head.

"Not just Earth. Existence. Everything that is or ever will be. Even death," Thoth looked to Azrael, clearly reading his thoughts. "We cannot allow him to continue to exist. He will be the end of us all…even you."

"Old friend, I think if you had seen the things that I have seen. With the sacrifices he made for Earth and the Celestial Empyrion, you may think differently. He fought to protect your host, Drucilla, and her comrades. He is actively protecting Earth from the Unholy. So much so that he has become a pariah to them and no longer rules the Infernal realm. I don't fully trust him, but–"

"Azrael," Thoth interrupted him.

Azrael stood silent.

"If what you say is true, and Lucifer is changed. I must seek counsel with the Thrones."

"I'm afraid that will be impossible." Azrael started to pace. "The Thrones are gone."

"How is this?"

"We don't know. When Calliope ended your life, the Thrones disappeared. We can't divine them in any way. It's as if they've vanished."

"They have moved on. I know where they are."

"Are you sure?" Azrael asked. "You've been away for quite a while."

"I'm certain. I will find them," Thoth reassured Azrael. "I will relinquish control to the human while deciding how to proceed."

"You can communicate with Drucilla?" Azrael asked, surprised.

"I sense her intentions, and I feel her will. In turn, I respond accordingly. However, before now, I did not know I was in the body of a human. I was certain I was inside of a Seraph."

"Although blind, you safeguard and empower her as you feel she needs it?" Azrael paced around Thoth.

"That is a rudimentary explanation, but essentially, that is correct."

"Are you aware you are keeping her alive, as well?" Azrael asked.

Thoth looked at Azrael peculiarly. "I am symbiotic with her essence. Curiously, she is of a higher frequency than any human we have ever created, apparently closely akin to a Seraph. I am not her life force."

Azrael seemed surprised by the answer.

Drucilla collapsed forward to the floor and caught herself with her hands before her face hit the ground. She rolled onto her side and sat up. Drucilla looked at the front and back of her hands, then looked up at Azrael. Azrael seemed to be struggling with something in his head. Drucilla got to her feet and brushed her hands off on her pants.

"Are you okay?" Drucilla noticed that he looked disturbed.

"I should be asking you that question."

"I feel fine."

"Could you hear anything that was said?"

"No, nothing. Sorry. Did you find out what you needed to know?"

"Unfortunately, yes. Things I didn't know that I needed to know. Things that necessitate I seek counsel to fully understand."

"That sounds bad."

Azrael turned his head toward Drucilla.

"No, not for you. But possibly for another... Lucifer."

"Lucifer?"

"We should return now."

146

"Oh, I will walk among your dreams when you think you are asleep." —Danzig

✝

"Dom, I am so sorry about what happened last night."

"Dru, don't. It wasn't your fault. Although, you gave Lucifer quite a scare."

"What, why?" Drucilla asked as she sat down on her usual old wooden swivel stool in Dominic's library. Dominic looked up from his laptop, leaned back in his chair, and folded his hands on his stomach.

"For a minute there, I think he really thought Azrael was going to deliver you to Drake."

"That's ridiculous. Lucifer should have known better than that," Drucilla lamented.

Dominic shrugged. "But hey, my brother thought that the Grim Reaper took you away. That was hilarious." Dominic giggled to himself.

"He saw Azrael?!"

"He didn't know what he saw. He was pretty hammered, so I wouldn't worry about it."

"What about your dad? Did he see anything?"

"Nah. We're good," Dominic reassured her.

"Did they head back to Seattle?"

"Not yet. They're over at Uncle Ivan's place. Apparently, there's a couple of crates of things that belong to Ford Bradshaw, so they're taking them to the shop."

"You're not helping?" Drucilla asked. She got up and walked over to the box that held the Book of the Dead, resting on the other of the table.

"Nah. Dad wanted to see his brother, and they offered to grab the crates, so who am I to say no to a couple of extra sets of hands."

Drucilla ran her hand over the box and looked up at Dominic. "Azrael spoke to Thoth last night."

Dominic blinked rapidly at Drucilla. "Really? How?"

Drucilla gave a slight shrug. "Azrael basically knocked me out. I guess the same way he did when Lucifer and I got into it. He was able to speak to Thoth. He probably put me in a coma to do it, but he did it."

Dominic stood up and walked over to Drucilla. He leaned against the table and crossed his muscular arms.

"Well?" Dominic asked.

"Well, what?"

"What did Thoth say?"

"Azrael didn't tell me much. Some things about Lucifer came to light. I don't know what it was. Azrael is trying to seek counsel about it." Drucilla made air quotes around seek council. "But the important takeaway is that the Thrones are still alive."

"They are? Is he sure?"

"Thoth knows where they are, but he didn't tell Azrael."

"Do you know why?"

"Honestly? I don't think Thoth can tell him."

"Why would you say that?"

"Because Dom, even though I can't talk to Thoth, I can feel him. I feel, I suppose, what I would consider emotions, intentions, maybe. In turn, he feels mine."

"I wonder what the deal is with Lucifer."

Drucilla shrugged. She flipped back the lid on the wooden box and peered down at the papyrus.

Dominic leaned his head to the side. He glanced at Drucilla, the papyrus sheets, and then back at Drucilla. He placed his hand under his chin and narrowed his gaze at her. She could tell he was deep in thought.

Drucilla's eyes darted around the room and then back at Dominic. "What?"

Dominic started to chew the inside of his cheek. "Hmmm…"

"Dominic, what?" Drucilla was becoming increasingly annoyed with him keeping his thoughts to himself. "You have that scheming face."

Dominic darted to his shelf and pulled down an old book about the Book of the Dead. He placed it next to Drucilla on the table beside the papyrus sheets. "Dru, what if I could put you in the same unconscious state Azrael does so you could talk to Thoth? Would you let me?"

Drucilla's eyes widened. "You want to knock me out? Like, take a big sledgehammer to my head? You can try," she smirked.

"Hear me out. In the Book of the Dead, there is a spell that allows you to enter the space between life and death. Sort of a modified version of what Azrael does, I think. But instead of me talking to Thoth through you—you and Thoth will exist in the same space together at the same time. Theoretically, if I can get you there, you can communicate with Thoth yourself."

"Why would we want to? And *theoretically*? I dunno, this sounds kind of dangerous."

"Thoth knows how we can find the Thrones and defeat Drake and his army. It's worth a shot. What's the worst that could happen? The spell fails?"

"I guess?" Drucilla said in an uncertain tone. "But if we do this, can you get me out?"

"Well, yeah," Dominic responded with assuredness. He opened the antiquated book. "The way the spell works is with essentially incense and rhythm. If I keep it going, you stay in the in-between state. As soon as it stops, you wake up."

Drucilla looked at the page in the book that Dominic had opened.

"What spell are you looking at?" Drucilla enquired, scanning the page.

"The spell isn't in here…" Dominic pointed over to the papyrus, across at the other end of the table. "It's in there." Drucilla looked at the papyrus.

"Okay, Dom, but hieroglyphs are super tricky. It's really easy to misinterpret—"

"Dru, I'm not going to translate them myself. I was hoping you would help with that part."

"I'm not very good at it, but I might know someone who is," Drucilla offered.

"…your mom," Dominic said.

"Yeah. But I don't exactly know how I'm going to spin this. She's going to have about five thousand questions."

"Is there anyone else you could ask?"

Drucilla looked down at the floor for a moment before looking back up at Dominic. She exhaled slowly.

"Yeah, my ex-boyfriend."

"Is that bad?"

"Bad? Not technically. I mean haven't talked to him in like ten years, but I know he still works for the National Archaeological Museum of Athens. I can try."

"It's up to you."

Drucilla nodded slowly.

CANTICLE FIFTEEN

"If you survive, don't do as we did." —The Fixx

"Hold that last one up again? The one prior to this one," Brandon asked. He squinted harder at the screen through his reading glasses at the image coming through the video call.

Drucilla protected her hands by wearing white archival photo gloves as she carefully handled the papyrus. She held up the Book of the Dead hieroglyphs before the webcam lens.

"Now that I've looked at the rest of them, I understand what the last ones mean."

"Okay, what is it?"

"That last cartouche is about, 'Ein al-Afreet.' It means Genie's eye. It's an explosive small red rock. You know, Dru, you could have just sent these to me as PDFs."

"I could have, but I figured you might enjoy seeing it on papyrus," Drucilla said while she typed Brandon's answers on her laptop notepad.

"I think that's all of them," Drucilla said. She scanned the three pieces of papyrus again to ensure she didn't leave anything out.

"Who are these translations for?" Brandon asked.

"My friend Dominic. He's an antique dealer. These are from an old book he acquired recently. He wanted to know what they were before he did anything with them," Drucilla said while thinking: *Technically, that's not a lie.*

"That's beautiful papyrus you have there. It almost looks real."

"Crazy, right? It's harder and harder to tell the fakes from the real ones anymore."

"Well, if anything, he has all the components of making ancient incense."

"Thanks for your help, Brandon."

"No problem. Oh, and Dru?"

"Yeah?"

"I was slightly surprised when I saw your email. I mean, with how things ended and everything."

"Brandon, I respect you as an archeologist and Egyptologist. Regardless of everything, you're a real asset."

Brandon nodded and smiled at her response.

"How is uh, Malva… is it?" Drucilla asked, knowing she probably should have avoided the question.

"Malva." Brandon thought for a moment. "That's right, it *was* Malva. Honestly, Dru, that lasted for all of three months. I took a teaching position, and she dumped me. I guess she was like an archaeology groupie or something."

Drucilla grinned to herself with some sick satisfaction at Brandon's misfortune.

"You know, if you ever get the itch to get back into the field, let me know. I can probably help you out. We're headed out to the Saqqara plateau next month. We think we've found Tutankhamun's nurse Maia."

"That's fascinating. You'll have to email me and let me know how it goes."

"Hey, if you need any more translation help, feel free to reach out."

Drucilla nodded and ended the call. She printed out the notes she had taken during the call, gathered up her papers, closed her laptop, and stuffed it into her backpack. She grabbed her keys and stood up to leave her office.

"What on Earth are you up to, Drucilla?" Lucifer asked. He materialized quietly and leaned against the doorway with a devious grin.

Drucilla's eyes shifted back and forth quickly as she reached for something to grasp onto in her mind, but nothing was coming.

"What do you need, Lucifer?" she asked, changing the subject.

"I thought I would drop by to say hello. I had not seen you since the birthday party."

Drucilla nodded and walked past Lucifer. As she passed, he plucked a sheet of paper from the stack of notes she held against her chest. He looked at the paper and smiled.

"Making an incense, are we?"

Drucilla nervously chewed the inside of her cheek.

"Cartouche spells. Habbet al-Baraka, Abou Kebeer? The gum extracted from the Alonjaddan tree is foul," Lucifer said. He contorted his face into a disgusted reaction.

"You can read Egyptian hieroglyphs?"

"What led you to believe I could not?"

"I dunno. I guess I never thought about it." Drucilla peered at Lucifer. She didn't know why she didn't think about asking him. Then again, the operation was relatively covert, and the fewer people involved, the better.

"What do you intend to do with the incense spell?"

"What makes you think I'm going to do anything with it?" Drucilla said in a nonchalant tone.

Lucifer turned his head to the side and raised an eyebrow as if to say, *'seriously?'*

Drucilla plucked the page out of his clawed hand and stuffed it back into her stack. She headed for the gallery door and searched for the door key on her keyring. She opened the door and motioned for Lucifer to exit the gallery. She remained silent as she locked the door behind them and headed for her Jeep. Lucifer walked beside her.

"Drucilla, what are you keeping from me?"

Drucilla scoffed as she opened the driver's side door. She reached over and dropped the papers on the passenger side seat before turning to face Lucifer.

"It's nothing, really. Dominic and I...."

Lucifer exhaled loudly.

Drucilla glared and shook her head. "Why do you always do that?"

"Come again?" Lucifer responded innocently.

"That! That disapproving sigh of yours. Whenever I mention Dominic or Azrael, you act all Pampers."

"Pampers?"

"Yeah, you know, diapers? Babies wear diapers?"

"Are you inferring that I am acting infantile?" Lucifer asked pointedly.

"Yes. You are acting like a baby."

"What has gotten into you, Drucilla?"

"It seems like whenever I bring them up, you get irritated with them. Are you jealous?"

Lucifer snorted and chuckled to himself. "You are all irritating. I do not favor one over the other."

Drucilla glared.

"I am committed to keeping you safe. If you are attempting to do something hazardous, I feel that it is my duty to step in—"

"Lucifer! I am twenty-nine years old. I think I can handle myself. Besides, I'm Divine."

"You can handle yourself; I do not mean to imply that you are incapable. However, if you are going to place yourself in a potentially perilous situation, I would prefer that you do so in my company."

"You're doing it again."

Lucifer folded his arms.

"You're saying I'm *capable,* and then you start talking to me like I'm *incapable.* You always do this."

Lucifer lifted his hand and was about to rebuke but folded his hand back down and nodded.

"Look, I get that I'm an amoeba in comparison to your bazillion years of existence, but I'm not in any danger, okay? You don't need to hover constantly."

"I apologize if I have made you feel inferior. That was not my intention."

"Good. Thank you." Drucilla nodded.

"You are not going to tell me the purpose of the incense?"

"It's just some translations from the Book of the Dead that Dom got from Azrael." Drucilla walked to the driver's side and climbed in the Jeep.

"I gathered that information already. Thank you, Drucilla. What I am asking is, what do *you* intend to do with the incense? You are acting extremely evasive."

"Because if I tell you, you aren't going to let me do it." The moment she admitted that fact, she instantly regretted it. *Oh great, here it comes…*

"Ah. In that case, stay safe," Lucifer stepped away from the Jeep.

"That's it?"

"You said it yourself, Drucilla. You are capable. I will leave you to your task." Lucifer blinked out.

Drucilla started her Jeep and darted her eyes around. *Well, now I don't want to do it…*

CANTICLE SIXTEEN

"Now I wonder where you roam; I've been here a thousand
times before." —2:54

Drucilla sat on the couch in her living room. The faint scent of fresh paint from the newly completed construction still lingered in the air. Adrian sat on the arm of the couch next to Drucilla, nervously looking around.

"Why are you so on edge?' Drucilla asked.

"I'm not sure how this is going to affect..." Adrian stopped mid-sentence.

"Affect? Affect what?"

Adrian clasped his hands, anxiously.

"Relax, Adrian. You know you don't have to be here if you don't want to be. I know you have a super covert life to return to." Drucilla taunted.

Adrian glared at her. "I told you I need to be here."

Drucilla exhaled. "It's going to be okay."

A crash coming from the kitchen interrupted their discussion. Adrian jumped up and hovered towards the dining room just as Dominic exited the kitchen. Adrian looked at him disapprovingly. Dominic sat down in the chair facing the couch. He pulled a small brass bowl, lighter, and a charcoal disk from his messenger bag and placed them on the table. Then, he pulled out his antiquated Book of the Dead reference book, a metronome, and a notepad. He lit the edge of the charcoal tablet and placed it into the brass bowl.

They all stared at the disc as the thin bright red line of heat penetrated the tablet's surface and burned down the sides. Dominic stood up and walked back into the kitchen. He quickly returned, holding a small plate with six small, round balls that looked like reddish-brown dirt combined with tiny twigs. He placed the incense balls on the table.

"It's dirt," Adrian commented.

"Is that it?' Drucilla asked.

"Yep, that's it," Dominic responded. "That was really cool that your archaeologist friend was able to find the main component."

"Yeah, I think I owe Dita a limb. Okay, so what do we do now?" Drucilla asked.

"First, I'm going to anoint you with Ahmar Osiris oil."

Dominic stood up and pulled the small bottle from his pocket. He put a dot on Drucilla's forehead and the insides of her wrists. He sat back down and picked up a ball of incense. He placed the incense on the charcoal disk and watched as the smoke swirl rose.

"Now I'm going to start the metronome. Do you remember how to astral project?"

"Yeah, but it didn't go so well last time," Drucilla recalled.

"This time, you'll let the rhythm and incense be your guide."

"What's the oil do?" she asked.

"I don't know, something about ensuring safe passage."

"Uh, isn't it important that we understand what the oil does?"

"It's just for good luck."

Drucilla lifted an eyebrow at Dominic before she leaned back and closed her eyes.

"Concentrate on the sound and just relax. When I stop the metronome, you'll wake up. Hopefully, with some answers. I'm giving you ten minutes, so talk fast."

Drucilla nodded, keeping her eyes closed. Within seconds she was unconscious.

"I've got a bad feeling about this, Dom," Adrian lamented.

"We did the translations right. I added and mixed the ingredients in the proper order: have confidence. Besides, what's the worst that could happen? She's immortal. It's not like she can die." Dominic spoke in a way to alleviate his own anxieties.

"Did you really just ask what's the worst that can happen?"

"Oh, don't be so superstitious!"

"Wait, did *you,* of all people, just tell *me* not to be superstitious?!" Adrian gasped.

"I get it…I get it." Dominic groaned.

Dominic sat opposite Drucilla and watched her chest rise and fall with each breath.

†††

Drucilla looked down at the floor beneath her. She stood on a ground consisting of raw textured metals that sparkled and shone, closely resembling the metallic crystalline-cubic structure of bismuth. Like a foggy winter day, the cloudy, white atmosphere felt cool against her body. There was no sound.

"Yoooooooo," she called out.

The sound disappeared as soon as it left her throat. There was nothing on which the sound could bounce. It was so quiet that Drucilla felt she might have become deaf.

She turned around in a circle to try and locate something tangible, something where she could ground herself.

"Hellooooo?"

Am I dead? Is this death?

"If you are dead, then as am I, and there would be no point to this communication," the voice answered back.

"Thoth," Drucilla said quietly.

"Female," Thoth responded. His voice was haunting, breathy—like a deep whisper.

"Drucilla works, too." She felt slighted that he referred to her by her gender. "I can't see you." Drucilla attempted to distinguish something in the clouded atmosphere.

A flicker turned into a slowly increasing glow as it emerged into view. Thoth appeared as a glowing star, with outward extending purple rays contained by rotating rings of light encircling the entity.

Drucilla peered at the illuminated presence with curiosity and confusion.

"Am I not what you expected?"

"No. I mean, no, you are, but I don't quite understand. You had a different form when I saw you in my retrocognition." Drucilla attempted to use Dominic's technical term to explain the event. "You had multiple eyes and wings."

"In here, you appear as your most basic form: energy or essence."

Confused, Drucilla stuck out her arms to look at her hands. In place of her arms were blue rays of light. Drucilla felt herself blink rapidly in disbelief.

"Your somatic body has limits and cannot travel here."

"Are you sure we aren't—"

"Dead? No." Thoth began moving about the space. He examined his human host's essence.

"Is this what Ophanim look like?"

"Ophanim take whichever divine form and human gender they find most appealing and representative of themselves. Calliope, Aurora, and Nova prefer feminine figures, while many prefer simpler energy forms. Yet others, like Min, prefer the form of a gigantic humanoid, and Urania prefers to take the shape of nebulae."

"And your names? Where did they come from?"

"We do not have names pronounceable by the human voice. However, humans attached names to us to help your kind understand who we are."

Drucilla moved about, attempting to make sense of her surroundings. "What is this place?"

"This place is not anything. It is between the realms. We are in an area of transition. Where we are, has no boundaries. We generally refer to it as, Nihility."

Drucilla looked around, hoping to see something familiar, anything. The emptiness was unsettling.

"You requested an audience with me. You have it," Thoth said.

"Well, if you're going to be living inside me, I thought we should figure out how to communicate without having to be here." Drucilla attempted to gesture about with her protruding rays of light. "You know?"

"You want to defeat the Unholy. Is that not the purpose of this meeting?"

"Well yeah, that's part of it. But I want to be able to communicate with you, as well. You are now who I am, and I know nothing about what we are or why. You and I together, I mean. Does that make sense?"

"You should not be alive."

"Yeah, and you shouldn't be alive either, so I guess we are at an impasse, Thoth. I don't have much time here before Dominic pulls me back, so we'll have to make this quick. I want to open a channel of communication. Can we do that? I mean, on Earth?"

"You request the ability to speak with me in the mortal realm? It is achievable. You will need the proper tools."

"No problem. Tell me what I need."

"Ancient artifacts that exist on Eorthe. A warning: the tools will not be easy to obtain."

"Ha, clearly you have no idea who I am," Drucilla chuckled to herself.

"On the contrary. I do know who you are and of which you are capable. However, these are not simple, pillaged artifacts from your meager archaeological sites. These are Divine relics. Like Nova's Erato Falx, they must cross paths with you.

"So, tell me what I need. I can get them," Drucilla reiterated.

"Your confidence is endearing but exceedingly short-sighted. However, I am willing to entertain your notion," Thoth said condescendingly.

Lucifer wasn't kidding. He is arrogant.

"Do you require my assistance, or do you wish to continue addressing me with your juvenile insults?"

Drucilla exhaled in annoyance and paced around before speaking. "Okay, ground rules, if we're going to share a body, you're going to need to stay out of my head. Emotions are one thing, but you don't need to know every thought that goes through my mind. We need to have some boundaries."

Thoth paused momentarily. "That is an ethical request."

Drucilla sighed. "Tell me what I need."

"As you wish. First, you will need a vessel. An adequate reliquary that can hold divine essence. There is such a caisson, the Tempest. A vestige of the Throne of the Storms."

"Aurora?! You mean as in one of the Queens of Hell?"

"Is that how she refers to herself?" Thoth scoffed. "I see.

Yes, you must acquire her cauldron, which may or may not have bonded to another human. This vessel you very well may be able to obtain given the correct set of circumstances."

"Okay, what else?"

"You must acquire my tome."

"You have a tome?"

"Of course. All Thrones have a vestige. I have an Alchemy Tome. Fortunately for you, Drucilla, you know of the custodian."

"Who?"

"She is called Adelia Castillo."

"Del? Del has your book?"

"Bring these items together. The Alchemy Tome will teach you how to enchant the Tempest."

†††

Ten minutes had passed, and Dominic stopped the metronome and extinguished the incense with a bottle of water. He sat beside Drucilla and picked up her hand to feel her pulse. Alarmed, he didn't feel it. He reached out to her neck–there was nothing.

"She doesn't have a heartbeat, remember?" Adrian piped in, noticing Dominic checking for vital signs.

Dominic exhaled with relief. "I had completely forgotten about that. Thank you."

"How long does it take for her to wake up?"

"I'm not really sure, Adrian."

Dominic quickly grabbed his book and started flipping hastily through the pages. A white spindly-fingered hand slapped down in the middle of the book and ripped it from Dominic's hands.

Dominic looked up at Azrael's face. Azrael glared down at Dominic. Even though Azrael lacked eyes, he still managed to look visibly angry.

"Do *not* tell me you used the 'Book of the Dead' on Drucilla." Azrael seemed to be speaking through gritted teeth.

Stunned at Azrael's sudden appearance and hostility, Dominic slowly said, "I didn't…not…use the Book of the Dead…on Drucilla."

"You simple child!" Azrael shouted as he dropped Dominic's book to the floor. Azrael's eye sockets began to burn with a purple glow.

"Why did you give me the book if I wasn't supposed to use it?! You know who I am and what I do!" Dominic shouted back.

"You were to be responsible with it!" Azrael shouted.

"I am the only one responsible enough to control this book!" Dominic shouted back.

"It would appear that you are not, because if you were, you wouldn't seek to 'control' it, and Drucilla wouldn't be stuck between the realms." Azrael's tone lowered and became flat. His words dripped with unspoken disappointment.

"What do you mean stuck between the realms?" Dominic's voice lowered.

Azrael took in a deep breath, cracking the bones in his chest. "I sensed her departure from Earth. In turn, I went searching for her. I searched for her in the Celestial Empyrion and Malakut. She is in neither."

"What about Hell?" Adrian asked.

"You cannot go to the Infernal Sphere. Admission is by invitation only, lest Cerberus destroy you. Regardless, she gave me her word that she would not attempt to enter Hell again. It is no place for human nor Divine."

"Really?" Dominic's voice was calm and empathetic. "So, you just don't go there for being a bad human?"

"No, that isn't how the Infernal Sphere works. Stop listening to your religious leaders. They have never died; they have no knowledge."

Dominic looked down at the floor, deep in thought, then back to Drucilla, who was still unconscious but breathing.

Azrael crossed his arms and glowered at Dominic.

"Where else could she be?"

"Most likely, Nihility."

Dominic furrowed his brow at Azrael.

Azrael paused and then nodded to himself. He then waved his arm, and four large, floating orbs appeared in front of him. One orb was orange, another blue, another purple, and the last one black. They rotated around each other in the air above them in a slow cosmic dance. "These four spheres represent the realms." He pointed to each orb. "This black one is the human universe. This orange one is the Infernal Sphere, Hell. This lighter blue one is the Celestial Empyrion, Heaven, and this darker blue one is Malakut, or purgatory, if you will."

Dominic and Adrian stood opposite Azrael in front of the orbs.

"Drucilla is somewhere in here." Azrael pointed to the spaces between the orbs.

"There's nothing there. What are you pointing at?" Dominic asked in case he was missing something.

"Exactly. There is nothing here. Nihility."

"How do we find her?" Dominic asked.

Azrael slowly shook his head. "I cannot see her. I will not be able to locate her."

Dominic's face fell.

"I can," Lucifer suddenly interjected as he seemed to be listening quietly in the background.

Azrael glared at Lucifer. "And just how do you suppose you can do that, Beast?"

†††

"I must advise you—the more Divine relics you obtain— the more of a threat you become to the Unholy. They will not hesitate to eradicate you to keep the balance in their favor," Thoth warned.

"You mean my brother..." Drucilla surmised.

"Ah yes, your sibling. The newly appointed King of

Pride now that Lucifer has abdicated his seat amongst the Kings. I sensed the demise of Belphegor, Asmodeus, and Hades at your hands. New kings are to be appointed soon to occupy the vacancy." Thoth hovered around Drucilla as if to study her closely.

"I'm not like Drake if that's what you're alluding to," Drucilla noticed his change of tone and movement around her.

"He is not my concern. It is the other in which that I am referring."

"Other what? I have no other brother."

"No, not a sibling…." Thoth continued to study Drucilla. "Something else."

"What do you mean? My mother?'

"The other that I am referring to is you."

"What? I don't understand what you mean?"

The area grew dim, as if the unseen sun was setting and the light was slipping away.

"What's happening?" Drucilla shouted. She frantically looked around.

"We are to take our leave," Thoth explained.

"No! I have more quest—"

†††

Drucilla's eyes popped open. She inhaled deeply and looked around her home. She looked down to see her legs, then held up her hands. They had returned to their standard, human shape.

"Dru! Dru, are you okay?" Dominic bent down and put his hands on her shoulders to look into her eyes.

"Just so," Azrael said, eyeless sockets boring into the back of Dominic's head.

"You gave me the book!" Dominic shouted.

"Perhaps a mistake. One to reconsider."

"No need to thank me. I am happy to do it," Lucifer said.

"What the Hell's going on?" Drucilla jumped out of her seat and faced everyone.

Azrael placed his thumb and forefinger against the bridge of his nose.

Dominic crossed his arms and rubbed his forehead.

"There was a bit of an issue. However, you are here, and everything is as it should be," Lucifer explained.

"What issue?" Drucilla looked at each of them with suspicion. "Someone better start explaining really quick."

"I, more or less, lost you, Drucilla," Dominic said.

"What do you mean you lost me?"

"Dominic learned an important lesson today. He learned that playing with an ancient Book of the Dead without understanding that time, space, and circumstance can change certain details. It proved enlightening," Lucifer responded.

"We did it right. I had the glyphs translated by one of the world's leading Egyptologists," Drucilla said.

"You did, and it was correct. But you didn't consider the purpose of the spell or its requirements. The spell you invoked was to pass a soul over into Malakut for judgment.

However, you are not dead, and so you failed a fundamental requirement and had no destination. You were flung between realms," Azrael explained.

"Judgment?" Drucilla asked.

"To decide whether you go back to the Agglomeration. It is an outdated practice. We do not do it that way anymore and have not for three thousand years," Lucifer explained. "Now, everyone goes to the Agglomeration. The Thrones realized that even the most unsavory individuals had something to offer in the way of growth for future humans."

"Azrael couldn't find you to pull you out. Good thing no one dies in there, or he wouldn't be able to do his job," Dominic said, slighting Azrael.

Azrael turned his eyeless sockets toward Dominic.

"It's resolved. Can we move on, please? Christ, for being omnipotent beings, you act like a bunch of damn children," Adrian piped in.

"How did I get out?"

"Lucifer could see you. He brought you out," Dominic said.

Drucilla looked at Lucifer. "You could see me?"

Lucifer crossed his arms and leaned against the door frame to the kitchen.

"Thanks," Drucilla said calmly.

Lucifer nodded.

"Did you see Thoth?" Dominic asked.

"I did." Drucilla looked at Dominic. "We have a way to communicate, but it's going to be a challenge. I need Nova's bowl and Thoth's Alchemy Tome."

"How do we get those?"

"Coincidently, I know the keeper of his tome," Drucilla responded.

"That's …that's great! What about the bowl."

"Yeah, uh, apparently, Divine relics need to be placed in our path."

"How do we get one in our path?" Dominic asked.

"Luck? I don't know. I mean, I managed to get two of them. Maybe I can locate the third?"

Dominic looked to Azrael and Lucifer for guidance.

"I cannot locate divine relics. I'm afraid I would not be of any help," Azrael replied.

"So, where do we start?" Dominic asked.

"Let's start with the Alchemy Tome. I know where that one is, at least."

CANTICLE SEVENTEEN

"We all have a monster within; the difference is in degree, not in kind." —Douglas Preston

Drake, Leviathan, and Persephone's assistant, Moloch, moved swiftly through the labyrinth of corridors that led from the Cathedral to the King's Quarter of Hell. They entered through the black, towering, arched doorway of Drake's residence. After taking Lucifer's position, Drake inherited Lucifer's large, elaborate stone-carved villa. Raziel sent word to the Infernal Sphere that the Seraphs found a solution to Drake's problem with containing the Throne and are now ready to present him with the result of their efforts.

Time was of the essence, and after ten Earth months, Drake could not afford to lose another day. The Throne of Death was slowly consuming his body. Every moment, every second was precious. He was eager to stop the clock. The power seething through his blood intensified with each passing week. Although he reveled in the Throne's power, he knew he couldn't retain control for much longer. He had begun having episodic blackouts. These blackouts became longer in duration as time passed. He would be having a conversation one moment, and in the next moment, he would find himself in another part of Hell, peculiarly, always in the same place after every blackout.

Alternately, his new fortitude allowed him to create changes within the realm he longed to create. His nearly year-long reign of unbridled power forced the Infernal Sphere into submission. He wielded Calliope's power like an angry god. Anything Drake wanted, he got. Every demon, every king knelt to him. He declared himself Imperator, and no being was strong enough to challenge him, save for Nova and Aurora, who seemed to have effectively hidden from his sight. This new Hell was out of their control. Drake was rapidly growing too powerful to confront. Those who questioned him would soon meet their demise with a snap of his fingers.

After entering the villa, Drake stopped short of his parlor. He exhaled and composed himself. He didn't want to appear weak or nervous, even though the thought of losing control terrified him. Moloch opened the door and held it open for Drake, Leviathan, and Persephone to pass through. The parlor's décor consisted of soft black textiles, like soot, with damask textured walls and black furniture featuring gold filigree and accents. Heavy intricate chandeliers hung from the fourteen-foot, classically painted ceilings depicting imps and cherubs. The room appeared only slightly dim, considering the dark textiles. The wall at the back of the room featured a variety of bourbon bottles that Lucifer collected from all over the world. The room smelled like bourbon and smoldering fire, much like Lucifer himself.

"Raziel should arrive any moment, Imperator," Moloch announced. Moloch was a humanoid demon, average in size, hairless, with large, red eyes. He was one of many devout followers of Drake. Drake kept him around because Moloch constantly showered compliments upon him and was adamant about following Drake's orders.

Persephone approached Drake and grabbed his wrist. She opened his palm in her heavy, gold and jewel-embellished hands. She examined the orange capillaries of light streaming through his fingers. She looked up at him affectionately. Drake looked back at her, lacking emotion.

"Drake, you will live through this. I assure you."

"Persephone…" Drake started. He snatched his hand away from her grasp. He sat down on the black velvet chaise behind him. "Now that we have a few moments, I have some concerns I want to discuss."

Persephone sat on the chaise opposite Drake. "Of course." She gathered the train of her long, red silk petticoat and draped it next to her over the cushion. She crossed her legs and folded her hands on her knees. "What concerns you?"

Drake leaned forward. "I understand you spend quite a bit of time on Earth."

"We all do. This should not come as a surprise."

"What do you do there? I'm curious as to why you take so many trips. Do you have a job or a family I am unaware of?"

Persephone felt a bit taken aback at having to explain herself. "No, I am not beholden to any human if that is what you are asking. I do have a wonderful seamstress and jeweler that I frequent. Why?"

"I've heard rumors that you speak to Drucilla and her friends. Is there any truth to that?"

Persephone appeared irritated but willing to compromise. She chose her words carefully. "My dealings with Drucilla are to simply monitor her transformation and stay apprised of any potential hazards or unfavorable outcomes that could affect our realm."

"Is that all?" Drake seemed unconvinced.

"My children reside in Hell. You do not think I want to protect them?"

"That is another story I heard. You have a child with Sariel: half-demon, half-angel."

Persephone's eyes widened momentarily at the notion that Drake would assume she was a demon. "Drake, we are not demons. We are Lilim," Persephone said firmly. "Yes, I have a half-Lilim, half-angel child—Not half-demon. Do not make that mistake. We are not the same."

Drake appeared confused for a moment. "You all reside in Hell. I thought all Unholy were demons."

"No, we are not part of the Unholy. We something else entirely. The Lilim reside here because I reside here. I made Hell what it is today, for Lucifer and my children. My children are part of me. They belong here alongside Lucifer's allies and subjects. I created this realm billions of Earth years ago." Persephone stood up and looked around the parlor. "Lucifer is gone, and you are here. Hell is yours."

Drake narrowed his eyes at Persephone. "If you want to continue our companionship, you must keep me apprised of everything. I want no more secrets, no more half-truths. Do you understand?"

Persephone met Drake's eyes with a narrowed gaze to match. "If you feel I have deceived you, it is because you have perceived it as deception. I have nothing to hide or gain from you. If I fail to disclose something, it is because I do not deem it worrisome or important enough to discuss. I do not concern myself with anything other than protecting my family. I had sixty-one children. Only eighteen have survived. My family is small, but we are strong. One Lilim can perform the task of a legion of demons easily."

"That sounds like a thinly veiled threat."

"It is no threat. It is factual."

Drake peered at Persephone curiously. "If the Lilim are so mighty, why are only eighteen left? Where are the other forty-three children?"

"The great war claimed many casualties. For every Lilim that fell, thousands more Seraphs died." Persephone looked down at the rings on her fingers and spread her fingers apart. She seemed not to want to recall the events.

Drake leaned back and crossed his arms. He studied the billions-year-old woman, attempting to make sense of her existence. "Your race intrigues me. Other than Sariel, who are the fathers of your children?"

Persephone raised an eyebrow at Drake. "I do not procreate as you do, Drake. I create the Lilim out of necessity."

"What does that mean?"

"Both Divine and Unholy are afflicted with burdens that even they alone cannot carry."

Drake frowned, unsatisfied with the explanation.

Moloch announced Raziel's arrival. He grabbed the door handle and pulled it open for the Seraph. Raziel hastily entered the room, accompanied by Valor. The beautiful, blond-haired Seraph was taller than Raziel but nowhere near a Cataclysm. She carried a sizeable silver ornate chest that seemed disproportionate for someone her size to carry, yet she moved it effortlessly. She placed it on the floor next to Raziel. She turned her gaze to Leviathan, curling her lip with disgust and scoffing.

"It's lovely to see you too," Leviathan replied to the gesture.

"Why must you mock us so?" Valor motioned to Leviathan's appearance.

"Must I change my appearance merely because I no longer exist in the Celestial Empyrion?"

"You are no Seraph!" she growled.

"And you are no Virtue," Leviathan casually responded. He didn't make eye contact and instead, straightened the cuff of his suit.

Persephone glanced at Valor. Valor side-eyed Persephone. Valor had no intentions of speaking to her.

Drake stood up and approached Raziel. He looked down at the chest and then back to Raziel. "Is it in here? The thing that's going to stop Calliope from taking over?"

"Yes," Raziel responded without hesitation.

Drake inhaled and exhaled deeply in relief.

Valor bent down, pulled the lid back on the chest, and stepped back. Drake glanced inside. A lead-black, armored breastplate with alchemical symbols etched on the surface lay neatly inside atop other pieces. Drake turned his gaze back to Raziel.

"A suit of armor? I already have a suit of armor. If you were only going to carve symbols all over it, I would have given you mine," Drake remarked.

Raziel scoffed. "The symbols are not the only aspect of the armor. The armor is made from celestial matter not found on Earth or the Infernal Sphere. It combines panguite and estrellaite, some of Ophanim's elemental compounds."

Drake bent down and picked up the breastplate. "It's light," he remarked. He turned it over and noticed more symbols inside. "So, how long do I have to wear it?" He looked back inside the chest at the other pieces of the set. He was hoping only to wear it for a short time.

"Indefinitely."

Drake shot Raziel a confused look. "You're telling me I can't ever take it off?"

"Correct."

Drake became irate and dropped the breastplate back into the box. "Is this really the best solution you could devise? A prison that I must wear for eternity?" Drake scowled and paced the floor. He crossed his arms and squeezed tightly to his biceps. "No, no, this is unacceptable. You'll need to design another solution," he demanded.

"Drake, there is no other solution. You must wear the armor if you want to survive."

"I'm not wearing it. You need to go back and figure out something else," Drake argued, clearly irrational.

"You must understand that we have provided you with the most effective and least invasive solution, short of exorcising Calliope. This was not an easy task. It took our Seraphs months to gather enough of the material from the outer ends of the cosmos. Very little of this matter exists anywhere. Given the time allotment, we have formulated the best solution possible. The wards are necessary to keep Calliope contained. Regrettably, you have no other choice."

Drake paced like a caged lion, desperately trying to find another solution on his own. He was unable to think of one.

"The armor is light and lean enough that you could wear your preferred garments over the suit."

Drake composed himself for a moment. He knew there had to be another way, but this was out of his realm of understanding. Facing the limited choices, he begrudgingly conceded. "And you are certain this will stop Calliope from taking over?"

"Yes."

Drake knelt down and pulled pieces of the light, airy armor out of the chest, inspecting each piece.

"You haven't much time, Drake. I suggest you outfit yourself immediately," Persephone stated.

"Are you sure?" Drake asked Raziel once more.

"As the arbiter of Celestial Law, I cannot mislead you. If I say it is an effective solution, it is guaranteed."

"One more thing, I request the utmost discretion in this solution. I request that no one else knows of our arrangement." Drake looked at the tall blonde Virtue. Valor's eyes shifted to meet Drake's gaze. She quickly looked away.

"Understood," Raziel said.

Drake loosened and ripped off his necktie. Persephone helped him with his coat and placed each piece of clothing over the chaise. She helped strap the breastplate to his body and legs. The armor fit Drake like a wetsuit, conforming to each muscle and tendon. As each piece snapped into place, Drake felt nothing was changing inside of him. The veins in his hands and arms still flowed with bright, orange light.

Raziel bent down and picked up the vambraces. He stepped over to Drake and held them out to him. Drake took the vambraces from him and opened them to place them on his forearms. As he opened them, he noticed a dozen two-inch protruding spikes lining the inside instead of warding runes. He looked at the vambraces dubiously. "What are these for?"

"These will keep Calliope locked inside of you. The material must pierce your flesh and enter your body. I am afraid it will be excruciating."

Drake's breathing became rapid in anticipation.

"Do it," Drake demanded. He held his arms out to Persephone.

Persephone picked up one vambrace and wrapped it around his arm. She looked into his eyes before slamming it closed. The barbs inside the vambrace punched through his flesh as Drake inhaled and stared straight ahead. She looked up at him. He nodded back to her to proceed. She placed the other on his forearm and shoved it closed. Again, the barbs pierced through his flesh. Drake held his emotions together and breathed deeply through the pain. The light from his hands dimmed down until it completely disappeared. His glowing white eyes turned to their natural orange state. He put his arms down to his side as small blood channels flowed down his hands and fingertips. A few drops fell to the floor.

"Beware! If you remove the armor, the transformation process will continue where it left off," Raziel warned.

"Am I also to understand that I can no longer access Calliope's power?" Drake asked.

"Yes, that is correct. You will no longer be able to access the Throne's power," Raziel responded. "But as a King of Hell, you retain your own. That has not changed."

"Imperator," Drake corrected. "I am the Imperator."

188

CANTICLE EIGHTEEN

"Time (shift) as we collide with the energy, in other ways."
—Deftones

Adelia pulled up to the old house on Bradley St. and exited the car. She popped open her trunk and pulled out her bags. She looked at her laptop bag and remembered that Marylin had told her the house didn't have electricity, so she left it behind.

She stepped onto the new front porch and noticed that modern mechanisms had replaced the door and locks. She searched for Marilyn's text message containing the access code to open the front door.

"They found a Copperhead den in yer backyard," a voice with a thick, Texas accent said behind her.

Adelia turned around to see who was talking to her. An elderly gentleman stood on the sidewalk with a miniature black dachshund.

"Snakes?" Adelia asked.

"Whole mess of 'em. Bit one of them landscapers. He's all right. I guess that's what insurance is for, right?" he chuckled.

Adelia set her bags down and walked toward the gentleman. The old man stuck out his hand.

"Roger. Roger Walker. I live across the street a couple of houses down. Y'all movin' in?"

"Adelia Castillo," she said and shook his hand. "My sister and I purchased this house almost two years ago. We're fixing it up."

"Castillo? You a Mexican gal?" he asked.

Adelia blinked at the blatant observation.

"Yes, on my mother's side. My father is from Spain. I'm from California. I moved to Texas for college a few years ago."

"We have a few Mexicans in the neighborhood, down't the other end of the road there. They're pretty quiet for the most part. They're all right, I guess. They don't cause much trouble."

"Well, thank you for sharing, Mr. Walker."

"Call me Roger. Mr. Walker is my father."

Adelia groaned to herself silently.

"You know who used to own that place?" he asked.

"A magician is what I heard."

"Yep! The Mysterious Ares Viorel," he said. "My father used to watch his performances as a young boy. Ares bought this property along with six other lots around it. Sold all but this house a month before he died. Seems like he knew he was going to die, I reckon."

"When did he die?"

"Oh, uh, I don't rightly recall, but I reckon it would have to be around 1930."

"Do you know how he died?"

"Was in Denver, was during a show, fell off the stage, and snapped his neck. Died instantly."

Adelia's eyes grew at the old man's story.

"He was estranged from his son, Cliff. Clifford didn't want nothin' to do with his father. Didn't do nothin' with this house neither. It's a shame, was a nice house at one time. One of the nicest in the neighborhood."

"So, it's not haunted, right?" Adelia smirked. She was only half-joking.

"Well, you never know. Some of these houses have stories to tell, and sometimes you can't get them to be quiet about it."

"That is, uh, that is unsettling."

"Aww, you'll be all right. Welcome to the neighborhood. If you need anything, jus' give me a holler. I'm right over yonder."

Roger tipped his baseball cap at her. "You have a good day, ma'am." Roger turned around and headed to his house with his little dog in tow.

Adelia pressed her lips tightly as she watched the peculiar old man walk away. She shook her head.

She stepped back up the porch and entered the house. The walls looked freshly constructed, with drywall and tape seaming them together. The stairwell was complete and sturdy. The musty smell had disappeared, replaced by dusty plaster, paint, and plastic construction debris. Piles of crumbled drywall and polyester straps from the packaging remained. She made her way to the dining room because she was concerned the floral walls didn't make it during the reconstruction. To her surprise, they were untouched. Parts needed repair, but the wallpaper looked even more amazing with the room cleaned. She made her way into the kitchen with its upgraded countertops, and cupboards consisting of quartz and oak. "Damn, Mare, you really know what you're doing." Adelia was impressed with the progress.

She returned to the foyer, grabbed her bags, and headed for the bedrooms. The master bedroom was habitable, not ideal, but it would do. She opened one of her bags and pulled out a few pillar candles. She placed them around the floor and a couple in the bathroom.

Adelia was suddenly caught off guard by subtle, yet rhythmic, rapping coming from downstairs. She headed back down the stairs and looked out the front door window. No one was on the porch or the sidewalk in front of the house. *I probably imagined it.* She shook her head and turned to head back upstairs.

Tap—tap—tap—tap

Adelia froze. She did not imagine this. It was coming from inside the house. She slowly turned her head in the direction of the tapping. It sounded like it was coming from the kitchen.

The sudden finger-snapping of the Addams Family theme song blasted from the pocket of her cardigan, nearly putting her into cardiac arrest. "Jesus!" she screamed.

She looked at the screen and saw Marylin's face. She quickly answered.

"My ringtone gave me a heart attack!"

"Hahaha. I was checking to see if you made it there okay. You didn't call."

"Yeah, I'm fine. I met our neighbor. He's an odd fellow. Apparently, someone working in the yard got bit by a snake, and I guess he figured I should know about it."

"Yeah, we had a copperhead infestation back there. It's been dealt with. The dude is fine. So, what do you think of the progress?"

"It looks really different."

"Be careful in that back office, I don't trust the floor. I haven't had a chance to repair that room yet, so you should probably stay out of it altogether. A lot of nails are lying around, so don't go anywhere without shoes on. Also, you might want to pick up a generator. The one we had at the house belonged to my boss, who took it back last week. Save the receipt for expenses. Oh and…"

"Mare, it's okay! I'm grown up. I know I'm your little sister, but I got it."

"Ok. Just be careful. I'll come up there as soon as I can."

"Oh, do you know of a café I can work from?"

"There's a coffee shop on Tennessee Ave. That's where I've been going."

"Rad."

"I gotta go, Del, call me later. Bye."

Adelia placed her cell back into her pocket. She squinted for a moment as if it helped her to hear better. She waited for a moment for the tapping to start again, but it had seemed to have ceased. She shrugged it off and headed to the bedroom.

†††

Tap-tap-tap-tap

Adelia blinked her eyes and opened them for a moment. She closed them and rolled over. She pulled the coverers up to her neck and started to drift back to sleep.

Tap-tap-tap-tap

Adelia sat straight up and looked around the room. The glow from the waning moon illumined the bedroom. She looked around, trying to figure out the direction of the sound. She reached over and looked at her phone. 5:15 a.m.

Tap-tap-tap-tap

"What the…."

Irritated, she flung the covers off her body and put on her robe. She lit the pillar candle on the nightstand, picked up her phone and candle and walked into the hallway. It was the same sound she had heard earlier. She used the candle to light another candle on the newel post at the top of the stairs and made her way slowly down the staircase into the foyer. It was a clear, quiet, late autumn morning. She remembered that the sound was coming from the kitchen earlier that day. She walked through the living and dining rooms into the newly constructed kitchen. *Maybe it's the wind.* She looked outside, but nothing was moving.

Tap-tap-tap-tap

The sound was coming from behind the closed office door. Marilyn told her not to go back there, but she also knew she couldn't sleep until she figured out where the sound was coming from. She approached the door and waited to see if the sound would happen again.

Tap-tap-tap-tap

There it was. She put her hand on the door handle and wondered if maybe an animal got stuck in there. Empathy took over, and she realized she needed to get the little guy out, if that was the case.

After entering the room, she noticed the room was cold, much colder than the rest of the house. She could see her breath when she exhaled. She set the candle on the desk and bent down to look under it, there was nothing there. She stood up, headed to the closet at the other end of the room, and flung the door open, but it was empty.

Tap----tap----tap----tap

Adelia froze in panic. The tapping was considerably slower that time. She slowly shifted her eyes to the left. The sound was coming from behind her, under the burned-out floor.

She inhaled and exhaled deeply. She pulled her phone from her robe, turned on the flashlight, and set it on the ground. It was bright enough to illuminate the immediate area. Adelia bent down and ran her hand over the scorch marks.

Tap-tap-tap-tap

Startled, Adelia fell backward onto her hands and stared, wide-eyed, at the floor. Something under there wanted out. She slowly sat back up and started to feel around to see if she could lift a wood plank. Surprisingly, she found three of the floorboards only loosely fitted in place. She needed something to pry the board up with. The two, thin silver rings, stacked on her finger might work. She slid one off and jammed it between the floorboards. She lifted off the board and grabbed her phone to look inside. It was too dark. She lifted off the other two boards and shined her phone back inside.

"What the Hell is going on?" she whispered.

She held her phone into the opening and stuck her head inside the space beneath the floor. Way back, under the boards, was a chest of some sort.

"Oh, screw this. I've seen enough horror movies to know something under there is going to eat me!" She sat out of the hole and contemplated whether she wanted to look inside the box.

She attempted to breathe through her anxiety.

"Adelia, this isn't a movie. Don't be stupid. It's just a box. Go get it."

She slowly stuck her arm into the space and felt for the box. It was just out of reach. She laid on her side on the floor, and shoved her arm back as far as it would go. She managed to grip the corner of the box and slowly slid it toward the opening. When she felt it was close enough, she reached in with both arms and pulled the box onto the floor. She used the light from her phone to examine the exterior thoroughly. Judging from the vintage travel ephemera, it appeared to be a piece of luggage from the late 1800s made of hard, brown leather. She loosened and unstrapped the buckles on either side that held it closed.

"Okay, all that's left now is to flip it open."

She stared at the container.

"Adelia, why are you not opening the box?" she spoke as if someone was in the room with her. She grabbed the candle from the desk and set it on the floor for additional light. "Okay, house, is this what the tapping was for? You wanted me to find the box?"

She waited for confirmation but heard nothing.

"Oooookay, here we go..."

She placed her hand on the side of the lid and flipped it back. She shined the flashlight into the case. On the lid was more vintage ephemera and a pocket with papers shoved inside. She reached her hand in and pulled out the small stack, setting them on the floor next to her. They were mostly magic show playbills.

"The Mysterious Ares Viorel and his Book of Magic," she read aloud. She continued to flip through the flyers. She found magazine clippings of reviews of his shows in various cities. There was also an article that claimed that Ares was a warlock and possessed by The Devil. Adelia chuckled to herself. There was a black and white photo of whom she assumed were Ares and his son standing in front of the house. She flipped over the picture. *April 5th, 1908, Bonfire,*

Texas, was the barely legible scribble on the back. She then turned her attention to the contents of the box. There was a purple scarf. She pulled it out and set it down beside her. Next was a long, black cape with a purple satin lining. She set that next to her—a pair of purple gloves. *The dude was really into purple.* She examined those and set that next to her as well. Next was a small, rectangular box. She popped the latch open, and inside was a satin, purple-lined box with a wand. The wand had silver symbols carved into it.

"Woah, this is cool!" she said. She held the wand up and twirled it in front of the flashlight.

Next were a couple of Victrola records in their sleeves. She turned to investigate the box again, and at the bottom there lay a book. She turned her head to the side to try and read the cover. She saw nothing but a bunch of random symbols.

"What the heck is this?"

She pulled out the large, heavy book from the case. She pushed the case back and placed the book in front of her.

"This must be the Book of Magic."

She examined the heavily-bound tome embellished with ornate, thick iron hinges. In place of a keyhole, there was a smooth, protruding sphere. She turned the tome repeatedly, trying to figure out how to open it. She ran her thumb over the sphere. The sphere reacted to her touch, and the locking mechanism sprung open.

"What?" she whispered. She was certain it would take more than that to open.

She gazed at the swirled galaxy pattern of the inner cover before she slid her hand under the first page and flipped it in amazement.

"What the? Ouch!" Adelia hollered. The paper-like texture slid across the inside of her index finger. Adelia shook her hand vigorously in reaction to the pain. She stopped and looked at the damage. A small blue spark shot across her hand. Stunned, she shook her head. *I must be exhausted. I'm seeing things.* She stuck her knuckle in her mouth to soothe the pain.

The pages weren't paper but rather a leathery type of substance. The texture was flexible and semitransparent but opaque enough that she could barely see the writing on the other side. The entire book seemed to contain nothing but handwritten symbols.

"Oh my God, this is the coolest book ever!"

A letter-sized slip of paper was sticking out from a few pages inside. She pulled the paper out. It was a letter to Clifford. It must have been wet at some point because the writing was barely legible.

The sky grew progressively brighter as the sun emerged over the horizon, casting a golden glow throughout the room. Adelia picked up the letter and walked outside through the back door. She sat on the newly constructed back deck and read the letter.

April 13th, 1929

To my son Clifford,

I am afraid that if you find this letter, it means that I have left this mortal coil and you have found my book. Clifford, this book is no ordinary book. It contains the secrets to the universe, all universes, at all times. You may think these are the ramblings of an old man, but this book is real. It is very real. My hope is that you learn about what it is and how to use it to help mankind. This book should only be in the hands of someone with strength and will, and a good heart. You, my son, are the one destined to carry the burden of this book. I believe you were born for this purpose. We both were. You are now its keeper. Learn to use it. There is a war coming between the Divine and the Unholy. Angels are real. Devils are real. But there is so much more. This book will show you how to prepare not only yourself but your allies that will be fighting alongside you. Good luck, my son.

Ares Viorel

"What? This is nuts—" Adelia dropped her arms and looked up at the horizon. Her phone started to vibrate in her hand. She looked at the screen. Her eyes widened in surprise.

"Dru!" Adelia said as she answered.

"Del! This is going to sound crazy, but bear with me."

"Doubt it could be any crazier than what I'm dealing with," Adelia said. She walked back into the office.

"What?"

"Nothing, never mind. What's going on, Dru?" Adelia sat down in front of the book and opened it again.

"The book, you have it, right?" Drucilla asked.

"Book?" *How does she know I have a book?* "Maybe. Can you describe the book?"

"It's a large, heavy tome. It is hand-written in weird symbols. It's written in angelic script."

"Angelic script?"

"Yes. Do you, have it?" Drucilla said impatiently.

Adelia's breathing became more laborious as she attempted to hold herself together. This whole thing was becoming increasingly terrifying. She inhaled and exhaled rapidly.

"Del? Del, are you okay?"

"Umm," she exhaled hard. "I just found it, just now. I don't know what's going on, Dru."

"Del, you're the keeper of the Tome, and I need your help."

Adelia was unable to form a single thought. This whole thing was spiraling.

"Del? Del, are you there?"

Adelia's eyes flashed with a blue flare of light. Something clicked inside of her. Adelia felt something big, bigger than she could have imagined, was playing out in front of her eyes. Everything from the inheritance to this moment of discovery was for a specific purpose, although she wasn't sure what it was.

"Yeah, I'm here," Adelia said apprehensively.

"Okay, what I'm about to tell you is going to sound unbelievable, but please try and be open-minded. The book you have is Divine."

"Divine."

"Yes. It's yours. It chose you."

"Of course, it did," Adelia responded in defeat as if her life couldn't be more complicated.

CANTICLE NINETEEN

"Whenever life sucks, remember you're going to die someday."— Oscar Wilde

†

"Dru, I still don't see why we had to fly down here." Dominic moaned as Drucilla drove their rental car from Dallas to Bonfire.

"I can't exactly go around teleporting from place to place. You don't think that would look a bit suspicious that we managed to get from point A to point B without transportation?"

"Okay, the car, I get it. But, flying? That took forever. And the people, and cramped seats. Dru, my knees were in my throat the whole time."

"If I'm going to appear human, I need to behave like a human, and that means I need to fly the old-fashioned way sometimes."

"I don't get it. Whatever. You do you, Dru," Dominic groaned. He leaned the seat back to get into a comfortable position.

"I always do," Drucilla smirked.

Dominic looked out the window at the "Welcome to Bonfire" sign they passed as they entered the historic small town. The area was flat and full of seasonal trees. Pecan and cottonwoods were abundant, but not a single pine, evergreen, or cedar tree was in sight. The air smelled dusty and devoid of anything fragrant. This wasn't something he was used to.

"Quite different from the PNW out here, isn't it?" Drucilla mused.

"What do people do here? I mean, there are no mountains, waterfalls, or glaciers. There's no rainforest. It's just all dead. It's all brown and flat. It doesn't even smell nice," Dominic commented.

"Drink. I think they drink and bar-b-que."

"Hah. Yeah, I think you'd have to," Dominic responded.

They pulled up to Adelia's house and got out of the car. They walked up to her front porch and rang the doorbell. Dominic looked behind them and noticed an older man waving at them from the front yard across the street.

"Why is that guy waving at us?"

"People in Texas are overly friendly and curious about anything that moves. Just be polite and wave back."

Dominic curled his lip and gave a slightly confused wave back.

"You are such a snob," Drucilla chuckled.

"No, Pacific Northwesterners are introverted. Loud people frighten us," Dominic corrected her.

"Dru!" Adelia yelled and threw her arms around Drucilla. "Come in, come in!" Adelia smiled at Dominic.

Fresh drywall and paint lingered in the air as they entered the house. Drucilla stuffed her keys in her pocket and looked around the foyer. Dominic dropped his laptop bag and looked around as well.

"Wow, this looks a lot different from when you first bought it. I remember the pictures you sent."

"Yeah, we're about five months late and probably end up being 60k over budget, but it's getting there," Adelia said. She looked around with pride.

"Do you still plan on selling it?" Drucilla asked.

"Dru, if you had asked me this last year, I would say yes, without a doubt. But now, now I can't. I plan on buying my sister out when it's complete."

Dominic looked at her inquisitively.

"I'm sorry, Del, this is Dominic. He's a linguist and expert in religious lore."

"Dominic, glad to have you join us." They shook hands. "Let's head to the dining room," Adelia said.

Dominic and Drucilla followed Adelia through the parlor into the dining room. Upon the table was Thoth's Alchemy Tome. Drucilla stood before the open tome, admiring the angelic script and detailed, gold bindings.

"May I?" Drucilla asked Adelia. Adelia nodded.

Drucilla carefully slid her hand under the open pages. She peered curiously at the strange paper. She could almost see her hand from the other side.

"I can't read the language the book is written in—" Adelia said.

"It's most definitely a form of angelic script," Dominic piped in.

"Dominic is an expert at translating angelic script since it relates to Catholic lore."

"How long will it take you to translate it?" Adelia asked.

Dominic glanced at the size of the book.

"It's lengthy. I want to read through it first and see what information this book contains. I have a cipher translator on my laptop that I could give to you."

"Take as long as you need."

Dominic nodded as he sat down and opened his laptop bag.

Drucilla turned to Adelia. "I suppose we should talk."

Adelia led Drucilla to the back office, where Adelia found the tome. She closed the door behind her and pointed to the burned floor and floorboards that lay nearby. Drucilla bent down and inspected the floor.

"This scorching looks like it came from underneath the floor rather than on top," Drucilla observed.

"Yeah, I noticed that too. I have no idea why. I don't know much about how fire spreads, but you'd think the whole house would catch if a fire started under the floorboards. Right?"

"You'd think," Drucilla responded.

Adelia pulled herself up onto the mahogany desk and leaned forward. "Dru, I have no idea what's going on here. I'm confused and just at a loss to grab onto anything rational. I don't know what's happening. You know, if the tapping hadn't drawn me to the floorboards, I might never have found the book."

"Tapping?"

"Yeah, I think my house is haunted," Adelia chuckled slightly. "There was tapping coming from under the floorboards. I thought maybe it was an animal trapped at first, but I found the leather suitcase with all this magician paraphernalia. The book was inside of it."

"Del, if your house were haunted, I'd definitely know about it," Drucilla said. She looked around the room and didn't see anyone other than Adelia.

"How could you possibly know that?"

"There's is a lot that I need to tell you. Some of it will be strange, and some of it will be terrifying. I don't expect you to understand all of it right now. I want you to ask as many questions as you need and understand that your reactions are perfectly normal. It will take some time to absorb everything I am telling you, but I ask that you keep an open mind." Drucilla took off her leather jacket and tossed it on the desk near Adelia.

"But I think the best place to start is here."

Drucilla closed her eyes for a moment, then popped them open. Her eyes blazing like stars, she clenched her fists as her wings burst from her back. The four wings expanded so colossally that they took up most of the room.

Adelia's first reaction was to scream at the top of her lungs.

Dominic glanced up at his laptop when he heard the scream, waited for a moment, then went back to work.

Adelia jumped down and stood in front of Drucilla, trembling.

Drucilla's eyes dimmed. "Be not afraid."

Adelia slowly walked around Drucilla, inspecting the wings. The eyes on Drucilla's wings followed Adelia's movements. Adelia crossed her shaky arms as she tightened them against her chest. "Does, does it hurt?"

"I showed you that I'm an angel, and my comfort is your first question?" Drucilla laughed. "Yeah, when I ruin an expensive shirt. Totally."

"How did this happen?"

"It's a long story. Basically, I died and came back. I'm an Ophanim," Drucilla answered.

Adelia stared for a moment. "You died? What? And what the Hell is an Ophanim?"

"Ophanim are essentially the highest race of Divine beings."

Adelia's confusion seemed to grow with each question.

"Okay, I'm really going to need you to explain all of this. The wings, especially. I mean, where do they go?"

"The wings aren't what you think they are. They are considerably compact from what they appear to be. When they close, they lay flatly against my back. You couldn't feel them. It's almost as if they are made of light and shadow. I don't feel them unless they are expanded." Drucilla retracted her wings. Her eyes returned to their normal state. "There's more. A lot more. That was the easy part."

Adelia's eyes widened. "More?"

"Yeah." Drucilla picked up her jacket and poked her arms through. "What do you know about the hierarchy of Heaven and Hell?"

†††

"Wait. Let me say this back to you to see if this sounds as insane when I say it. So, God isn't real but, rather, a committee of ten Thrones that created everything," Del started, emphasizing the nouns as if trying to force her belief into them. "Lucifer is real. Adrian lives in your house as a ghost. Azrael, the Angel of Death, looks like Dave Vanian, the singer from The Damned. Drake is in Hell as the Throne of Death that was once Calliope, and you're the Throne of Infinite Knowledge and Wisdom that once was Thoth, that you gained by absorbing Divine blood that killed you, but now you're back on …Eothre? Is that how you say it?" Adelia asked with an upturned eyebrow.

"In a nutshell."

"And there are Divine relics scattered around the world, and you have found two of them?" Adelia confirmed.

"Three, counting yours."

"Now I am the owner of the Thoth's book?"

"Yeah."

"And that fine specimen of a human in my dining room is *not* your boyfriend?"

"No."

Adelia grinned. "So, *does* he have a girlfriend?"

211

"Del, focus," Drucilla demanded.

"Honestly, this all sounds like a fever dream. Wait, am I asleep? Punch me or something."

Drucilla groaned.

"Seriously, Dru, shouldn't you own the book?" Adelia asked.

"No, that's not how Divine relics work. I shouldn't even be Thoth. I sort of impulsively lucked into it."

"Uh, okay. I am not even going to pretend to understand any of this. So how does the tome fit into this?" Adelia asked.

"That's why I'm here. That's why I need your help. I can only talk to Thoth in the human realm with the alchemy in your book. Once we have it, I can use Aurora's bowl to summon Thoth when we need him, I think."

"Who has the bowl?"

"We don't know. But you were the first stop on our insane tour."

"I want to help. I mean, whatever you need, I'll do what I can," Adelia offered.

"What I need for you to do is learn how to read the tome. It's going to help us in saving the realms from my brother. Learn as much as you can from it."

"That's what the letter said."

"Letter? What letter?" Drucilla asked.

"The previous owner, the magician, wrote a letter to his son that was never delivered. He said the same thing you are saying. Something about the book holding the secrets to the universe and that he would need it for this coming war."

"Del, from what I understand, this war has been prophesized for centuries and is just now coming to fruition, in our generation. I believe all the relics will be found right now."

"Dru," Adelia slowly leaned against the closed door and crossed her arms. "How did you know I had found the book? You called me just minutes after I found it under the floor."

Drucilla exhaled. "I didn't. I took a chance after being told it was in your possession."

"Who told you I had it?"

"He did," Drucilla answered, pointing to her heart. "There was a bit of a mishap with an ancient spell. I did get to speak to him briefly, but that way is closed now. I had to find another.

"Wait, he's alive inside of you, like a parasite?"

"He is."

Adelia scrunched her nose. "What's that like?"

"Stressful."

CANTICLE TWENTY

"Start by destroying the world you know. Take away all the things that you control."—God Module

A few days had passed since Drucilla and Dominic met with Adelia in Bonfire. Dominic rubbed his eyes as he sat up from the chair in his library. He exhaled, pulled himself away from the table, and headed for the coffee maker in the kitchen. Drucilla sat hunched over the dining room table, flipping through one of Dominic's multitudes of antique Catholic reference books as she rested her head in her hand.

"Refill?" Dominic asked. He motioned to Drucilla with the coffee pot.

Drucilla shook her head as she kept her eyes on the book.

"Dru, you should really go home and get some rest."

"It's Saturday night. Am I really living my best life if I'm not out of my house until four a.m.?" Drucilla smirked.

"Okay. I guess."

"At least half of this chase is over," Drucilla said on a positive note.

"True, we have the thaumaturgy to summon Thoth. We got lucky that your friend had the book. I don't know what the chances of that were, but that was a huge stroke of luck in our favor."

"What do we have so far on the cauldron?" Drucilla asked.

Dominic returned with his cup and placed it before himself. He sat back down at the table. "It looks like we have fourteen references to the Tempest and five visual Tempest interpretations. All different. The only consistency is that it's a cauldron or a ceremonial bowl. You really can't remember anything?"

"As I said, Belphegor told me that I had it. Lucifer made the implication that I might not have it yet. Thoth said I needed to obtain it. If we average Belphegor, Lucifer, and Thoth, that means we'll find it."

"That's about as logical an assumption that someone half-asleep is going to offer. Go home, Dru. We can work on this tomorrow."

Drucilla picked up her leather jacket off the back of the chair and poked her arms through the sleeves and untucked her long black, hair from her collar to free it from the coat. She pulled keys from her pocket and pressed the unlock button on the remote. Dominic snorted.

"What?"

"It's just amusing that you can teleport to anywhere in the world, yet you still drive."

Drucilla scrunched her nose. "I like driving, okay?"

Dominic raised his hands as if to say, *whatever*. Drucilla shook her head and turned away. She halted as she came face to face with Lucifer.

"Leaving so soon? You are so close!" Lucifer smiled.

Dominic glanced up at Lucifer. "What are you talking about? We've been at this for hours."

Lucifer crossed his arms and looked over the reference books, both antique and newer, spread across the table. "I understand you have a way to summon Thoth?"

"We do, well, partially," Drucilla answered.

"Is there anything I can do to help?" Lucifer asked.

"No, not right now. I mean, unless you could just tell us where to find the Tempest," Drucilla said.

"I cannot. Divine relics are to be found, not given."

"Um, you're Lucifer. You actively bend the rules whenever you feel like it. Can you at least give us a hint?" Drucilla pleaded.

"Celestial Deals, Drucilla," Lucifer reminded her.

Dominic placed five open books in front of Lucifer with sketched depictions of the cauldron. "Do any of these cauldrons look even close to what we are looking for?"

Lucifer shook his head no. "I will offer you this, since it is not technically violating the rules. Drucilla, you have seen it. Not only have you seen it, but you have held it in your hands at one time."

Drucilla's eyes darted around in thought. Lucifer turned to Dominic.

"Dominic. *Vio siete quell oche noi eravamo, noi saimao quelo che voi sarete.*"

Dominic repeated the words in his head as he mouthed them to himself.

"*ooDAchi,*" Lucifer said as he blinked out.

Dominic quickly flipped open his laptop and typed the words into a search engine. He put one hand over his mouth and navigated with the other.

"Do you know what he said?" Drucilla asked.

"It's an Italian phrase. Unfortunately, Italian is a language that I am not good at. I'm translating it now."

Drucilla sat on the swivel stool behind Dominic and looked over his shoulder.

"Okay, it basically translates to: *You are what we were, we are what you will be*."

"And *ooDAchi*?" Drucilla asked.

"That's Lucifer's way of being droll by saying *good luck* in Russian." Dominic sat back and pondered the phrase.

Drucilla bit the inside of her lip and paced the floor. She stood before the large, plate glass window and looked out into the dark backyard. "Heed these words as you pass by, as you are now, so once was I. As I am now, soon you will be. Prepare for death and follow me."

"What?" Dominic asked. He looked up at Drucilla in confusion.

"I read it on a headstone at the Boothill Graveyard in Arizona. One of the random trips we took with Mom as kids. It was an inscription. That sounds like it's potentially the same thing. It's probably an inscription on a grave."

"So, we have to find a headstone with that inscription? Sounds like a plan. I guess we would only need to sort through about ten billion," Dominic complained.

"Maybe not. He said I had it in my hands at one point."

"How many cauldrons have you handled in your life as an archaeologist, hundreds?

Drucilla walked around. "The inscription is Italian. We can assume that the grave is in Italy or Sicily, right?"

"True, or possibly the Vatican," Dominic added.

Drucilla raised her eyebrows. "I know who might be able to help. Dominic. What time is it in Florida?"

"Uh, three hours ahead, so about seven a.m."

"Great! Mom is awake." Drucilla pulled out her phone and called Fiona. She stepped outside onto Dominic's front porch.

"Drucilla!" Fiona said as she answered.

"Hey, Mom."

"What are you doing up so early on a Sunday?" Fiona asked.

"Mom, I have a question for you. Does the phrase "you are what we were, we are what you will be" mean anything to you? Perhaps you saw it inscribed on something? I remember a similar phrase inscribed at Boot Hill in Arizona. Do you remember a mausoleum or anything with that inscription in Italy?"

There was a long pause on the other end before Fiona spoke again. "No honey, it doesn't sound familiar."

"What if it was in Italian? Would you know it then?"

"My Italian isn't very good, but that sounds like something similar written on the door of the Capuchin Catacombs."

Drucilla's jaw dropped. She knew which cauldron Lucifer was attempting to get her to remember. "Mom, thank you so much. You just solved a mystery."

"I did?"

"Yeah, I love you. I gotta go." Drucilla hung up.

"Dominic!" Drucilla yelled as she ran into Dominic's house. She slammed her hand down on the book that Dominic was reading. "Wanna go to Palermo?" Drucilla asked, her eyes wild with excitement.

†††

Drucilla and Dominic appeared in an alleyway near the front of the entrance to the catacombs. It was a dry, sunny afternoon in Italy. It was roughly three p.m., nine hours ahead of the time zone from which Drucilla and Dominic came.

Random tourist swag and maps were lined up along the sides as they walked up the pathway, which led to the flat, yellowish-beige entrance of the rather unimpressive outer building of the crypt. Dominic noticed the sign on the front door. "Vio siete quell oche noi eravamo, noi saimao quelo che voi sarete," he read aloud and nodded.

An elderly friar dressed in brown, linen monk robes opened the door for Drucilla and Dominic to pass through the corridor. Inside, the crypt was cool and dry. Drucilla remembered the familiar, unpleasant scent of dust, tattered moldy fabric, and stagnant air. Heavy clanging sounds reverberated with every step of Dominic's hiking boot against the steel scaffolding that lined the floor protecting the delicate stone underneath. Walking along the hall, he looked up to see infant mummies displayed in long dresses. They looked like small, skull-faced dolls as they hung peacefully overhead. The walkway was narrow as high steel fencing kept the mummies safe from the tourists. They turned down another corridor where stacks of mummified remains lay in spaces that looked like book shelving. Some mummies had dehydrated skin, mustaches, and beards, while others were merely skeletal remains. Some wore burlap clothing, and others wore velvet and elaborate pattern textiles. Dominic noticed that, curiously, many that hung overhead had their feet and hands bound with rope.

"Why are their hands tied?" Dominic observed as he slowly walked by Drucilla's side, taking in the surroundings.

"Probably, so an arm doesn't fall off into someone's latte." Drucilla shrugged.

Dominic pressed his lips together and gave Drucilla a disgusted look.

"Out of everything you've seen as an EMT, that's appalling to you?" Drucilla blinked in disbelief. "Down the end of the east hallway is the museum's office."

Drucilla and Dominic headed down a set of stairs to a short hallway that terminated at a tall, white door. She opened it, and they stepped inside. A younger gentleman stood behind a desk and looked up at them.

"Hello, can I help you?" he asked with an Australian accent.

"Hi, I'm looking for a woman named Caroline Dixon. She used to work here as a funerary specialist. Do you know if she's still here?"

"Who is asking, please?"

"I'm Drucilla Blackwood. This is Dominic. My mother, Fiona Blackwood, was her collogue."

"I'm sorry, but we don't have anyone by that name here."

"Would someone else know how to find her? It's important that we speak to her. It's, um, related to an archaeological discovery that has to do with these catacombs."

"I might be able to help. What is it exactly?"

Drucilla glanced at Dominic, and Dominic glanced back at her.

"Some artifacts were discovered here about fifteen or sixteen years ago when the new corridor opened. My mother and I were here for the excavation. Could you tell me where they would have placed the artifacts?"

"Usually, if they were found here, some would remain here in the museum," he responded.

"Like on display? I'm looking for a specific bowl or cauldron. It would be about fifteen inches wide and four inches deep. It would have been made of brass or gold. It has symbols on the outside. They look like scorch marks," Drucilla explained.

"I haven't seen anything like you're describing. Perhaps it was sold to a private collector."

"You do that? You sell the artifacts?" Dominic asked.

"Of course. It's common practice. We keep some and sell some at auction to help maintain the museum. You know to pay salaries, maintain the grounds, and keep the lights on."

Dominic looked at Drucilla with concern.

"If you did sell this piece, would you be able to tell me to whom you sold it?" she asked.

"I can see if such a piece was auctioned. It was a bowl, you said?"

"Yeah, or cauldron, if you rather."

"Give me a moment. I will see what I can do. Please have a seat." The clerk motioned to the benches on either side of the doorway. He disappeared into another office.

"Dru, if they sold it, would that mean the relic has attached itself to a new owner?"

"Yeah, I think so. If my understanding of how relics are placed in your path is correct."

Dominic thought to himself for a moment. "But it was placed in your path first. Wouldn't you be the rightful heir?"

"I dunno, Dom. It seems likely, but I don't think we've begun to scratch the surface of how all this works. Remember, I had the pen first, but it was given to you because you're supposed to wield it."

"That is true. However, you seem to be the lynchpin in this whole discovery process. Why you? I mean, what is it about you that is setting these things into motion?"

"Maybe because I freed a Throne? Because I cohabitate with a Throne? Maybe there are more Thrones locked in various artifacts, and I can pull them out? I don't know, Dom."

Dominic crossed his massive arms and leaned back against the wall. He appeared consumed with the unknown and trying to understand it all.

The clerk returned with some papers and walked over to Drucilla. "Since 2000, we have sent three bowl-type artifacts to auction, and two remain within the catacombs." Dominic reached for the stack of papers and flipped through them. Drucilla looked over his shoulder.

"Any of these look familiar?" Dominic asked.

Drucilla bit her lip and shook her head as he leafed through them.

"Wait! Stop! That's it! This is the one we are looking for!" Drucilla took the paper from Dominic and held it up to the clerk's face. The clerk took the printed sheet with the catalog number and description. Dominic looked at the image of the bowl. It was just as Drucilla described.

"So where is it?" Dominic asked.

"Regretfully, that particular item was sold at an auction five years ago," the clerk said.

"Can you tell me who bought it?" Drucilla asked.

"That information is private. I apologize. However, I could relay your information to the current owner if you like. I can't guarantee they will respond to your request, but it may be worth a try if it's that important to you."

Dominic and Drucilla looked at each other and nodded.

O that they were Wise, that they vnderstood This,
that they would Consider their latter End! *Deut: 32.29.*

———— MORS sola fatetur
Quantula sint hominum corpuscula. ———— *Iuvenal:*

CANTICLE TWENTY-ONE

"Some people have no idea what they're doing, and a lot of them are really good at it."—George Carlin

"Del! Help me with these paint rollers 'n stuff!" Marylin shouted from the front door. Her arms held bags overflowing with items from the local hardware store.

Adelia emerged from the back office barefoot and briskly made her way to her sister.

"Great, take these," Marylin said. She off-loaded herself to Adelia's hands. "I got a couple more bags."

Marylin quickly stepped off the porch steps and headed for her truck. Adelia set the bags on the floor and picked through the items in the bag. She held a small container of spackle in her hands and looked up at the crown molding to see where it needed to be repaired.

"We're in the home stretch," Marylin announced as she entered the house with the remaining items.

"Yeah, pretty close. Painting and tacking down the floor trim. We should be there," Adelia acknowledged. She walked around the parlor and continued to check for spots on the crown molding.

"So hey, I think I'm gonna get the realtor out here on Monday to give us an estimate on how much we should list it for," Marylin proposed.

Adelia set the spackle container on the floor and turned to her sister. "Mare, I don't think I want to sell it."

"The house? Why not?"

"We put so much work into it. I don't think I want to let it go."

"Del, we can't afford to keep it."

"Why not? We didn't put that much of our own money into it. It was mostly inheritance."

"But I thought the plan was to double our investment?"

Adelia walked slowly through the parlor and into the dining room. She looked at the exquisite, floral, hand-painted, patterned wall treatment. She had hired a local artist to restore it to its former beauty. "I just don't want to. I really like it."

"So, you want to live here, in Bonfire?"

"Yeah."

"You're going to leave your life in Austin to live in a small, rural town?"

"Yeah, I think so."

"Del, you need to think about this. This is a lot of house and you're quite a hike from Dallas, let alone Austin."

"I know."

"We're in the hole about sixty thousand, plus there's my two hundred thousand investment," Marylin reminded. "How are you going to come up with that?"

"I can come up with it by selling my house," Adelia responded. She sat down at the dining table.

Marylin crossed her arms and leaned against the wall. "Are you sure? There's not a whole lot out here for someone your age."

"I know, but I think I need to be here right now."

"I'll sell you my half for three hundred. That's a hundred less than I had planned on making."

"Fair."

"It also needs to be inspected. You can't live here legally until then, and that could take a few weeks to a couple of months."

Adelia nodded.

"Del, are you sure?"

"I'm positive."

Marylin glanced at her sister suspiciously. She walked over to the table and sat across from Adelia. "What's going on with you lately?"

Adelia looked uneasy. She didn't want to tell her sister everything that had been going on with Drucilla and the tome.

"I know something is going on," Marylin pried.

"I'm just attached to this place, and I have been wanting to get out of Austin for a while."

Marylin looked surprised at the comment. "You love Austin. Isn't that why you applied to the University of Texas in the first place?"

"…I did. Now, I'm ready to move on."

Marylin exhaled and leaned back in her chair. "All right." She threw her hands up. "I'm not going to fight you. You're twenty-nine, and you can make your own decisions."

†††

Adelia sat alone in the dark, quiet back office of her home. The only light was emitting from a single desk lamp and her laptop. She looked to the previously burned-out floor, where she'd found the Alchemy Tome. She could still see a slight discoloration of the wood surrounding the new hardwood floor section. On the wall across from her, she had framed ten of the old show flyers of The Mysterious Ares Viorel. Behind the door on a hook was his cloak and collapsed top hat. His wand lay at the end of the desk, still inside its box.

Adelia opened the modified Enochian-Ophanim cipher application she received from Dominic. Dominic also provided a corresponding alphabet to help her learn the symbols. She remembered that Dominic told her Enochian has twenty-one symbols. Although quite similar, the Ophanim script has thirty-two.

"Okay, upload images," Adelia said as she read the instructions. "I guess I need to take photos of the pages." She pulled the heavy Alchemy Tome from her desk drawer and opened the book to a random page. She took a couple of photos with her phone and uploaded them to the cipher. She flipped the pages and took a few more photos. Adelia watched the cipher as it decoded about three hundred characters from a single uploaded image.

Line by line, English words began to emerge inside a text box below the images. Adelia peered closer at her screen and read the words aloud.

"Tempers, Infernals, and Cambions are lesser daemons within the hierarchy of the Infernal Sphere. They are ranked as foot soldiers and work in service of the Seven Kings. These vengeful creatures can be arrested through the summoning ritual of the seraph Azrael the Exorcist or by reciting the captive Rite of the Immure. The rituals go as follows..."

Adelia looked at the English words and then at the angelic script in the book. She quickly began to make associations in her head between the symbols and the letters. The more she stared at the script, the more she understood what she was reading. Adelia's eyes began to glow slightly with a pale, blue light as she read the lines of symbols in the tome.

"The Rite of the Immure is a violent spell," a voice said from her doorway.

Startled, Adelia jumped to her feet. "Roger?" she said as she glared at him. "What are you doing in my house?"

"Oh, your backdoor was open," he said nonchalantly. His small dog was at his side.

"Roger, you can't just come into my house like that! What were you thinking?" Adelia shouted.

Roger snickered to himself as he walked into Adelia's office. He sat halfway on the corner of her desk.

Adelia glared at him and the audacity that he could just enter her house whenever he wanted.

"Roger, you should leave!"

"Or? What are you gonna do? Use that banishing spell on me? You can barely read that tome," he chuckled.

Adelia's anger turned to fear as she stared at Roger and his knowledge of the tome. Her breathing became rapid. "Who are you? How do you know about the book?" Adelia asked. She struggled to get the words out.

"It is not a secret. All Divine and Unholy know of its existence." Roger's façade faded to a bald, orange-skinned being with short, black claws and a finely tailored black suit. He stood up and straightened his jacket. He looked down at his small black dog. The small dog grew in height and girth as his collar snapped under the pressure of his enormous neck. His fur became dense and his back rigid. His eyes emitted a red glow as his fangs elongated. He thrashed his head as his façade faded into a massive wolf demon. He snarled at Adelia.

Adelia stepped behind her chair to create an additional barricade between herself and the Hellhound.

The dog growled and snapped at Adelia. "Not yet, Lycanis, patience," he said to the enormous beast. The Hellhound calmly and slowly growled and circled the desk like a predator watching his prey. He did not take his eyes off Adelia.

"My apologies. Lycanis tends to get excitable."

Adelia's bottom lip trembled, staring at the former Roger. She was taken aback by his appearance and sudden change of dialect and speech.

"You aren't Roger, are you?"

"No, Adelia, Roger is no more. My name is Melek. I am one of four princes of Hell. This beast is Lycanis, of course. He is the Grand Marquis of Hellhounds."

"Are you here for the tome?" she asked, her voice quivering.

"Are you offering?" a devious grin stretched across his face. Adelia stood silent, trembling with fear.

"The tome holds many secrets to the realms and the cosmos. Did you know that?"

Melek paced around Adelia's office with one arm tucked under his elbow and one hand stroking his chin with his black claws. "That book could destroy the Infernal Sphere as well as the Celestial Empyrion with a single canticle, a single verse. It would all come crashing down."

Terrified and unable to move, Adelia followed him around her office with her eyes. Melek continued to pace until he finally stopped in front of Ares' show flyers. "Your tome, Adelia, is highly coveted. But it will only work for the wielder. The tome chose you."

"Yeah," Adelia whispered.

"Of course, you know. But did you know you can surrender the tome to anyone? Even a demon." He smiled. "We can utilize its power as well."

Adelia remained silent.

"Your friends, the ones that visited you last week. Where are they now? I do not sense them."

Adelia shrugged. She didn't want to give Melek any more information than she needed.

"The woman who was here with the large fellow. She is unfathomably strong, clearly Divine, though I do not know who she is. Seraph? No, more than a Seraph—Virtue possibly. I have not sensed anything like her in eons. What does she call herself?"

"I'm not telling you anything," Adelia muttered.

Melek gazed into Adelia's eyes, he seemed to read her thoughts. "Drucilla!" he announced. "Yes, that is right, Drucilla. I am fascinated by her."

"What do you want?" Adelia asked. She struggled to get the words out of her mouth.

Melek quickly hopped on the desk and sat directly in front of Adelia. She gasped and tried to stay as calm as possible, but inside, she was in the throes of a full-blown panic attack.

"What do I want? Yes, what do I want…" he stroked his chin again.

"Clearly, I am interested in the tome. It holds great value, and Drake would be most appreciative if I were to bring it to him. He may even make me a King!"

Adelia stood as still as possible.

"Unfortunately, since it will not work for me if I take it, you will have to offer the tome to me."

Adelia took short and rapid breaths.

"So, what do you say? May I have the book?" Melek's eyes emitted an eerie flicker as he grinned. Lycanis growled deeply and exposed his fangs at Adelia as he crept closer to her from the other side.

Adelia reached over to the desk and closed the tome. She picked it up and held it against her chest, trying to hide her trembling.

Melek held out his clawed hand.

Adelia moved her eyes to her laptop at the open transcription of the banishment spell. She looked at Melek and then back to her screen. She slowly opened her mouth. In a shaky voice, she uttered the words. "Iviam lo esu, eh ewey. Giza tai drun…"

Melek dropped his hand and blinked a few times at Adelia. He crossed his arms and seemed offended.

"Did… did you just try to banish me?" he questioned. He smirked at the presumed weak attempt.

"No." A low baritone voice came from behind Melek. Startled, Melek quickly got to his feet. He turned to face the voice behind him.

"She summoned me," the voice finished. The looming, scarf-clad skeletal figure dwarfed Melek, even more so as Melek cowered and began to shiver within the shadow cast by the Angel of Death. Azrael positioned his scythe to the side, its blade glinting in the darkness. For a moment, time seemed frozen as the angel's presence dominated the Prince's, forcing the Unholy to break the tension and skidder backward. At the moment Melek began to move, Azrael brought down his scythe upon Melek, the blade slicing him into two equal parts with an effortless swing. The halves of Melek tumbled through the air once before they burst into flames and hit the floor. When the flames died down, nothing remained.

Lycanis cowered in the flash of light and transformed himself into the small, black dachshund. Lycanis whined as Azrael glowered at him and turned the point of his scythe toward him. "Begone," Azrael said, as he revealed his free hand and snapped his fingers. The Hellhound dissipated within an orange flame and flickered out.

Adelia's jaw hung open as she looked up at the enormous seraph. She couldn't believe what had appeared before her. She couldn't move. She couldn't blink.

"I am Azrael," he said, turning his eyeless gaze to the woman. "I assume I have fulfilled my summoning."

Adelia opened her mouth, but not a sound would come out. She stared at Azrael in bewilderment. She finally managed to snap herself out of her trance and breathe.

"Y-yeah," she nodded. She slowly let go of the tome and set it on the desk in front of her. She looked back up at Azrael as he stood, looming over her. "I'm, I'm sorry I didn't mean to summon you. I—I meant to use the banishing spell. I mean...."

Silence met her as a reply. "I mean, I'm glad you showed up and got rid of him—"

Azrael turned fully toward Adelia.

"It's just that I am learning how to read the tome, and I got confused and—"

He shifted the scythe into his other hand.

"You're… you're not here to take me, right?"

Azrael stared at Adelia for a moment. "No, Adelia, it is not your time."

Adelia took in a deep breath to quell her anxiety. She glanced down at the tome and back to Azrael. "Will he come back?"

"Melek has been banished, as has Lycanis. They can no longer enter the realm of Earth."

Adelia put her hands over her eyes and ran her hands down her face. She slowly sat down in her chair.

"Will more come for the tome?" she asked.

Azrael looked at the book and slowly nodded. "Word will travel fast that another Divine relic is in play. Already others are planning how to seize it from you." He reached out and tapped the tome's cover. "You appear to be able to read and understand the incantations. You may yet keep them at bay with the secrets inside."

"It's starting to make sense, a little at a time."

"Good. Keep at it." Azrael put his scythe on his back. "Drucilla needs you."

"You do look like Dave Vanian," Adelia joked.

Azrael almost grinned slightly through his gaunt facial features. "I will see you again, Adelia," he said.

Azrael disappeared.

CANTICLE TWENTY-TWO

✝

Dominic entered Drucilla's gallery and briskly walked over to Drucilla standing behind the front counter. Drucilla looked up from her laptop to see Dominic's confused expression.

"What's up?" she asked.

"Can you leave?" Dominic asked.

"I have people here right now. Can we meet at Sirens in about an hour?"

Dominic looked around the gallery, at the patrons standing around admiring various paintings on the wall. Dominic turned back to Drucilla with an impatient stare.

"Fine. I'll get Ash to lock up." She threw up her hands. "Ash! I gotta step out. Can you mind the front and lock up?"

Ash appeared from the back office. He straightened his collar and sat behind the counter. He smiled at Dominic. Dominic curled his lip at him.

Drucilla grabbed her bag from behind the counter and walked to the gallery's front door. "You still have that weird Stepford kid working for you?"

"He's not weird, Dom," Drucilla said.

"He's absolutely weird. He looks too perfect. Have you ever, in your life, seen someone with every single hair perfectly in place? Have you ever seen him with as much as a single speck of lint on his clothing? No, you haven't. He creeps me out."

"Did you actually pull me out of the gallery on one of our busiest days of the month to complain about Ash? Tell me you didn't."

"No, I didn't. But he's still creepy."

"Fine, he's weird. But he's also kind of endearing." Drucilla grinned. "Anyway, why are you so agitated?"

"I found something."

"Okay?"

"I think I know who's invading my dreams. I think it's a Seraph."

"What makes you say that?" Drucilla asked. They made their way up the stairs to the pub and took their usual table.

Dominic sat across from her and put his hands on his face. "I don't know how to explain it, but the dream has changed. You know how I would see a woman, and she would call me 'Dominic the Guardian,' right? Last night I had the same dream, but it was different. This time she handed me a shield. It was made of energy."

"Go on."

"Then I woke up. But the dreams are evolving. It's like every night, I get another piece of the puzzle. I just don't know who the Seraph is or why they are trying to contact me through my dreams.

✝✝✝

Drucilla and Dominic exited the bar and stepped out onto the sidewalk. The chilly winter evening made the air feel sharp, even the slightest breeze stung Drucilla's cheeks.

"It's gotta be twenty degrees out here," Drucilla complained as she shoved her hands deeper into her pockets. Dominic pulled his collar up higher.

"Eighteen, but what's a couple of degrees, right?" a feminine voice came from behind.

Drucilla looked around to see who was talking to them. She shifted her eyes to Dominic. He also searched for the voice. Persephone appeared from around the corner of the gallery building and approached them.

"Dominic, Drucilla." Persephone nodded slightly as she wrapped herself tighter in a floor-length, black mink coat. Her huge, gaudy gemstone rings reflected the streetlights above.

"What do you want, Persephone?" Drucilla asked through gritted teeth.

"I cannot tell if you are angry or cold," she chuckled.

"Both," Dominic answered in Drucilla's stead. "Why are you here?"

"You know, I can't figure out what you're doing. Are you here to help or cause chaos? Because so far, it's been nothing but chaos," Drucilla added.

Persephone shrugged slightly. "That is fair. However, you might want to listen before you burn me at the stake to keep yourselves warm."

"Doubt it," Dominic responded.

"Whatever, make it quick." Drucilla glanced at Dominic.

"You don't think you can actually win at this game, do you?" Persephone said.

Drucilla raised an eyebrow. "Persephone, go back to Drake, okay? I'm not interested in debating you right now." Drucilla turned and stepped off the curb to cross the street.

"You trust Lucifer?" Persephone spoke up louder. Dominic and Drucilla looked at each other, and she stepped back onto the sidewalk.

"Trust is a complicated term that we don't use with Lucifer. We have a mutual understanding. We have the same goal. We work together, but separately. Is what you want to know for your report?" Dominic asked.

Persephone disregarded Dominic's remark and turned to Drucilla.

"Trust shouldn't be complicated. You should either have it, be working to earn it, or have it broken. And I'd like to build a little between you and me."

"And how would you even begin to build that trust with me when I know you're at Drake's side?"

"How about some answers Lucifer doesn't deign to tell you? Right now, more of the Divine relics are being discovered by those who are close to you, Drucilla."

Drucilla quickly stepped up to Persephone. "Wait, wait a minute, you know who all of the keepers of the Divine relics are?"

Persephone leaned her head to the side. Her glistening, pomegranate red lips stretched slowly into a mischievous smile. "Of course, I do."

"Who possesses the Tempest, Aurora's cauldron?" Drucilla blurted out without hesitation.

"Katia van Vliet. You know her by her former name, Katia Thomson," Persephone confidently responded.

"Katia?!"

"Who's Katia?" Dominic asked.

"She was my best friend in High School, before the um…." Drucilla made a motion with her hand around her wrist. "The rosary incident."

Persephone quickly turned around, seemingly spooked by something. "I must take my leave. I will speak to you again soon." She disappeared.

The door to the gallery quickly swung open. Ash turned around, closed the door, and locked it behind him. He sang quietly and softly to himself. A strange and eerily beautiful Latin song in a soprano choirboy voice. He abruptly stopped as he looked up to Dominic and Drucilla, who stood a few feet from him. "Hello," he said, surprised at their presence.

"Even Persephone is creeped out by him. I told you he was weird," Dominic said quietly.

Maledicta Terra in opere tuo, in laboribus comedes
cunctis diebus vitæ tuæ donec revertaris.

CANTICLE TWENTY-THREE

✝

Dominic sat in Drucilla's living room as she paced the floor, trying to figure out the best way to breach the subject with Katia about her Divine relic.

"What if we show up at Varstadt in San Francisco?" Dominic asked.

"At her office?" Drucilla responded.

"Sure?"

"No, that would be weird."

"No, really! Check it out. So, you said she's a genetic scientist, right? Let's tell her I have a weird gene that causes me to become larger and taller as I age," Dominic suggested. "I mean, no one has that. She'd definitely be interested."

"What? How do you know you'd be the only one?" Drucilla enquired.

"Because I've researched it. Endlessly."

Drucilla creased her forehead. "Huh?"

Dominic nodded. "It appears that way."

Drucilla sat down on the couch beside Dominic. She peered at him curiously. "We're not talking about hypotheticals anymore, are we?"

Dominic ran his hand over his head.

"You're just now telling me about this?"

Dominic stood up, paced around the room, and crossed his arms.

"When I was born, I was average size for a baby. Nothing out of the ordinary. However, my dad noticed that I wasn't growing at the same pace as the other kids. See, kids shoot up in growth spurts, they can literally grow three to four inches in a year right after puberty, but they would eventually slow down. I didn't. My growth was explosive. I'd grow six inches a year at times. I was 5'9" when I was twelve. When I graduated high school, I was 6'1". No big deal, right? Drucilla, I was 6'4" five years ago. I am currently 6'6" and still growing. If I'm not growing taller, I'm growing bigger. I don't even work out as much as you'd think, maybe twice a week, if that. Yet my biceps and chest seem to increase as if I'm constantly lifting."

"And your dad knows?" Drucilla asked.

"He couldn't explain it. He's pretty much stopped trying."

"So, you've never stopped, ever?"

"It slows down, then speeds up. But it's almost like I have no upper limit."

"That's gotta be scary," Drucilla said.

"I figure I'll start panicking when I hit eight feet. Or my heart starts giving out. I've got time."

Drucilla shook her head. "If it's all the same to you, I rather not have you not become Katia's science project."

"Have any better ideas?" Dominic asked.

"As a matter of fact." Drucilla stood up. "Adrian."

"Huh?" Adrian asked. He overheard his name and glided into the living room.

"Do we still have the invitation to Sierra's wedding?" Drucilla asked.

"Uh, somewhere. Why? Are we going to the wedding?" Adrian said with a bit of hope in his tone. He loved weddings.

"What does your cousin's wedding have to do with this?" Dominic asked.

"Sierra is marrying Killian, who happens to be Katia's brother. She'll obviously be there. I can't think of a reason why she would miss something like this. She's quite close with her brother, the opposite of Drake and me."

"Where is the wedding?" Dominic asked.

"In an old hotel in San Francisco," Drucilla responded.

"*Le Palais de Cristal*, it's in the Presidio Heights area. I actually think it's tomorrow," Adrian chimed in.

"Looks like we have our in," Dominic said.

"Get ready, Adrian," Drucilla said.

"Why are you bringing Adrian?" Dominic asked.

"In case she needs further convincing," Drucilla responded.

CANTICLE TWENTY-FOUR

"I feel like the rules been changed. Sometimes I feel like a ghost in chains."—††† (Crosses)

Drucilla dashed out of the cab, into the rain, and up the red-carpeted stairs to the entrance of the hotel before the doorman could help her out of the car. Adrian kept close pace behind her. She shook her umbrella away to avoid getting her dress and shoes wet. One of the doormen took her umbrella from her and closed it. Another held the door open for her.

"I'm here for the Thompson-Blackwood wedding?" Drucilla said to the doorman.

The doorman pointed to the black, velvet sign with white lettering that said *Thompson Blackwood event* and an arrow pointing left down a corridor. "Thanks," Drucilla said as she walked briskly past.

"Have you planned out what you're going to say, or are you just going to wing it?" Adrian asked.

Drucilla glanced slightly at Adrian. She found a small alcove outside of a banquet hall and stepped behind the floor-to-ceiling curtain, pulling him in with her.

"Okay, rules—no being corporeal," Drucilla said as quietly as possible.

"Don't you think I know that? Christ, most of these folks were at my funeral," Adrian said with little patience.

"True enough. And no, I haven't thought that far ahead. I guess we'll see how far I can get without you. She's going to have a heart attack if I have to bring you in."

"At the very least," he said.

"Okay, radio silence from here on out. I can't have people see me talking to myself. That would make me look weird."

"Oh, you think *that* is what would make you look weird?" Adrian snarked.

Drucilla groaned. She moved away from the alcove and took off her coat. She handed it to the coat check clerk. Drucilla was dressed in a short, black dress with sheer, black lace sleeves. Her usual long, straight, black hair rolled down her shoulders in neat, silky, black curls. Around her neck was a long, silver chain that held the vial and another chain with Calliope's amulet.

"There's my other baby!" a woman shouted. She quickly approached Drucilla.

"Hey, Aunt Darla" Drucilla said. Darla wrapped her arms around Drucilla.

"Drucilla, this is my boyfriend, Victor," Darla introduced the male companion that stood behind her.

"Nice to meet you," Drucilla said. She shook Victor's hand before turning her attention back to her aunt. "So, where is my uncle?" Drucilla leaned around Darla to see if she could see him down the hall.

"Silas? Oh, he's around. Hovering around the bar, most likely. I know he'd love to see you," she responded.

"And Sierra?" Drucilla sked.

"She's probably still upstairs with Katia."

"What room are they in?" Drucilla asked.

"Sixth floor. Rooms 620-622. It's a presidential suite. Here, take my keycard. Give it back to me before you leave." Darla handed Drucilla a white and gold key card. "The wedding is in forty-five minutes, so don't get drunk beforehand."

"Me?" Drucilla said in a shocked tone.

"Don't you give me that innocent tone; I remember my second wedding to Spencer." Darla made the sign of the cross across her chest. "You kids were drunk on champagne, and Sierra could barely walk down the aisle."

"That was fifteen years ago!"

"You're still children to me!"

Drucilla giggled as she recalled the incident.

"Your mother should be here any minute. She texted me from the airport an hour ago."

"Okay, I'll be back soon," Drucilla announced. Drucilla headed for the elevators.

†††

The elevator doors opened, and Drucilla headed down the hall to Sierra's room.

"Just what do you plan on telling her about me?" Adrian asked. He glided alongside Drucilla.

"Honestly, I'm hoping I don't."

251

"Am I some sort of fail-safe in case she doesn't believe you?"

"Pretty much. If it comes to it, then yes."

Drucilla stopped in front of the presidential suite and shoved the keycard into the slot. The door made a clicking sound as it popped open. When she entered, she noticed the tall, bright, arched windows all around. It was a corner room with spectacular views of the town that could be seen from every angle. At least fifteen different floral arrangements sat around the room, consisting of bold, blue, and red roses. The heavy scent of rose was almost overpowering. The carpet and living room furnishings appeared to date from the 1920s. They were elegant, yet comfortable. Drucilla heard shuffling and rustling coming from the open door at the other end of the room. Sierra bolted out with her dress gathered up in her arms so she could move quickly.

"Dru!" she shouted.

"Hey, you!" Drucilla shouted back.

Sierra dashed over to Drucilla and threw her arms around her. "You came! You didn't RSVP! I didn't think you were coming!"

"Yeah, sorry about that. Funny story: I lost the invitation and found it last night and noticed that the wedding was the next day, so I took the first flight out."

"Wow! You got lucky that you caught a flight that quickly!"

"Um, yep. I have pretty good luck when it comes to teleportation, er, I mean, transportation!" *Damn it!*

"Dru, hey," Katia said as she emerged from the bedroom.

"Hey, Katia."

"Glad to see you could make it," Katia said.

"Yeah, me too. So how have you been? I haven't seen you since Adrian's funeral."

"Oh, has it been that long?" Katia thought to herself. "Yeah, I guess it has."

"Is Todd here?" Drucilla asked.

Katia looked at the carpet and then away to the curtains, seemingly apprehensive of the question. "Todd and I are on a break."

"Oh no. I'm so sorry."

"It's fine. We're just in different places."

"Tell her the truth, Katia," Sierra said, messing with the hem of her dress.

Drucilla looked at Katia curiously.

"Theodore wants Katia to quit her career and make babies," Sierra interjected.

"Theodore?" Drucilla giggled. "His name is Theodore?"

"Shut up, Dru," Katia smirked.

"How's Killian?" Drucilla asked.

"Uh, nervous. I saw him about 20 minutes ago. He was pacing around the reception area." Katia responded.

"Nervous?"

"Yeah, you know how high-stress weddings can be. Your aunt and my mom are overbearing and controlling. They're acting like it's their wedding instead of Sierra and Killian's wedding," Katia explained.

"Mom just wants me to have the fairytale wedding," Sierra said.

"How do you feel about it?" Drucilla asked.

"Honestly, I'd be fine having it in the woods during a camping trip."

Drucilla laughed. "Wearing backpacks, I suppose."

"Hey, there's nothing wrong with backpacks. I can eat snacks while I exchange my vows!"

✝✝✝

The wedding was beautiful and went off flawlessly. Drucilla sat next to her mother. Fiona consistently made random comments such as *When you get married, we should have it here too.* Drucilla rolled her eyes so often that she thought they were going to fall out of her head.

After the ceremony, Drucilla sat at a table closest to the window in the reception area, which was within a huge white and gold ballroom. She stared at the rain rolling down the outside of the windows and ran through multiple scenarios in her head about how she could get Aurora's bowl from Katia. Live chamber music played at the other end of the room. The tall calla lilies were big and intrusive and obscured anyone that tried to approach the tables. It was easy for her to hide in a corner, unseen, until now.

"Mrs. Mikhailov?" Killian said as he turned his head to the side to read the small white place card on the table in front of Drucilla.

"Huh?" Drucilla said as she snapped out of her trance. She looked up at Killian and back at the place card on the table. "Oh!" she laughed to herself. "I'm sorry, Killian. I'm a little out of it." Drucilla stood up and picked up her black clutch.

"Are you okay?"

"Yeah, yeah, I'm fine. I just have a lot going on lately."

"I totally get it, but your place is over with the family near the back wall at the long table," Killian pointed.

"I just needed to take a breather. Family can be a lot at times."

"Oh my God, right? Sierra and I didn't even want to do this huge, elaborate wedding. This was all Verona and Darla's bullshit."

"Why didn't you say something?"

"You know, Sierra and I really didn't care about a wedding. It's really not important to us, so we just let our parents run wild with it."

"That they did! Well, Killian, welcome to the family."

"Ha, you too, Dru! Hey, I know I haven't spoken to you in years, but I'm really sorry about Drake. He was a good dude."

"No, he wasn't," Drucilla rebuffed. She started to walk away from the table.

"Dru, I know you hate talking about him. You always have since high school, but you know he loved you, right?"

"What makes you say that?" Drucilla asked. She turned to him a put her hands on her hips.

"Because I ran into him just after he won the city congressman seat. We sat and talked after the election. He told me that he was setting you up for life, that he had all kinds of plans to make sure you were well taken care of if something were to happen to him. I asked him why. He told me you were the other half of his soul and that if he died, half of him still would go on through you."

Drucilla gritted her teeth. "You know it's really pathetic he couldn't tell me that when he was alive."

"I don't know why he never kept contact with you. But I do know he cared."

"Yeah, well, now he wants me dead, so I don't know what to tell you."

"He what?" Killian said. He gave Drucilla a puzzled look.

Drucilla realized what she had said but was too angry to take it back. "It's not important, never mind. I'm just exhausted. It's been a long day."

"That was smooth," Adrian scoffed. Drucilla shot a glare at Adrian.

Killian noticed Drucilla was glaring at something that wasn't there. "Uh, okay, Dru. See you later," he said, clearly confused by her mannerisms.

Drucilla hastily exited the reception area and into the hall and ran almost face-first into Katia.

"Oh, Dru, I'm sorry," Katia said as she turned to move around Drucilla.

Drucilla grasped onto Katia's arm. "Katia, can we talk?"

“Uh yeah, sure, Dru.”

“Privately?”

Katia nodded.

†††

Katia sat down on the couch of the presidential suite, and Drucilla paced around in front of her rubbing her hands together anxiously.

“Dru.” “Katia.” They spoke in unison.

“Go ahead,” Drucilla said.

“No, you go.”

“No, Katia, go ahead.”

“I’m not angry with you if that’s what you’re concerned about. It was a long time ago, and I know that you didn’t poison Belynn. I mean, I wasn’t sure at the time, but there was no evidence tracing anything back to you. I mean, you were there with me, and when you weren’t, you were with Adrian. You didn’t even see Belynn until…you know.”

Drucilla crossed her arms. She blinked rapidly at Katia.

“Is that what everyone thinks happened? That I poisoned her?”

“Well, she was poisoned, and you being a weird goth girl and the public display of hatred you had for one another was suspect. But it came out that it was clearly someone else, totally random. You were nowhere near Belynn until the moment she died.”

"Wow, I had no idea. I mean, I remember going to school and everyone looking at me like I was a murderer or something, but I had no idea that's what everyone thought."

"They didn't think that for very long. Dru, no one is mad at you."

Drucilla curled her lip as her eyes darted around the room. She still couldn't believe what she had heard.

"What did you want to tell me?" Katia asked, breaking the tension.

Drucilla shook her head and continued to pace and rub her hands. She stopped, sat at the edge of the chair, and faced Katia on the couch. "I guess there's no better way to come out and say this." Drucilla exhaled deeply. "Okay, here we go. When Belynn died, she wasn't poisoned."

"Of course, she was. There was a toxicology report."

"The toxicology report was falsified, and if I had to guess by whom, I would assume Drake had something to do with it." Drucilla figured there was no other way since Drake was the only other witness.

"What are you talking about?"

"Katia, what do you remember?"

Katia looked at the floor for a moment, then lifted her eyes back to Drucilla. "She had kicked you, and you were on the ground. Your lip was cut, and I got down to help you. I remember I called her a bitch or something, and then she started choking and fell over."

"What else?"

"That's it."

Drucilla stared at Katia. Katia wouldn't look Drucilla in the eyes. She almost seemed scared as she stared at the ground.

Drucilla reached for Katia's hand. "It's okay. You can talk about what you saw."

Katia ripped her hand from Drucilla and stood up. She straightened her dress and started to pace. "Dru, you have to understand. I was in a bad place back then. I was using drugs and drinking. I was really depressed; my parents were constantly fighting. Remember? That's why I spent so much time at your house. It was a lot."

"It wasn't a hallucination."

"Yes, it was, Dru! I'm a scientist. I know I was manifesting. It's normal to do that in times of crisis."

"Katia, what did you see?" Drucilla said as she stood up.

"I didn't see anything, Dru!" Katia yelled.

"Yes, you did! Say it!" Dru yelled.

"You want me to say I saw a demon rip Belynn's heart out?!" Katia yelled back.

"She was blue. She flowed like the wind, and when she screamed, she shrieked so loud you felt like your eardrums would rupture!" Drucilla recalled.

Katia dropped down on the couch, put her hands on her face, and started sobbing loudly. Drucilla sat down in front of her again, grabbed her hand, and held it.

"I had to go through years of therapy! Years Dru! Depression medication, meditation, anxiety management, all to get through something you're telling me is true!?" Katia said between breaths.

"There was nothing wrong with you, Katia. You saw what I saw. It was real."

"No. No, I can't right now." Katia stood up and wiped her tears with the back of her hand. She headed for the door and put her hand on the door handle.

"Katia, don't leave."

Katia stopped and stared at the door.

"You are so important," Dru continued, "You have no idea how vital you are to the universe."

Katia turned around at looked at Drucilla, puzzled. "What does that mean?"

"It means you have a big role to play in what's to come."

Katia sniffled. "You sound insane, Drucilla."

"Maybe, but if you won't listen to me, maybe you'll listen to him." Drucilla nodded and motioned with her eyes for Katia to look to her side. Confused, Katia looked to her left.

"Hey," Adrian said as he leaned against the wall near the door.

CANTICLE TWENTY-FIVE

†

"Oh shit, we're losing her!" Adrian said. Katia's face drained of color, and her eyes rolled back into their sockets.

Drucilla dashed over to Katia to catch her before she hit the ground, but Katia dropped like a sack of flour. She collapsed to her knees and then to her side. Drucilla wrapped her arms around her chest, and Adrian grabbed her legs. They carried her to the couch.

"Katia?" Drucilla patted Katia's hand.

"She is out!" Adrian remarked.

"Damn it," Drucilla groaned.

"Could have been worse; you could have brought Lucifer instead of me. But that probably would have killed her."

Katia's color slowly returned to her face as she blinked and looked around.

"Katia?" Drucilla said again.

Katia pulled herself up to a seated position. She looked at Adrian, and her eyes grew wide. "You're dead!" Katia yelled, trying to make sense of his presence. "I don't understand what's happening. How are you here?" Katia reached out to touch his face.

"It's going to be okay. You're okay," Adrian said as he attempted to comfort her.

“You’re not dead?”

“I am dead, but Drucilla has a special ability that allows me to be here with you.”

“Like a ghost?” Katia whispered.

“A little bit more than a ghost, but more or less.”

Katia looked at Drucilla curiously. “Are you dead too?”

“Me? No. I mean, yes. Well, I was. I did die about a year ago. A little after Drake, actually. I came back—”

“Ohhhh, I need a minute to process.” Katia stood up and took deep breaths.

“Take all the time you need.”

“Dru, do you know how ridiculous and insane this all is? This is totally improbable and completely—”

“Crazy?” Drucilla interrupted.

Katia paced for a moment. “Is there anything else you want to tell me? I mean, if there is, let’s just get it all out there!” Katia said, making large hand gestures.

Adrian leaned back on the couch and glanced at Drucilla, who nodded and stood up.

“I'm sorry I pushed so much on you so soon, I just wish I had the time to ease you into everything. But you have something I really need, and just asking you for it wasn't going to cut it. You have an antique metallic bowl. I believe it is made from gold or silver. It has etched markings that were created by something hot. They’re burned into the surface—they look like glyphs. You may have picked it up from an auction a few years ago. Does that sound familiar?”

Katia thought for a moment. "Yeah, I have something like that. It's an old ceremonial cauldron or something significant like that. It has markings on the outside and inside the center. But I didn't buy it. Todd gave it to me as a wedding gift. He told me that it was an ancient artifact. It belonged to someone called Brân the Blessed in Welsh folklore. He used it to heal the sick and did something about resurrecting the dead in medieval times. How did you know *I* had it?"

"That's an even longer story. We'll save that for another time. Where is it now?"

"It's on my shelf in my office."

"Your home office?" Drucilla asked.

"Oh God, no. Todd bought it at auction for nearly a million dollars. It's in my office at Varstadt. It's way more secure there than any museum could be."

"I need to use it. It's important."

"You need to use my million-dollar art piece?" Katia said in a preposterous tone. "No, Dru, you can't play with my cauldron. No one is touching it. I don't care how many dead people you bring into this room."

"Girl! I can hear you!" Adrian hollered.

"Forget it, Dru," Katia said firmly.

Drucilla exhaled loudly and was frustrated at Katia's reluctance to participate. "I really didn't want to do this today, but you've literally left me zero choices." Drucilla backed away from everyone and stood in the middle of the room."

Katia looked at her peculiarly.

Adrian tapped Katia on the arm. "This is cool, watch this," Adrian said with a grin, anticipating Drucilla's display.

"I really like this dress, too," Drucilla said. Drucilla rolled her shoulders forward, then forcefully pressed them back. Four massive, barely bluish-grey tinted wings burst through her back as she expanded them out as far as she could. Her glowing blue veins appeared through her party dress's sheer, black lace sleeves and down her legs. Small, blue veins crept across her cheeks and forehead. She opened her eyes which blazed like burning stars. The wing-eyes along their lengths opened and closed as they looked around the room.

Katia inched towards Drucilla, trembling and unable to speak. She slowly crept around her wings and examined her body. She came to a stop in front of Drucilla.

"What…what are you?" Katia whispered.

"Ophanim," Drucilla responded. She collapsed her wings as her body died down to its natural state.

"How is this…" Katia's voice quivered.

"I told you. I died. I came back as sort of a celestial being. There's a lot more to it, but this is what I am," Drucilla answered before Katia could finish. "The being you see before you is the combination of myself and a Throne. Do you know what a Throne is?"

"I remember learning about them in Sunday school. They're one of the highest order of angels, just below Seraphs. Seraphs being just below God."

"Almost, but that's not quite right. There are ten Thrones. A Throne is a title; they are all Ophanim, the highest celestial being in existence. Seraphs are products of Ophanim, and God doesn't actually exist. God is essentially putting a face to the council of the Thrones."

"Are you a god?" Katia asked, not sure if she wanted the answer.

"*He* is. The Throne that occupies my body. His name is Thoth. See, I can't communicate with him. We can only react to each other's emotions. That's it. Your cauldron, along with a tome that Adelia has, will allow me to create a way to communicate with him."

"So, this is why you need my cauldron. Wait, Del knows?"

"Yeah. She has offered to help. She, too, plays a vital role."

Katia contemplated for a moment. She wasn't too thrilled with surrendering such a unique and expensive artifact, but she also knew something greater was happening. She exhaled and threw up her hands. "Okay."

"You'll let me use it?" Drucilla asked.

"I want to help. What do I need to do?"

"The cauldron is bound to you. It won't work for me, only you. You were chosen to be its owner. You'll have to control it."

"Control it? I don't even know what it does, let alone get it to do something."

"Don't worry. I have a friend who can help with that. He's a bit of a specialist in these types of artifacts. I'll call you in a few days. We'll need to get Adelia as well. Maybe we can meet at my house in a couple of weeks?"

Katia nodded.

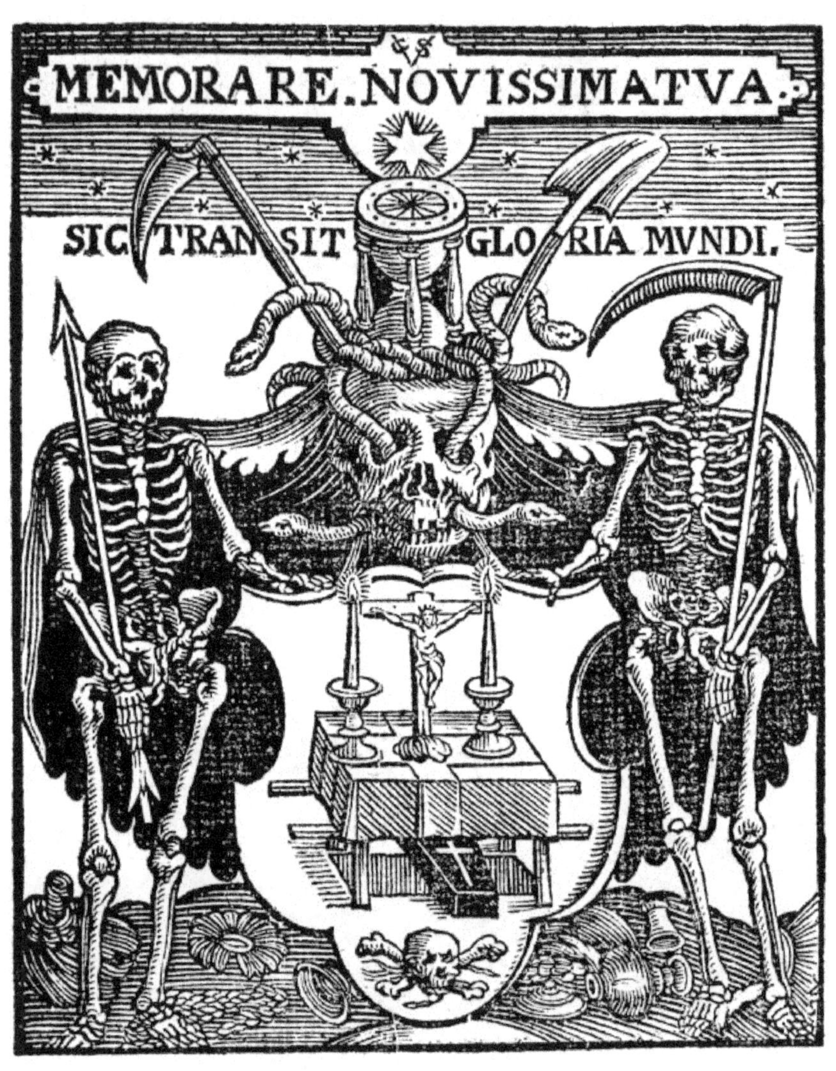
MEMORARE . NOVISSIMA TVA .
SIC TRANSIT GLORIA MVNDI.

CANTICLE TWENTY-SIX

"Grant me those secret songs that shall lull the stars to sleep."—Nightbringer

✝

Adrian moved swiftly through the kitchen, adding ingredients to a large bowl. He loved baking in death as much as he did in life.

"You know what the frustrating part is? Not only am I unable to consume any of it, but I also can't even smell it. I gotta rely on your unrefined palate to tell me if it's up to expectations."

"Yeah, but I at least get super granular about it," Dru said. "I mean, what I can taste and feel. And I am not unrefined!"

Adrian put his hands on his hips and smirked at Drucilla for a moment.

Drucilla sat with her elbows on the dining room table. She leaned her head on her hand, watching Adrian glide about the kitchen, adding random ingredients into a large, steel bowl before stuffing frosting into a pastry bag.

"What?" He stopped and looked at Drucilla with the piping bag hovering over his four-layer orange cream cake.

"Nothing. Just watching you do your thing."

He studied her face for a moment, then went back to piping delicate peachy curls along the top of the velvety, smooth cake.

"Something on your mind?" he asked. He didn't look up at Drucilla but instead contemplated the placement of his next curl.

There was a long pause before Drucilla spoke.

"Why do you think you hang around? Here, I mean," she asked. "You didn't cross over into the next phase. You didn't go into the Agglomeration."

"I had the option. I declined it."

"Well, I know that, but why?"

"You will understand in time."

Drucilla groaned, "You know I hate vague answers."

Adrian grinned to himself.

"What's the cake for anyway?"

Adrian threw his hand up and looked at Drucilla like she had lost her mind. "The cake is for your mom! She's arriving tomorrow. Tell me you did not forget!"

Drucilla sunk down in her seat.

"Dru, how could you forget that?" Adrian scolded. He dropped his piping bag and put his hands on his hips. "Did you think this cake was for you?"

"You bake all the time!" Drucilla shrugged.

"Yes, but I don't put this much effort into it unless it's important." Adrian picked the piping bag up again.

Drucilla got up and walked into the kitchen. She leaned against the cabinets and stared down at his masterpiece.

"Is that vanilla buttercream?" she asked, hovering her finger above it.

"No, it's honey orange blossom, and I will thank you not to touch it." He slapped the back of her hand.

Drucilla pulled her hand back to her chest and glared at him in discontent.

There was a sudden, rapid banging at the front door. The sound drew their attention to the living room. Drucilla glanced at Adrian and shrugged. "I wasn't expecting anyone." She headed to the front door and peeked through the peephole.

"It's Ash…" Drucilla swung the front door open. Ash was standing on the porch with a folder and a small stack of papers in his arms.

"I am sorry, Drucilla; did I interrupt anything?" He asked, poking his head in and looking around her home.

"No, it's fine. I was, uh, just baking a cake." Drucilla shifted her eyes around nervously.

"I closed the gallery, and I was … May I come in?" Ash asked.

"Yeah! Yeah, sorry, come in." Drucilla moved out of the way for Ash to walk past. He looked slowly around the living room, at the walls, the ceiling, and the various artifacts on Drucilla's mantle and shelves.

"Wow, this is astounding. It is an accurate presentation of a Victorian parlor from the 1880s. Complete with Egyptian artifacts. Victorians were obsessed with death, just like the Egyptians. These artifacts appear to be flawless replicas."

"Yeah, um, historically accurate reproductions." Drucilla glanced over at Adrian, who was halfway up the staircase. He shook his head at Drucilla.

"What brings you by, Ash?"

"I have news. Our gallery was selected as one of the finalists to showcase Beverly LeMay's '1960s Zeitgeist Future Visions of Architecture' exhibit." Ash jutted out the small stack of papers toward Drucilla's chest. She took the papers from him and flipped through them.

"It's a photography exhibition," he said.

"I know who Beverly LeMay is, Ash. Thank you." Drucilla walked away with the papers in hand.

Ash slowly walked around the dining room, heading toward the home's original fireplace beyond the formal dining table. He glanced above the fireplace to the left, at the neoclassical painting of Madame Perroux, and then to the right, at Marie Antoinette. Drucilla peered up at him and watched as he made his way into the kitchen. It was almost like he hadn't set foot in a house in his life, as if he was looking at everything with new eyes.

"Beautiful! Did you make this yourself?" he said loudly, in an impressed tone from the kitchen. He was clearly looking at Adrian's cake.

"Drucilla…?" Lucifer entered through the open front door. Startled, Drucilla squeezed the papers in her hands and looked at him.

"Oh, I am sorry, it was in fact, open," Lucifer said apologetically. He glanced over his shoulder at the open door.

Drucilla shrugged.

"I was pondering your quandary about contacting Thoth—."

Lucifer stopped mid-sentence. He sensed something in the air. He glanced at Drucilla for a moment. Drucilla looked at him and furrowed her brow. He frantically looked around the house. His face contorted from confusion to instant rage. His eyes began to glow as his long, black claws stretched out beyond his fingertips. He made a dash to the kitchen. Drucilla dropped the papers to the floor and ran in behind him in an automatic response. Lucifer ran up to Ash, grabbed him by the neck, and slammed him onto the breakfast bar. With the extreme force of Lucifer's attack, Ash's body broke off a part of the counter, demolishing Adrian's cake as it splattered to the floor in large chunks.

"NOOOOOOOOO!" Adrian yelled from the stairwell. He dropped to his knees and covered his face with his hands.

Ash's arms and legs thrashed and struggled to break free of Lucifer's grasp. Lucifer lifted him slowly off the ground, his feet dangling in the air.

"Lucifer! What are you doing?!" Drucilla yelled. "Put Ash down! Now!"

"Ash? Is that what he told you his name is? Ash? Ash, what?" he asked. He squeezed Ash's neck. Lucifer's eyes glowed with intense orange light; his bright orange veins showed beneath his skin. Lucifer's long-serrated tail whipped out and wrapped around Ash's chest in a double spiral holding him even higher.

"What do you mean, 'Ash what'? Ash Palm! He is my assistant! You're gonna kill him! Put him down!" Drucilla yelled. Drucilla's eyes began to glow as well. She grabbed Lucifer's hands to pry them off Ash's neck.

Lucifer turned his attention to Drucilla and then back to Ash, who was still struggling to break free.

"No. This scourge isn't human, Drucilla! Why are you here? How did you break out of the Infernal Sphere!? Answer me, or I will incinerate you where you stand!" Lucifer yelled. He refused to let Ash go.

Drucilla let go of Lucifer's wrist. She turned to Ash and looked at him curiously. He held on to Lucifer's arm, still writhing in his grasp.

"Ash Palm. His name is an anagram," Lucifer said. He slowly brought Ash down but kept him immobile with his tail that was still wrapped tightly around Ash's body.

Drucilla mouthed the words to herself, attempting to unscramble them.

"Slapsh…Mash.. uh…" Drucilla muttered.

"Malphas," Lucifer said through gritted teeth.

"Malphas?" Drucilla asked. "You guys are really into letter scrambling." She remembered how Belphegor and Asmodeus named themselves.

Ash didn't say a word. He peered at Drucilla out of the corner of his eye and then back at Lucifer.

"Who are you?" Drucilla asked calmly.

"He's a scourge, a lesser demon," Lucifer snarled. "Nothing more than a familiar to a Lilim."

Malphas didn't say a word.

"Lilim?" Drucilla asked.

"Not all residents of Hell are demons, Drucilla."

"Let him go, Lucifer," Drucilla said. "I think he knows he can't run from us."

Lucifer looked at Malphas and then complied. He loosened his tail's grip and released Malphas.

"Malphas, this is extremely important; I need you to answer me. How did you get out of the Infernal Sphere? Please tell me," Drucilla asked as calmly as possible.

Malphas looked at Drucilla and back at Lucifer. "The containment spell is broken."

"I knew it," Drucilla threw her hands up. "How long ago?"

"I do not know, but I believe shortly after it was put in place," Malphas responded apprehensively.

"I f-ing knew it. He's biding his time." Drucilla paced uncomfortably.

"Why are you here?" Lucifer asked.

"I heard that Thoth was alive here on Eorthe; I had to see if it was true. Then, I found her."

Lucifer groaned and rubbed his forehead. "Right, of course, you would look for Thoth."

"What? You don't believe him?" Drucilla asked.

Lucifer made his way to the staircase and sat down. He placed his elbows on his knees and his head in his hands. Drucilla looked at Lucifer suspiciously, then back to Malphas. There was a long silence.

"Is someone going to say something?" Drucilla asked, looking around the room.

Malphas looked at Lucifer.

"Malphas is Thoth's ward," Lucifer said calmly.

"Wait, you're like his kid or something?" Drucilla asked.

"I am not a child. Thoth was my mentor. Who, I suppose, is now you," Malphas explained. He ran his hand through his hair. He straightened his coat and brushed off his pants. "I will have you know I am..." He looked up and thought to himself. "I am roughly 66,000 in Earth years."

"Well, that's still 66,000 years older than I am. If anything, I'm the child." Drucilla admitted. "So, why did you come looking for Thoth?"

"He needs to go back," Lucifer interjected. "He does not belong here, Drucilla. Earth is not his domain. Need I remind you that we are in the middle of a potentially catastrophic war between the realms? It is not safe for anyone here who cannot fight. He will prove to be a hindrance more than an asset," Lucifer said firmly.

"He's basically Thoth's acolyte. He must be useful in some capacity. Thoth had to have taught him something." Drucilla looked at Malphas. "What did Thoth teach you to do?"

He paused for a moment and thought about the question, hesitant that what he could say would be of any value.

"I can do this," Malphas looked at Adrian's ruined cake on the floor. The cake miraculously came back together and placed itself back onto the breakfast bar. "And I suppose this," He turned his attention to the breakfast bar countertop. The counter was repaired as the pieces came flying back together as if compelled by some magnetic force.

Drucilla's eyes widened as she watched in awe.

"Malphas is what you humans would call a magician or an illusionist," Lucifer said.

"Low magick, mostly. But with a proficiency in spatiotemporal manipulation," Malphas interrupted.

"Can everyone manipulate time except for me?" Drucilla moaned.

"Yes," Lucifer responded.

Drucilla pressed her lips together and glared at Lucifer.

"I can do other things. For example, I can do simple spell-work like alchemy, potions, and rearranging matter."

Drucilla looked hopeful at Lucifer.

"No! Absolutely not! He is going back to the Infernal Sphere."

"I cannot go back. He most likely knows I've been gone," Malphas said.

"Drake?" Drucilla said.

"...and he most likely knows where I am."

"Lucifer, we can't let him go back. There's no telling what Drake will do to him. He seems like he genuinely wants to help. Our hands are kinda tied here."

"Where have you been hiding, Malphas?"

"His father's house," he said, gesturing to himself. "The father of the man who this body was."

"Wait, the story that you told me about yourself is true?" Drucilla asked.

Malphas nodded to imply that he had told her the truth.

"Where is your host now?"

"Drucilla," Lucifer cut in. "You must understand that the previous owner vacates whenever an Unholy or Divine takes a host body."

"Vacates? Like until you're done with the body?"

Lucifer glanced at Malphas and then back to Drucilla.

"No. The Cosmic Essence is released from the host, permanently."

"You mean, you took someone's life when you inhabited their body?"

"Possession does not work as your human stories indicate. Possession is to take up residence in the host body. Permanently," Lucifer explained.

"But you don't take bodies," Drucilla said, looking at Lucifer.

"I am a King of Hell, Drucilla. I do not need your human flesh. Many lesser demons are summoned manifestations and are largely intangible. They must possess a human host to reside on Earth."

"What about Calliope? She possessed a human," Drucilla asked, attempting to wrap her head around the possession process.

"Some lesser Divine and Unholy lack a physical form even in their home realms, and even those that do, cannot take them into Earth. They don't have the power to coalesce a physical body. To exist here in any sort of physical way, they must take over a body. And, unfortunately, send the human soul they replace to the Agglomeration. I am of a level of power that I can take my form anywhere and alter it as I wish. I could possess a human, but that would be unnecessary and cruel. Calliope, on the other hand, took a body to solve the opposite problem. She had so much power within her essence that should she manifest here, her very presence would have caused destruction all around her, as you saw when she broke through the Hellgate. She took a body to conceal her power, to artificially stunt it. And it was temporary. No human vessel could contain a Throne's power for more than a few minutes before it'd tear at the seams. You experienced that, too, when you took in Thoth," Lucifer explained.

Drucilla peered at Lucifer curiously.

"The realm of the Infernal Sphere is populated by tangible and intangible beings and entities. You cannot apply your Earth physics to our realm. They are not comparable."

"So, to be here, you had to sacrifice a human being?"

"It was necessary," Malphas replied.

"I'm gonna be sick." Drucilla sat down and put her face in her hands.

"It is done," Lucifer continued, "There is no need to ruminate upon this incident any longer. I suggest we decide what we will do with Malpas now that he is on Earth."

"Drucilla is right. I want to help. I will, in any way I am able. Drake has taken over Hell, and I cannot go back," Malphas said.

"Taken over? How has Drake taken over? The queens nor my brothers would ever allow such an act," Lucifer said.

"They probably would not allow it; if the kings had not formed an alliance with Drake."

"What are you inferring?"

Malphas crossed his arms and leaned against the kitchen counter. "I am saying that the kings have sided with Drake and elected him Imperator."

"What?" Drucilla asked.

Lucifer stood silently, pondering the new information.

"What does that mean, Malphas?" Drucilla asked.

Malphas looked at Lucifer. "It means exactly what Lucifer understands it to mean." Malphas turned to Drucilla. "Drake has absorbed Queen Calliope and is now a Throne. The remaining kings have sworn fealty to him. Drake rules Hell in its entirety."

Drucilla placed her hand over her mouth as her eyes widened.

"Shortly after Hell broke the containment spell, I took my leave. I have no idea what his plans are, but I do know he wants you, Drucilla."

"There's no way I would ever join him."

"He knows. He also knows how strong you are and that you and Lucifer joined efforts along with Azrael and Sariel's legions. He is going to be very strategic and effective when he comes for you. It appears that Drake does not like for things to become large and messy. His mission will be covert, straightforward, and efficient. I would expect the unexpected. He will strike quickly and most likely when you are most vulnerable, that much I know," Malphas stated.

"What do we do?" Drucilla asked Lucifer. "Our only move now is to find the Thrones with Thoth's assistance."

"I do not think that will be an option," Lucifer responded.

"Why not? I mean, this is their universe; I thought they wanted to protect it?"

"Protection was left in the hands of the Seraphim. No, Drucilla, I do not think the Thrones would be of assistance, even if we did manage to locate them."

"Sariel said this war is theirs now. Does that not include the Thrones?"

"Drucilla, the Thrones are not concerned with Earth anymore. That is evident in their departure. Trust me when I say that if Earth were to fall into the hands of the Unholy, the Thrones would recreate the experiment elsewhere. Which I am certain, is what they are doing at this moment."

"He speaks the truth," Malphas said. "The Thrones have innumerable planets in the universe to utilize. This is just one. And one universe, too, for that matter."

"But this is the first; this has to mean something?"

"But only to the Infernal Sphere and the Celestial Empyrion. Not to the Thrones," Lucifer responded.

"What about you, Lucifer? Can't you do something? Can't you take away Drake's power? You did give it to him, after all."

"Though a Celestial Deal, Drucilla. He has my power until I return, and the deal is complete. But he has a Throne's power now, too. Completing the deal would be to no avail."

"Thoth will know," Drucilla said with certainty. "He has to."

CANTICLE TWENTY-SEVEN

"The blackest days are waiting up ahead."—Danzig

✝

Fiona glanced at her phone, placed it face down, and turned to her daughter. Drucilla sat across from her mother, picking at her Turkish stuffed eggplant. Dinner at Port Townsend's local steak house was quiet and uneventful, aside from Fiona constantly checking her phone for messages. Drucilla glanced to the other side of the street, at the ocean, through the large plate glass window next to their table.

Drucilla ran multiple scenarios in her head, trying to decide how to break the news that she was an Ophanim. Every one of them ended with Fiona either passing out, screaming, or going insane. None of the options presented in Drucilla's mind made for a good dining experience.

Drucilla broke the uncomfortable tension. "You know, Mom, you can just call Grandma."

"What if she is unable to answer the phone?" Fiona retorted.

"Mom, she's fine."

"You think I'm being paranoid?"

"I know you're being paranoid. I think Grandma is far more rugged and capable than you give her credit for being. How's your steak?"

"Good, it's good. How's your eggplant?"

"It's fine." Drucilla leaned back and crossed her arms. She looked back out the window to the clear, dark evening sky. The roads were wet from the rain earlier that afternoon, and the cold temperatures prevented the roads from drying. Drucilla exhaled and decided to breach the subject slowly and indirectly to gauge her mother's potential reaction.

"Mom?" Drucilla started.

Fiona looked up from her phone again and placed it face down on the table. "I'm sorry, honey. This weekend was for us to spend together. I'll call Grandma later." She smiled and took a sip from her glass of red wine.

Drucilla chewed the inside of her lip and exhaled. "So, I've been pretty interested in Western religions lately. Ancient Catholic theology, mysticism mostly."

"That's interesting. What do you like about them?"

Drucilla shrugged. "Celestial lore. Mostly pertaining to demonology and angelology; theories on what they are and where they came from."

"You know your grandmother is very interested in angelology. Ever since I told her that I spoke with one before you were born. She loves that stuff."

"So, you really believe in all of that?" Drucilla asked.

"A lot of it, yes. I believe that when we die, we become angels and live with God. I know we do. Why the sudden interest? Is it because I raised you and Drake without religion? I wanted you to discover and learn about that on your own. I wanted you to make your own decisions about faith. Granted, I didn't think you would be nearly thirty when you did."

"I guess it's better that I show you." Drucilla stood up and pushed her chair into the table. She put her hands on the back of the chair and put her head down. She rolled her shoulders back as four massive wings burst from her back, violently expanding outward, knocking over chairs and tables, and smashing through the large plate window next to them. Glass and debris went flying at high speed out into the street. Alarmed by the sudden cacophony of crashing, restaurant patrons jumped to their feet, screaming at the sight of Drucilla's wings and glowing body. Terrified, they scrambled to get out the door. The eyes along the ridges of her wings gave a 360-degree view of the room. People were yelling, climbing over each other, running through the back kitchen, and breaking windows with chairs to get out. Drucilla turned her attention to her mother, her eyes blazing with blue fire. Fiona screamed, turned pale, and fainted, her head hitting the table and her neck loudly snapping, killing her instantly.

Upon seeing her mother's lifeless body, Drucilla screamed in a high-pitched, vibrating tone that rang out so loudly the building shook, car alarms down the street went off, and car windows burst outward down the street. The townsfolks' heads exploded on their shoulders like overinflated water balloons full of blood, painting the buildings and streets red. Cars crashed into each other as others jerked the wheel to avoid a wreck, only to break through the barricade on the side of the road and crash into the icy, dark ocean below the nearly invisible cliff.

✝✝✝

"Dru?" Fiona waved her hand in Drucilla's face to refocus her attention. "Drucilla?"

Drucilla shook her head as she snapped out of her trance.

"Where did you go, honey?" Fiona laughed.

Drucilla looked around at the restaurant patrons eating and quietly engaged in their own conversations. "I'm sorry," Drucilla mumbled.

"Are you okay?"

"Yeah. Um, what did you ask me?"

Fiona smiled. "I asked you about your sudden interest in religion."

"I uh, just find it interesting. My friend Dominic is really into the occult, and he kind of sparked an interest."

"Oh, that's right. Your Russian friend owns the antique shop. Grandma knows his family. I never did meet them. Will I get to meet him this time?"

"Yeah. Yeah, if you want to. I'm sure he's around. I'll call him later."

"Good evening, ladies." A pleasant, yet cheerful voice that could only be Lucifer's appeared behind Drucilla.

Fiona looked up at the well-dressed gentleman behind her daughter and smiled brightly. "Good evening!" she said in response.

Drucilla turned around to see Lucifer smiling over her. Drucilla stood up. "Uh, this is my—"

"The matriarch of the Blackwood family. Yes, Fiona! It is a pleasure to finally meet you." Lucifer held out his hand to Fiona. She offered hers and smiled back.

"Are you Dominic?" Fiona asked.

Drucilla snorted.

"No, no, I am not. I am much more attractive. I am Lucifer. A friend of your daughter."

"Mom, he's an art collector. I do, uh, business with him frequently." Drucilla was trying to utilize the first thing that came to mind.

"Lucifer? That's interesting. Dru and I were talking about angelology. Did you know that Lucifer was the first angel?"

Lucifer's eyes lit up as he amusingly glanced at Drucilla. "I did know that! You do not go through life with a name like *Lucifer* without hearing all the stories related it."

"I take it your parents are Catholic?" Fiona asked.

Lucifer grinned at Drucilla again. "No, no, not Catholic. But close."

Drucilla shook her head and bit her lip.

"Would you like to join us?" Fiona asked.

"He can't, Mom. We gotta take off now if you want to make it to the photography exhibit at my gallery. It starts in fifteen minutes. I also kinda need to be there."

"Well, perhaps you'd like to join us in taking in the exhibit?"

"Mom, I'm sure he's really busy." Drucilla stared Lucifer down.

"Oh! Well, another time," Fiona said.

"Absolutely," Lucifer grinned.

Fiona stood up and looked around for the waiter. "We need to pay our bill."

"Do not worry about that. I will take care of it," Lucifer offered.

"Lucifer, you don't have to. It's cool, I got it," Drucilla interjected.

"I will not hear of it. Please allow me."

Fiona smiled. Drucilla opened her mouth and promptly closed it. She didn't want to argue in front of her mother, especially since her arguments with Lucifer tended to get heated. "Fine. Thank you," Drucilla relented.

†††

Drucilla opened the door to the Corvidae Gallery for her mother to pass ahead of her. Fiona's eyes lit up as she took in the displays of local artwork around the gallery. Colorful paintings in abstract patterns, faces, and landscapes adorned the walls. Elaborate jewelry rested within three large, glass-covered pedestals in the center of the room as pendulum lighting hovered overhead, reflecting off the surfaces of the faceted gems. Fiona stopped in front of the vast display of black and white photographs depicting concrete buildings from the 1960s featuring an architectural style known as Brutalism. Neo-classical darkwave played quietly throughout as the slight scent of oil paint and turpentine could be vaguely detected, depending on how close you stood near a painting.

"Dru, this is beautiful!" Fiona exclaimed.

Drucilla pressed her lips together and smiled, beaming like a child would when their parent congratulated them on winning a softball game.

Fiona walked around the gallery slowly to not miss a single display. Drucilla watched from afar. Malphas walked over to Drucilla's mother and introduced himself as Ash. Fiona greeted him by shaking his hand and pointing to Drucilla, probably bragging that she was the owner's mother. Lucifer made a sudden reappearance and stood next to Malphas and Fiona. They engaged in a friendly conversation.

Drucilla looked out the front window and watched Dominic as he crossed the street with his hands shoved in his pockets. He glanced over to Drucilla. She pointed with her chin to acknowledge his arrival as he entered the gallery and stood next to Drucilla.

"How did it go?" Dominic asked.

"I didn't tell her," Drucilla responded. She continued to watch her mother's interaction with the Unholy.

Dominic exhaled and nodded. "She needs to know, Dru."

"I know. It just hasn't been the right time."

"When is the right time?" Dominic badgered.

"Dom, I don't know. She's barely stable now. I think she's been channeling her loss of Drake into Grandma. It's like it's killing her to leave Grandma alone. I mean, look at her."

Fiona pulled out her phone to check for messages, then promptly put it back in her pocket and went back to her conversation.

"You know she's checked her phone every ten minutes since she got off the plane yesterday? She's compulsive."

"I doubt she's checking it every ten minutes," Dominic scoffed.

"No, you're probably right. I think it's every five to seven," Drucilla retorted. "I don't think she can handle me telling her something like this."

"Why don't you think she'd be able to handle it?"

"Have you told your dad?" Drucilla rebuffed.

"No, but that's different. Dad is a doctor. He's a scientist."

"My mom is a scientist, too!"

Dominic acknowledged her response by giving a slight nod.

"Dom, I basically have to tell her that I *also* died, and I'm not who I once was. I know my mother and have run multiple scenarios in my head. Every one of them has been less than optimal, and by less than optimal, I mean catastrophic. I've thought about showing her my wings, I've thought about having Adrian appear, I've thought about having Lucifer reveal himself, and I've even thought about demonstrating some of my abilities. I think it might be best to leave her in the dark."

"That's your decision Dru, but I thought the whole reason for her visit was so you could tell her."

"It was."

Dominic glanced at Malphas and curled his lip. "Dru, you should consider finding a new assistant."

"Yeah, about that. That won't be happening any time soon."

Dominic raised his eyebrow at Drucilla.

"Apparently, he is my ward," Drucilla said. She made air quotes with her fingers when she said ward.

"He seems a bit old for you to adopt," Dominic mused.

"Ash is actually Malphas. Malphas is a lesser demon."

Dominic abruptly turned to Drucilla. "He's what? How? I mean, how did he get out of Hell? Why is he here?" Dominic turned his attention to Malphas, with his jaw slightly agape.

"The barrier spell is broken. I was right. Drake is biding his time."

"Shit," Dominic whispered.

"Yep."

Dominic pondered the consequences of the broken barrier. He looked at Malphas in confusion.

"How exactly is he your ward?"

"He was Thoth's apprentice. Now mine."

"Dru, you can barely control your own rage issues, how are you supposed to teach him anything?"

Drucilla glared at Dominic.

Fiona approached Drucilla, noticing the abnormally large gentleman standing next to her daughter. She stood in front of him and then turned to Drucilla. "Is this Dominic?"

Drucilla looked at Dominic and exhaled. "Yes. This is Dom. Dom, this is my mother, Fiona."

Fiona looked up at the handsome, muscular man. "*Dobryy vecher*," Fiona said.

Dominic nodded and responded with "*Dobryy vecher. Kak dela?*"

Fiona laughed. "I'm sorry. I don't know any other Russian phrases past simple greetings."

"That's okay, Ms. Blackwood. Everyone starts somewhere." He smiled.

Their brief conversation was interrupted by the ringing of Fiona's phone.

"Oh, thank God. It's my mother. Will you excuse me?" Fiona asked.

"Mom, take my keys, and you can talk to her in my office."

Fiona took Drucilla's keys and nodded. She headed down the long gallery hall to the back of the building.

A low vibration trembled the wall of black and white prints. They shimmied slightly on their mounts. Drucilla glanced at the odd shaking. The vibration intensified and became more obvious. It was enough to catch the attention of Malphas and Lucifer, who stood with their backs to it. They slowly turned to face the wall display as the shaking turned violent, causing the eighteen photos encased in glass to bang relentlessly against the wall. A rush of silence took over the room. The gallery patrons stopped their conversations to witness the shaking wall.

"What the Hell is going on?" Drucilla asked quietly.

"It's not an earthquake. It's just affecting one wall," Dominic said, matching her confused tone.

The shaking stopped as abruptly as it had started. It was eerily silent. The atmosphere in the gallery felt tense, heavy, and wrong. There was an obvious and foreboding presence in the room. Reflexively, Dominic pulled out his stylus and held it to his side. He stepped in front of Drucilla to act as a barrier of protection against the unseen entity.

"Dom," Drucilla whispered.

Dominic slowly moved toward the center of the room. He glanced at Lucifer and Malphas. Malphas backed away. Lucifer's eyes shifted around the gallery, trying to make sense of something unseen. The gallery patrons spoke in confused, hushed tones.

"Dom?" Drucilla whispered louder.

Dominic turned to face Drucilla.

Drucilla stood rigidly in place, almost afraid to move. "Dom, it's right next to me…."

Lucifer turned to Drucilla. His eyes widened. He could see it too.

A long, semi-transparent black figure slowly materialized and stood at Drucilla's side. The entity's scarlet eyes burned with rage and fire. Its shoulders expanded as they heaved with every breath. Wispy trails of smoke emanated from every direction of its translucent body. It slowly raised its arms as long tendrils of branch-like fingers elongated into a twisted vine of black smoke. It reached out toward Lucifer.

Lucifer stood a few feet in front of the entity. His serpentine eyes flickered as he shook his head disapprovingly.

The smog apparition dropped his jaw and let out a dreadful, blood-curdling scream as it rushed Lucifer. The glass-encased photographs exploded one by one as the entity rushed past. The pedestal displays that stood in the center of the room shattered into millions of tiny, glittering shards of glass that rained down throughout the main gallery.

The patrons yelled and screamed, shoving each other out of the way as rushed out of the gallery.

Lucifer held out his hand and grabbed the entity by its neck. The entity tried to free itself from Lucifer's grasp by shifting into multiple shapes to no avail.

Lucifer's snake eyes emitted a bright orange glow. He studied the entity for a moment before releasing it. The entity shot upwards through the ceiling and disappeared.

Drucilla spoke in a loud, staggered cadence, "What, the ever-loving fuck, was that?"

Dominic looked up at the ceiling and back to Lucifer for answers.

"It appears you have a wraith," Lucifer said confidently.

"A what?" Drucilla asked.

"A wraith. You have a wraith. Well, not you specifically, Malphas has one. The wraith is the result of Malphas' possession," Lucifer explained.

"What the Hell is a wraith, and why does it belong to Malphas?" Drucilla demanded.

"It does not belong to Malphas, personally. The previous inhabitant of the body that Malphas is currently occupying has returned. Or quite possibly, never left."

Dominic pushed Erato Falx back down into the pocket of his jeans. He crossed his giant arms and creased his forehead at Lucifer's explanation.

"I thought that when Malphas took over this body, the soul from it goes back to the Agglomeration?" Drucilla asked.

"Unfortunately, that is not always the case. Usually, the soul will go back to the Agglomeration. But there are some instances when the soul refuses; the personality of these souls, their sense of self and will, can be too strong for the pull of the Agglomeration to take at first. Or the circumstance of their death can get them caught in a cognitive loop that resists the pull. These are wraiths." Lucifer looked around at the destruction caused by the angry spirit. "It's Azrael's job to collect them and convince them to move on, though sometimes he'll let the less dangerous ones linger for a time and burn themselves out."

"Less dangerous?"

"Most are just ghosts who want to stick around longer," Malphas added, "or they end up becoming little more than echoes as Lucifer said. They'll eventually weaken enough for the Agglomeration to take them."

"Then what was this one's problem?" Dom asked.

Some wraiths can become consumed by bitterness and rage when their lives end. They lash out at the living, generally those that had a hand in their death. This is the probable outcome of the *Fractured*."

"Fractured?" Dominic inquired.

"Malphas pushed this soul out of this body to take it over. Such an ejection breaks the soul off from where it was connected to the flesh. The soul is now damaged, fractured, and that kind of damage tends to corrupt it. It's more likely to give into its anger and become a threat."

Dominic and Drucilla exchanged confused glances.

"What does it want?" Drucilla asked.

"It wants revenge. Or to return. Wraiths can very rarely return to their bodies if the possessor vacates, though it won't heal the fracture. It will forever be incomplete, hence why they are called the Fractured," Malphas answered.

"Why? I mean, it's rejoining its missing piece," Drucilla prodded.

Lucifer pointed to the shattered glass that littered the floor in the center of the gallery. "Drucilla, the glass jewelry display case pieces are here. We can attempt to adhere them together, but they will never be whole again. It will always be fractured."

Drucilla exhaled and nodded in understanding.

"Lucifer, why did he come after you?" Dominic asked.

"I would assume to inhabit my body. He learned rather quickly who I am. He will undoubtedly come back. He will keep returning as long as Malphas retains in control of the host body, and it has the energy to resist the Agglomeration. Or until Azrael does his job and collects it."

CANTICLE TWENTY-EIGHT

"I've shed my skin, and my disguise, and cold on the naked eye." —The Chameleons

Malphas sat at a desk in Drucilla's parlor at home, updating the website with photos of the current exhibit at Corvidae Gallery on his laptop.

"Thank you for getting the images on the website, Ash. I have no idea when power will be restored at the gallery. These Pacific Northwest windstorms are no joke."

"It's lucky that the storm rolled in when it did. It's a pretty good cover-up for the wraith attack."

"Yeah, but you know you could have just taken the day off."

"And do what exactly? I still have tasks to complete," Malphas said. He didn't look up from the screen.

Drucilla was always impressed with Malphas' work ethic. Then again, being thousands of years old, he has the time to do just about anything.

"I have some guests arriving shortly. Dominic and I will be in the dining room with them, so we won't disturb you."

"You are going to attempt to communicate with Thoth again, are you not?" Malphas turned his attention away from his work and looked at Drucilla.

Drucilla nodded.

"You have obtained the bowl and the tome?"

“We have.”

“Good.” Malphas turned his attention back to his work.

Drucilla’s eyes darted around the room. “Is there something I should know before we start?”

“Nothing, in particular, stands out.”

Drucilla sensed that Malphas was being a bit cagey, but she couldn’t figure out why. The knock at the door broke her concentration. Dominic looked up from the dining room table and closed his book. He stood up.

Drucilla swung open the door to greet Katia and Adelia. Katia stepped inside and dropped her bag. Adelia followed behind her.

“Wow, I haven’t been here since I was thirteen!” Katia remarked as she walked in. Her eyes were wide with nostalgia as she took in the surroundings.

“You remember coming here the summer before high school?” Drucilla asked.

“Yeah, it was when my parents were going through counseling, and they thought it was a good idea for me to get out of the house. It was the first time in about a year I had experienced quiet with no one screaming. How is Miriam?”

“She’s doing okay,” Drucilla said.

“This is great, Dru! Everything seems the same but, at the same time, different. The décor mostly.”

“Well, Dominic helped out with a lot of that. You should see his antique shop. It’s very cool and interesting.”

“Dominic!” Adelia shouted as she ran over to him to hug him. Dominic embraced her and glanced awkwardly over her shoulder at Drucilla. Drucilla gave a sarcastic smirk.

†††

Dominic, Drucilla, Katia, and Adelia stood around the table in Drucilla's dining room. Adelia opened Thoth's tome and set it in front of Dominic. He flipped through the pages slowly. Katia placed a large, black, weather-proof case on the table.

"Is that it?" Drucilla asked.

"Yep," Katia responded. She rolled her fingers over the combination locks, pushed the buttons, and flipped the lid back. Encased in black foam was the metallic cauldron.

Drucilla noticed the bandage on her thumb. "What did you do to your thumb?"

"I sliced it on the edge of the cauldron when I was packing it. It's fine."

Dominic peered at Drucilla. Adelia also glanced at Drucilla.

Katia removed Aurora's cauldron and set it atop a thick, ceramic block in the middle of the table. The bowl was much cleaner and brighter than Drucilla remembered, it had clearly been polished to a pristine shine. She hadn't seen the bowl in so long that she had forgotten how deeply the glyphs were scorched into the sides. This was also the first time she noticed glyphs on the inside at the bottom.

"Todd paid a million for that?" Adelia asked.

"Kind of a bizarre wedding gift, right? But it's pure platinum and super old. Apparently, it's unable to be dated since they have nothing to measure it against. The archaeologist that Todd spoke to is assuming it's probably older than Mesopotamia. Protohistoric, it would seem. They said the cuneiform script is one of the oldest they've seen," Katia grinned.

"Del, there is a transmutation spell in this book. It's the only spell in the book that utilizes Aurora's cauldron. If my translations are correct, which I am pretty sure they are, we need a subject. A trinket, an object of some sort," Dominic said. "We'll place the item into the bowl and use the spell in the tome to enchant it."

"Okay, so let's brainstorm here for a minute," Katia said. "Dru, you will need something small but not too small to fit inside. Can it stick out?"

"It doesn't say anything about that. Just that it needs to be placed in the bowl," Dominic responded.

"But portable, right? So, you can talk to him where and whenever you want," Adelia stated.

"Okay, something portable, small, preferably lightweight, but that's more of a want than a need," Drucilla said.

"Like a compact mirror," Adelia added.

Drucilla side-eyed Adelia. "Del, you want me to essentially communicate like *James Bond* to a God?"

"You gotta be able to speak to him when and wherever you are. Why not?" Adelia questioned.

"I can teleport. I can literally attach the communication spell to anything. Hell, even that painting of Marie Antoinette," Drucilla said, pointing to the portrait on the side of her fireplace.

"What about a mirror? Like that one over your buffet table?" Adelia asked. "No one said it had to be submerged in the bowl, right? Put, like, a corner in it."

"Del, you are not shoehorning a chunk of glass into a Divine artifact!" Katia scolded.

"But the painting was, okay?" Adelia shot back.

"I didn't mean that literally. I meant that, as in the item isn't super important. I don't think it needs to make sense. It can be like a spoon or something," Drucilla said.

Dominic scoffed and crossed his arms at the ridiculous ideas being thrown out.

"All right, Dominic. What do you suggest?" Drucilla asked pointedly.

"I don't know. I do agree that portability would probably be optimal. You might be in a situation where you can't just port out. Also, it has to be indestructible. I don't think we want to keep doing this spell over and over."

"Hmm, point taken," Drucilla said.

"What about a quartz crystal?" Adelia said.

"What about a cell phone?" Katia asked.

"A cell phone is fragile. I mean, it hits the water and it's game over," Adelia said.

"It's not like you'd be using it for its intended purpose. Besides, it would look like Dru was actually talking to someone versus looking like a weirdo who talks to objects," Katia replied.

"So portable, indestructible, doesn't make me look like a weirdo… Anything else?" Drucilla reiterated.

"What about a demon?" Malphas interjected quietly as he leaned up against the door frame to the kitchen.

Drucilla and Dominic looked at each other. Katia raised an eyebrow at Malphas.

"Is...is that even possible?" Drucilla asked.

Dominic's eyes widened as he shrugged. "Well, theoretically, he does check all of the boxes."

"Excuse me, who are you?" Adelia asked.

Malphas grinned a maniacal grin as his façade of a clean-cut, well-dressed young man turned into a bald, translucent-skinned being with bright yellow eyes and perfectly gaunt facial features.

Adelia stepped backward into the table. "What?!" she screamed.

"Del, it's okay, it's okay. He's sort of one of us." Drucilla attempted to calm Adelia.

"But he's a demon?!" Adelia yelled anxiously.

Katia seemed more curious than afraid. She approached Malphas and stood in front of him. She turned her head to the side and studied him intently.

"You're the very last person I thought would be okay with this," Drucilla quipped.

Katia continued to inspect Malphas. She turned to Drucilla. "Dru, after what you revealed, you thought *this* would upset me? Besides, this isn't the most bizarre thing you've presented me with." Katia turned her attention back to Malphas, "Can I have a vial of your blood? I mean, would that be something I could get from you?"

Malphas looked at her inquisitively. "For what purpose?"

"Katia is a genetic scientist. I think your blood would keep her busy for the next fifty years," Drucilla answered.

"At least," Katia added. "I even have blood collection tubes in my backpack!"

"Katia, why would you bring blood collection tubes with you to Port Townsend?" Adelia asked.

"Drucilla is an ophanim, and we're using Unholy relics to summon an entity that lives inside of her. What part of this whole thing would make you think I wouldn't bring collection tubes?"

Adelia shut her mouth and blinked a few times.

Malphas peered at Katia suspiciously. Katia grinned back.

"Does possession actually cause physical changes to the host body, or is Katia going to get human blood out of you?" Dominic asked.

"Possession alters the composition of the human body to allow lesser celestial essence to be contained within it. To what degree? I am unsure. This is my first human."

IEVSNEZ
ET FAICTES
PENITENCE.

CANTICLE TWENTY-NINE

"My guests have arrived, Moloch," Drake sensed, peering up from his cathedra at the opposite end of the oratory. He sat at the head of a long, gilded, embellished, carved oak table. The oratory boasted sixty-foot-high, gothic arched ceilings and was decorated in the Renaissance style with tapestries, three large alcoves, and a spiral stairwell that led to a large basilica.

Drake ran his hand over the seam of his bracer. Although he could no longer access Calliope's power, he knew he could immediately remedy that if the need arose. He pulled his shirt sleeve over the armor to conceal it.

Moloch opened the tall, heavy oratory door inward. Drake stood up and straightened his suit. A tall, raven-haired gentleman dressed in an elegant brocade suit nodded to Moloch as he walked past him and approached Drake. He stopped in front of the table.

"It appears I am a bit early for our meeting," he said. He folded his hands in front of him and glanced around the room.

"Please, have a seat, Count Ronove," Drake instructed. "We'll begin shortly."

The door opened again as two more gentlemen entered. One appeared middle-aged with copper-colored hair, the other one older with pure white hair, both in suits. They quickly approached Drake and stood across the table from Count Ronove.

"Marquis Apollyon," Drake said, addressing the white-haired gentlemen. "Viscount Marchosia." Drake nodded to the copper-haired gentleman. "Please sit down."

Everyone took their seats. Persephone abruptly entered the oratory and hastily made her way to Drake. She sat down beside him, crossing her legs and folding her gem-incrusted hands on her knees. Persephone had grown accustomed to being at Drake's side and made herself available when important matters were being discussed, by invitation or not.

Drake raised an eyebrow at Persephone inviting herself. "I assume you all know Persephone," Drake said as he listlessly motioned toward her. Persephone casually leaned back and crossed her arms. The gentlemen nodded and seemed confused by her attendance.

Drake turned to Persephone, "Persephone, we have urgent matters to discuss. Would you mind giving us a moment?"

Persephone appeared disappointed in the request but conceded. "Yes, of course," she exhaled under her breath. She slyly glanced at the count, viscount, and marquis as she walked past them. She closed the heavy oak door behind her with a reverberating *clunk*.

Count Ronove turned his attention to Drake. "An alliance with Persephone? That is quite an audacious and brazen partnership."

Drake glowered at Ronove. "Count Ronove, Persephone is not your concern. I will request that you choose your words carefully when it comes to my personal associates. Do I make myself clear?" Drake's eyes flashed with a blaze.

Ronove nodded in response. "Yes, of course, I apologize; I meant no disrespect. However, as someone who knows Persephone, please understand that she will always choose her own family above all else."

"How so?"

"The Lilim are her children. There are very few remaining. Delphyne is her favorite. Should it ever come down to choosing between you or her children, it will not be you."

Drake's eyes narrowed at the response. "Persephone has been nothing but devoted to me since I took Lucifer's position. I don't want you or anyone here to think that Persephone isn't loyal. Quite the contrary, I trust her implicitly, as should all of you. She is to be my consort eventually."

"I think I speak for all of us when we say we only want what is best for the realm," Count Ronove responded. He looked directly into Drake's eyes.

"Why have we gathered here?" Marchosia asked, clearly growing impatient with the seemingly irrelevant chatter.

"I wanted to congratulate you in person and inform each of you that you have been chosen as the new Kings. Viscount Marchosia, you will assume mantle of the King of Wrath. Marquis Apollyon, you have been appointed King of Constitution, and Count Ronove the King of Acumen. I wanted to thank you for your unwavering support and allegiance to the new order. Each of you has been pivotal in establishing the new era in the Infernal Sphere. We couldn't have done this without you. Congratulations, gentlemen."

Marchosia, Ronove, and Apollyon looked at each other and smiled. They clapped for one other then stood up and clapped for Drake.

"There is to be a formal coronation in a few weeks; then, you will be officially instated in your roles within the Seven Kings. Gentlemen, the old regime is dead. Hell will be in a much stronger position to overthrow the Celestial Empyrion and finally take possession of Earth for ourselves. Lucifer's kings attempted and failed for eons. So did our queens. I will raise the Infernal Sphere and bring the Celestial Empyrion to its knees. Next year, Gentlemen, we will be drinking champagne in the skulls of the Seraphs."

"Agreed!" Count Ronove hollered. He pounded his fist on the table.

"But what are we to do about the queens? They surely will not bend to this new regime. They will not be convinced," Apollyon said.

"They will not be an issue. I assure you," Drake responded. "I have festivities in mind after the coronation; I will be announcing a contest. We have one more role that must be filled within the Seven Kings—"

"Lucifer's seat," Marchosia interrupted.

Drake looked at Marchosia. "Yes, as the new Imperator, I will no longer be occupying Lucifer's vacated seat."

"What is the contest?" Ronove asked.

Drake slowly grinned. "I will make the announcement at the coronation. You are free to go, gentlemen."

Ronove, Marchosia and Apollyon stood up to exit the oratory.

"A moment Count Ronove?" Drake said.

Ronove stopped and turned to Drake, as the others continued out.

"I am not asking you to be diplomatic; I want a straight answer. Must I worry about Persephone?"

Ronove stood silently for a moment as he chose his words. "No one knows from where she came. From what we understand, she is not a creation of the Thrones, nor Lucifer. She's something else entirely. We may never know, and that makes her formidable. You're wise to keep your alliance with her, but maybe even wiser to keep her in the dark."

"You're telling me that Persephone has no history?" Drake pried.

"That is correct. She is not an angel, not a demon. She is something else."

MYOTOMIA
REFORMATA

CANTICLE THIRTY

"I must have said a thousand prayers, but I never got one answer."—Screams for Tina

Katia held the small vial of black, slightly opalescent demon's blood up to her eyes. She gently swirled it and watched the blood twist within the glass tube. "This is incredible," she remarked. Katia's mind was racing with possibilities.

"Okay, so how would this work? Do we just put the bowl on his head or something?" Adelia asked.

Malphas put his hands on his hips and gave Adelia a confused glare. He held up a clawed hand, wiggled his fingers, then plunged his hand into the bowl.

"You sure you want to do this, Malphas?" Dominic asked.

"What better option do we presently have? No one was closer to Thoth. I had studied under him for eons. I am certain Thoth would agree that I would be the best vessel for communication. Additionally, I can sense Thoth in any realm. Locating Drucilla would not be an issue should it come to that."

Drucilla noticed the sarcasm directed at Dominic over losing Drucilla in Nihility. Drucilla snorted as she pressed her lips together and side-eyed Dominic. She was trying not to laugh.

Dominic exhaled. "Okay, if you're sure?"

"I am. Let us begin," Malphas pulled the chair up to the table and sat in front of the bowl.

Dominic stepped away from the open tome and looked at Adelia. "Adelia, you are the keeper of the tome. You will have to read the incantation."

"Why can't you?" Adelia asked.

"Because you're bonded to it by blood. It chose you; only you can utilize it," Drucilla interjected.

"Uh, I don't know if I can do this," Adelia lamented.

"Del, you can. You've been practicing with the cipher, right?" Dominic asked.

"Yeah, but this is like a first-year French class. What if I screw up the words and conjure up something bad?"

"You can do it. I assure you. The tome will listen to you."

Adelia exhaled and nodded.

"Katia, since you have bonded with the cauldron. Only you can utilize it. You will have to place Malphas' hand into the bowl. The bowl is useless to anyone but you."

"Acknowledged," Katia responded. She held her hand out for Malphas to take it. He stiffly placed his long-clawed hand in hers. Katia held it for a moment. She had never touched a demon before and was feeling a bit confused yet fascinated. His skin was soft but warm. His nail beds were black, but the tips turned white, thick, and sharp as the nails grew outward. She placed his hand into the bowl gently. The bowl reacted to Malphas. The symbols on the outside morphed into other symbols as if they understood Katia's intent.

"Wow," she whispered.

"Okay, Del. You're up," Dominic said.

Adelia stood in front of the tome and put her hands on the open pages. She inhaled and exhaled deeply, lifting her eyes to the bowl.

"Le ot tu avenu. Te kah, neue, udesha nisa sumenswega. Nu dioh tu eheh kai. Kadu kosei," Adelia chanted.

The bowl began to burn brightly from the inside, shooting rays of light outwards to the ceiling. Malphas eyes began to droop and finally close.

"It's working!" Drucilla shouted.

"Keep going, Del," Dominic urged her. "Finish the chant."

Adelia looked at the bowl; her eyes began to emit the familiar, celestial blue glow.

"Le ot tu avenu. Te kah, neue, udesha nisa sumenswega. Nu dioh tu eheh kai. Kadu kosei! Aniyah nayewah!"

Malphas eyes remained closed. Adelia looked around the room panicked. She gritted her teeth before hurling the last chant.

"Nisha avena!"

Malphas eyes burst open with bright white beams of light that blasted throughout the room. Dominic put his hands up over his eyes to block the glaring barrage until Malphas' eyes slowly dimmed to a soft white. The illumination from the cauldron diminished as Malphas stood up before Dominic, Adelia, Katia, and Drucilla.

"Thoth," Drucilla said. She stepped closer to him.

Malphas looked at Drucilla. He appeared to be studying her human form. "Drucilla."

"I don't believe it," Katia said in amazement.

"Thoth, do you understand what has happened?" Drucilla asked.

"Yes. You have adapted Malphas as a communication conduit. I am impressed at your ingenuity."

"Actually, this was Malphas' idea," Drucilla said.

"I was speaking to Malphas," Thoth said.

Adelia's eyes shifted to Drucilla as she bit the inside of her lip. Drucilla exhaled.

"Then, I suppose you know why we're communicating," Drucilla asked.

Thoth turned his attention to Dominic. He squinted slightly, then turned his attention back to Drucilla. "You request my aid in the location of the remaining Thrones."

"Yeah. You said you knew where they were. So, where are they?"

"There is one, here, on Eothre."

"Great! Who and where?"

"Gaia."

"How can we find her?" Dominic piped in.

"I do not recall you. Are you a recent delegate to the Seraphs?"

"Um, no. I'm a human," Dominic responded.

Thoth stared at Dominic for a moment, unconvinced. He then turned his attention to Drucilla. "Gaia moves with the Eoethrian seasons. Her preferred season is spring. You will assuredly find her there."

"Right now, that could be anywhere in the southern hemisphere," Katia chimed in.

"Yes," Thoth responded.

"Okay, uh that's a really big area to cover," Katia responded. "Can you be just a smidge more precise?"

"The deserts are barren; you will not find her there. You will find her in areas of new growth and new beginnings. Drucilla and Malphas will locate her. As far as the others, you must scan the stars with the Cosoculous lens. It is the only lens powerful enough to view the entirety of the universe."

"Like a telescope?" Adelia asked.

"That is a very abecedarian way to describe such divine apparatus; however, if that is how you must understand it, so be it."

Adelia frowned at the slight against her intelligence.

"Thoth, is Malphas permanently enchanted? I mean, if he's not, how do I speak to you again?"

"Drucilla, you simply ask Malphas. Malphas has agreed to be the conduit in our communications until a more suitable conduit is chosen."

Drucilla nodded. "Thank you for your guidance."

Thoth's eyes closed and then sprung back open as Malphas' usual, amber eyes. Malphas changed his appearance to his human façade. He straightened his cuffs and checked his hair in the mirror over the buffet table.

"You look great," Katia proclaimed. Malphas side-eyed Katia and grinned to himself.

Adelia and Drucilla stood shoulder to shoulder and glanced at each other.

"Someone is trying to get her flowers pressed," Adelia muttered. Drucilla smacked Adelia's stomach with the back of her hand to shut her up.

"Oof! ...bitch." Adelia whispered.

"So, this Cosoculous lens. What do we know about it?" Katia inquired.

Drucilla shrugged and looked at Dominic.

"I'll, uh, I'll get on that," Dominic said.

"I may be of help," Malphas offered.

"You've seen it?" Dominic asked.

"Not only have I seen it, but I have used it."

"…and Gaia?" Drucilla asked.

"That will be tricker," Malphas said.

"I hate to do it, but we're gonna need *him* for this," Dominic confessed.

"Who is *him*?" Katia asked.

Drucilla looked at Dominic. "Let's concentrate on one thing at a time. Malphas, what can you tell us about the lens?"

"The Cosoculous is the vestige of Urania. She is the Throne of Astronomy, celestial objects, and anything that has to do with the cosmos. The lens was created to fit into a standard spyglass telescope. You may know them as the type seafarers used centuries ago."

"I think I have one of those in the shop," Dominic offered.

"How would we find out who would become the keeper of the Cosoculous lens?" Adelia asked.

"We can speculate, quite accurately, that every relic that has been recovered so far has one thing in common; Drucilla," Malphas responded.

Drucilla nodded.

"You are the linchpin," Malphas said.

"I figured. Well, I'll need to find out if any of my other friends or family have found an object recently that cut them and if they witnessed a blue spark jumping into their skin."

Katia started breathing heavily. She pulled the bandage off her thumb. To her surprise, her thumb had healed.

"Hey, are you okay?" Dominic asked.

"My thumb. I sliced it on the cauldron. I saw the blue bolt." Katia started to pace. "This is becoming scary. It's too real. Is this really happening?" She started hyperventilating.

"Katia. You're going to be okay. This is a good thing. These relics have done nothing but good things for us. These are helpful." Drucilla explained.

"Yeah, but I don't believe in all these celestial folktales. I never have, and now my world is being turned upside down because they're real, and I have no scientific proof for it other than what I'm seeing with my own eyes. I mean, you're an angel, there's a demon standing right next to me, and now

I'm having Divine objects hurled at me that I'm being told are from the Gods of the universe and—" Katia drew a deep breath. "I feel like I'm losing control."

"You're losing control? Are you serious, Katia? Dru is an effing God, and you're scared that you're losing control?!" Adelia growled.

"Del—," Drucilla interjected.

"Katia, this is happening. You've spent your entire life denying that any of this is happening. Hell, you've put yourself on pills for years to forget. Why can't you just accept that you don't know everything?" Adelia shouted.

"Because I can't! I'm not like you and Drucilla!"

"Like what? Accepting?" Adelia yelled.

"Unafraid!"

"Katia, we're all going through this with you. I was actually dead for a few days. Don't you think I was scared too? If what Malphas is saying is correct, we're a tribe. We'll deal with this together," Drucilla said.

"But, what's the point of all of this? Why do we have these relics? Why are we being cursed with them?" Katia said.

"We don't know, but we do know that something big is coming, and these relics are going to put us in the best position to fight it."

"I don't want to fight, Dru."

"Katia," Dominic started. "Fighting doesn't always mean with your fists. Fighting also means protecting, strategizing, and using your mind. You're the keeper of the

Tempest because you were chosen out of everyone in the universe to be its keeper. The cauldron has attached itself to you. You're the right person to harness its power."

"But why me?"

"I dunno, why Dru? Why Dominic? Hell, why me?" Adelia said. "We'll know when it's time, but right now, Katia, you're the keeper of a Divine relic. That has to say something about you."

"Katia, we have each other, okay? We're experiencing this together. We're a tribe. There will even be more of us. You aren't alone," Drucilla said.

Adelia and Dominic nodded to Katia.

Katia exhaled and nodded, slowly calming herself back down. "Thank you. I think that's what I needed to hear." Drucilla put her hand on Katia's shoulder.

"So, what happens tomorrow?" Adelia asked. "I mean, we just go back to our normal lives?"

"Take the normalcy as a gift. We don't know how many more normal days we have before it becomes abnormal. But I know, in the end, we were chosen for a reason, and since we were chosen, we're the best hope for whatever is going to come our way," Drucilla said.

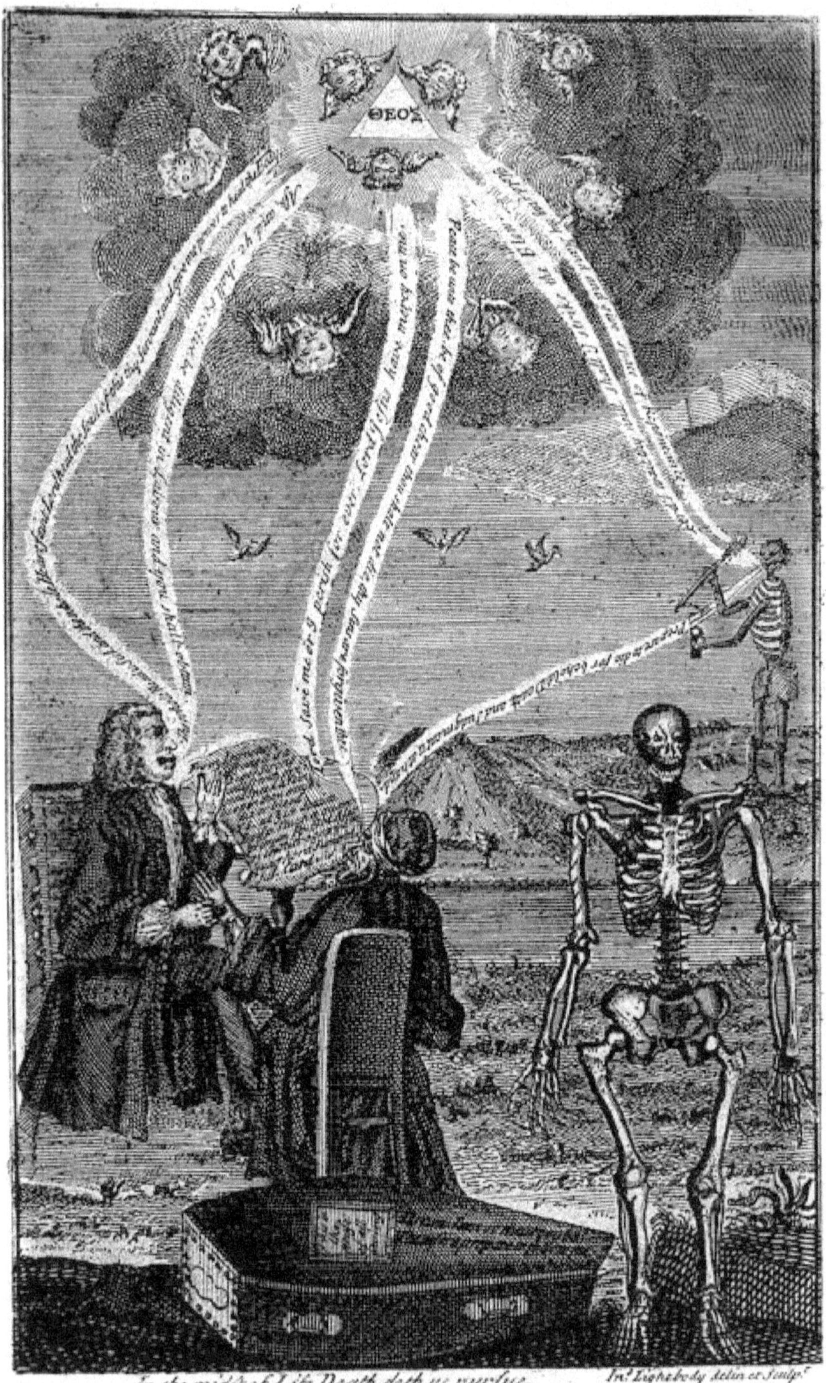

In the midst of Life Death doth us pursue,
Let each therefore with Speed for Mercy sue.

Jn.º Lightbody delin. et Sculp.

CANTICLE THIRTY-ONE

"Such a strange numb. And it brings my knees to the Earth."
—Deftones

Marylin shuffled down the stairs of the newly renovated Victorian, tying her long pink hair into a loose bun. She quickly entered the kitchen and searched for her tool bag. Her girlfriend, Camille, was rushing around the kitchen, making pasta. Marylin spotted her tool bag near the back door, grabbed it, and set at the counter. She began sifting through the bag.

"We don't have parsley," Camille said. She hung onto the cupboard door handle and gazed inside. She got on her tiptoes and looked back as far as she could.

"I'll text Del and tell her to pick some up on the way back," Marilyn said, picking up her phone.

Camille leaned over the counter, folded her hands, and faced Marylin. "You're really gonna do it, huh? You're going to sell it to her?"

Marylin looked up at Camille. "What choice do I have, Cammy? She doesn't want to sell the house, and I can't force her."

"Yeah, but there's literally nothing out here."

"I told her that, and she's determined. I mean, I technically have to give her the right of first refusal. She wants it, and that's it." Marylin pulled out a few random Phillips head screwdrivers and pliers.

"Why didn't we keep it, you and I?" Camille asked.

"You didn't seem interested. Are you?"

"At first? No, Hell no, but you did such an amazing job..."

"Okay, but Cammy, you would have to either A. leave Houston or B. keep up two houses. You and I can't afford two mortgages."

Camille thought about it for a moment. "Can't you, like, rob a bank?" Camille jested.

"Oh! Of course, honey, I'll go do that in a bit. But right now, I want to open that lockbox I have in the dining room," Marylin responded sarcastically.

"Lockbox?"

"Yeah, we found it in a house we were demolishing in Houston a couple of weeks ago. It looks at least seventy or eighty years old. I am dying to know what's in it!"

"Doesn't that belong to someone?" Camille pushed back.

"The previous owners said they had never seen it before. It looks old. They told me to take it, so I'm going to crack it open. Maybe there are diamonds inside…"

Camille grinned and shook her head. She went back to the stove to check her pasta. Marilyn headed into the dining room and sat down in front of the lockbox. She picked up the small box and held it in her hands, examining all sides. The box was heavy and covered in chipped, black ceramic paint. It was about the size of an eight-by-ten picture frame. She shook it as vigorously as she could, considering its weight. She tapped the end of her screwdriver around the outside of the box in search of a weakness. She set the box on its backside with the handle and locking mechanism facing her and shoved the smallest screwdriver into the hole to feel for any obstructions.

"I don't think you're going to open the lock with a screwdriver," Camille commented. She leaned against the doorway, watching Marilyn.

Marilyn glanced up at Camille briefly and went back to inspecting the box.

"I'm gonna get us some wine." Camille returned to the kitchen.

Marylin studied the box, thinking about how to break the lock.

"What's with these weird-ass wines? Bitchy Redhead? Slaughterhouse Floor?" Camille yelled from the kitchen.

"I dunno Cammy, Del likes that weird wine, I guess." Marilyn kept her eyes on the lock. She decided to try and pry the plate surrounding the keyhole with pliers. To her surprise, the plate popped right off, exposing part of the locking mechanism. "Hmmm..." She stuffed the screwdriver into the exposed mechanism to try and move it. With a sudden creak and a clunk, the box lid popped open. "Oh, no way!" she shouted.

"You get it open?" Camilla yelled.

"Yep!" Marylin set the box down and flipped the lid back. Inside the box was a worn, leather pouch about the size of her hand. She reached inside and set the pouch on the table. She opened the pouch and dumped the contents onto her hand. A small gold object that resembled a pocket watch-sized sundial rested in her palm. Many strange sigils were carved into the edge of the top of the dial in a uniform pattern. It looked like a calendar to Marilyn, but there weren't enough months or days.

"What inside?" Camille yelled.

"I dunno, come look at this, tell me what you think it is."

Camille entered the dining room with two glasses of red wine. "We're drinking Slaughterhouse Floor." She set one of the glasses in front of Marilyn and sat beside her. She looked curiously at the strange object in Marilyn's hand. "Is that a tiny sundial?" Camille asked.

"I dunno, maybe."

"What's all the writing around the edge?"

"No clue." Marilyn grasped the gnomon with her thumb and index finger and attempted to turn it like a dial.

"Ouch!" she yelled. Marilyn accidentally pricked her finger at the point on the end. A small, blue spark jumped from her finger and disappeared up her wrist. Marilyn furrowed her brow at the spark. "Is there a battery or something in here?"

"Where would you put it?" Camille asked.

"Did you see that?" Marilyn asked.

"See what?"

"That bolt of electricity?"

"No?"

Marilyn shook off the weird occurrence and grasped the gnomon again, this time with better care. She cranked the gnomon halfway around; it moved effortlessly. She peered at the dial with suspicion. "I didn't think these were supposed to move." She looked at Camille for confirmation, but Camille had vanished. Marilyn quickly looked around, stunned that she seemed to have vanished in a blink of an eye.

"Camille?"

Camille entered the dining room with two glasses of red wine. "We're drinking Slaughterhouse Floor." She set one of the glasses in front of Marilyn again.

Marilyn's eyes widened in panic. She stared at Camille in shock.

"What's wrong with you? Why do you look like you've seen a ghost?" Camille asked. She sat down next to Marilyn. Marilyn's eyes were still wide like saucers. "Is it my hair? It's my hair, isn't it? I need to wash it. I'm a mess," Camille laughed.

"Cammy, did you bring me a glass of wine two minutes ago?"

"Huh? I was in the kitchen two minutes ago. Are you okay?"

Marilyn's eyes were fixed on Camille. "I.... I don't know," Marilyn said quietly.

"Heh, weirdo. Show me what you have."

Marilyn creased her forehead and looked back down at the small, golden sundial. She grasped the gnomon again. Once more, she turned the gnomon halfway around the dial. "So, you disappeared when I did this the first time." Marilyn looked at Camille, but Camille had vanished again.

Camille entered the dining room again with two glasses of red wine. "We're drinking Slaughterhouse Floor." She set one of the glasses in front of Marilyn once more.

Startled, Marilyn jumped to her feet, hitting the table so hard the wine glass fell over. "Oh my God!" she screamed.

Camille jumped up, "It's okay, it's okay, I got it." She ran to the kitchen and quickly returned with a towel. "Mare, are you okay? What's wrong?" Camille asked. She laid the towel over the pool of spilled wine.

Marilyn stood stunned, unable to form a sentence or a single word. Her breathing became rapid and shallow. She looked terrified.

"Mare! Mare, what's wrong? Talk to me. What's wrong?" Camille pleaded.

Marilyn dropped the small sundial onto the table. "Camille, I'm freaking out. I think I'm having an aneurysm or something."

"What?! Are you in pain? Do you need to lie down? Let's get you over to the couch."

Camille led Marilyn to the couch and pulled off her shoes. She felt Marilyn's head. "How do you feel?"

"Confused. I don't know what's happening." She looked at Camille in panic.

"You're okay, Mare. You're fine. I'm here. Just breathe."

The abrupt click of the front door opening broke the tension. Adelia walked in with a grocery bag. Marilyn sat up and looked at her sister in terror.

"What's wrong with you?" Adelia frowned.

Camille grabbed the groceries from Adelia. "She's having a panic attack, I think. Maybe you can calm her down. I need to finish dinner."

Adelia sat on the other end of the couch from Marilyn and put her sister's feet on her lap. "Hey, you all right?"

Marilyn sat up. "Something weird is happening." Marilyn rubbed her eyes and exhaled.

"It's like the world is glitching out. I swear to God that Cammy put a glass of wine in front of me three goddamn times."

"What?" Adelia squinted at Marilyn.

Marilyn stood up and walked to the dining area. She returned with the small pocket sundial and sat on the couch beside her sister. "This thing. It's a weird sundial thing that I found in that old lockbox." Marilyn pointed to the dining room table. "I found this lockbox in a house that we tore down in Houston. I brought it here to open it and this is what I found inside." She handed the dial to Adelia. Adelia slowly took it from her and peered at it curiously.

"Okay so, what's so weird about it?"

"I turned the gnomon, and time reset. Like when I moved the gnomon, I reversed time, and it started over again…"

"Huh?"

"I'm explaining this wrong. Okay, when I moved the gnomon, this fin thing here, I cranked it to the left, and Cammy came out with a glass of wine. Exactly like she did before I turned it, I did it again, and she came out with the wine again. I mean, it's like I'm resetting time, and she's repeating the same action from a few minutes before. Three times, Del!"

Adelia blinked a few times, attempting to understand the issue. She turned to Marilyn. "I have a really weird question to ask you. Did you at any time cut yourself on the object?"

"Uh, yeah, I accidentally stuck myself with the gnomon."

Adelia gasped and then composed herself. "This is important. Did you see a blue spark of light?"

Marilyn's eyes grew wide again. She nodded slowly and maintained eye contact with her sister.

Adelia exhaled. "Oh no."

†††

"Del, are you sure?" Drucilla asked.

"I didn't see it happen. But yeah, that's what she told me. She's manipulating time somehow. She's really freaked out by this. Dru, I don't want my sister involved," Adelia said.

"Unfortunately, we don't get to make that decision. Where is she now?" Drucilla asked. Drucilla leaned against a chair in the dining room.

"She left with Cammy back to Houston this morning. I don't expect to see her for a couple of weeks."

"Did she take it with her?"

"No, she left it here. I think she's really scared of it. It's over there in the drawer." Adelia pointed to the buffet table at the other end of the dining room. Drucilla headed to the table and opened the top drawer. She saw the small, gold object resting on a worn, leather pouch. Drucilla picked up the object and moved it around in her hands.

"What exactly did she do? How does it work?" Drucilla asked.

"She just turned the dial, er, the gnomon, and that's it."

"So, If I turn the dial…" Drucilla grasped the gnomon, but it wouldn't budge. She furrowed her brow and tried again, putting more effort into it, but still, the gnomon wouldn't move.

"Well, I can't make it work. I'm afraid if I push harder, I'll break it. You try." Drucilla handed the sundial to Adelia.

Adelia took it from Drucilla and attempted to turn the gnomon. "I can't move it either," she said. She set the sundial on the table in front of her. "Is it another one of those angel objects?"

"Is it a Divine relic? I think so. The only way to know for sure is to get Marylin to move it again."

"I don't think you'll ever get her to touch that thing again."

"Del, if she's meant to have it, she's the only one that can control it."

"Even if that is true, I think we're kind of on our own here. I know my sister. She isn't going to touch it."

Drucilla exhaled. "If she was chosen, she might not have a choice."

CANTICLE THIRTY-TWO

"Stuck halfway between the unsightly and the serene."
— Crispy Ambulance

Drucilla walked briskly down Water Street with two cups of hot coffee as she shuffled her way through the fallen leaves on a typically crisp, autumn morning. She attempted to hold both cups while trying to press down on the door handle of Ford Bradshaw and Co. The door wouldn't budge. Drucilla's brows knitted as she looked up at the closed sign in the window.

"What? It's ten a.m. on a Monday."

Drucilla set the coffee cups on the ground in front of her and fished her cell phone out of her handbag. She called Dominic's number, and the call went to voicemail after a moment. She ended the call without leaving a message. "What is going on?"

Drucilla picked up the coffee cups and quickly walked across the street to her gallery. She noticed as she approached Corvidae's main entrance that a peculiar-looking gentleman was leaning against a tree roughly thirty feet away. He was unusually tall and had albinism. Drucilla glanced at him a couple of times before reaching for the front door handle of her gallery. The man nodded, turned away from her, and walked across the street in the opposite direction.

Drucilla unlocked the door and closed it behind her. She looked out the large display window, the gentleman had disappeared. She shook it off and pulled out her phone again.

She attempted to call Dominic one more time. "Pick up, pick up," she said as she paced.

"Problem?" Lucifer said as he appeared and leaned against the front desk. He grabbed the coffee that was meant for Dominic and lifted the lid to smell the aroma.

Drucilla put her finger up as if to shush Lucifer while she waited for the call to go to voicemail.

"Ooh, La Victoire Coffee." Lucifer smiled as he placed the lid back on and took a sip.

"Dom, call me as soon as you can." She pressed the end button and turned to Lucifer. "Where is he?" Drucilla asked, pointedly and without hesitation.

"Dominic? He isn't here."

"Well, no shit Lucifer. I mean, do you know where he—" Drucilla's phone rang. She quickly answered.

"Dom! Where are you? I went by your shop, and it's closed. Are you okay?"

"Hey, Dru. That's uh, that's a long story. I'm in Milan, in Italy."

"What? When? Uh, why?" Drucilla had a lot of questions but struggled with which one she needed first.

"I received a distressing call about two a.m. on Sunday. I needed to take the first flight out."

"What happened?"

"I'm trying to get to the bottom of that right now. My mom's ossuary is destroyed. It looks like arson. Maybe. I'll call you when I get more information." Dominic hung up.

Drucilla stuffed her phone in her pocket and looked at Lucifer.

"That is a pity," Lucifer said, presumably hearing the conversation. He took another sip of the coffee.

Drucilla shot dagger eyes at him and put her hands on her hips. "What do you know about it?"

"Me? I had nothing to do with it."

"Okay, do *you personally* not have anything to do with it, or do you, *Charles Manson,* not have anything to do with it?"

"I am sorry?" Lucifer gave Drucilla a confused glance.

"You know what I mean."

"Are you referring to whether I orchestrated this? Why would I do that?"

"If I find out this is part of your game, I will throw you through every wall on this street, not just mine."

"This was not me. I swear to you. I do not know what this is about. I have no knowledge of a desecrated ossuary, Dominic's mother's tomb or otherwise. I would hazard a guess that it would be someone from Drake's entourage," Lucifer stated confidently.

"Why would Drake even care about Dominic's mother?"

Lucifer took a sip of coffee. He seemed to be stalling.

"Answer me, Seraph!" Drucilla folded her arms and stared into his serpentine eyes as if she was attempting to burn a hole into his brain.

The corner of Lucifer's lip turned and snarled at the slur.

"What are you not telling me about Dominic's mother?"

†††

"Mr. Novikov?" A well-dressed, dark-haired gentleman approached Dominic with an outstretched hand. "I am Alessandro Benevento, welcome to Cattedrale di San Milanesi." He spoke perfect English and Italian when he pronounced the cathedral's name.

"Hi, thank you for meeting with me. Uh, call me Dominic." Dominic shook his hand.

Alessandro, still holding on to Dominic's hand, seemed to react negatively to his touch, He peered at him, confused for a moment. He looked down at Dominic's hand, then quickly dropped the connection. "You're quite a rarity," he said slightly concerned.

"I'm sorry?" Dominic said.

"Tell me, who else has companied you on your travels?"

"It's just me."

"I see. Very well, thank you for coming all this way, Dominic." Alessandro changed his demeanor. "I apologize, but you were the only one listed as kin to your mother. We did not have anyone else to contact. This way, please." Alessandro motioned for Dominic to follow him.

"My father should have been listed as a contact, not me," Dominic said.

"I'm sorry there was no spouse on file. It could have been a misfiling of contact information. You are the owner of the Ford Bradshaw antiquities shop?"

"That's right," Dominic responded. "But how did you get *my* number? You didn't call the shop."

"I am not sure how your number was obtained. You may need to speak to the office."

Dominic furrowed his brows; something wasn't adding up.

The gentleman led Dominic through the grand cathedral. The outside of the church was impressive with its elaborate and highly detailed white spires and arches, but it was even more beautiful on the inside. Dominic turned his gaze to the high-arched alcove that spanned sixty feet above the altar. The church had five naves, one central, and four laterals, with about thirty pillars throughout. The central nave was adorned with detailed, baroque tapestries that depicted angels and worshipers with arms stretched outwards to the sky. The highly detailed stained-glass window was made of hundreds of smaller images of saints and followers, accumulating into a beautiful motif of fleur-de-lis patterns encircling the center rosette. The church had a distinct smell of frankincense that had been burned so often that it had stained and seeped into the walls over the centuries. The atmosphere felt intrusive and judgmental. Almost like you had to be on your best behavior, or God may come down and damn you to Hell.

"My sincerest apologies that this has happened, such a tragic accident. Ossario de San Milanesi is one of the oldest ossuaries in Milan. I can assure you nothing like this has happened in our 600 years," Alessandro said.

"Was the tomb destroyed or just the ossuary box?" Dominic asked.

"The tomb, I am afraid."

Dominic inhaled sharply.

Alessandro led Dominic through a heavy wooden door that opened to a corridor. Multiple, lighter wooden doors lined either side of the walls for the length of the corridor. At the end was another set of wooden doors, like the one they came through. Dominic and Alessandro made their way to the end and pulled the doors open. Below was a stone staircase leading into a downward spiral. Alessandro flipped a dated, bulky, double pole throw switch to light the stairs. The lights buzzed for a moment and flickered on to a steady glow.

"How does a fire just start down here?" Dominic asked. He quickly followed Alessandro down the staircase.

"It was intentional, most likely, given the circumstances."

The staircase went down four flights and terminated at a long, stone, arched hallway. The hallway was dim and frigid. It smelled of decay and mold. As they moved toward the end of the corridor, the black soot and the odor of charred wood began to overtake the heavy scent of decay.

Dominic felt a lump in his throat as they approached the entrance to the tomb, Alessandro picked up a battery-operated lantern and turned it on. What was once the wooden door to the tomb lay before them in chunks of charcoal, part of it still hanging on its rusted hinges. The door was burned out so badly that they could easily walk through it into the room. Alessandro turned on a few more battery-operated lanterns laid around in various places. The room was small and circular, lined with multiple pointed segmental arches. Between the arches were small alcove shelves with remnants of candle wax. There seemed to be runes, or some sort of cuneiform etched into the stone columns but peculiarly gouged and chipped away as a crude way to erase them. In the center at the back of the room was his mother's ossuary. The three-foot, intricately carved limestone box was open with the lid leaning against the outside. Dominic looked at Alessandro.

"This was opened," Dominic observed.

"Yes. We noticed that as well. I am uncertain why they would desecrate the ossuary and set fire to the tomb. I assume they could either not find what they were looking for or they needed to destroy whatever was in here."

"Why would you assume something like that?" Dominic asked.

"I do not have a better explanation as to why your mother's tomb was the only one that was vandalized. Tell me, Dominic, was your mother royalty?"

Dominic bent down to inspect the ossuary. He looked inside the box at the charred bone remains that were once his mother's body. He placed his hand over his mouth and closed his eyes. "No. I mean, I don't know for sure. She died of heart failure when I was twelve years old. I don't know much about her family. The only thing I know is that this is the place where her remains were to be interred. This was in her Will. Arrangements were made before her death."

"It is peculiar; no one had been placed in these catacombs for centuries until your mother. I am curious about the connection she has to this place, let alone the permissions and bureaucracy she would have had to go through just to be allowed here," Alessandro commented.

"I, uh, I couldn't tell you." Dominic stood up and walked around the ossuary, inspecting it for clues as to why the tomb was desecrated.

"What do you think she would have been interred with?" Alessandro asked.

"I—" Dominic waved his hand and shrugged. "I mean, we had the funeral in the states, and my father brought her here to rest. From what I remember, she just had what she was wearing and some photos in her casket."

"No jewelry, artifacts, or anything of value?"

"That would be a better question for my father. I'm sorry, I don't know."

"Ah, perhaps you were not the best person to ask. We should have asked Edik." Alessandro shrugged.

Dominic placed his hands on his hips and continued to stare down into his mother's ossuary.

"Yeah, I guess—" Dominic stopped and looked up, quickly turning his attention to Alessandro.

"How did you know my father's name if no spouse was listed?"

Alessandro crossed his arms and scoffed as the light from the lantern caught the orange flash across his eyes. His façade faded into an orange-skinned being.

"Oh, Hell no—" Dominic pulled the stylus from his pocket and thrust it outward. The javelin fully expanded. Dominic stared down Alessandro.

"How fortunate. We had hoped you might bring Erato Falx," Alessandro said, admiring the ancient relic, "we planned to kill you after we obtained the cuff. Since you don't appear to have it, the javelin is a nice consolation prize."

Dominic held his stare, unflinching.

"Unfortunately, in addition to killing you, we must keep searching. This will undoubtedly be more work for us." Alessandro let out a heavy sigh.

"It's under the ossuary." A feminine voice whispered over Dominic's shoulder that only he could hear.

"What is?" Dominic asked, confused.

Alessandro laughed maniacally and summoned a font of fel fire and flung a ball of fire at Dominic. Dominic dodged the streak of flame, just barely, and watched it collide with the archway behind him and erupt in a blaze.

Dominic raised his javelin and poised to throw it at Alessandro but was once again caught too slow and could only brace for impact as he saw another fireball arcing his way. With the javelin brought before himself, Dominic prepared for the coming heat and pain, but hesitated when the javelin appeared to catch and soak up the otherworldly fire. Like a candle wick set aflame, the fire sped down the length of the javelin and engulfed it completely.

Dominic could not let go of the javelin in time and watched the artifact burn with the light of fire that laced through the fingers of his clenched fist. The heat from the fire didn't burn him, even as he could see it billowing the air around it with ferocious intensity. Dominic, in disbelief, eyed Alessandro and measured his reaction.

Alessandro took a step back. His face was blank, betraying his sudden lack of confidence.

Dominic seized the opportunity to close the distance between them and thrust the javelin. In the few steps it took to come into range, Alessandro readied another attempt at fel flame and shaped it to his hands, bringing them up in a shield of energy to block the attack. The weapon's fire-coated tip pierced the shield effortlessly, sliced along the inside of his arm, and pierced the demon's chest.

Alessandro's eyes widened. Though the blow of the weapon stung, it wasn't deep enough to cause a fatal wound. However, the torn flesh left behind burned like a white-hot ember, and the pain spread quickly. Staggering backward, Alessandro could only watch as the empty slit in his chest lit aflame and, like a fire uncontrolled, raced over his body. Alessandro flailed, trying in vain to put out the fire.

Dominic readied the javelin again, bringing it up over his shoulder and lining up a throw. Alessandro did not see the line of fire streaking from Dominic's hand as the javelin impaled him in the neck. As before, the intense burning possessed of the javelin transferred itself onto Alessandro, matching the gravity of the blow, instantly igniting his head and shoulders upon impact.

Alessandro laughed maniacally. "You think you've won? This is nothing compared to what you will suffer, you vulgar abomination!" Alessandro cackled until he could no longer get a sound past the ash in his throat. He collapsed, and the fire took him, leaving little more than greasy char and the smell of burning fat.

Dominic glanced down at the former Alessandro and picked up his javelin. He examined the iron weapon closely.

"Well damn, that's new."

Dominic collapsed the javelin and stuffed it back into his pocket. He turned his attention back to the area of the ossuary.

"Persephone?" he yelled, looking around the tomb. "What is under the ossuary."

There was no answer. Dominic got down on his knees before the limestone box. He placed both hands on the sides and slid the ossuary backward to expose the flooring underneath. Nothing was noteworthy—just the deliberate placement of small square limestone blocks in a circular pattern around the room.

"There's nothing here."

He ran his hands over the squares, hoping one of them might be loose. He felt the edges of each block to see if any of them wiggled. They were all solidly in place. Dominic stood up and chewed the inside of his lip in contemplation.

"Under the ossuary. The whole ossuary?"

Dominic grasped the limestone container and tipped it onto its side. He lost his grip; it hit the floor, cracked, and then collapsed under its weight. The charred remnants of his mother's bones scattered across the floor. Dominic grimaced and squeezed his eyes closed. He opened his eyes in time to see a thick, silver cuff roll out and land on the tip of his hiking boot.

"What in the Hell?"

†††

"Lucifer. I'm asking you a question. What are you not telling me?"

"It is not that I do not want to tell you. Rather if I do tell you, it will add difficulty to the already enormous quandaries we currently have at hand."

"Are you still hung up about The Temperance Flame thing?"

"No, this is about Dominic. It adds another level of complexity. Damn it, Drucilla. Have you not figured out that some things must be kept away for the sake of Dominic and you?"

"No, I'm an idiot. Tell me anyway," Drucilla snarked.

Lucifer paced the floor for a moment. He crossed his arms and put one hand to his chin. He thought to himself before stopping and looking at Drucilla.

"Dominic has uncovered something that belonged to his mother."

Drucilla stood quietly as she watched Lucifer pace. Lucifer put his hands in his pockets. He looked out the back window to the ocean behind the gallery. He seemed concerned and moderately paranoid. He appeared to be cautious with what he wanted to say.

"Do you remember last year after we fought Hell's army, when we walked back to your home, we discussed a myriad of different subjects spending just a short time on each? You seemed most interested in how Sariel composed himself around Dominic. Do you remember?"

Drucilla nodded.

"Do you remember what you said?"

Drucilla's eyes darted around the room as she attempted to reconnect the neural pathways in her brain to recall the exact words she used.

"Do you think—and you said that he's Divine in some way? You finished my thought."

"Yes. That one."

Drucilla looked at Lucifer suspiciously. Her eyes grew wider at the thought.

"What are you saying?"

Lucifer crossed his arms and looked at Drucilla.

Drucilla felt a cold chill run up her spine. Lucifer was right. This was something that she wasn't ready to deal with.

"Dominic's identity has been discovered. The chatter among the infernals is that a Nephilim had expelled a demon from the human realm and sent him back to the Infernal Sphere."

Drucilla's breathing became labored. She knew the fate of the Nephilim.

Il faut sans diferer me suivre
Tu dois être prêt à partir
Dieu ne t'a fait si long temps vivre
Que pour t'aprendre à bien mourir
MEMENTO MORI
A AMSTERDAM.
Chez HENRI DESBORDES.

CANTICLE THIRTY-THREE

"Heaven knows nobody." —Southern Death Cult

Katia sat alone in her laboratory, examining the vial of Malphas' demon blood that she had brought back from her trip to Washington State. The laboratory was bright and quiet, save for the humming of computer fans. Katia's mind was racing with possibilities of what kind of plasma, platelets, and blood cell types she would discover. *Maybe this would be a new blood type.* She was eager to unlock its secrets. She leaned back in her chair and held the vial up to the light. The blood was black and viscous, closely resembling tar, with a vague iridescence to the fluid. Light from the ceiling could not penetrate the contents of the vial. She set it down and looked over her shoulder into her office across the hall. Aurora's cauldron sat peacefully inside a locked glass shelf. She glanced at the vial and back at the cauldron again. She got up from her chair and pulled out her keys. Katia unlocked the glass case and removed the cauldron. She held the cauldron in her hands and slowly examined the exterior as if she were seeing it for the first time with new eyes. She ran her finger over the jagged, inconsistent, deeply gouged symbols. She carried the cauldron back to her lab and set it on the table in front of her.

Katia exhaled slowly.

She picked up a hypodermic needle package from a basket on her desk. She unwrapped the package, plunged the needle into the top of the vial of blood, and pulled the plunger upwards to draw blood into the barrel.

"What am I doing?" she said. She placed the vial into a test tube holder and set the needle down. She rubbed her eyes, leaned back in her chair, and crossed her arms. She stared at the cauldron as she tried to figure out its secrets.

"I don't know what I'm supposed to do with you. I don't know why you chose me."

She shook her head and picked up the needle again. She hovered the needle over the bowl and pushed the plunger down until a single drop of blood slowly formed and released. It splashed to the bottom of the bowl. The symbol on the bottom began to glow brightly. Katia quickly stood up and slowly took a step back. The drop of black blood began to grow and quickly filled the cauldron. Katia took a few more cautious steps back as the cauldron continued to fill itself. It stopped just short of overflowing. The blood in the bowl was still and placid. Katia felt her heart race and her breathing become more rapid. She took a step closer and then another step, creeping up to the cauldron so as not to disturb it, she stood over the bowl and looked inside.

"What is this?" she whispered.

She gazed into the bowl. The blackness of the blood slowly cleared and gave way to an image. As the image became brighter and clearer, she could see a cathedral. It was large, black, and had multiple spires. It looked quite old. She gazed at the open door. The blood seemed to respond to Katia's eyes, and the image focused on the door and expanded.

"What's inside?"

Again, the bowl responded to her, and the image moved from the door into the cathedral. Inside were hundreds of people, but they didn't quite look human. These people sat at multiple tables–it looked like a feast or ceremony. Katia looked from the head of the cathedral to a long table at the end. There were four people sitting at this table, facing the crowd. She couldn't see who they were. She focused on the man that seemed to be talking and moving his arms around. He appeared to be giving a speech or explaining something. Katia couldn't hear a sound. She quickly realized that the man looked very familiar.

"Is that…" she whispered, as she tried to understand at whom she was looking. "Is that Drake?"

Katia watched as Drake moved to the head of the table and stood in front of three golden crowns. He reached over the table and picked up one of the crowns.

"What the Hell?" Katia said loudly.

Drake looked up to the ceiling from where Katia was viewing him. He glared as if he could see her. Katia gasped and stepped back. The image became dark and clouded until she couldn't see anything anymore. The pool of black liquid quickly dissipated into nothing. The cauldron was empty.

"What is going on?" Katia said.

"Scrying," a woman's voice said behind her.

Katia quickly turned around and stepped backward into her desk. She gripped the desk in fear at the being that stood before her.

The being, made of white light, dimmed to a soft glow. Katia could see it was a young woman in a white, fitted suit, tall with pale blond hair that flowed like waves from her head to her waist.

"Scrying?" Katia managed to get out the single word.

"Yes. The Tempest has many functions. Scrying is one of them."

"Are you an angel?" Katia asked, almost afraid of the answer.

"My name is Valor," she said. "I am not here to harm you. I am here to warn you." Valor's voice came in soothing, soft waves.

"Warn me about what?"

"Aurora's cauldron has bonded to you by blood. According to Celestial Law, that makes you the keeper of the divine relic. You are bound to it until your death."

Katia followed Valor's movements as she slowly walked around Katia's lab.

"Katia, the cauldron has more power than you could comprehend. Understand that when you use the cauldron, you are opening a window into other realms. Windows are open on both sides. Not just your side. Do you understand?"

Katia nodded slowly.

"How did you know to scry with the demon's blood?"

"I didn't. I swear I didn't. It just seemed like something I should try," Katia explained.

"The idea came from the Tempest. It spoke to you in a way that made you think you produced a theory on your own—everything from obtaining the demon's blood to using it with the cauldron. You are already working in tandem. The demon's blood you used allowed you to view the Infernal Sphere. Alternately, Divine blood would grant you the ability to view the Celestial Empyrion."

"What else can you tell me about the cauldron?"

"The cauldron has many functions. Many of which I do not know. However, I do know that water from the cauldron can be used for healing and transmutation."

"Transmutation?"

"Joining two objects together or changing one object into another."

Katia's mind was racing. "Valor, why was I chosen to be the keeper of the Tempest?"

"The relic has chosen you. You have been selected as the human that has the knowledge and courage to use it."

"I'm just a laboratory director. I'm not anybody important."

"I am sorry, Katia. I do not have more information for you."

"Valor, you came all the way from Heaven to warn me about creeping on other realms?"

"I came to you because I was sent here by my father, Sariel."

Katia wrinkled her forehead. She sat down in her chair and crossed her arms. "Who is Sariel?"

"Sariel is the General of Virtues in the Celestial Empyrion, Heaven if you will. The Seraphs are the protectors of this realm, Earth, along with every planet and galaxy within the universe. Earth is special as it is the first planet to have been populated with humans. Both Divine and Unholy covet this planet."

"I see."

"This planet has value to all Celestials since it is the starting point for every experiment the Thrones ever created. It was created with the capacity to make the strongest terrestrial beings, vegetation, and elements in the universe. Every being that has been created here is the blueprint for creating and populating new worlds. If the Unholy gain control of Earth, they would be unstoppable."

"It seems to me like the power is the favor of the Divine."

"What are you implying?" Valor asked.

"I mean, there hardly seems to be a balance. What if your dad decided to just blow up the planet and every one of us because he's having a bad day? He could just do that, right?"

"Virtues will not end Earth over a fit of blind rage," Valor scoffed.

"So, are you a Virtue too?"

Valor paused for a moment before answering the question. "I am a Seraph—Virtue in title only."

"What does that mean, in title only?" Katia pressed.

Valor put up her hand to stop Katia, "It does not matter. Katia, I was sent here to learn what I could from you and to get you to entrust me with the Tempest cauldron and, in turn, surrender it to me."

Katia stood up and looked at Valor in confusion. "Are you telling me that surrendering the relic to you would gain you the official title of Virtue? Is that what this is about?"

Valor paused for a moment before answering. "It is complicated. Sariel hoped that you to surrender the relic to me, and I would give the relic to him." Valor began to pace around the laboratory uncomfortably. "Presumably to gain an advantage over the Unholy and shift the balance in favor of the Divine."

"But the Divine already have possession of Earth. Why would they need the cauldron?"

Valor seemed visibly frustrated. It never crossed her mind that her father would use her in this way. It seemed nefarious.

"Valor, can I ask you why we, humans, have possession of the relics? I mean all of us, not because we are chosen, but why do they exist here on Earth at all?" Katia inquired.

"They were stolen. We do not know by whom. When the Thrones departed, their vestiges were left behind. I assume they were not needed. They were entrusted to Lucifer long before the war. When Lucifer was exiled, the relics disappeared along with him. Multiple missions were carried out in the Infernal Sphere, and it was concluded that Lucifer did not have them. However, they would randomly show up from time to time in the possession of a human. The Thrones made these relics sentient, in that they would bond by blood to whomever the relics deemed worthy."

"You know I can't surrender the Tempest to you, Valor. If this were even just four weeks ago, I would have. Now that I understand that I am part of something bigger…"

"Katia, I believe my father was wrong in sending me on this mission. Seraphs are entrusted with the protection of all life on Earth. I would never do anything to endanger your lives. I believe that taking this relic from you would impact humankind in the most detrimental way."

"Jesus and I thought I had daddy issues," Katia groaned.

"No," Valor said abruptly.

"…No?" Katia asked.

Valor exhaled, her eyes seemingly processing something in her head. "No, I will not take the Tempest cauldron from you, Katia. It belongs to you. You are its keeper."

"Okay, I mean, I wasn't gonna anyway…" Katia blinked at Valor blankly.

Valor seemed distraught. Lucifer's words echoed in her head about her worth and that she belonged in a place of power.

Katia noticed the change in Valor's demeanor. "Valor, are you okay?"

The corner of Valor's mouth curled up slightly in an almost devilish grin. She nodded at Katia. "Thank you, Katia. You have helped me see things clearly."

"I did?"

"Good luck to you, Katia van Vliet. You will do a great many things before your time on Earth comes to an end."

"Uh, okay."

Valor's eyes flashed a yellow glint once more.

CANTICLE THIRTY-FOUR

Drucilla sat down in one of the overly designed, turquoise chairs in her gallery and placed her face in her hands.

Lucifer crossed his arms, rested his clawed hands on his biceps, and glanced out the front window, presumably at the townsfolk going about their day.

"Tell me what we're dealing with," Drucilla demanded, lifting her head.

"What do you want me to tell you, Drucilla? You know the fate of the Nephilim."

"Yeah, but that was long ago," Drucilla responded.

"A long time ago for you. For Celestials, it was last Tuesday."

Drucilla got up and stood next to Lucifer, looking out the window beside him. "You aren't going to let this happen, right?" Drucilla said.

"Extermination is not my position."

"Yeah, but—," Drucilla caught a glimpse of what Lucifer was intensely focused upon. There was the gentleman with albinism again, standing across the street, watching them. Feeling uneasy, Drucilla took a step back.

Lucifer looked over at Drucilla. She didn't take her eyes off the gentleman.

"Lucifer, who is that?" she said quietly. "I've seen him before."

Lucifer turned his attention to the gentleman, who nodded at Lucifer.

"His name is Orias. He is Grigori," Lucifer responded.

"Why is he stalking me?"

"He is not stalking you. He is doing what you would refer to as surveillance."

"That's stalking," Drucilla interrupted.

"A Watcher's role is to keep tabs on Celestials. That is why you see him. If you were not celestial or even to become one, you would not see him."

"Why?"

"Because it is what I require of them."

"That doesn't make sense, Lucifer. I had a science teacher in high school who had albinism. Everyone saw it."

"Yes," Lucifer responded.

Drucilla raised an eyebrow at Lucifer. She wanted to wrestle with that answer, but a more pressing matter needed attention. She recalled the incident when she was a teenager when the Grigori attacked her.

"Why does their presence concern you so? You are not in any danger," Lucifer added.

"How could you possibly say that? You know why!" Drucilla snapped.

Lucifer didn't respond.

"So, you aren't going to say anything?"

Lucifer turned to Drucilla. "What would you have me say?"

"I almost died!"

Lucifer scoffed and then chuckled to himself. "That is doubtful."

"Lucifer, you know I was attacked by them! You were there! You are the one that told me to break the rosary bead and summon the dead? Remember, in the cemetery?"

"How do you know that was me?" Lucifer asked, surprised.

"Who else could it be? You basically did the same thing in Egypt."

"Drucilla, you must understand that although the Grigori have a specific role, they do not swear allegiance to anyone, Divine or Unholy. They are bound to Earth for eternity but not to a faction. No one controls the Grigori."

"Why are they bound to Earth?"

"It is their imprisonment for treason handed down by the Celestial Empyrion," Lucifer explained. "They have been stripped of their wings and the ability to leave, but maintain much of their strength and immortality."

"What did they do that stripped them of their wings?"

"Fornicated, and some even procreated with humans."

Drucilla stepped back and stared wide-eyed at Lucifer. "All of them?"

"Yes, all of the Grigori."

Drucilla nodded in acknowledgment. "How many Grigori are there?" Drucilla turned her attention to the Grigori outside.

"Not many. They are scattered around Earth. There are around one hundred left, possibly less."

"You said they watch us because that's what you require them to do. What does that mean?"

Lucifer stood silently for a moment before speaking again,

"I maintain relationships with some of the Grigori. They are in my employ. They provide surveillance by warning me of any impending threats, and in return, I provide them with adequate living arrangements."

"Okay, but why is he watching me?"

"He is not watching you," Lucifer said. "They are waiting for Dominic."

"Why?"

"I suppose they want to see the Nephilim. They are dubious to his presence, possibly even resentful."

"Dubious of his presence? Are there no other Nephilim?"

"Not anymore. Not that we know, anyway. Except for…"

"Do they know I'm Thoth?" Drucilla cut Lucifer off.

"Yes."

"Then they shouldn't worry about Dominic."

"Again, Drucilla, they are autonomous. It matters not what I say. They will study his intentions, and if they find him to be non-threatening, they will most certainly leave him to his affairs."

"I don't like this," Drucilla stated.

"What would you have me do?" Lucifer asked.

Drucilla glanced at Lucifer. She turned in the direction of the gallery entrance and stormed her way to the door. She flung it open.

Dominic stood in the doorway, almost like he came out of nowhere. He noticed the aggravated look on Drucilla's face.

"You okay, Dru?"

Drucilla attempted to look around Dominic's massive physique. Dominic turned around and looked behind him before turning his attention back to Drucilla.

"What are you looking at?"

"Dom, did you see a tall, lanky guy with albinism when you came here?"

"Oh, that guy. Yeah, I see him all the time. He seems to be a fixture around here lately. I've seen him nearly every day for the past week. Do you know him?"

Drucilla glanced at Lucifer, but Lucifer was already gone.

CANTICLE THIRTY-FIVE

"You're shooting stars. From the barrel of your eyes. It drives me crazy." —Deftones

Dominic sat in his library with his chin on the table, staring at the bracelet from his mom's ossuary. He reached over and tapped the thick, weighty silver cuff with his index finger.

Drucilla stared at Dominic. She looked him over as if she was seeing him for the first time. His enormous physique that kept growing, his higher intelligence that allowed him to understand multiple languages, and how he could wield Erato Falx like he'd been using it his whole life. She was looking at pieces that fit perfectly. She had just never put them together before.

"What?" Dominic asked, taking notice of her intense stare.

"Uh, nothing," she responded. His words snapped her out of her fixation. "You were asking if I knew what period this came from? Other than the possible face of Jupiter embellished on the front, I honestly have no idea. Clearly, it's Roman, but I haven't seen anything like it. Romans didn't start using silver until 220 BCE. This appears to be much older. I'm sorry I can't be of any more help."

Dominic groaned as he stood up. He walked over to his bookshelf and stared.

"You know what's messed up? I have something about everything, but I can't even tell you about a piece of jewelry my mother owned. I sent dad a picture, and he said he had never seen it before. I don't know anyone on my mother's side, alive or dead. She doesn't even have family in Santa Maria. It's like she didn't exist."

Drucilla stood next to Dominic, crossed her arms, and looked at him empathetically. "Well, I don't think it's stupid. Why else would a demon fight you so hard for it?" She leaned her head against the bookshelf and looked up at one of his hideously grotesque catholic art paintings. "These things are really ugly."

Dominic snorted and grinned.

"Do you think we should try to find out if your mother had friends in Santa Maria? I mean, there has to be someone."

Dominic looked at Drucilla curiously.

"Maybe Lucifer—" Drucilla started, then stopped.

"Of course! He has to know about this. I didn't think about that!" Dominic looked up at the ceiling and shouted, "LUCIFER!"

"We could figure this out ourselves. What's wrong with research? You love research, right? We don't need to get Lucifer involved."

"LUCIFER!" Dominic shouted again.

"Really, we don't!" Drucilla bit the inside of her lip.

"I heard you the first time," Lucifer said. He appeared in a chair at the dining room table, examining his claws.

Without hesitation, Dominic asked, "What do you know about that cuff?" He pointed to the jewelry sitting on the table.

Lucifer looked at Drucilla. Drucilla shook her head as if to tell Lucifer not to divulge anything. He then glanced down at the cuff on the table and back to Dominic's face. "That cuff belonged to Minerva, Jupiter's daughter."

Dominic and Drucilla looked at each other.

"What? Minerva, the Roman goddess of war?" Dominic asked.

"No. Minerva is a Seraph. Well, she was a Seraph," Lucifer said. He attempted to correct himself and use the right tense.

"Why was it hidden underneath my mom's ossuary, and who put it there?"

"Presumably so no one would find it. However, you managed…"

"Where did it come from? Don't be cagey with me. You know what I'm asking you."

"Dominic, maybe we should let this go and find out for ourselves," Drucilla begged.

"Dru, what is up with you? You've been acting really weird since I came back."

"No, I haven't!"

"Yes, you have. You've been treating me with this sort of unusual kindness that's super out of the ordinary for you and looking at me like I'm a defenseless puppy. You haven't made a single sarcastic comment at my expense, not one!"

"Well fuck you sideways, Dominic!" Drucilla said, overcompensating.

"She's been attempting to delay the inevitable," Azrael said. He emerged towards the table. "Drucilla, Dominic, …Beast." Azrael nodded in greeting everyone.

"There is no need for you to be here, Tobit. Carry on," Lucifer said.

"I cannot," Azrael said.

"You can and you will," Lucifer said. His eyes flickered with orange light.

"What are you guys talking about?" Dominic asked.

Azrael looked at Lucifer and Drucilla in confusion. "He doesn't know?"

Drucilla shook her head aggressively. Lucifer looked up at Azrael under his brow.

"Dominic. Place the cuff on your wrist," Azrael ordered.

"Why?"

"So, we may all know for certain."

Dominic glanced at everyone and picked up the cuff. He examined it momentarily and contemplated whether it would fit him. He slid his wrist through, and to his surprise, the cuff fit his massive wrist perfectly. He turned his wrist from side to side, admiring the heavy piece of jewelry.

Azrael pulled a heavy scythe from behind his back. He wielded it high above his head and looked down at Dominic. Dominic looked up at him just a second before Azrael brought the blade down. Dominic instinctively threw his arm up to block the blow. An enormous, transparent, bright blue ethereal shield expanded outward from his wrist, blocking the blow with a massive *Klang*. Azrael lowered his scythe.

"Holy—!" Drucilla cried out.

Lucifer stood up and got between Azrael and Dominic. "We saw what we needed to see. Thank you for that demonstration."

Dominic looked at the glowing ethereal shield in shock and disbelief.

"Only the Divine can activate the shield," Azrael stated.

"What are you saying?" Dominic looked to Lucifer and Azrael for answers.

"What he's saying is that the cuff was your mother's. Your mother was Minerva," Drucilla stated.

Lucifer nodded slowly.

"Wait, does that mean that I'm...?" Dominic looked around the room.

Drucilla looked at Azrael and shook her head.

"I'm a Nephilim." Dominic studied the shield on his wrist.

"You are," Lucifer confirmed. "That is precisely why Azrael is here. Word must have reached critical mass between the Spheres."

Drucilla's body began to heat up. Bright blue branches began to glow through her skin, expanding across her face as her eyes became bright beams of light. She stared down Azrael as if to tell him that he would need to go through her to get to him.

"Drucilla," Azrael stressed, "I must."

Drucilla's four wings burst outward from her back as books and random objects went flying across the room from the force of her wings expanding. The eyes on the ridges of her wings blinked randomly.

"I'm making the decision here. I outrank you! You will not touch him!" she screamed.

"You do not, host," Azrael stated, his black, cavernous eye sockets glowed with an eerie purple radiance as his black wings slid outward. "Nephilim cannot suffer to live."

Lucifer stood near Dominic. "I cannot put them into a deep slumber like Azrael, but I can take you out of the equation." Lucifer grabbed Dominic's wrist and blinked out.

"Drucilla, do you not understand who I am? My station?"

"I know exactly who you are! But he's my friend, Azrael!"

"Divine law is immutable!"

"I don't give a shit about any fucking law! You will not touch him!"

Azrael sighed and lowered his scythe. Drucilla's eyes began to dim, and her wings relaxed. She looked around the room only just realizing that Lucifer had taken Dominic.

"You do not understand," Azrael started, "if I refuse to kill him, another Cataclysm will. It doesn't end with me. Either I, a friend, do this, or he will face an enemy who doesn't know him. And doesn't know you."

Azrael stowed his scythe again. Drucilla opened her mouth to protest but stopped when Azrael raised a hand.

"The Divine, The Unholy, and The Cataclysms now

know of his existence. By law, he cannot be allowed to live. It's not a choice any of us can make."

"Why?! He's never hurt anyone. He wouldn't even be involved if it wasn't for me. Why kill him?" Drucilla shook her head in disbelief.

"Nephilim are not allowed to exist in this universe. They are dangerous."

Azrael looked to Drucilla, somehow showing a slight hint of pain in his otherwise void-sent eyes. "They were all decried to die by the Thrones, led by the one that now resides in you."

Drucilla paused trying to collect her flood of thoughts. She squeezed her eyes shut for a moment to slow herself down and refocus. She looked back up at Azrael.

"Did you really not know? I mean, about Dominic?"

"I knew since I first saw him. But Nephilim haven't existed in eons, and Dominic posed no threat. As long as his lineage remained secret, I bent the rule of my station to help keep it that way."

Azrael turned his face away, looking to where Dominic was seated earlier.

"I took a risk and believed it to be the right call. But now he is known, and his life will be forfeited. It won't be long before word is sought of his demise. And if none comes, my fellow Cataclysms will seek to remedy that."

"Is that why the Grigori are interested in him?" Drucilla probed.

"They are most likely resentful. Dominic lives while

their offspring do not.”

Drucilla pondered for a moment before speaking again.

“When I was a kid. I lived in Los Angeles. After Drake left, I was in a bad place emotionally. I didn’t know who or what I was. I only knew I had this weird ability. I thought I was a witch. Of course, this all stemmed from my rosary. But one time, when I was alone, two of those Grigori attacked me, a man and a woman. They also had colorless skin with red eyes. I think they were named Armaros and Gadreel. They spoke Latin to each other. They said I wasn’t Divine and something about angel’s blood. They knew about my rosary; they tried to get it from me. I managed to summon the dead in a cemetery, and the corpses pulled them down into the ground. I don’t know who helped me that night. Someone told me to break a bead and summon the dead. I am pretty sure it was Lucifer even though he refuses to confirm it.” Drucilla pondered that last sentence. “Come to think of it, you didn’t show up.”

“I recall the incident.” Azrael nodded. “I did arrive afterward, but I never intended to reveal myself to you.”

“I suppose that makes sense.” Drucilla shrugged. “Since the Grigori live among us, are there more Nephilim that we don’t know about yet?” Drucilla asked.

“As far as I know, Dominic is the only one.”

“But we didn’t tell anyone; we just found out ourselves.”

“That’s not how the universe works. You fail to understand that everything is connected by a network of here and now, tomorrow and yesterday.”

"What are you talking about?"

"Time moves differently in different realms. The best way that I can explain it would be two days here, is two years in the Celestial Empyrion, and two years in the Infernal Sphere. Save for Malakut. Malakut has no concept of time, and it does not exist in those realms. The point is that the infernals know and have known since the demon was expelled back to Hell. All celestial beings know.

"Wow, I didn't know it worked like that," Drucilla whispered. "Is there a way to save Dominic?"

"Maybe," Azrael speculated.

"Tell me?"

"Only a Throne could save him."

"What about me? Could I do it?"

"No...I..."

Azrael peered at Drucilla in contemplation.

"I honestly don't know."

The WAGES of SIN is DEATH. Rom VI. 23.
Man that is born of a Woman, is of
few days, and full of trouble.
He cometh forth like a flower, and is
cut down: he fleeth also as a shadow, and
continueth not. Job XIV. 1, 2.
All flesh is as grass, and all the glory
of Man, as the flower of grass. I Peter I. 24
They spend their days in wealth, and
in a moment go down to the grave. Job XXI. 13
This their way is their folly.
When he dieth, he shall carry nothing away,
his glory shall not descend after him. Psa XLIX.
Verily every Man at his best state
is altogether vanity. Psalm XXXIX. 5.
The lofty looks of Man shall be humbled. Isai II.
It is appointed unto Men once to die, but
after this the Judgment. Heb IX. 27.

Here in the rich, the honourable, famed and great,
See the false scale of happiness complete. Pope
HERE LIES THE GREAT. False Marble! Where?
Nothing but poor and sordid Dust lies Here. Cowley
REMEMBER DEATH

CANTICLE THIRTY-SIX

"My only weakness is a list of crimes. My only weakness is, well, never mind." —The Smiths

Dominic looked around the expansive gilded room. The room featured Renaissance artworks on mahogany walls, Persian rugs, and tall, burgundy Queen Anne chairs that were situated around a large inglenook fireplace with highly detailed carvings of gargoyle faces. The room had the distinct scent of polishing oil and firewood. Everything in the room was opulent and refined. Dominic felt like he was in a time capsule from 1900. It was clear that this home was built for a wealthy magnate.

"Is this your new place? I mean, Drake's old place?" Dominic asked.

"Do you like it?" Lucifer answered with his own question. Lucifer stood in front of a small table near the fireplace and poured himself a drink.

"It's incredible."

"Yes, this mansion is the former residence of Drake Blackwood. It is technically Drucilla's home now as per the terms of his Will. Alas, she appears to have no interest in this place. I will remain here until she decides what she will do with it. The ample closet space is more than enough for my habit of collecting fine suits. Perhaps I will purchase it from her one day. Sadly, it does not hold a candle to my former place in Hell, but it will do." Lucifer smiled at Dominic and motioned to his glass to offer him a drink.

Dominic nodded. "Yeah, please." He was clearly nervous.

Lucifer poured whiskey into a carved crystal highball glass and handed it to Dominic. "Have no fear; this place is impenetrable to Divine and Unholy without my expressed permission. Please, sit down." Lucifer motioned to the chairs in front of the fireplace.

Dominic took the glass and sat down. Lucifer sat in front of him in the opposite chair and propped his feet up on the matching footstool. He straightened the cuffs on his suit and leaned back. Lucifer glanced at the fireplace and the logs contained within. The logs abruptly burst into flames.

"I want to tell you a story," Lucifer began.

"Uh, okay." Dominic's eyes shifted around uncomfortably.

"It was many years ago. Back before you were born, well, rather before Drucilla and Drake were born, I met a beautiful young woman. She had long, curly chestnut hair and the most beautiful bright blue eyes. She sat in one of the last rows of the Sistine Chapel one warm summer's day. She was sad, confused, and felt she had nowhere else to turn. She told me that she came here to talk to God in hopes of finding an answer. She had devoted her life to her profession, which she loved dearly. However, what she really wanted was children. Her conundrum was that she felt she had to choose between the two, which she had no intention of doing.

Without a partner and the inability to hold lasting relationships due to her constant traveling, she felt defeated. I explained to her that although the bible clearly states that physical relations before marriage is a sin, pregnancy out of wedlock is not a sin since children are a blessing. There is no distinction between a human life born in marriage or a human life born out of wedlock. Sort of a loophole, if you will."

"I've heard this story. This is about Fiona, isn't it? Wait, you were that angel?" Dominic's eyes shifted as the pieces clicked in his head. "You aren't going to tell me that you're actually their father, are you?"

"No! Of course not! Their donor is a gentleman named Fazel Atef. He is a proctologist or something, I do not know, that is not important. Regardless, it is important that you understand what I am about to tell you," Lucifer said, cutting Dominic off.

Dominic leaned forward and interlaced his fingers. Lucifer got up and stood in front of the fireplace, staring into the fire as the flames danced upon the logs.

"I was responsible. I was the one that pushed Fiona into artificially conceiving these children."

Dominic looked concerned. "Why would you do that?"

"I am so glad you asked," Lucifer said. He slowly walked to a heavy mahogany desk and leaned against it, crossing his ankles. He took a sip of his whisky and sat it down next to him.

"Every protégé I have had was a complete and miserable failure. Every single one of them. They either did not have the heart to perform the tasks or lacked intelligence. Never have I had one that could do both to my standards. With my influence, I was able to craft a being that was worthy of becoming my apprentice. Someone who would be my reflection, my human equivalent."

"What are you saying?"

"I think I've made myself clear. Drake and Drucilla were manipulated by Unholy influence. My influence."

Dominic sat in silence, processing what Lucifer had explained. "I don't understand how Drucilla was affected. Why didn't she turn out like Drake?"

"When Drake became of age, I offered him a deal in exchange for my coin that he found. When Drucilla came of age, she came upon the Queen's vestige. Both relics provided different paths. You see, they represent both sides of me. Drake reflects my Unholy side, while Drucilla represents my Divine side. Both are equal, but opposite sides. Drucilla is intelligent and cunning in her own way. She has been able to successfully outmaneuver me on multiple occasions. Including, but not limited to, becoming who she is now. I did not account for her taking in Divine blood. That was her free will."

Dominic leaned forward. "Why would you give Drucilla the rosary of all relics?"

Lucifer stared at Dominic for a moment. "Drucilla is a tiny thing. If done correctly, controlling an army of the dead would grant her the strength, confidence, and security she would need in the future. The rosary was the only relic that offered such incredible power."

Dominic appeared uneasy. He wasn't sure what to make of everything that he heard.

"However, at this moment, we must decide what we are going to do with you, don't we?" Lucifer said, changing the subject. "You are Nephilim. That is a fact, and it is out there in the universe. I will not end your life. I like you, Dominic. You have become an asset, and Drucilla loves you deeply. I would never take you from her. Since Drake has transitioned, Drucilla has become my sole purpose, and you are a large part of her life. If Azrael does not eradicate you, understand there are three more cataclysms that will. I assume Mot will come for you next."

"Mot?" Dominic inquired.

"Samael would not trouble himself with a minor issue like one Nephilim, Abaddon, well she only responds to plagues and disregards everything else. Mot would see your existence as a slight against the Thrones and will adhere to the ancient order."

"Well, I can't just hide here forever. I assume you have a plan for this too?" Dominic asked.

Lucifer paced the room. He stopped in front of the window and looked out onto the expansive vineyard that had gone dormant for the year. "What do you know of the Nephilim?"

"Pretty much everything that's been written," Dominic responded confidently. "My knowledge in celestial lore is pretty decent if I do say so myself."

Lucifer nodded slowly. He sat back down in the chair opposite Dominic and crossed his arms. "Dominic, I would like to offer you a deal."

"You want to offer me a Celestial Deal?" Dominic's eyes blinked rapidly in disbelief.

"I can save your life. If you accept my offer, I can prevent your demise."

"Will that work on me? I mean, I'm not supposed to exist."

"You are half-human, are you not?

"Well yeah."

"I do not see an issue."

Dominic stood up and paced the room. He was unsure whether this was a good idea, but given his limited options, which were currently none, he decided he should at least hear what Lucifer had to offer.

"Okay, how would this work?"

Lucifer smiled brightly. "Dominic, I offer you one hundred years of human life. The cataclysms will not be able to remove you until one hundred years are complete."

"In exchange for what?"

"I need an assistant. Since the demise of Belphegor and Asmodeus, I have no one to carry out my mundane tasks."

"What does that even look like?" Dominic asked, wrinkling his forehead.

"The matter of collecting owed debts. Those kinds of tasks."

"You're asking me to be your hitman?"

"You have a gift. You are infinitely powerful and a skilled fighter. It would be a tragedy to let that go to waste."

"I don't know about this, Lucifer."

"Your only other option is to live out your days here, in this house."

Dominic felt uneasy. He didn't want this, but it may be his only choice. "I need time to think about this. Can you grant me a couple of days? Is that something you can do?"

"Yes, of course. It is done. I will see you three days from now, at five o'clock, for your answer. I will make sure the Cataclysms know of your pending deal. You are free to return."

"Deal," Dominic said. He stood in front of Drucilla and Azrael. They looked surprised at Dominic's sudden appearance. Dominic quickly looked around the room. He realized he was back home, standing in his library.

Drucilla's eyes widened at the word deal that came out of Dominic's mouth the second he reappeared.

"You didn't!" she yelled.

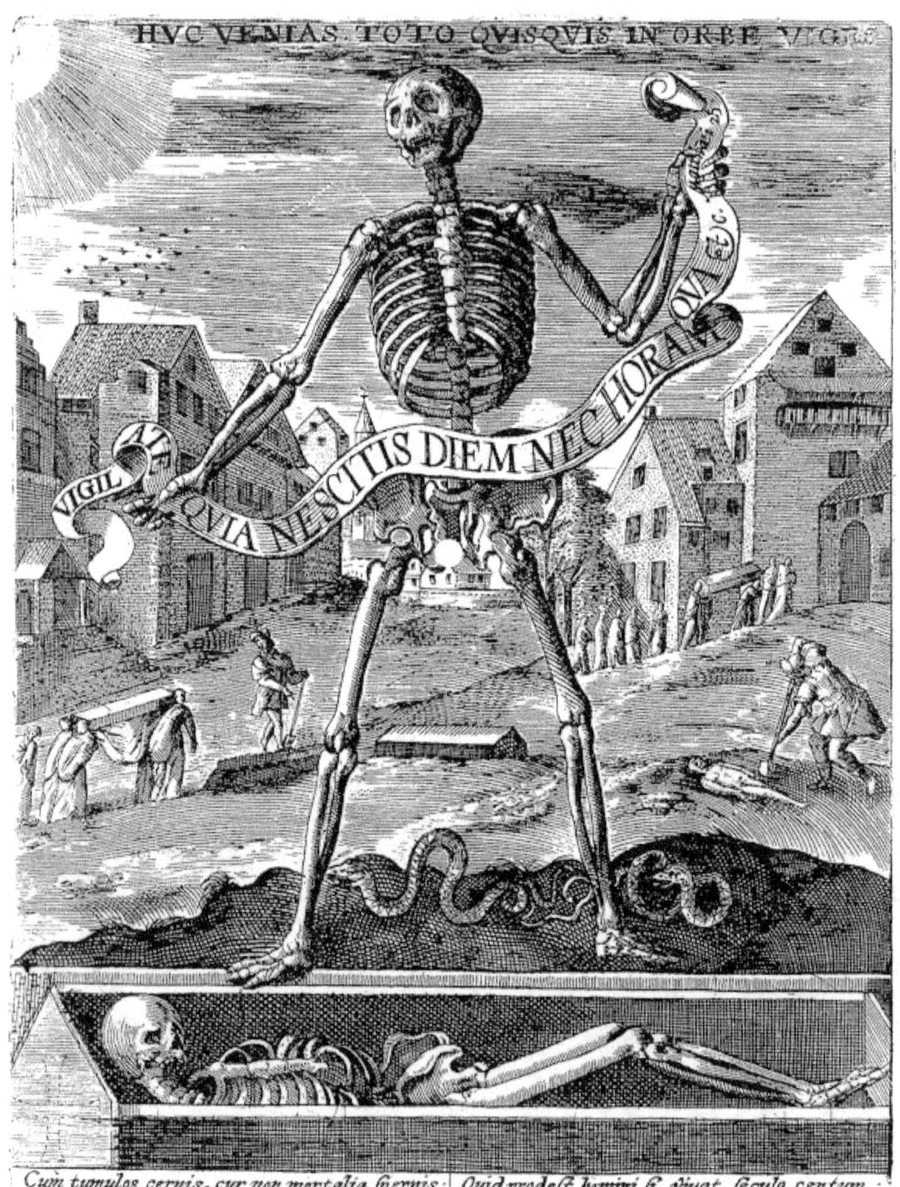

Cum tumulos cernis, cur non mortalia spernis;
Communis mors est, quod cunctis debita sore est.
Quid prodest homini si vivat secula centum;
Cum moritur, vitam transisse putat quasi ventum.

CANTICLE THIRTY-SEVEN

*"I see you slither away with your skin, tail, flickering tongue,
and rattling scales."*—The Church

Drucilla and Dominic sat across from each other in Siren's pub, drinking craft beer from bottles. Dominic relayed the information that Lucifer had given Dominic about Drucilla and Drakes' arrival into this world. Drucilla sat quietly and remained calm.

"I'm sorry I didn't tell you sooner. I had been dealing with… you know."

"I get it," Drucilla acquiesced.

"You don't seem nearly as upset as I thought you would be."

"You know, I think it's because I already knew that. My mother had told us the story of how we came to be a few times. The last time we talked about it was after Drake disappeared. It was the first time I asked her to describe the angel. Of course, it sounded nothing like Lucifer but then again, with the facades and stuff, who knows? The whole thing was just too weird and too random for it not to be Lucifer." Drucilla took a sip of beer and set it down in front of her. "Did he say how he did it?"

"No. But your donor is, in fact, your donor. He was adamant about that. I guess he's a proctologist?"

Drucilla giggled to herself and shook her head. "Figures he'd say that. No Fazel is a pediatrician. Well, he was. I think he's retired by now. He's gotta be like seventy years old. I know my mom used to keep him up to speed with our lives."

"I haven't seen my dad since my birthday. But hey, Aleksei, quit drinking. Seeing Azrael really messed him up," he grinned.

"I miss the days when these were bizarre supernatural stories and not real life. Granted, that was all before I was eighteen, but I remember the blissful ignorance of it all."

Dominic nodded in agreement.

Drucilla leaned back and crossed her arms. "It's been three days. Do you know what you're going to tell him?"

Dominic set his bottle on the table, looked at his hand, and fidgeted with an antique Russian prayer ring on his middle finger. "I don't think I have any other choice. I can't leave my dad, Baba, and Aleksei."

"How much time do we have left?" Drucilla asked.

"He's going to want his answer within the hour."

The waitress showed up with their bank cards and receipts. They signed their slips of paper and went back to their conversation.

"Gimmie your hands," Drucilla commanded.

Dominic looked at Drucilla confused and slowly slid his hands over to her across the table. She grabbed each hand and looked into Dominic's eyes. The room began to quickly melt around them from the ceiling down to the floor. Dominic stared in shock at the room seeming to disappear, and another room reappeared underneath. To his surprise, Dominic was sitting in his library at his dining room table. Drucilla looked around and smiled.

"You've been practicing!" Dominic exclaimed.

"Yeah, I have," Drucilla said as she beamed with pride.

"That's really great, Dru. I, uh, I like the melting effect. That's kinda cool."

Drucilla got up and stood behind the chair. She leaned over it and clasped her hands.

"Dom, do you remember when we discussed Celestial Deals, and you told me that one deal can overwrite another?"

"Yeah, what about it?"

"If you take Lucifer's deal, what's to stop you from making another one?" Drucilla asked.

"I can't initiate deals. He has to initiate them."

"If you're half Seraph. Why can't you make your own deal?"

"I'm a product of a Seraph and a human. Not a Seraph; that's a title. I'm a half angel."

"That is correct," Lucifer said. He entered Dominic's library. "Being a product of a Divine and a human does not grant you the abilities of the Divine. You essentially have some of their physical attributes, such as superior strength, dexterity, and agility. The Nephilim are stronger than Seraphs but lack immortality."

Dominic stood up and looked at Lucifer. Lucifer leaned against the doorway of the library. The room was tense with anxiety and unknowns.

An abrupt, heavy thump was heard from the roof of Dominic's house. The sound traveled like heavy footsteps across one side of the roof and then another heavy thump as it hit the ground below. Dominic and Drucilla watched the ceiling as the sound moved downward.

"Is that him?" Dominic asked, looking at Lucifer.

"Unquestionably," Lucifer answered.

Dominic walked out of the library, opened the backdoor, and headed down the steps to his newly landscaped backyard. Drucilla and Lucifer followed behind him. In the dim light of the evening sky, a hooded figure loomed in the middle of the yard. He was tall, like Azrael, and held a long, sliver scythe over his shoulder.

"Mot," Lucifer said.

"Lucifer. How are you faring?" Mot asked. His voice was deep and powerful.

"I do not think we will be in need of your services tonight," Lucifer said.

"Has there been a deal?" Mot asked.

"I believe we are coming close."

"You have but a few moments to close your agreement," Mot explained.

Drucilla felt the familiar coldness and distinct scent of wet Earth behind her. She smiled slowly; she knew that Azrael was there. She slowly turned and looked over her shoulder. Azrael turned his head down to meet her gaze and nodded. She turned her attention back to Mot.

Dominic looked at Drucilla peculiarly and then at Azrael.

"Why is Azrael here?" he whispered to Drucilla.

Drucilla just smiled to herself. The short musical chime from the church bell was heard in the distance, followed by the first gong ringing out.

"Five o'clock," Dominic whispered.

"Dominic, do we have a deal?" Lucifer asked.

Mot stood silently and stared at Dominic. Dominic's eyes shifted back and forth. He knew it was now or death.

The second gong reverberated throughout the town. It curiously seemed louder.

Lucifer exhaled deeply and turned to Dominic. "Take the deal. You won't get another."

Dominic desperately searched his mind for a way out, but as the last three days had proved, he had no other recourse.

The third gong reverberated; it was, in fact, louder than the two previous gongs.

"I—," Dominic started.

Drucilla darted in between Mot, Lucifer, and Dominic. She turned to Dominic. "Dominic! I offer you a deal!"

"What?" Dominic and Lucifer said in unison.

The fourth gong reverberated louder.

"I offer you immortality, invulnerability, and impenetrability from any weapon, curse, or spell from either mortal, Unholy, or Divine in exchange for one strawberry cupcake," Drucilla shouted as fast as she could.

"I accept!" Dominic blurted out without even thinking.

The fifth gong rang loudest. With the final sound, the atmosphere turned still.

Lucifer's face fell into a mixture of confusion and calculation. His eyes darted around as he turned his head from side to side, trying to sort out the offer and its validity.

Mot began laughing. His laugh, deep and bellowing, made the ground tremble.

"What's so funny?" Drucilla asked with a level of annoyance in her tone.

"You cannot possibly think you can offer him any of that, do you?" Mot mocked.

"Why not?" Drucilla asked.

Lucifer's eyes shifted back and forth in contemplation. *Could she?*

"Child. I know who you are. But perhaps you were not aware of the Celestial Bargain made among the Thrones at the beginning of time," Mot said.

Drucilla moved closer to Mot. She was so small that she barely stood past his waistline. She leaned her head back to look at his face. Unlike Azrael, Mot had eyes. His irises radiated a subtle purple glow.

"Oh, you mean the deal that they made that in order to keep the universe in balance: they wouldn't offer each other invulnerably. Just in case one of 'em decided to go nuts and start committing mass genocide in the universe. That deal?"

Mot peered at her suspiciously. "Yes, that is the deal in which I speak."

"Yeah, so let me explain something to you. Thoth died. According to Celestial Law, the deal is done once you die, right? Am I right?" Drucilla looked around at everyone for confirmation. No one spoke in disagreement. "That holds true for all Divine and Unholy regardless of rank, correct? So, now that he's been reborn inside of me and we work together in a symbiotic relationship, I speak for us. We are Thoth." Drucilla stared into Mot's eyes as her four wings burst outward from her back. She levitated upwards as she slowly flapped her wings effortlessly back and forth to meet Mot's face. She put her finger up and pointed to his eyes. "I did not make that deal with anyone. I am not part of that pact."

Mot's eyes radiated in anger.

"Drucilla is correct. I am here to confirm that according to Raziel, the arbiter of Celestial Law, Drucilla's deal is valid," Azrael said.

"Dru, you planned this?" Dominic asked, stunned.

Drucilla lowered herself and collapsed her wings. She looked at Dominic and nodded.

Lucifer burst into laughter. He put his hands in his face and laughed harder than anyone had heard him laugh before.

"This is deception! Azrael, you cannot confirm this barter! You are prohibited from involving yourself in Earthly matters apart from death. How can you possibly discern the restrictions and allocations of a Celestial Deal?" Mot shouted. "I will not allow this mockery of our Divine creator's wishes!"

Furiously, Mot brought his scythe up over his head and brought it down upon Dominic. Dominic reflexively covered his head with his arms. The ethereal shield burst from his bracelet as the scythe hit Dominic's arm. The scythe shattered upon impact as if it were made of thin glass.

Everyone fell silent as they watched the shattered shards of Mot's scythe fall to the floor like dry leaves. Dominic quickly inspected his arms for damage, but there was none. Mot slowly looked at the partial scythe that he still held in his hands before turning his gaze back to Dominic as a new scythe materialized from the remnants of the old.

Mot pointed his scythe at Dominic. "AFFLICTION!"

Everyone stood around silently. Dominic looked at Drucilla and Lucifer. "What's supposed to be happening?"

"I believe he is trying to infect you with a disease," Lucifer said, studying Mot.

Mot's demeanor turned to frustration and ire. "SENESCENT!" he shouted.

"Now he's trying to age you rapidly," Lucifer crossed his arms, amused at the demonstration.

Drucilla looked at Mot. "Well, well, it looks like I can, and I did. I think we're done here."

Clearly frustrated with his lack of power over Dominic. Mot lowered his scythe, raised his other arm, and pointed at Drucilla. "YOU and you alone have created an abomination and brought forth your demise," Mot warned. He vanished in a blink.

Drucilla looked back at Dominic. "Where's my cupcake?"

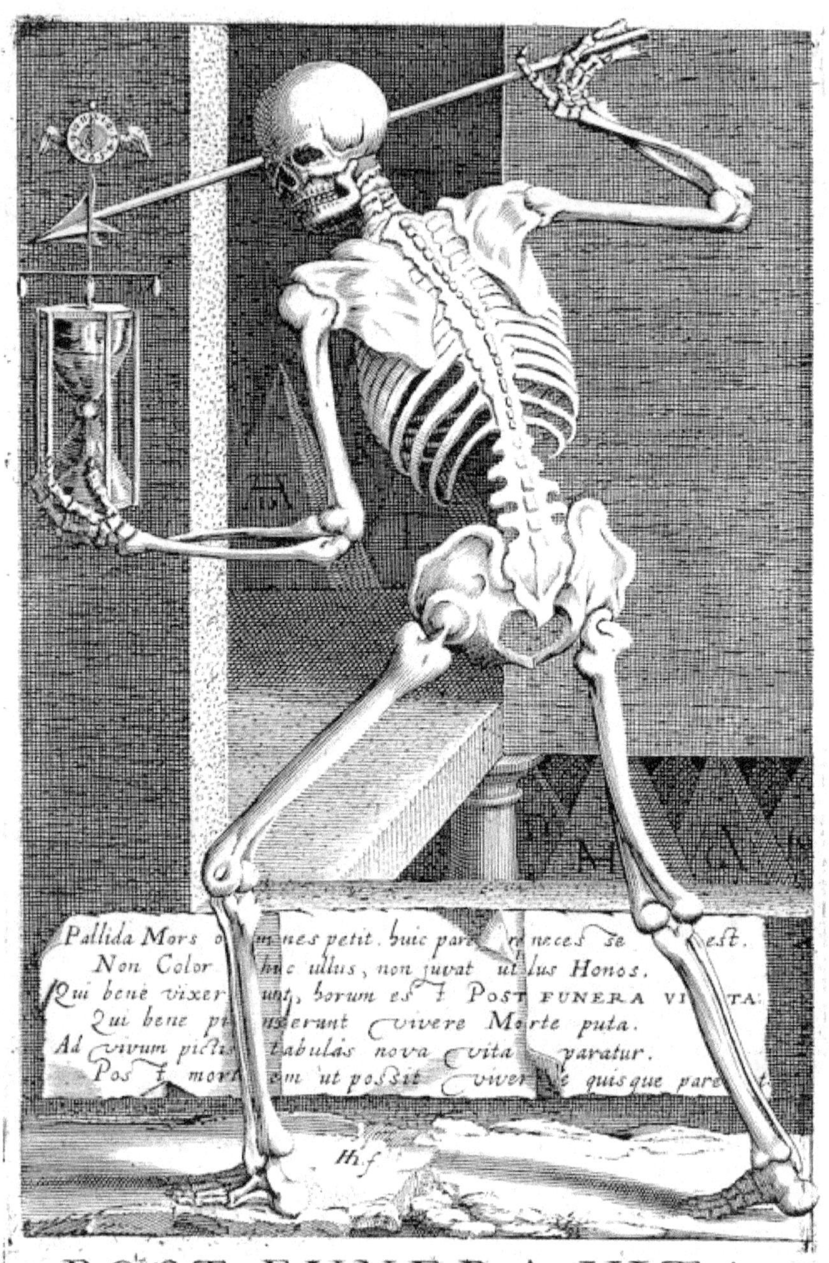

POST FUNERA, VITA.

CANTICLE THIRTY-EIGHT

"Stark screaming curses on the card deck."
—Tamaryn

Drucilla sat quietly at the breakfast bar in her kitchen. She held the bright pink cupcake with a mound of frosting over the top in her petite hand. With the other hand, she slowly tore away the wrapper exposing the soft, spongy, pale pink cake. She ran her fingertip through the frosting and placed her finger in her mouth. A few days had passed since the deal was struck, and she was finally enjoying her prize. Dominic and Adrian leaned against the opposite kitchen counter, watching Drucilla slowly pick apart the cupcake, nibbling and examining it as if to take in every sprinkle, every wave of frosting. It was almost uncomfortably sexual. Diablo sat on the table, hoping for a bite.

"What's uh, what's the deal with the cupcakes?" Dominic asked Adrian.

Adrian shrugged. "She's always had this weird, almost emotional connection to them."

"So, this is normal?"

"More or less."

Drucilla looked up at Adrian and Dominic and smiled.

Adrian turned to Dominic. "So, tell me, how does this whole immortality thing work for you? Aren't you already immortal because you're a Nephilim?"

"Nephilim aren't immortal per se. They do die but after a significant amount of time. About five times more than a human. I've read that Nephilim live anywhere from 500 years to a thousand depending on which book you consult, but to err on the side of caution, I'm going with the lower number."

"Safe," Adrian acknowledged.

"The deal that Drucilla offered goes beyond life. I am unable to be harmed by any object, regardless of which realm it derives from. I'm immune from sickness, curses, and spells. I'm not even sure I age anymore. However, I have noticed a few strange side effects."

"Like what?"

Dominic glanced at Drucilla, who was still deeply involved in her cupcake, and then back to Adrian. He walked out to the living room to move out of her field of view. He pulled his shirt over his head. He held his large, heavily tattooed arms up to Adrian. "My tattoos. They're fading. I imagine they'll be gone by the end of the week."

Adrian grabbed Dominic's wrist and studied the babushka nesting doll on the inside of his forearm. The ink had significantly faded. Only light grey outlines were visible.

"You're healing," Adrian said.

Dominic put his shirt over his head and slid his hands through the sleeves. "My hands were covered in scars and callouses from years of bodybuilding and boxing. I haven't seen my hands look like this since I was fifteen. I have more energy and…." Dominic looked perplexed.

"And?" Adrian asked.

"…and I haven't slept in two days. It's as if I have no use for it. I'm never tired. I spend my evenings just reading. I have so much extra time I'm not sure what to do with it."

"That's peculiar."

"Does Dru still sleep?" Dominic asked.

"God, yes, she sleeps. You get her up before ten o'clock on a Saturday; you better have a damned good reason. She doesn't mess around."

"Even though she's Ophanim? Hmm, I guess she would. She's still human on the outside," Dominic said, answering his own question.

"Does Dru know what you're experiencing?"

"I haven't told her. I'm trying to wrap my head around it first." Dominic paced the living room in thought.

"Dominic, are you ok? I mean, with this?"

"Honestly? I'm not prepared. Dru is supposed to be immortal. Not me."

"You sound almost resentful," Adrian observed.

"I understand Dru had her heart in the right place, but I can't help but question if I took the wrong deal," Dominic pondered. "I suppose I feel like she did this more for herself and less for me."

"I've known Dru since the sixth grade. She absolutely has a warped view of reality, but I can assure you she would do anything, including self-sacrifice, for the ones she loves. Even Drake," Adrian assured.

"I hope she learns how to use her abilities responsibly," Dominic lamented.

"Oh really? You don't think I'm responsible?" Drucilla said as she caught the tail end of the conversation. She stuck the edge of her thumb in her mouth and then brushed her hands together.

Adrian backed away from Dominic and glided out of the room. He didn't want to be a part of the conflict.

"Dru, I don't mean that you're totally irresponsible. But maybe you should've told me what you were planning. I didn't have a chance to make a choice. It was taken from me."

"You we're seriously considering Lucifer's deal, really? Tell me, Dominic, what do you think your life would have been like as his attack dog?" Drucilla refuted. "He's Lucifer. You wouldn't be able to refuse him. He could tell you to kill your own brother."

"You're being ridiculous."

"Tell me I'm wrong!"

"It wouldn't benefit him to have me do something like that," Dominic protested.

"The point is you have no idea what he would have asked of you. All I did was make you invulnerable."

"Dru! I shouldn't even be alive!" Dominic retorted.

"Neither should I!" Drucilla hollered.

Dominic and Drucilla stood staring each other down. Fuming, Drucilla broke eye contact, sat on the couch, and crossed her arms. She gave herself a few moments to compose herself.

"But here we are. And now we need to figure out how to navigate our existence," she mumbled.

Dominic leaned his head to the side. He blinked a few times, studying Drucilla. Drucilla slowly lifted her head to Dominic's gaze. "What?"

"Dru,"

"What?"

"Dru, you didn't detonate."

"Huh?"

"Ever since you've become an Ophanim, you explode when you get angry."

"So?"

"So? You're learning to control your anger," Dominic commended.

Drucilla blinked a few times, then turned her attention to the newly installed French floral patterned wallpaper. "Not like going all hellfire and brimstone on you would do anything anyway."

"But this is a new ability! Dru, you are controlling the entity."

Drucilla groaned.

"Dru, you're communicating with your emotions. He's not reacting to you because you don't feel threatened. You're actually getting a handle on this!"

"You mean I'm being responsible?"

"You're not going to let this go, are you?" Dominic asked.

Drucilla shrugged at Dominic.

"Okay, fine. I apologize that the comment came off that way. You're not irresponsible. I shouldn't have alluded to that. I understand your perspective. I honestly think you did what you did to protect me." Dominic exhaled and paced the floor for a moment. "Now that I'm thinking about it, I probably would have done the same thing in your position. I would have done whatever it took to protect you. However, I am not entirely sure I need invulnerability for myself."

"I accept that. In hindsight, I probably should have told you what I was planning, but honestly, I didn't know I was going to be able to pull it off until the moment that Azrael arrived."

Dominic looked surprised. "You mean it got down to the last few seconds?"

"Yeah, it was that close. He consulted the Arbiter of Celestial Law and got confirmation moments before he arrived."

"Wow," Dominic exhaled.

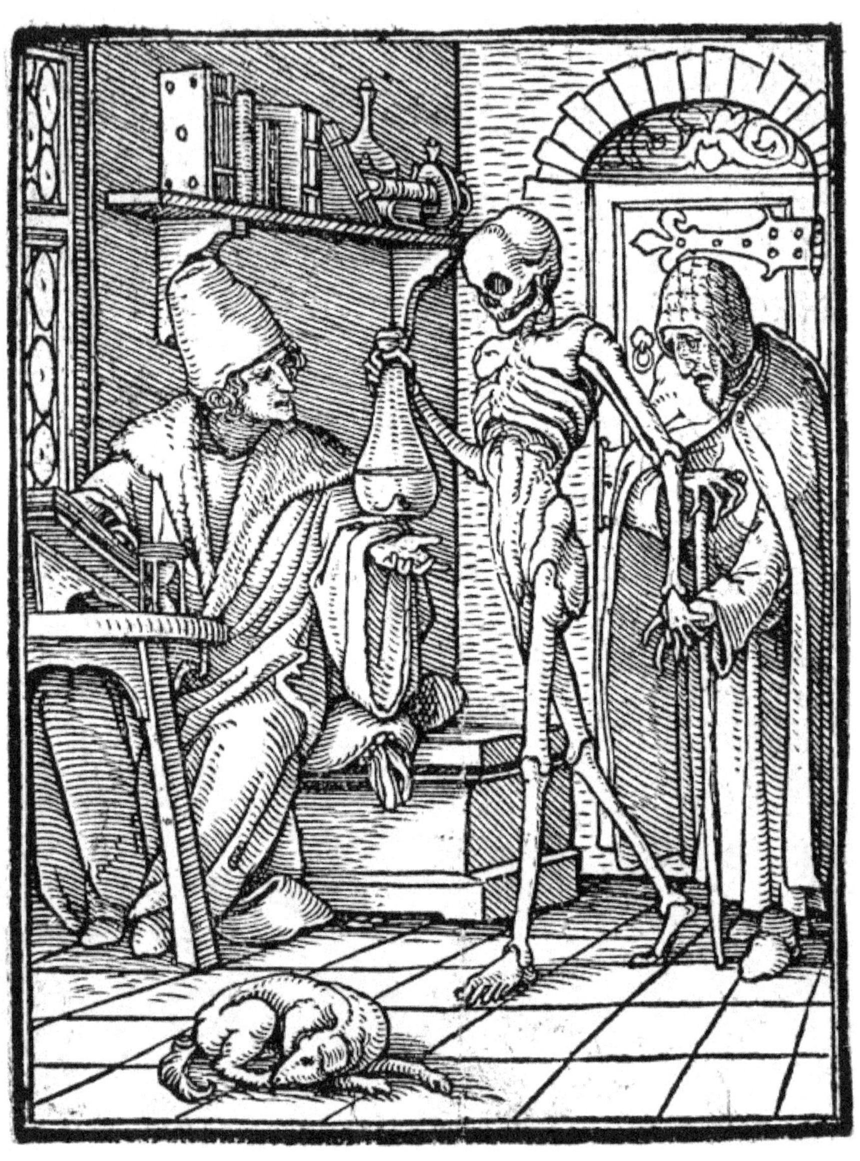

CANTICLE THIRTY-NINE

"I lost all my faith in what was right, no one is honest"
—The Revolution Smile

Dominic stood in the center of Ford Bradshaw & Co, debating on which crate to open first. He chose the one closest to the door. It seemed logical to get it out of the pathway. He shoved a three-foot pry bar under the lip of a large wooden crate. He barely pushed down on the unfinished wooden lid, and it gave way with a creak and a pop. The top abruptly flew to the ground next to Aleksei's foot.

Aleksei's eyes widened at the vulgar display of power Dominic had shown opening the crate. "Watch it, bro. You almost took out my shin," Aleksei protested.

"Oh, stop, it's a foot away from you," Dominic groaned as he pulled clumps of wood shavings from the box and placed it in a large, plastic receptacle.

Aleksei lifted an eyebrow at his brother's demeanor, he seemed off. Aleksei picked up the prybar and crammed it into the lip. He grunted and shoved as hard as he could to get the lid off the second crate. He wiped his forehead and looked at Dominic for help. Dominic grabbed the bar and barely pushed down as the lid popped. He moved away so Aleksei could finish taking it off. Aleksei grabbed the corners of the lid and placed it on the floor against the crate. He glanced curiously at Dominic.

"Ramping up pounds on the free weights? You've gotten bigger."

"No?" Dominic responded with an influx in his tone. He shook his head and went back to unpacking.

"Is something going on?" Aleksei speculated.

"Just want to get these crates dealt with before I open tomorrow."

Aleksei leaned against the crate. He studied Dominic's mannerisms. Dominic stopped what he was doing and put his hands on his hips.

"You wanna say something?" Dominic questioned.

"Yeah. Yeah, I do. You seem different. You seem to be lost in your head."

"I'm fine." Dominic went back to the crate. He pulled out a large, silver oval ornate mirror. He held it in his hands and examined the detailed floral scrolls around the edges.

"That would look delightful in Drucilla's home," Lucifer said. He quietly emerged from the back of the shop. Dominic glanced at Lucifer.

"My apologies; your front door was locked."

"That's because I'm not open on Tuesdays and Wednesdays," Dominic explained. "Aleksei, can you give us a minute?"

"Uh, I'm gonna grab lunch anyway. You want anything?"

"Sure, whatever you're getting is fine."

Aleksei looked at Lucifer and nodded in greeting as he slid past him. Dominic waited for the audible click of the back door closing before he turned his attention back to Lucifer. "What brings you by?"

"I suppose a sort of wellness check. How are you faring?"

Dominic shrugged and put the mirror down on the countertop. He went back to unpacking the large crate. He bent over and reached inside for the next object.

"I assume by now you are noticing a few effects to your invulnerability."

"My tattoo work has faded. There were areas on my head where my hair was receding; it started to grow back. Also, I haven't slept in a week. It's unnerving but nothing I can't handle."

Lucifer pulled himself up onto the countertop and crossed his legs. He placed his hands on his knee. "You have not asked about your mother. Is it because you do not want to know, or you are afraid to know?"

Dominic groaned and stood upright. He turned to face Lucifer. He threw his hands up and shrugged. "I dunno, you tell me, what am I feeling?"

Lucifer looked uneasy as his eyes darted around the room. He cleared his throat. Dominic's eyes narrowed at Lucifer's uneasiness. Lucifer avoided Dominic's gaze.

"Something wrong?" Dominic asked.

"Wrong? No, not wrong. More…unanticipated."

"Unanticipated?"

"I cannot read your thoughts anymore, Dominic. Your mind is…barricaded."

Dominic's eyebrows rose.

"Clearly, it is an effect of your invulnerability," Lucifer concluded.

"Oh." Dominic's face went blank. He didn't realize that Lucifer would be affected by the deal.

"You must tell me verbally," Lucifer conceded.

Dominic pulled himself up and sat on one of the unopened crates. He placed his hands on either side and leaned forward. "I have thought about asking you about Mona."

"Minerva," Lucifer corrected.

"Minerva, yeah, I need to get used to that. I wasn't sure how to approach the subject but I'm also not sure that I would understand the answer."

"Mmm, hmmm." Lucifer examined his claws for a moment as he thought, then put his hand down. "Minerva had gone by many names in the past. Athena, Anat, Neith, to name a few. She was a Seraph, and she belonged to the order of Virtues. I assume you know of Virtues."

"Uh, high Seraphs?"

"Correct. The high council of Seraphs. Many of your demi-gods are Virtues. Minerva was very competitive, combative, and jealous to a degree. I am certain you have heard of the many competitions she had with Neptune to name the city of Athens and Poseidon to decide which god the seaside towns would worship."

Dominic nodded.

Lucifer grinned. "The realms were different back then. Many angels were competitive. There was a celestial competition every millennium or so to determine which Seraph could gain the most followers. That was an amusing time. You know, she wielded your javelin for a while." Lucifer pointed to Dominic's pocket. "After we had taken our leave of the Celestial Empyrion, Minerva was one of Hell's most highly regarded generals. She was Countess Minerva in the Infernal Sphere. A prestigious title that Queen Aurora had bestowed upon her. She fought on our side for eons."

"She was Unholy?" Dominic asked.

"Not exactly. She was always a Virtue, but some Seraphs did cross realms when the occasion called for it. Hell was, and is, a fractured place. It has divided multiple times, and on occasion, there would be a need to call upon Divine Seraphs to help keep the peace, as it were. At one time, Minerva controlled forty infernal legions and, at other times, twenty Divine ones. The Hell you see now, as of the last three thousand years, is quite different than it was prior to that. We did not just descend to Hell and rule from day one. There were many battles and many conflicts, as any growing nation would experience here on Eothre. Switching sides was not uncommon."

"Where did the shield come from? One of those battles?" Dominic asked. "I've never seen it mentioned in any of my books."

"Ah yes, the shield. You see, when she left the Celestial Empyrion during one of those periods of peril, Jupiter gifted it to her. Many Seraphs have shields from Jupiter. He had been her mentor. Although Jupiter did not join us, he wanted to make certain that Minerva and the Seraphs had protection. The shields are created by none other than Vulcan himself. The shield not only offered impenetrability but also...." Lucifer stopped. A wild grin stretched across his face. "I think you should find that out for yourself. That is part of the fun. Is it not?"

Dominic pressed his lips together.

"But let us get to the burning question, how did Dominic come to be? That is what you want to know, am I correct?"

"Wait," Dominic halted. "Does my father know any of this?"

"No. Edik knows nothing of your mother's past. The human façade and cover are falsified to keep your mother's identity hidden from anyone outside of the Infernal Sphere that may want to harm her. She chose a country that did not keep birth records."

"Why did she want to leave? Heaven, I mean," Dominic questioned.

"Minerva had grown fond of, maybe even infatuated with human beings. She requested the queens release her of her status. She no longer wished to be a Seraph. She wanted to live among you. The queens denied her request. Minerva became withdrawn and refused to participate in her responsibilities. She stated if we did not help her, she would ask the Celestial Empyrion to release her. You must understand, only a Thone could release her. She pleaded her case to Min, the Throne of Spirit and was subsequently released with his blessing. You know what happened after that."

"She renounced her angelhood to be human?"

"I don't know what is so special about you humans and why anyone would want to be like you. You are kin to lunar moths. You emerge from your chrysalis, flutter around for a week, and then perish. Seems like a waste of existence, but perhaps that is why so many of us chose to live in Hell."

"Yeah, that seems like something you'd feel, Lucifer. It isn't about how long you live; it's about how you live and the relationships you cultivate. It's about love, happiness, friendship, unity, and working together to make the world a better place for all of us. Clearly, my mother understood that. Sadly, you don't," Dominic sneered.

"Love? Do you think I do not understand love? Child, I invented love."

"Maybe, but it's obviously never been reciprocated."

Lucifer's snake-like eyes flickered orange at the remark. He jumped down off the counter and approached Dominic at lightning speed. He stopped just inches from his face. "You think this newly granted invulnerability will allow you to protect the ones you love? Do not make that mistake. No human is immune to death. You can ask me for a new deal at any time, and believe me, you will. Eternity can become agonizingly lonely for an immortal." Lucifer's eyes beamed brightly and then died down to his usual serpentine irises.

Dominic's mouth curved into a half smile. "Okay, man."

Lucifer disappeared just before Aleksei opened the back door.

Dominic dropped his bravado the moment Lucifer left. He inhaled and exhaled deeply to quell his anxiety.

Aleksei looked at him strangely as he handed Dominic a sandwich wrapped in white butcher paper.

"Dom, you've been out of it today. Go home, bro. I can do this on my own."

"I'm fine."

"You're not fine, though," Aleksei argued.

"Damn it, Aleksei!" Dominic snapped.

"You on the 'riods?"

Dominic threw his hands in the air and stared at his brother. "When the Hell have you ever known me to take drugs?"

Aleksei put his hands up as he backed off, "All right, all right, *uspokaivat'*!"

Dominic took a moment to breathe. "*Chto by ni*. Lock the back door when you leave." Dominic picked up his jacket and walked out.

l'Etat de la Mort.
SOUVIENS
TOY
QUE TU
ES POUDRE
ET QUE TU
RETOURNERAS
EN POUDRE

CANTICLE FORTY

"I'll wait for you, set the world on fire and watch it burn."
—Cancerslug

Drucilla and Malphas had hung the final photograph of Herman Grivere's 'Textures in Nature' series on the gallery's main wall. The collage of framed prints created a modern and tantalizing pattern.

"You're really good at this, Malphas. You have a unique gift at seeing displays in your mind and producing them brilliantly."

Malphas looked up at the wall and sighed. "I cannot take credit for this. I recreated this display seventeen times in the last hour before I found the best assemblage."

Drucilla blinked a few times. "You reversed time over and over until you found the one you liked? So, is it like Groundhog Day while this goes on?"

"Beg pardon? A groundhog? There were no groundhogs."

"It's an, uh, human expression. It's from a movie. You know, living the same time over and over? Like someone is experiencing making a cup of coffee repeatedly in a loop that doesn't end?"

Malphas looked at Drucilla curiously.

"You know what? Never mind."

Malphas shrugged. He picked up his coat from behind the counter and put it on. "Are you going to be leaving soon?" he asked.

"I'll be leaving shortly."

Malphas picked up his laptop and tucked it under his arm.

"Thank you for your help, Malphas. I appreciate it."

Malphas nodded and exited the gallery. Drucilla locked the door behind him. She walked through the gallery and opened the large, double glass doors that led to the deck. She leaned over the railing and looked down to the ocean below. It was a mild and cool evening. One of the rare days when it wasn't raining. It was uncommon for this time of year.

"I was human once. Did you know? It was a long time ago."

Startled by the sudden voice out of nowhere, Drucilla's eyes flared up in a bright blue glow.

"I apologize for startling you."

"Persephone?" Drucilla's eyes returned to their normal state.

Persephone smiled and stepped out of the shadows from behind Drucilla's gallery.

"I envy you. I look at you and remember what it was like to be small and vulnerable. You exist until you do not. Your short lives are consumed with status, wealth, and family. Temporary things that do not add up to much in the end. But it is those small human joys that I miss so desperately. Blissful moments that I will never get to experience again."

Persephone gazed out to the open ocean as the sun set in vivid hues of gold and magenta, followed by a blanket of white-speckled, navy-blue sky forcing the light past the horizon.

"I'm not exactly human anymore," Drucilla responded.

"You are, but also different. You have the best of both worlds. You are immortal with the privilege of living as a human. You still get to experience human life."

Drucilla stared at Persephone, trying to figure out where she was going with her story.

"You want to know why I am here." Persephone turned away from the waning light and faced Drucilla.

"I don't think you're here to chat about my mortality," Drucilla said.

"You and Lucifer have grown quite close." Persephone took a few steps closer.

"I guess."

"He is quite fond of you."

"I don't know what you want me to say here, Persephone."

"I would suppose he has not told you everything about himself."

"He doesn't tell me anything. I know he's older than time, but apart from that, he tends to keep things to himself. Well, unless he has no other choice and it's forced out," Drucilla said. She crossed her arms, annoyed by Lucifer's elusiveness the more she thought about it.

Persephone smiled and nodded. "That is true."

"Why do you ask?"

"I came to warn you about him."

"I can handle Lucifer."

Persephone sat down on a deck chair, crossed her ankles, and folded her hands on her lap. "No, child. I do not think you understand. Lucifer is not who he says he is."

Drucilla frowned. "He's not a Seraph? Not a king of Hell?"

"He *was* a king; no, he is not a Seraph. Lucifer is Ophanim."

"He's a Throne?"

"No. He has not the title of Throne. Lucifer is the child experiment of the Thrones."

Drucilla looked confused. She sat down on the chair opposite Persephone and listened intently.

"There was a desire to create a being that was the sum of all Thrones. Lucifer was created with but a fraction of each. For scale, if a human is a blade of grass, a tree is an angel, and a planet is an ophanim. Lucifer would be considered a country or a continent. Lucifer can create human life; he cannot create a universe. He is unique, special; he is the only one of his kind."

"For what purpose?"

"Lucifer was created to be what humans would refer to as a God. His purpose was to be the avatar of Earth. Unfortunately, he could not be. With their free will, humans created and devoted themselves to other Gods, making

Lucifer one of many gods. This led to Lucifer's purpose being discarded. Eventually, he ranked among the Seraphs."

"Why would he keep this a secret?"

"Only Lucifer knows why Lucifer does what he does. There is more..."

Concerned, Drucilla leaned back in her chair. She folded her arms.

"Go ahead," Drucilla said reluctantly.

"Your relic, along with the other vestiges of the Thrones, were not put in human paths by the Thrones. Lucifer put them there. He is responsible for you finding Calliope's rosary and Adelia finding the Alchemy Tome. There are others. It is your tribe that will carry them."

"Calliope didn't put the rosary in my path?"

"Did you ever think to ask why an Ophanim, a Throne, would need to place a Divine relic in your path?"

Drucilla squinted as her eyes shifted back and forth. "I...I suppose they wouldn't."

"Believe me when I say that Calliope's death was no great loss to anyone in the universe. She was cruel, and her demise only created a sense of relief for the Divine most of all. Interfering with human lives is not a priority for any Throne."

"I didn't kill her; I mean, I tried."

"True. But now we have a bigger problem, don't we?"

"Drake."

"Yes. But that's not what is important right now. You and your tribe are on a set path."

"What do you mean?"

"Your friend Dominic already has Erato Falx. Urania's Cosoculous Lens will be appointed to Hazel. The Galothian Crystal is in Dita's hands. Kairos Fatia's Aeon Article will belong to Marilyn. Brandon has recovered Judicium, and Min's Temperance Flame will be Aleksei's to find. The cauldron, of course, is in the hands of Katia."

"Hazel? I don't know a Hazel."

"You will."

Drucilla stood up. She paced the deck of her gallery. She put her hand to her chin and attempted to process the information.

"You are wondering to what end? What is the point of this?" Persephone asked.

Drucilla shot Persephone a glare. "Why should I believe you?"

"I have nothing to gain by deception," Persephone responded. "You have nothing I desire."

"We literally killed your boyfriend."

"Ah, Hades." Persephone laughed to herself. "His demise was merely a footnote. I had no affection for him. I am not mourning his death."

"Why would Lucifer orchestrate this?"

"He simply feels he deserves what he is owed."

"Godhood," Drucilla whispered.

"Yes. That is correct. He intends to create a new council of Thrones that your tribe will fulfill with the Divine power of the relics."

"But how? Calliope's relic no longer exists." Drucilla pointed out.

"As long as Drake exists, so does Death. Drake is not that far out of Lucifer's grasp. He may think he's in control, but his deal could be terminated anytime Lucifer sees fit."

Drucilla's aggravation was replaced with visible paranoia.

"Lucifer allowed himself to become careless. He underestimated humans. He thought he could place objects in your path, and you would toy with them like a cat would a ball. He would wait to see if you could unlock its secrets. The ones that did would ultimately become his council."

"But I'm not the first to own Calliope's rosary."

"No, you are not. This is his game. It moved from human to human until it came into your possession. You had unlocked its secrets and hence became worthy of his new council."

"Lucifers isn't careless. If anything, he's been overly calculating," Drucilla argued.

"Lucifer is exceptional at recalibrating. However, two things happened that he had not anticipated. First, you took the Ophanim blood into yourself. You lived when you should not have."

"What's the second?"

"His unexpected love for you."

Drucilla blinked rapidly as if she had misheard.

"What do you mean his love for me?"

"He loves you as a companion, whatever you humans call it this century."

Drucilla's eyes widened as she shook her head. "I mean, I thought he was joking—."

"He intends for you to be at his side when he takes over the universe."

Drucilla inhaled deeply, "This is a lot. How do you know?"

"I have a reputation for obtaining vital information." Persephone smiled. She seemed pleased with herself.

"Any other bomb you want to drop on me? I mean, we may as well get this out. Is Drake planning on killing me soon?"

"You are a hindrance. You're nothing more than an obstacle to Drake."

"An obstacle?" Drucilla gritted her teeth. "I'm his sister!"

"Your existence is essentially a nuisance. After all, what would he do with—"

"That is enough of that," Lucifer said. He quietly appeared behind Drucilla, who turned to look at Lucifer. Lucifer pressed his middle finger against his thumb and flicked a spark outwardly toward Persephone. Drucilla turned to Persephone to see the spark hit her center mass, instantly consuming her body in a bright orange flame and dissipate.

"What did you do to her?" Drucilla demanded.

"Sent her home," Lucifer said calmly and directly.

Drucilla stared at Lucifer with uneasiness. Lucifer wasn't smiling. His demeanor was different, grim. His usual jolly self was replaced with a serious and intimidating semblance. He quietly and slowly moved towards the edge of the deck. He leaned back and placed his elbows on the railing. He intertwined his fingers against his stomach.

"Ask me," he demanded.

"No," Drucilla said quietly.

"Why not?"

Drucilla shook her head.

"You want to know if all of this is true; ask me."

Drucilla's eyes darted around. She wasn't sure she wanted the answer. She inhaled deeply and let the words fall out of her mouth without thinking about them. "I don't want to believe these things about you. I don't want them to be true."

Lucifer studied Drucilla's face for a moment and folded his arms.

"Do you think it's true?"

Drucilla opened her mouth as if to respond and quickly closed it.

Silent and motionless, Drucilla stared into Lucifer's serpentine eyes. Lucifer held her gaze. She searched for the right words to explain her feelings. At that moment, she felt betrayal, disgust, anger, depression, and hatred all at once. Drucilla reflected on every unwilling pawn affected by Lucifer's game. She knew that Persephone could also have a stake in this game. But Drucilla could put an end to it. All of it. If she did, Drake would win; if she didn't, Lucifer would get what he wanted. Either way, the universe was going to shift, not for the better.

"Why couldn't you let this go?" Drucilla blurted out.

"We have come entirely too far to stop now."

"I mean, in the beginning. Before this game of yours. It didn't need to get this far."

"It is done. It cannot be undone."

"Why can't we just end it now?"

"Drake's power grows with every passing moment. We have a way to stop him together."

"And make you a God."

Lucifer said nothing.

"This was part of your plan, too, wasn't it? Drake was created to be an adversary for you to defeat with the help of the tribe. We were locked in from the moment we were born. You created a problem for the sole purpose of emerging the hero."

Drucilla dropped her arms stiffly.

"God, how much of an ego-maniacal asshole are you? You even have Heaven convinced that you're this savior to Earth. But this, this is just...."

Lucifer watched Drucilla pace. Drucilla stopped and stepped up to Lucifer.

"Why me? Why Drake? Why did you choose us?"

"Your lineage mainly. You are the strongest option for success. Your mother is a direct descendent of Theodora,

Empress of the Byzantine Empire, and your donor is the direct descendent of Mark Antony and Pharoah Cleopatra.

As for the others….” Lucifer put his hand to his chin. “Aleksei and Dominic’s second great-grandfather was Rasputin. Adelia and Marylin are direct descendants of King Philip II of Spain. Katia is the direct descendant of Mary Queen of Scots; Brandon is the descendant of King Sejong. Your friend Dita is a great-granddaughter of Vlad Țepeș and Sierra, same as your mother but on her father’s side, a great-granddaughter of General George Washington.”

“The only reason you chose us is that we’re related to leaders?”

“These leaders do not exist out of random chance, Drucilla. All of them have been affected by Divine influence.”

“So why didn’t you start with my mom or my grandma?”

“It is not enough to merely exist. That is only half of it. I place the relics in your path. You choose to take them or leave them. The relics had either been unintentionally avoided or the ones that found them had failed until now. As you know, you are the first to unlock the power of the rosary. You far exceeded any expectations I may have had.”

The familiar scent of cold, damp Earth permeated the air around them.

Lucifer rolled his eyes and crossed his arms. “Tobit.”

Azrael walked past Drucilla and stood towering over Lucifer. He looked down at Lucifer in what could only be described as sheer disgust.

"What is your plight?" Lucifer asked him.

"I thought this was over. I thought you had abandoned those intentions eons ago. I allowed this to go on because I thought it was just a game at this point," Azrael said. He seemed to have forced himself to calm his tone.

"Allowed? Tobit, what could you do to stop me?"

"I had Calliope's ear. I was in her employ. I kept your secret, but had she known about your rouse, she would have ended it. But that's not all you've been keeping from us, is it?"

"Which part?" Lucifer inquired.

Drucilla's eyes shifted to Lucifer.

"You didn't leave Hell. You were exiled." Azrael crossed his arms and looked down at Lucifer.

"Take care what you say, Tobit."

"You couldn't stay with the mess you created."

Lucifer raised his finger to Azrael. "Do not do this, Azrael," Lucifer said quietly but sternly.

"She has the right to know. Although I will say, I only recently figured it out myself."

"Christ, what now?" Drucilla glowered at Lucifer.

"Yes. You are right. I was asked to leave. But Drucilla, you must understand, you need to exist; you and Thoth."

"Oh my god, will you just say it already?" Drucilla blurted out impatiently.

Azrael looked down at Drucilla and went back to Lucifer. Lucifer's eyes pleaded for him to stop.

"It's bad, isn't it?" Drucilla asked.

Azrael gazed at Drucilla through his hollow eyes that radiated a deep purple glow. The glow settled into visible eyeballs. This was the first time Drucilla had seen his real eyes, not his skeletal, ocular cavities. Azrael shook his head. "This has gone too far. I'm done." Azrael pulled his scythe from his back and dropped it at Lucifer's feet.

"What are you doing?" Drucilla asked.

"I am done with this allyship. I will no longer be a part of this."

Drucilla grabbed Azrael's hand to get his attention. "Azrael, what's going on?"

Azrael looked at Drucilla's hand and then back to Lucifer. "I could not fathom why I would sense Drucilla in the Infernal Sphere but also here on Earth. I thought it was Drake's human essence but realized that was not the case. I am embarrassed to admit that it took me this long to put it together."

Lucifer exhaled and nodded slowly. "You may as well tell her. Go ahead; I will not stop you."

"No. You wish to play God? *You* will tell her, and revel in the consequences of your deceit."

Azrael took his hand from Drucilla and placed his hand on her shoulder. He looked down at her eyes. "But, before he does, I do not want you to blame yourself or think it had anything to do with your decision."

"My decision?"

"He was referring to when you took the Divine blood," Lucifer said.

"Come what may, I will be your friend and will be here for you."

Drucilla looked at Lucifer. Lucifer shook his head. Drucilla looked at Azrael.

"Ask him the question—ask him what Thoth meant when he said the 'the other is you'."

Drucilla forced herself to breathe calmly and directed her attention to Lucifer. "Lucifer, what was Thoth talking about?

Lucifer inhaled sharply and looked at Azrael in betrayal.

"Drucilla, you are so vital to the universe. You must understand that your existence is imperative. Without you…" Lucifer stopped and searched for the right words to say. "Drucilla, when you died. Your death was horrific. It was felt throughout the realms. I tried to get to you as soon as I could, but I was a moment too late." Lucifer focused on a nail protruding from the wooden deck plank on the floor. He pushed it with the tip of his shoe while he fought to find the right words.

Drucilla's eyes narrowed. "Too late? What does that mean?" She looked up at Azrael, but Azrael stayed locked on Lucifer as if he wouldn't allow him to escape without explaining himself.

"I searched for you for three days while you lay dormant on a cold slab in a morgue. I searched everywhere in every universe. I finally found you. Since you and Drake are twins, your essence is nearly identical; differentiating is difficult. I assumed I was sensing Drake. But it was you. You were firmly at Drake's side. Drake took you the moment you died. I could not get you back."

"So, cut to the chase, you got me back, but you made another deal with Drake to do it? What are we talking about here?"

Azrael looked to Drucilla, his dark eyes searching her face.

"Not exactly, no," Lucifer answered.

"So, how did you get me back in my body."

Lucifer glanced at Azrael. Azrael only stared coolly back in return.

Drucilla's eyes flickered blue. She knew that whenever Lucifer hesitated to tell her something, it was going to be devastating. She braced herself.

"Drucilla, I remade your essence, placed the new, identical essence back into your body, and revived you."

"The other is you," Drucilla repeated Thoth's words. "The other is me!"

Drucilla stood stunned. Branches of bright blue light began to stretch across her face and hands. Her eyes grew increasingly brighter as she pressed her lips tightly together. She clenched her fists and screamed as her wings burst from her back into their full expanse.

"I'm a fucking duplicate!" Drucilla shouted. Her powerful Ophanim voice reverberated like a gigantic tree crashing to the ground throughout the surrounding area.

"Drucilla, your role in the universe is too vital for you not to be a part of it! Your essence is an identical duplicate of your former self. One version of you resides in Hell, the other standing before us. I had no other choice!" Lucifer yelled. His serpentine eyes were glowing.

"I exist in two realms!" Drucilla yelled.

Drucilla slowly bent down and picked up Azrael's scythe. She held it tightly in both hands and glowered at Lucifer. Her eyes were filled with bright white fire as blue branches of light grew across her face. The long shaft and blade glowed with an ethereal blue light. She swung her hands back and, in a supernatural blinding speed, brought the blade down upon Lucifer.

Before the blade struck, Azrael grabbed the shaft and stopped it mere inches from Lucifer's head. Drucilla looked at Lucifer in anger.

"Drucilla, this is not how we solve this." Azrael slid the scythe from her grip.

Drucilla's hands burst into blue flames as she lunged at Lucifer. Moving like a blur, Lucifer raised his hands to the side, bent at the elbows, fingers like claws scraping upwards. From the wooden planks of the deck erupted fiery infernal chains that sought out and wrapped a dozen times around Drucilla's wrists. Drucilla was suddenly stopped and noticed the new weight on her arms. As she looked at them, the chains retracted and pulled her down with surprising strength and forced her to her knees.

Drucilla felt a rage that built up in her chest. She flexed her wings and buffeted Lucifer, blowing him backward a step. The chains tightened. Lucifer flicked his wrists, and the chains slid across the planks to anchor behind him, and with a pull of his hands, they responded by retracting down into the wood and pulled Drucilla stumbling toward him.

"Dru—" Lucifer began, drawing her close to him. Drucilla's rage deepened. She pulled and twisted against the chains. Hearing Lucifer uttering her name felt like a rush of fire in her brain and she lashed out. Her wings raised and cut downward, the edges of them sliced through the air like blades, the force of them splitting the links in the chain and cutting her loose. Despite Lucifer's look of surprise, Drucilla advanced on him and swung wide with her hand aiming to scratch his face, the tips of her nails grazing the glamoured flesh, causing ripples to slide through it.

"You will NOT!" Lucifer's voice boomed, and with it he flung out his hands. An invisible wall of energy slammed into Drucilla and propelled her backward. The thud resounded through the air and reverberated through the wood and other physical matter. Drucilla crashed through the back wall, crumpling under the pressure, and folded over on herself as she fell to the floor.

"You..." Drucilla rolled to her knees. "You son of..." Her rage built; her eyes locked on Lucifer, their light shown as points of white-hot fire. "YOU SON OF A BITCH!" Drucilla screamed. Her voice cut the air and split the atoms apart. Angelic fire, full of blue and white hues, lurched forward and ignited the open air. The span of blazing sound and fury washed over Lucifer, and he brought his arms up to shield his face. His clothes caught like kindling and paper, incinerating away, and fell from him in clumps of ash and cinders.

"Ha…" Lucifer laughed softly. "I haven't had to brace myself in centuries. Well done, Dru. Well done."

Lucifer lowered his arms and stood tall, his glamour damaged and peeling away from his form as it dissipated. Red flesh began to replace the translucent skin. His mass began to grow. Where his head was once bald, now a set of large horns of slick black bone was revealed. His fingers stretched, blackened, and sharpened. He loomed, dwarfing his former size by more than double as a long red tail and black barb snaked across the deck floor.

"If this is how you want it," Lucifer looked over his form, "then so be it."

He lunged at Drucilla, spanning the distance between them in a blink and tearing the wind behind him. The debris of their fight caught up in the flow, following him like shrapnel animated of its own volition. He brought his talons down, tips poised for blood. Drucilla's wings swung into place defensively, taking the raking down their length and spilling blood across the feathers.

Drucilla spun underneath her wings, turning to rise with an upward strike at Lucifer's chest. The thud rang solid, and he was knocked a step back and to one side. He leaned into the forced turn and whipped his tail toward Drucilla. Through her winged eyes, she saw the attack and spun again to slice her wings downward and cut through the tail. Despite

Lucifer's demonic reliance, her wings sliced to the bone and sent pure pain up into Lucifer's spine.

Drucilla screamed again, channeling her anger into her body. She rushed Lucifer's mass and slammed a shoulder into him. Despite his imposing size the impact flung him off his cloven hooves and backward several feet. He landed squarely on his hooves and continued to slide a foot more. He hugged his chest with one arm and winced. Drucilla pressed on, closing the distance, swinging blows one after the other, each connecting with a power that dented Lucifer's flesh and bruised bone. He took a few of these hits, attempting to quell his own rising anger, but was pushed ever further by each blow. Finally, he would take no more.

Erupting in a blaze of fel fire, Lucifer released a controlled explosion, sending Drucilla flying back and splintering the deck into bits. Drucilla tumbled to the beachfront below, but had no time to make it to the ground before Lucifer appeared next to her and grabbed her falling body, wrenching it over his head and slamming it down. Drucilla coughed up blood, spattering it across the rocky shore. Lucifer raised his arms up, the fire intensifying in his fists as he tensed to bring them down.

Like the shadow of death Azrael crossed in front of Lucifer, his hand wiped across Lucifer's face, his fingertips within an inch of his flesh. The gesture chilled the fel fire and smothered it along the trace of his fingers. From somewhere deep within him, Lucifer felt something wrong. His energy, and his fire, evaporated. He watched as wisps of his soul rose like smoke and left his body, called to Azrael's hand. Lucifer fell to his knees, unable to keep focus. His bones were cold.

Azrael turned toward Drucilla, dismissing the hold he had on this bit of Lucifer's soul and letting it return to the demon, except for a tiny, lingering puff that traced around his finger and was drawn within the flesh.

Drucilla got back on her feet. Taking Azrael's interference as allyship, she bared her teeth and made ready to continue her attack. But, with a point of his finger Drucilla also fell to her knees, feeling the chill creep over her as she watched her soul seep out of her like a cool mist on a sunlit pool. It, too, was called to Azrael's presence as if it belonged to him. And, as before, he sipped only a taste of it before letting the rest return to her.

"That is more than enough," Azrael spoke, "this fight serves only to worsen the situation. Get your answers, and then get on your way. Leave this playing about to the children."

"Why would you do this to me? Why—" Drucilla yelled.

"I was not the one that did something so short-sighted! No one told you to take Divine blood into yourself! You did it for your own selfish reason. Start taking responsibility for your actions!" Lucifer yelled back.

"Are you serious? You're blaming me? Nobody told you to remake me! You did that for *your* own selfish reasons!" she shouted.

"Enough!" Azrael boomed. The air darkened around his form as if the light was sent away in fear of him. Drucilla and Lucifer both stepped back, feeling their soul energy quiver and recede from the cold Azrael now radiated. He held their attention completely.

"If you must feel, then feel for the plight of Drucilla in Hell. There she exists, shackled to the man that was once her brother and is now, most assuredly, her captor and tormentor," Azrael began. "If you must rage, then rage against that which you all so furiously deny, that it is you three that are at the heart of it in your triangle of self-destruction." Azrael's voice cooled as he calmed, and the light returned. "But, if you must berate, berate yourselves, for neither of you have taken responsibility for who or what you are, and your flippant displays of power and will have damned an innocent soul to a Hell that did not exist until you created it. Drake, with the power of Calliope, is the most powerful entity the realms have ever seen." Azrael's voice lowered into a growl. "Now, what are you going to do about it?"

Lucifer paced the shore and pointed to Drucilla. "Azrael's right. Regardless of what you may think of me; we need to work together if we are going to stop Drake's regime—"

"A regime where you had direct influence!" Drucilla yelled, cutting him off.

"Drucilla!" Lucifer's eyes blazed with Hellfire. "You have the potential to be infinitely more powerful than Drake."

"What about you? You're an Ophanim and have a part of every Throne. Wouldn't that make you more powerful than any of us?"

"Drake is calculating, resourceful, and knows how to manipulate and influence. It's not just about my abilities; it's the entirety of the Infernal Sphere against us. Understand the Infernal Sphere has hundreds of legions made up of thousands of individuals, consisting of fallen cambions, demons, infernals, and humans per legion. This is not considering kings, princes, or generals. No, Drucilla, Hell's power is more than one Ophanim could conquer!"

"With the Thrones relics, you think we could defeat them?" she said, hoping for confirmation.

"That is precisely why you are all necessary."

"What about the Seraphs?" she asked. She pointed and looked upwards. The moon was vacant. Millions of points of light in the sky shimmered like tiny diamonds against a sheet of inky blackness.

"Getting them to side with us will prove to be difficult. The Seraphs would most likely let the Infernal Sphere destroy us if it meant they would not have to be involved. Their only concern is Earth. That is why they appeared when Hell broke through. Outside of protecting the planet..."

"I don't believe that."

"Drucilla, you should be dead. Dominic has no right to be here, yet you forced his existence. Now tell me again, why would they care?"

"My death wouldn't have changed anything. You said it yourself. You need us to use the relics. Right now, we need to get *me* out of Hell."

"Drucilla, I could not retrieve *you*. What plan do you have?" Lucifer asked.

"I'll have to get her myself," Drucilla responded. "Dominic's stylus."

"That is a terrible idea. What makes you think they will not anticipate your arrival?"

"You got a better plan? You're banished, and Malphas refuses to go back. Besides, I wouldn't force him. What other choice do we have?" Drucilla asked.

"Drucilla, listen to me."

"No!" Drucilla shouted. "I'm done listening to you. You've done more than enough. I don't need you anymore. Goodbye, Lucifer."

CANTICLE FORTY-ONE

"But she's just not that way; her little soul is stolen."—The Offspring

Drake paced the grand foyer of his palace; he appeared agitated and restless. He stopped and stood in front of the open door to the balcony and looked out to the courtyard.

"Imperator, she still isn't in her chamber," Moloch said. He approached Drake from the opposite end of the chamber.

"I know she is here. Find her, Moloch!" he shouted.

The abrupt clank of the heavy, large, ornately carved door creaked and swung open as Drucilla quickly entered the room. She hastily approached Drake and stood in front of him. Her eyes filled with annoyance.

"Well? I'm here!" Drucilla threw her hands up and looked at Drake with hostility. "What was so important that you literally had every demon in Hell looking for me?"

Drucilla glared at Drake. She was dressed in a dark-red vintage, button-down pleated shirt, and a long, tight-fitting burgundy pencil skirt and heels. Her long, black locks were loosely curled, tousled, and pinned to the crown of her head. Her deep-red lips and smoky eyes were entirely out of her comfort zone.

Drake looked pleased with her appearance. "Dru! This is a good look for you."

Drucilla gritted her teeth. "I look like a madame for a brothel that caters to oligarchs! Did Persephone tell you to dress me like this?"

"I assure you, she didn't, and you don't look like a madame."

Moloch grinned menacingly and stared at Drucilla as if he was eyeballing a thick, juicy steak.

"Look you, creepy little Renfield fucker—," Drucilla seethed.

"That's enough, Moloch." Drake turned and glared at him. "Oh, and speaking of Persephone, if you see her, remove her, and make sure she is barred from entering again. I no longer wish for her to be present in Hell. You are free to go," Drake commanded.

Moloch closed his eyes and sniffed deeply in Drucilla's direction. Drucilla glared. As he turned and headed out of the room, Drucilla curled her lip disgusted. She turned her attention back to Drake.

"Wow, exiling Persephone. That's a ballsy move."

Drake ignored his sister and diverted his attention back to the courtyard.

"Damn, why are you so agitated?" Drucilla asked, trying to loosen the tightness of her shirt collar.

"I will not tolerate deception in my realm. Nor will I tolerate someone using my sister for nefarious purposes. Speaking of, have you been in contact with Lucifer?" Drake asked pointedly.

"Lucifer? Why would I talk to Lucifer? I haven't seen him in years."

"You wouldn't be lying to me, would you?"

Drucilla creased her forehead. "I don't see how I owe you any explanation as to whom I speak, but if I had, I would have no problem telling you. Why would I care if you approved or not? I'm not one of your lackeys, Drake."

Drake's eyes narrowed at Drucilla's response, and he chose to disregard her blatant insubordination. "Drucilla, I love you. You are my twin, and because of that fact, you have been extended a rare offer. To rule at my side. No human would ever hold such a position."

Drucilla's eye shifted. "What are you saying?"

Drake turned away from her. "The coronation is this evening. Three new kings are to be instated to fill the vacant roles within the seven kings. I want my sister to start looking the part of my advisor. I can't have you draped over a cathedra wearing a G.G. Allin tee shirt and black skinny jeans."

Drucilla threw her hands up and exhaled. "It was Andrew Eldritch! They look nothing alike. They're not even in the same music genre! Do you even know how difficult it is to get Western civilization clothes in Hell?"

"I don't care. This coronation is very important. Do you remember the gentlemen you met recently?"

"Vaguely," she responded.

"I need you to remember their names and their positions. Marquis Apollyon has been chosen as the new King of

Constitution, Viscount Marchosia has been chosen as the new King of Wrath, and Count Ronove is the King of Acumen."

"Fine. Marquis Apollyon, Viscount Marchosia, and Ronove. I got it."

"Count Ronove. Drucilla, Count Ronove is the Great Earl of Hell, commanding thirty-one legions. Please attempt to be respectful."

"Can I go now?" Drucilla said. She tapped her foot and crossed her arms, becoming increasingly impatient with her brother.

"Two hours, Drucilla. I expect you to be in your formal gown and waiting for me in the sacristy—ready to walk out to the great hall at my side. Do I make myself clear?"

"Wouldn't you much rather take a date to one of these things and not your sister?"

"Typically, this would be a position for the Imperator's mother, but since you are what I have, you will have to fill that role."

Drucilla scoffed and turned to walk away.

"Two hours, Drucilla. Don't be late."

Drucilla quickly walked away from Drake's chambers into the hall. She closed the door behind her. Her expression changed from annoyance to terror as she walked briskly down the hall and the long, gilded spiral stairs. She swiftly moved across the elaborately embellished main hall that separated Drake's side from her side of the villa. The walls were full of tapestries, gold furnishings, and a large fountain that poured pure gold into each tier, with finely woven rugs placed randomly over quartz crystalline tile. She bolted up the stairs to her bedroom where she opened the door and locked it behind her. Persephone turned to Drucilla as soon as she heard her enter the room.

"Well?" Persephone asked.

"The kings are being appointed tonight—two hours from now. Ronove, excuse me, Count Ronove, Apollyon, and uh, Marchosis or something," Drucilla divulged.

"Viscount Marchosia? As expected," Persephone responded.

"One more thing, he plans to have you exiled. He doesn't trust you. I don't know how we're going to keep in contact after tonight."

Persephone laughed. "I would not worry about that. No Unholy knows the ins and outs of this realm better than I do."

"Persephone, I have a request." Drucilla sat down on her bed. "I want to see her."

"Drucilla, I am not sure that, presently, that's the best course of action. She has only now learned of your existence."

"I don't care. If she has become who you say she's become, she can stop this. Whatever Drake is planning, it's bad. Drucilla is basically all we have now. Besides, if I'm going to continue to be your confidant, I want something in exchange. I need to see her."

"Are you extorting me?"

"No, that's not what I meant. I have no way out of here; I'm dead. I'm not powerful like you all are. I can't move between worlds, so I need your help. Look, if she's really me, then she'll want to see me too. Please, Persephone. I can't spend eternity here! You're my only option."

Persephone looked at Drucilla empathetically for a moment. "Very well. After the coronation. We must go at a time when Drake would be unaware of your disappearance, and it must be a very short visit. Drake will undoubtedly sense your absence."

"I'm not afraid of my brother."

"Drucilla, it would behoove you to reevaluate your opinion. Drake is the single most powerful being in the Infernal Sphere. Do not think his affection for you will be enough for him to keep you safe. Do not be a fool. As his strength grows, his humanity wanes. Love is a human emotion; of which he has very little remaining."

"Drake won't hurt me."

"But clearly, he had no issue abandoning you, did he?"

Like a gut punch, the comment caught Drucilla off guard. She had never felt more alone than she did at that moment.

"After the coronation, excuse yourself. Meet me here. I will take you to her," Persephone directed.

†††

Drucilla paced the sacristy, wobbly in her five-inch, golden heels. She wore a floor-length, tight-fitting gown embellished with exquisite, gold sequins and lace. The bottom of the dress flared out into a long train. Her raven locks rolled down her shoulders like an ink-black waterfall. Her neck was adorned with hundreds of diamonds looping multiple times around her neck. She looked like royalty.

Drake entered the sacristy in a finely handcrafted gold and silver threaded Victorian tailcoat with a high neck collar and embellished, silver buttons down the front. On his head was a golden crown encrusted with white and yellow diamonds. He pulled on his cufflinks and offered his elbow to his sister. She put her hand through his arm, her large, gemmed rings catching on his sleeve. Drake turned and looked into her eyes. "How amazing do I look right now?" he asked. "Do I look like a ruler?" He pointed to his long sword strapped to his side.

Drucilla blinked slowly at his arrogance and turned her attention to the double doors ahead of them. "What are we waiting for?"

"Oriens. He is one of the four demons that oversee the cardinal directions. He will announce us, and we'll walk to the grand table. You will take a seat closest to me, next to Leviathan and the other two kings."

"Cardinal directions?" she asked.

"He rules the East. Honestly, Drucilla, you must learn these names and positions. You are among the highest-ranking officials in the realm."

"The Imperator Drake and his sister, Countess Drucilla," Oriens announced from the other side of the doors. Two small demons pushed the doors outwards to reveal Drake and Drucilla to the great hall.

"Countess?!" Drucilla repeated.

Drucilla looked up to see the great hall filled with applause from hundreds of demons and fallen dressed in formal attire. Drucilla and Drake stepped down the short flight of steps to the ornate marble tiled floor. Drucilla struggled to keep her balance as she gripped her brother's forearm.

"You okay?" he whispered.

She glanced at Drake. "Aside from these heels and not being able to move more than six inches at a time in this dress?"

"You look like a queen." Drake grinned. He kept his attention facing forward. After they reached the bottom, Drake motioned for his sister to take a seat at the large table in front of him, upon which sat three golden crowns. She sat down and looked up at her brother.

"Will Count Ronove, Marquis Apollyon, and Viscount Marchosia please approach the floor?" Drake requested. Drake moved to the front of the table in the middle of the great hall.

The three gentlemen in formal wear stepped away from their tables, then to the middle of the great hall, a few feet from Drake.

"Count Ronove, Marquis Apollyon, Viscount Marchosia, are you willing to take the oath?"

"I will," they said in unison.

"Will you solemnly promise and swear to govern the Infernal Sphere according to its respective laws and customs?"

"I will," they said in unison, again.

"Will you use your power in Law and Justice to be executed in all your judgements?

"I will," they said in unison, again.

"Will you, to the utmost of your power, maintain the laws of the realm in true profession, preserve inviolably, in doctrine, discipline, and government thereof, as by law established in the Infernal Sphere?"

"I will," they said in unison, once more.

"Gentleman, please face the commonwealth."

The three demons turned and faced the crowd. Drake picked up the first crown. He abruptly glanced at the ceiling. Count Ronove looked at Drake and then looked to where Drake's attention had been drawn. Drake glared and turned his attention back to Ronove. Drake placed the crown upon the head of Ronove. "Count Ronove, I crown you the King of Acumen." Drake moved to Marchosia, picking up the second crown. "Viscount Marchosia, I crown you the King of Wrath." Picking up the third crown, Drake stepped over to Apollyon. "Marquis Apollyon" I crown you the King of Constitution." Drake walked back behind the table next to his sister.

"Long live the Kings!" he shouted.

The crowd erupted into cheers for the newly crowned kings. Drucilla looked up to the parapet above the great hall and saw Persephone watching the ceremony from above. Drucilla kept staring until Persephone felt her gaze. Persephone finally looked at Drucilla. Drucilla motioned to the door with her eyes, asking if she should leave. Persephone shook her head at Drucilla to indicate that it wasn't time. Drucilla nodded slightly.

Drake waited for the cheers to die down before speaking again.

"As you all know, I have recently vacated the seat held by Lucifer. Since I was chosen as the Throne of Death after Calliope's tragic demise, I have taken the position of Imperator. That means that there is one position available within the seven kings. I know many of you are worthy of this position. We have a realm full of brilliant scholars, fierce warriors, and ardent protectors. Now is the time for you to prove your allegiance. I have made the decision to open a contest. This contest is available to any citizen of the Infernal Sphere. Any man, woman, demon, fallen, lost soul—any of you. If you want to hold this coveted position, then this opportunity is for you."

"What do we have to do?" someone shouted from the crowd. A cacophony of murmurs erupted from others in the hall, asking the same question.

Drake grinned. "I am so glad you asked!" he yelled as he paced, "I ask but one simple task. Just one. It may even take you five minutes to complete. The first one to complete it will become the King of Pride. Right here, right now, this night."

The crowd murmured in hushed tones.

Drake turned to the great hall and folded his arms. A slow and devious grin spread across his face. "Capture and bring to me the queens Aurora and Nova!" Drake yelled.

The crowd erupted again in cheers as many demons and fallen jumped to their feet and rushed out, shoving each other through various entrances of the great hall. Some demons unfurled their wings and flew out through open windows, all hunting for the remaining queens.

"What if there are two contenders for Lucifer's seat?" Leviathan asked.

"A duel to the death, of course!" Drake yelled and laughed.

Drucilla's face went pale. She looked up at Persephone. Persephone looked panicked. She turned and ran away from the parapet. Drucilla was terrified. She stood up as the crowd rushed around and past her. Drake turned to his sister. His eyes were blazing orange as he smiled a devious grin.

"Drake, what are you doing?" she asked, but it was too loud for him to hear her.

A loud, thunderous explosion was heard outside in the courtyard. Many cheered and screamed outside. Drucilla jumped to her feet in terror as the Great Hall doors swung open. Four winged demons appeared at first, then a bright, white light slowly emerged through the towering doors of the Great Hall. Drake moved to the center of the hall. The light dimmed down to an ornate silver armor-plated humanoid with a thick, flaming yellow chain over their shoulder as they dragged the bound and restrained light being into the center of the hall. The humanoid figure stopped and dropped the end of the chain in front of Drake's feet. Drake looked down at the chain that burned in front of him and then at the head of the armored humanoid.

"Who are you?" Drake asked.

The humanoid took off their gloves one at a time and dropped them to the floor; they put their hands on their head and slowly removed their helmet. Valor shook her head as her hair fell from the helmet to her shoulders.

The room fell silent.

"It's a Seraph! It's Valor!" Count Ronove yelled.

"A Virtue, to be exact," Valor corrected.

The crowd gasped and chattered in disbelief. Drake's eyes widened. He recognized her as the Seraph that accompanied Raziel when Drake was given his armor to contain Calliope.

"Virtue, what are you doing here in the Infernal Sphere? Your kind is banned from entering!" Count Ronove demanded.

Valor glanced at Leviathan. "Do you want to tell him what I am?"

Leviathan stood up and turned to Count Ronove. "She is Lilim. She is the abomination of Sariel and Persephone."

Drake quickly turned back to Valor in disbelief. "Wait, you? You're Valor? Persephone and Sariel's daughter?"

"I am. You said this competition is open to any citizen of the realm. I am a citizen just as much as anyone else here."

Drake turned back to Leviathan. Leviathan nodded to Drake in agreement.

Drucilla nervously looked back up to the parapet, but Persephone had vanished.

"And why would I allow you to take Lucifer's place among the Seven Kings?" Drake asked.

"Because I won it fairly. I brought you, Nova." Valor turned around at the restrained light being. The protruding rays and rings were slowly rotating but were unable to break free from the binds.

"You are a Virtue. You belong to the Celestial Empyrion. Why would I entrust a Virtue to be a King of Hell? How could I trust you to even so much as to exist in this realm?"

"We already share a bond of trust." Valor held Drake's stare and nodded slowly to imply that she knew the secret of the armor he was using to contain Calliope.

Valor turned to the Infernals. "Misplaced allegiances. I chose the wrong side. I apologize; I was wrong."

Drake paced the Great Hall back and forth in front of Valor. "Are you here to swear your allegiance to the Infernal Sphere and to me as your Imperator?"

"I am."

The hushed tones of hundreds of demons could be heard among the crowd. Drake walked back to the table and sat down next to Drucilla. He placed his elbows on the table and interlaced his fingers. He looked at Leviathan. He quietly asked, "Do you believe her?"

Leviathan looked at Valor for a moment and then back to Drake. "My understanding is that her title is in token only. Sariel refuses to grant her a seat among his council of Virtues," Leviathan said.

"Is it true, Valor, that because you're a Lilim, the Virtues will not accept you?"

Valor's bottom lip began to quiver; she pulled her lip into her mouth and bit hard to feel a different kind of pain. A small trail of cobalt blue blood fell from the corner of her mouth down her chin. "Yes." Her eyes briefly flashed yellow.

"How do you intend to prove your word?" Drake asked and stood up.

Valor's bright white wings broke out from her back, fully extended. She reached back between her shoulder blades and pulled out her sword. The sword burst into a blue flame, engulfing the blade from hilt to tip.

More murmurs and gasping were heard from the crowd. Drake narrowed his gaze at Valor.

Without batting an eye and with a quick swipe over her left and right shoulder, her wings fell to the floor with a heavy thud. She dropped to one knee as the blue blood slowly flowed down her back and dripped to the floor. She drove the tip of her blade into the floor and bowed her head before Drake.

A slow grin stretched across Drake's face. "Bring me Aurora!" Drake shouted. The crowd erupted in cheers again as the demons rushed back out of the Great Hall.

Drucilla stood up and bolted for the sacristy. She kicked off her heels as she ran up the stairs. Drake saw his sister leave but turned his attention back to Nova and Valor.

Drucilla tore her dress along the side to give her the ability to run faster. She ran to her side of the villa.

"Persephone!" Drucilla yelled as she ran up the stairs. She hoped Persephone could take her away.

✝✝✝

Persephone, waiting in Drucilla's room, heard Drucilla yell from down the hall. She stood up and headed for the door. Persephone flung open the door to meet Drucilla in the hall.

"Drucilla!" Persephone yelled.

The door abruptly slammed in front of Drucilla on its own just as she was about to rush into the room. Persephone grabbed the doorknob and tried to open the door from the inside. The room suddenly flooded with bright light. Persephone turned away from the door to see a bright, yellow light being in the shape of a woman's figure. She shielded her eyes from the illumination. The being quickly grabbed Persephone by the throat and squeezed as Persephone tried to scream and pull away.

Drucilla continued screaming and pounding on the other side of the door.

Persephone tried to fight the being by kicking and shoving, but the being was too powerful. The light being lifted Persephone off the floor into the air high above its head.

Chovin

CANTICLE FORTY-TWO

"Can you feel these spirits passing, though? It's such a lovely way to die"—Cancerslug

Dominic laid on his queen-sized bed and flipped through a heavy-bound antique book about Nephilim. He took off his glasses and rubbed his face.

"I'm not going to sleep. I don't even know why I bother." Talking to himself, he looked at his book without his reading glasses. He squinted and put them back on. He took off the glasses again and looked at them curiously. "I guess I don't need these anymore." He tossed the glasses on his nightstand and sat upright. Out of the corner of his eye, he caught the words *Interitis* scribbled in Ophanim script on a slip of paper protruding from the top of one of the books piled on his nightstand. He pulled the book from the stack. The cover had the word *Galgallin* written in Hebrew.

Dominic examined the front and back cover of the book. He had not seen this one before. It was new to him. He saw the slip of paper sticking out of the top and pulled it out. *What's Interitis?*

There was a sudden and aggressive banging at his front door. His phone began ringing in his pocket as the pounding on the door intensified.

"All right!" he yelled. He ran down the stairs and opened the door to see Drucilla pacing frantically with her phone in her hand.

"Were you calling me and banging on my door at the same time?"

"Dominic, we have a huge problem." Drucilla huffed. She stormed through the front door past him to his library.

"Um, okay," Dominic followed her. He leaned against the doorframe and crossed his massive arms. Dominic noticed her lip had been cut, her cheek bruised, and there were droplets of dried blood sprayed across her face and neck. "Jesus, Dru! What happened?" He reached out to her face to examine her injuries.

"This? It's nothing. Lucifer and I got into a fight," she turned away from him.

"Tell me he looks worse than you."

"Dominic, I need your help. I need Erato Falx."

"Why?"

"Because I need to get into the Infernal Sphere."

Dominic scowled, "Dru, we talked about this. No, you don't, and you're not going—"

"Dominic! Listen to me! Do you remember when I died last year? I'm still dead."

"What are you talking about? You're still dead?"

Drucilla paced for a moment, wringing her hands. "I found out tonight that when I took the blood, and I died, Drake took my soul. He took me to Hell."

"How did you come back?"

Drucilla looked at Dominic anxiously. "I didn't. I'm not the original Drucilla. Lucifer remade me."

"What?" Dominic whispered in shock. "Why?"

"He needs Thoth. He needs me alive to host Thoth. That's all I know. But I do know we need to get me out of Hell. So please, I need Erato Falx."

"Are you sure? This isn't one of his games, is it?" He pulled himself away from the doorframe and reached into his pocket. He pulled out the stylus and examined it before looking back up at Drucilla.

"No, it's true. Azrael found out when I did. I am another incarnation, Dominic."

There was a sudden crash in his living room, like a small meteor hitting and exploding to the ground. The explosion bored a hole into the center of the hardwood floor. A bright, orange glow bathed the walls of the inside of his house. Dominic shielded his eyes.

He squinted at the enormous hole in his living room floor, the bright light was coming from his basement. Drucilla and Dominic ran through his kitchen and flung open his basement door. They dashed down the stairs. Rock and debris lined a five-foot hole in the floor, emitting orange light from the center. Dominic thrust his stylus into the javelin. He held the javelin close to his body as he slowly approached the carved-out ground. The light began to dim, and Dominic could see the figure of a woman standing in the center.

"Persephone," Dominic spoke. He noticed the familiar long, black mink coat and the light reflecting off the surfaces of the gems on her fingers.

"Persephone, what's happening? Are you okay?" Drucilla asked.

Persephone lifted her eyes to Dominic as they blazed with the intensity of a hundred suns.

"What the—" Dominic said.

"Un tai gonef seh," the natural deep frequency of her voice set off ripples of vibration around her. She took a step out of the rubble. She looked down at her body and back up at Dominic. "Aleph'res."

"Aurora," Dominic whispered.

Drucilla's eyes grew increasingly wider at the presence of the Throne of Storms. "Oh my God," she whispered.

Aurora turned her attention to Drucilla, "T'oth," she said.

Aurora reached her hand out to Drucilla with a pulling motion. Drucilla's body began to burn with intense blue light. The blue branches of lightning came closer and closer to the surface. Her skin began to stretch as the blue veins of lightning forcibly exited her flesh. She let out a horrible and excruciatingly painful scream as her flesh tore, and the blue lightning left her body and reached itself closer to Aurora. Drucilla's chest intensified with light as her heart grew and moved closer to the surface. It too ripped a gaping hole in her chest as it exited her body. Drucilla collapsed to the ground.

"NO!" Dominic screamed. "You're killing them!"

Aurora turned to Dominic.

"They're symbiotic. They can't exist without each other. You're killing Thoth!"

Thoth grew in intensity as the bright blue orb of light regained its protruding rays of light, and rings of eyes encircled its center.

Aurora turned her attention back to Thoth and lowered her arm.

As quickly as Thoth was freed from his host, his light began to wane. He rapidly became dimmer, and his rays of light grew shorter as they collapsed into themselves.

"He needs her! You need to put him back," Dominic shouted. "He is going to die!"

Thoth's celestial essence bolted towards Dominic. He slammed himself into Dominic's chest. The entity could not enter due to his impenetrable skin. Dominic stared in shock as the Throne failed to possess him. Thoth's light was fading quickly.

Aurora, now realizing that Thoth was terminal, reached out to Thoth again, grabbing him and thrusting his energy back into Drucilla's unconscious body.

Dominic rolled Drucilla's limp body onto her back as he held her head in his hands. The light sunk deeper into her chest. The blue light stretched out from her center mass, filling her limbs as it gained a hold of her body from the inside.

"Dru! Dru! Are you with me?" Dominic shouted.

"Et vivet." Aurora spoke in Latin that she would live.

Drucilla twitched as her chest heaved with every forced inhalation.

CANTICLE FORTY-THREE

"I won't become this thing I hate." —Stabbing Westward

†

Drucilla slowly opened her eyes. She focused on the ceiling, at the white, crossed beams that formed large squares. The beams ran from her living room to the dining room and into the crown molding. Her eyes were fixated on the hand-painted floral wallpaper that Adrian had spent a month searching for and painstakingly installed. The ornate hues of silver and light blue flowers flowed softly to the hardwood floor below. She felt cold, but the comfort of her couch gave her a sense of calm. She clung to the soft, pale grey blanket around her chest.

"She's awake!" Adrian yelled. He brushed the lock of hair off her forehead.

Malphas rushed to Drucilla's side. Drucilla's head felt strange, like someone had reached into her skull, ripped out a deeply rooted plant, and attempted to put it back haphazardly. It was jarring, and she felt dizzy. She turned to her side and tried to prop herself up.

"Easy, Dru, you've been through a lot," Adrian said.

"What happened?" Drucilla groaned and placed both hands on either side of her head. "My head is killing me."

"Not surprising," Malphas said.

"You're okay; you're going to be okay," Adrian comforted her.

Drucilla tried to shake off the dizziness and get her bearings.

"Drucilla, you were briefly separated from Thoth," Malphas explained.

"What, how?" Drucilla frantically tried to recall the events that put her in her current state.

"Aurora," Dominic responded. He leaned against the fireplace mantle with his muscular arms crossed.

"Oh yeah, Aurora," Drucilla winced through the throbbing pain in her skull.

"Aurora attempted to free Thoth from you. She found out rather quickly that you and Thoth are symbiotic. Thoth nearly died, and you..." Dominic paused; he appeared to get emotional for a moment. "We thought we lost you for a minute there."

"Yeah, well, I'm not a stranger to death. We're old friends at this point," Drucilla snarked. "Dom, why would Aurora come to your house, of all places?"

"I can only speculate, but presumably, it is because Dominic's house is warded against The Unholy," Malphas said. "It is a highly effective ward against me, I cannot enter."

"Just something I pulled out of the Book of the Dead," Dominic added.

The corners of Drucilla's eyes crinkled, "Where is she now?"

"She is still in my house."

Drucilla grabbed onto the couch arm and stood up slowly. Dominic moved quickly to her and held onto her arms to steady her.

"How are you feeling?" Malphas asked.

Drucilla slowly met Malphas' eyes. "Amazing," she said sarcastically.

"Dru, we really should get you to bed," Dominic insisted.

"No. There's no time. I need to get *Me* out of Hell." Drucilla lumbered towards the dining room.

"There's plenty of time, Dru."

"Dom, Aurora possessed Persephone to escape the Infernal Sphere; I can only imagine what's happening to the other me."

Drucilla's hands began to glow as the bright blue branches stretched across her face.

"Dru, what are you doing?" Dominic demanded.

She gritted her teeth as she attempted to force the wings from her back. She grabbed hold of the doorway to the dining room to steady herself. Gasping for breath, her hands waned, and her eyes returned to normal. Her breathing became erratic; she was unable to force the transformation.

"Dru, stop!" Dominic yelled. "You're too weak, and you need to rest. You and Thoth. You aren't strong enough."

"Dom, I need to get Drucilla." Drucilla gritted her teeth again. The blue veins barely came to the surface of her skin.

"Stop! Stop! Just stop it!" Dominic yelled again. Frustrated, he ran his hand over his head.

Drucilla clung to the door frame. She looked up at Dominic, weak and in excruciating pain; her breathing labored.

"Dom..," she said.

"Damn it!" Dominic exhaled in frustration. He paced her living room. "I'll do it; I'll get Drucilla."

Malphas looked up at Dominic. "I will do it."

Dominic shot Malphas a concerted look. "Malphas—"

"You stay with Drucilla. I will go."

"Nuh-uh. It's too dangerous. Besides, there's no telling what Drake will do to you if he finds you."

"How do you plan on going?" Malphas pried.

Dominic reached into his pocket and pulled out Erato Falx.

"Do you know where you are going?" Malphas asked.

Dominic looked up at nothing in particular; he appeared to recall a scene that Lucifer had put into his head. "Where I saw Drucilla. It's a big, tall room with seven chairs around a table. Drake was sitting at the head, and Drucilla was at his side. It had a couple of spiral staircases in the background, lots of stained-glass windows near the ceiling…."

"That is the oratory and the very last place you want to enter! That will put you directly in front of the Seven Kings!

"Fine, where should we go?"

"Delphyne. We will go to Delphyne. She will know where to find Drucilla."

"Who is Delphyne?" Dominic asked.

"She is my mother, essentially. Delphyne is Persephone's daughter."

"Whoa, wait. Persephone, is your grandmother?" Drucilla blurted out.

"No, it does not work like that in Hell. We are creations, not kin. I do not have a somatic body. In the beginning, Delphyne created me to be her familiar, if you will. I am of no relation or creation of Persephone."

"Uh, kay?" Drucilla wrestled with the information trying to make sense of it.

"Okay, let's do it," Dominic said. He looked over to Drucilla, listless and leaning against the doorframe. "Adrian, make sure she gets some rest."

Adrian nodded. He wrapped his arm around Drucilla's waist and led her to the staircase.

Malphas turned to Dominic. "Dominic, this is essentially a chess match. You are attempting to remove the queen from the king without his awareness. This could have a catastrophic outcome for all of us."

"Yeah, I know. But we're all she's got."

"Are you ready?" Malphas asked.

"Do it."

Malphas placed his hands on Dominic's head. He inserted a vision of Delphyne, much like Lucifer did when he transferred images of Hellscapes to Dominic while teaching him to use Erato Falx to open portals.

Delphyne was tall and thin with long, silver hair. She looked to be roughly twenty years old in human years. She was standing near an alchemy table. She seemed to be creating concoctions from dark plants that bled purple when she cut them. Dominic pulled away from Malphas; he readied his stylus and tore a hole in the fabric of reality.

"Dom…" Drucilla said.

Dominic looked at Drucilla and held her stare for a few moments. She blinked slowly and pressed her lips together. He could tell that she was scared and couldn't find the words. He nodded to Drucilla. He understood their silent communication.

Dominic stepped through the tear with Malphas close behind. The hole resealed itself. Drucilla collapsed to the floor.

†††

Dominic and Malphas stood in the center of a small, dark room. The room smelled overwhelmingly of dirt and dried foliage. It was almost suffocating. It was cold and dusty, with shelves of small jars of tinctures, elixirs, and bottled plants lining the walls. The windows were made of deep purple glass that barely let in light. This place appeared to be a sort of greenhouse or potting shed for plants that needed to be in low to zero light.

Startled, Delphyne quickly turned around when she felt the presence in the room. She readied a boline knife to protect herself.

"Malphas?" She could detect his essence but seemed shocked to see him in a human body. She lowered the boline.

"Delphyne."

Delphyne furrowed her brow at Dominic. She slowly approached him. She raised her hand to touch the massive, imposing, muscular man. "Nephilim," she said. Delphyne seemed intimidated but curious. She placed her hand on his forearm and stared directly into his eyes.

"Delphyne, we are looking for—" Malphas started.

"Drucilla," Delphyne nodded. "You plan on taking her?"

"You plan to stop us?" Dominic asked.

"No; I swear no allegiance to Drake. Aside from Valor, no Lilim does."

"Valor," Malphas said to himself.

"Drake does not let Drucilla out of his sight, ever. He knows that you will be coming for her. You must understand that he is prepared. He will throw everything Hell has at you to keep her from you. If this is your attempt, you will not succeed unless you plan on bringing the entire Celestial Empyrion with you, and that will start an epic war that's been teetering for millennia. Understand when I say you will save the realms from a catastrophic loss if you turn back now. All realms."

"I can't go back to Dru without her. There's gotta be a way," Dominic pleaded.

Delphyne placed her hand over her mouth in contemplation.

Delphyne put her boline on the black wooden alchemy table. "I may be able to create an illusion elixir. Something to change her appearance to a demon. However, getting close enough to get it to her could be challenging."

"What about you?" Malphas asked. "Can you get access to Drucilla?"

Delphyne suddenly froze. Malphas nervously looked around.

"What is happening?" Malphas asked, picking up on her senses.

"She is here, Valor. She is coming. If she knows I am helping you, she will execute me!"

"Valor would not kill her sister," Malphas said.

"She takes orders from Drake. She is his general. If that means killing me, she will."

"We have to leave, Dominic," Malphas pleaded.

"It is too late; she already knows you are here. She will kill me." Delphyne backed away slowly in terror.

"Not if she thinks we attacked you," Malphas responded.

Malphas' hands began to glow as illusionary cuts and bruises appeared all over Delphyne's body. "Lay down, quickly."

Delphyne complied and threw herself to the floor just as the double doors to the purple glass greenhouse flung open.

Valor stood statuesque. Her long, blond hair flowed like streams of golden fire around her new black armor. Five heavily armed demons accompanied her. Her fiery, piercing eyes narrowed their gaze at Dominic. A slow grin stretched across her face.

"Well, if it is not the only living Nephilim. You, sir, are a legend. You found a way to circumvent a death sentence; impressive." Valor drew her sword and placed the tip against the floor beside her. The sword burst into a Divine, blue flame. Valor slowly approached him as she dragged the tip along the ground. Blue sparks shot off wildly in different directions. She held Dominic's stare with a maniacal grin.

"Do you remember when I said this is essentially a chess match? They have introduced a dragon," Malphas said loud enough for Dominic to hear.

Dominic expanded Erato Falx into a double-bladed javelin. "I've fought an Ophanim; this is nothing." Dominic grinned smugly. He felt confident with his javelin and impenetrability.

"Look, Valor, we don't need to get messy. Give us Drucilla, and I'll go away peacefully. I will leave you and your realm intact." Dominic moved slowly toward Valor.

As Dominic moved further from Delphyne, Valor spotted Delphyne's seemingly lifeless body on the floor behind him, covered in blood and gashes.

Valor's face turned to instant rage.

Instinct and anger blinding her, Valor rushed forward. Her blade had no time to ready as she crossed the distance, sliding across the stone floor and splitting it under the intense heat of the blue flame. Bounding forward a single step, she brought the sword to bear, arcing it upward from the stone and through the air in front of her with an eye to slice up through Dominic's chest.

Dominic saw the advance and stepped out of the way. He knew a wild swing when he saw one, and this one went wide enough for him to shift to the side. The movement was fluid to him, and he felt the rush of adrenaline kicking in. But he knew to keep his head clear in the fight and watch for her next attack. He knew he needed to understand what he was fighting.

Valor gave Dominic another swing, leveling the blade horizontally to strike his side in the direction he had moved, sure that she predicted his next movement despite her clouded senses. Yet, the swing came up too short once again as Dominic twisted out of the way. This is what she needed to snap her out of her fervor.

"Nephilim," she growled, "too dumb to hide behind a shield, too smart to die standing still." She used her words as misdirection, hoping to catch his attention wavered as she swung once again, this time remembering herself and guiding the attack with honed precision.

Dominic barely heard her words. He saw the sword approaching him again. This time it was too centered, too on-the-mark. He couldn't dodge it, but he was ready to deflect it and saw an opening. Letting the thrust of her sword travel, he pivoted the Erato Falx before him and swung one of its blades into hers, pressing his strength into the motion and altering its path. In the same motion, the other blade of

Erato Falx moved into position for a thrust of his own, and he jammed it forward towards Valor's center of mass.

Valor's eyes widened. She pulled in her stomach and leaped back, narrowly avoiding being pierced. *Such a reckless attack,* she thought, *and yet effective.* She did nothing to hide her disgust.

Dominic saw no counter and continued his attack. He kept the leading tip of Erato Falx level and turned to brace the weapon in both hands. Turning his torso and planting his feet, he swung the weapon overhead. His hands slid together during the motion, and he brought it down like a broadsword at Valor's head.

Valor flung up her weapon as a shield and took the blow. She slid on her feet under the force and took to a knee. The speed and power of the attack chilled her to the core.

"Abomination!" She spit at his feet. "Vulgar power!"

She stood, and in the same motion, her sword blazed its blue fire with renewed intensity as she delivered a flurry of thrusts and strikes aimed first at the Erato Falx and then Dominic's extremities. Dominic backpedaled, struggling to keep his balance. His hands ached from the repeated connections of the relic against Holy metal. When her focus shifted from his weapon to his flesh, he couldn't help but let out a smirk of confidence. Fighting with his instincts and training as a mortal man, he still did not want to test his invulnerability against her blade needlessly, but he could not contain the thought that he had an upper hand.

"It seems we both have legends that precede us," Dominic chided. "Me the last of a failed experiment, and you a warrior with a millennium of blood on your hands. Tell me, Valor, you hate me for my blood, but I respect you for your skill." He paused, watching her eyes. "So where is it?"

Valor seethed. "How dare you? You mistake your unearned power for skill and for lack of mine. Were you not of cursed blood, I'd have sundered you before you could have raised that crutch you call a relic in defense." She gripped her sword tight, her knuckles whitening. "You *will* make a mistake, and I *will* end you."

"Maybe, but not before I do what I came here to do."

Dominic tensed his legs and then unleashed them, shattering the stone beneath him with a sudden surge and sending him forward with blinding speed. Leveling one point of Erato Falx before him, Dominic willed it to form a lance with a serrated bladed tip with the forward quarter covered with spikes, a change that, combined with his size and mass, rendered him into a deadly wrecking ball. Three hundred and forty pounds, enhanced with untapped Nephilim power, moved as though mass had no meaning. Valor, unthinking, evoked her shield. Her silver cuff flickered into existence, the ornate barrier that formed fully an instant before impact. Dominic met no resistance against it, and together they propelled through the intervening space, the greenhouse wall, a stone structure just outside it, and spilled out into the courtyard beyond.

Valor tumbled and rolled across the red grass, her shoulder jamming into the ground as she righted herself back onto her feet but still sliding from the inertia. Not waiting to stop skidding, she lunged forward, overpowering the momentum and directing herself back at her prey. Bringing her sword before her and pointing downward, she met Dominic and collided with him. Sword against lance, she banged it out of the way before swinging it up and crossways down to strike at his neck.

Dominic kicked a leg forward to push off against Valor's thigh and arched his back to dodge the blade. He flipped over backward and landed squarely on his feet. Parrying sword strikes with lance jabs as he met Valor blow for blow. As both combatants learned from each other, the fight morphed into a dance, and neither seemed capable of landing a deciding blow.

Valor's rage boiled. She would not suffer this indignity any longer. Calling upon the power of Lilim, she commanded time to heel. All around her, the flow of the continuum slowed, and tendrils of blue fire bore their way out of her eyes as the toll extracted for the effort. Gritting her teeth through the pain, she willed all of creation to draw as close to cessation as possible, and she accepted the bargain with an offering of blood as the fire digging through her eyes gushed rivets of blood down her cheeks. In this moment, she brought her sword to bear against an unprotected and sluggish Dominic. She slashed at his throat.

With all the strength she had left to muster, the blade connected with his flesh, but neither yielded. Surmising his Nephilim skin to simply be denser than most, she turned the edge deeper and pressed on, anticipating the inevitable gaping wound. Instead, her blade buckled, and before she could pull the attack, the metal sundered on Dominic's body.

Dominic blinked, and in the span of the flutter, two things became truths to him; Valor, who had just a moment before been in his face and keeping pace, had turned into a blur of supermotion beyond his comprehension and landed a blow he had no hope of parrying. And that the blow proved his invulnerability, shattering the holy sword into pieces that littered the ground at his feet. Smugly, he looked at Valor, whose blood-tear marred face was locked in shock at the broken hilt in her hand.

"Oh," Dominic started glibly, "did I forget to mention that I'm impene—"

Valor screamed. Boiling, blinding, white-hot rage fractured her mind. *You. Must. DIE!* The only thoughts she had left were fixed on this single desire. She flung herself at Dominic, projecting herself upward and slamming a gauntleted fist into his face. The punch landed harmlessly, Dominic's enchantment valid against Hell-forged steel, but Valor would not relent and continued hammer-fisted strike after strike. Dominic fell to the ground. The force of each punch still carried weight enough to pressure and topple him but did no real damage. Still, Valor would not relent and pummeled Dominic, her hands bloodying within their casings.

Between the punches and Valor's scream, Dominic could hear the clanking of her gauntlets as they warped under the onslaught. Each blow bent the metal until a link finally broke and fell away, and an exposed knuckle collided with Dominic's jaw. He felt a snap and a sharp pain. Valor had fractured his jaw.

Dominic scrambled to throw Valor off him and get to his feet. Valor grabbed his shirt with one hand and continued punching him with the other, the gauntlets all but loose metal around her wrists. Each punch sent shocks of pain through Dominic. His kidneys, his back, and then his face when he turned to push Valor away, all were reddened and blackened by her blows. And then his nose broke, and with it came a gush of blood.

Dominic flung himself to the ground and covered his face with one arm. With the other, he retracted Erato Falx into a small blade. Gouging the dirt under him, he ripped a tear in the fabric of reality and fell through it.

Valor thudded to the ground in the space Dominic once was. Her breath strained her chest, and her vision blurred, but she rose to stare at the disheveled Earth. Between the blades of grass, blood glistened gently in the darkness.

Drucilla and her allies will return in book three.

The Raze of the Infernal Imperator

Coming October 2025

ACKNOWLEDGEMENTS
References and acknowledgments

- Unsplash.com, wikimedia.org, Vault Editions
- Antique illustrations by Vault Editions
- Cover photo provided by Pexels
- Additional artwork designed by Michelle C. Stewart
- *A Dictionary of Angels* by Gustav Davidson
- *Book of Enoch* by R.H. Charles
- *Fractured* by Brian Blackwood
- Brian Blackwood wrote Azrael's voice.

MUSIC

Some songs I listened to while writing The Hallowed Blood Bonds of the Eternal

- *I Am Nothing* by Stabbing Westward
- *Fear No Evil* by Bloody Hammers
- *Vivien* by †††† (Crosses)
- *This is Heresy* by Christian Death
- *Love Like Blood* by Killing Joke
- *NC-17 (Matte Blvck remix)* by HEALTH
- *Shadows* by Twin Tribes
- *Daydreams* by Tempers
- *Never Had No One Ever* by The Smiths
- *Floodgate* by Soft Kill
- *Unknown to the I* by Drab Majesty
- *Secret Scream* by The Black Queen
- *Come 2 Me* by Johnny Goth
- *Transgender* by Crystal Castles

Along with copious amounts of dark techno, stompy industrial, and demonic deathcore.